Praise for

IN THE MOUTH OF THE WOLF

"Bill McCausland deftly weaves a complex and compelling story that shows the long-lasting effects of war. Beautifully written, *In the Mouth of the Wolf* is a pleasure to experience and will make all readers look at human conflicts in a new way."

—ANN HOWARD CREEL. Award-winning author of nine novels, seven for young adults and two for adults

"*In the Mouth of the Wolf* is an honest, provocative and complex narrative full of adventures along the California coast and road trips to Laguna Salada and Santo Tomás in Mexico. Through an astute understanding of his own emotional terrain, Memo makes sense of his odyssey. From the depths of war's aftermath and a compelling love affair, he discovers within himself the ability to navigate life's dangerous opportunities."

—JEANMARIE MORELLI. Magazine and newspaper writer

"*In the Mouth of the Wolf* explores the collateral damage of war inflicted upon soldiers, and their loved ones, after returning home from Vietnam. Heartbreaking, riveting, astonishing, and beautifully rendered, this story is a major stoke. McCausland is a Big Wave story teller. He masterfully evokes the battles that engulf Memo and his Vietnam vet buddies and their families after returning home from the war. With compassion, voice, pace, and riveting tension, McCausland takes us on an unflinching, powerful journey of discovery, healing, and redemption. His book deserves a place on your bookshelf, right between *For Whom The Bell Tolls* and *The Things They Carried*. McCausland is the real deal."

—GUY BIEDERMAN. Playwright, actor, creative writing professor, and author of *House Samurai*

"In narrating the psychological damage of an unpopular war, Bill McCausland has expanded our horizons of an era we thought we knew well. This story of three soldiers struggling to find their way back to their wives after serving in Vietnam is by turns harrowing and hopeful, sorrowful and, in the end, life-affirming."

—JOHN PAINE. Professional book editor of many
New York Times best sellers

IN THE MOUTH

OF THE WOLF

Bill McCausland

McCAA BOOKS • SANTA ROSA

McCaa Books
1604 Deer Run
Santa Rosa, CA 95405-7535

First published in 2016 by McCaa Books, an imprint of McCaa Publications.

LIBRARY OF CONGRESS CONTROL NUMBER: 2016902795
ISBN 978-0-9960695-5-7

Printed in the United States of America
Set in Minion Pro
Cover design by Duncan Long

www.mccaabooks.com

TO

First Sergeant David McNerney

In the Mouth of the Wolf is dedicated to First Sergeant McNerney who was awarded the United States highest decoration, the Congressional Medal of Honor.

1SG McNerney was my first sergeant in the company where I was assigned in the United States before being deployed to Vietnam. At that time he was a celebrity on post. He was awarded the Medal of Honor for his heroism in the battle of Polei Doc and taking over the company when the commanding officers were killed.

The area was named, "The Valley of the Tears," and later a documentary film was made about the battle that was called *Honor in the Valley of the Tears*. There were many wounds and casualties and 1SG McNerney single-handedly took out a machine gun nest that was causing the impact on his company. He then gathered up explosives and detonated trees to make a landing zone for helicopters to evaluate and evacuate the casualties. The men in this battle are considered to be the most highly decorated during the Vietnam War.

In 2008, I reestablished contact with 1SG McNerney, and we had frequent telephone conversations. During one conversation in October of 2010, he reported that he had lung cancer that required hospice care. I called him days later, and his telephone was out of service.

PROLOGUE

November 1970, 1100 hours

I'M DRIVING DOWN THE WASHBOARD ROAD running next to the Rio Santo Tomás on the way back to our camp at Arboleda de los Robles, spacing out on Baja's bright blue sky and the late morning sun flashing through the leaves and branches of the gnarly oaks and brilliant yellow-green willows and sycamores that line the road . . .

"Jesus, Memo, slow down! Are you trying to get us killed after all we've been through?"

Jack's voice snaps me back. I smell the fish and saltwater from our trip to the coast. I muscle the FJ40 Land Cruiser around a sharp curve just a centimeter clear of a pickup full of pigs and chickens. I glance in the rearview mirror and see nothing but dust.

Jack white-knuckles the door handle in case I change my mind and drive us into the next oncoming vehicle. "What's going on, man? You haven't said a word since La Bocana."

I take a last drag on my Camel, flick it out the window, and keep my eyes on the road.

"You're an asshole. You came back in one piece, man. You're alive. We're in Mexico, man."

Jack laughs, doing his coyote howl. "*Me-hi-co! Me-hi-co!* Let's eat." He points up the road.

"Right." I slam on the brakes and jerk the rig to a stop in front of a rustic bleached-wood shack. A hand-lettered sign across the door says *Refrescos*, soft drinks. Maybe they have some ice that has been trucked in for cold beer.

I punch Jack in the shoulder and manage to rough a smile. "Time for Carta Blanca!"

We jump out of the truck and wander over to an open fire, where two little, brown leathery-skinned old women are squatting, cooking tortillas on a flat iron plate. They glance up at us. Little smiles. I smell hot cornmeal and burning oak. This really is heaven. What the hell is wrong with me?

Jack says, "I'll get a six-pack and see if they'll make us some chicken tacos." We head for the shack. Half a dozen chickens jump out of our way, squawking. I hear the sadness and grief-filled, scratchy old recording of Lola Beltrán from inside the shack, singing *El Crucifijo de Piedra*, the crucifix of stone. I still feel twitchy, but yeah, it's good to be here.

"*Al contemplar mi tristeza—*" To contemplate my sadness.

Then something flashes in front of my eyes—there and gone—and the music is washed out by the rush of blood from my head to my heart. My eyes are popping wide to take everything in, and I see a dark, scrawny guy come stumbling quickly out of the shack, carrying a rusty old rifle. Is it like the weapon I'd seen once before on a Mexican soldier? The Heckler & Koch G3 seems to glow, growing larger as my heart thrashes in my chest—shit oh shit, oh shit—the muscles in my arms and legs vibrating like ten thousand watt electric tension coils as the dumb pendejo lifts the rifle to his shoulder. What the fuck is wrong with this guy, and click—CLICK . . .

I'm back in the jungle with the Hueys from hell tearing holes in my brain. I grab the rifle's barrel, the cold steel burning my hand like napalm. I jerk it out of the pendejo's hands, lift it up, rotate the butt down and back, and smash it forward full force, cracking his ribs.

That's right, mother fucker, but why don't you scream?

"Inocencio!"

At the edge of my vision I see a terrified young woman running out of the shack, carrying an infant, and behind her are two screaming children.

"Inocencio!"

The man moans, staggering toward her, gasping for breath.

But I'm not done.

Still holding the rifle in my left hand, my free hand swings around to drive a hammer-fist strike to the left side of his neck, his sweat and blood mixing with mine. Now the man is on the ground, where I want him, and his wife is running at me, pushing me—

"Memo! Shit. Get off him!"

I'm standing over the guy, poised to finish him off with another rifle butt to the skull. And I'm the one who's screaming now.

"You motherfuckin' gook!"

"*¡Párese, Señor, párese!*" More bodies are pouring out of the shack, the tortilla ladies are running around, the wife is shrieking, and the children are wailing.

"Memo!" Jack's voice is cutting through the rotor blades. For a split second my sanity flashes in, and I know how badly off I am. How did a guy who had every advantage—a charmed life—get this way?

He's grabbing me by the arm, trying to pull me off balance, pounding on my hand so I'll drop the rifle. But I can't let go.

"Memo, for God's sake, stop! We're in Mexico! Stop before you annihilate this guy!"

CHAPTER 1

LOS MILAGROS

Friday afternoon, October 1970

OUR CARAVAN DRIVES EAST on Mexican Highway 2. The stretch of human-chewing road parallels the United States-Mexican border between Tijuana and Mexicali. Kate and I are sandwiched between two vehicles. Chet and Suzanne are upfront. For a second I take one clinched hand off the steering wheel to rub the back of my neck. My eyes are pinned on their bumper moving back and forth through the twisty turns. I look at Kate, wanting to connect with her and then I turn away. I keep sight of Jack and Diane in the rearview mirror.

Chet is a different brand of harbinger than Jack. Jack is a man who gives a sensation of providence.

Chet and I drive FJ-40 Land Cruisers. Good for what's ahead. Chet's rig has off-road modifications and a powerful winch to rescue him or anybody else from being stuck. Good rig. Good setup for handling the rugged Mexican backcountry, and it's ironic he has the best rig, but among us Chet has the most misdirected touch on salvaging himself from his war traumas.

Jack's air cooled rear engine VW camper van leverages against the rough roads—the nemesis of a city vehicle—and the desert terrain to come. Jack was inextricably snared by treating the grisly wounds and dismemberment and witnessed incalculable deaths that would make any other man permanently numb.

The caravan snakes through the curvy, potholed conduit between La Hechicera and La Rumarosa, headed via the mountains to an abrupt descent leading to the Laguna Salada desert. We'll travel off-road to the south once we reach the desert plain. The destination is an oasis with hot springs and desert palm trees, Cañón de la Virgen de Guadalupe.

Twisted grayish-green juniper trees lean down over the cliff edges around us. Kate points up and says, "I love the berries and cones. The trees are so sculptural."

"Yeah."

"The rock formations bring a prehistoric look to the moment. They're so cool."

"Sure are."

Kate turns towards me. Deep furrows between her eyebrows disturb her naturally angelic face. "Come on, Memo, you haven't spoken since we crossed the border at Tecate an hour ago."

"I hadn't noticed."

"You're in your element. It's Mexico." She raises her hands and lets them fall back down in her lap. Her tresses drape across her left eye, and the sunlight through the rear window catches the delicate wispy highlights in her hair. "Think of everything your mother has done to make you love Mexico. You should be happy to be here."

I can't stand Kate's pressure. I grip the wheel. She needs to let-up. The white of my knuckles stands out against the flesh color of my hand.

"Yeah, I know I should be happy."

"Is it about being down here with Chet and Jack?"

Her pestering questions start to annoy me, like a gnat hovering in front of my eyes. "I don't know." My lips press together to make what feels like a white slash.

"Memo, you're stonewalling me." She fidgets and twists her wedding ring around her finger.

"I swear to God, I don't mean to," my voice is a pressured knot.

Kate grimaces and shakes her head. "I know you don't mean to."

I glance at her. Kate's eyes are wide. Her chin pushes up, turning her mouth into a frown. I remember her looking this way when we found out I was going to war. "So what do you want me to say?"

"It's not that I want you to say anything in particular. I just want you to say something." Kate draws in a full-size breath. She lets it go. "Jesus, you're like my father. He didn't talk either. Or he didn't talk because he wasn't around. How do you think that makes me feel?" She tugs at her collar.

I try to frame a smile, like my old charming self. "Would it do any good to call you Sweet Cakes?" I take a fleeting look at Kate.

A flash comes across her face. Charm does the trick. Her face softens. Then the attempt to win over Kate wears off. She says, "No Sweet Cakes stuff. And don't try the thing with the bedroom baby blues, either." Kate gets serious. "That Sweet Cakes stunt worked on me for two seconds, just like when you used it in France, until—"

"Okay. But I am at a loss." I jerk back having trouble being articulate.

Kate looks straight ahead. "Yeah, I believe you."

A huge, ear-splittingly loud, old truck—no muffler—going in the opposite direction drifts over to our side of the road. I swerve off the pavement, hitting the dirt with the two right tires. "*¡Que pelotudo!*"

I immediately pull our rig back. This is a piece of shit potholed road. The truck almost clips Chet's rig. It misses Jack's van.

Kate pants. She looks like she's trying to pull herself together from the fright of nearly getting axed. "What?"

"Hm? *Que pelotudo* means, 'What an idiot.'"

"That was really scary!" She has an incredulous dazed look.

I snap back from the shock of almost getting nailed. "No big thing."

Kate raises her eyebrows. "That's what I mean." She gives me a glassy stare.

"Huh? You're talking over my head." My words have a hard choppy sound.

"You were jazzed the first couple of days you were back. Then something curiously weird happened." Kate cocks her head. "Like your brain checked-out, but you left your body behind."

I hear Kate talking, but I don't know what she's saying.

She keeps it up. "Take right now. You get pumped up. Guy's an idiot! But then you go flat. It's no big deal. What's going on with you?"

I haven't been wearing my seatbelt since we left San Diego. I click it on. Adjust the rearview mirror. I see Jack and Diane's image in the rear view mirror. The sun is at my back, not in my eyes. There's no need for sunglasses, but I put on my Polaroids to hide-out.

There's a pressure behind my eyes. Tightness in my temples forces a couple bats of an eyelid. I say the first thing that floats to the surface of my torn-up mind. "I remember one morning, maybe three or four days after I got back. It was around eight in the morning. You were still asleep, and I was driving around aimlessly. Maybe I was trying to find something—didn't know what it was—maybe desperately trying to land back home—scratching for a sense of ballast. Don't know how I got there, but I was in a depressing, ticky-tacky housing tract. Probably the result of aimless wondering." I pause. Don't know if my answer makes any sense, or I'm a lunatic who is a tangential mess. I look at Kate for some sort of backup, but she just waits for me to finish. "All the houses looked the same, except for being painted dreadful dirty shades of yellow, pink or beige. There were beaten-to-shit cars parked in front of the houses. A guy wearing an old white t-shirt turned shabby gray had the hood of his car up, and his head was buried in the engine. His butt crack showed."

I glance at Kate, who's studying my lip movements. Despite my state I can't help but notice her refined cheekbones are smoothed over by softy textured fine skin. She blinks her stunning hazel eyes—now strained by my story.

The high desert terrain changes. We approach the descent. I'm too close to Chet and Suzanne's rig. I back off the gas and concentrate.

I grind my teeth, making an ache. My jaw loosens. "And then I saw some woman watering her front lawn in the fresh morning light. It was as though I were a million miles away, looking through a movie camera. She was a flabby, barefoot bitch wearing dingy shorts and a horizontally striped tank top. Udder-like tits falling over the woman's blubbery stomach. Her hair was up in gigantic pink curlers." I had felt unreal. The scene was surreal. What the hell did I come back to after being in Nam?

I take a quick look at Kate again. Her eyes are wide. I wonder if she is connecting with the story. And connecting with me trying to inch my way back to sanity.

We start to make the precipitous, sinuous four thousand-foot descent of Cuesta La Rumarosa at the eastern edge of the Sierra de Juarez escarpment. We catch our first glimpse of the dry Laguna

Salada in the San Felipe Desert valley floor below. The purplish mountainous tectonic lift of Sierra Cucapá is in the distant background. The vista is loaded with muted shadings, contours and dimensions. I can hold the view, almost touch it. And seeing the imposing impressiveness in front of me sets off the thought I should react to the panorama by feeling something or having a sensation. But I don't—just a blunted sense of oblivion. The next thought is I don't feel enough since I got back from war. Or really, I probably feel too much. Or I feel something, but I don't know what it is.

I restlessly drum the steering wheel with my fingers. "A few days earlier, I had been in the crawling anthill called Saigon, sweltering in its steamy rot. Thinking of that piglet watering her brown lawn... Was that why I went to war – to defend our country for a flabby utter-breasted woman so she could water her dead lawn? Fuck! I sure as shit hope those first few days aren't a preview of what's to come." I pound the steering wheel once with my fist.

"I've never, ever heard you sound so twisted up like this before." Kate looks straight ahead. The strain in her eyes release. Huge tears form and trickle down her blushed cheeks.

I can't deal with this shit right now. I tap the brake and steer the rig around the hairpin curves of one of the most dangerous roads in Mexico.

Kate's look bounces from place to place for a second. "I understand you pretty well," she goes on, her voice misted with tears. "You're not a bad person; you're a really good person. I love the charming side of you." Kate places a hand on my shoulder. "But where's that good person?"

I feel the skin bunch up around my eyes. "I don't know." I keep my eyes on the road.

"When are you going to find out?" She sounds strident.

"I really don't know." I feel helpless with Kate putting the squeeze on me. I wring the steering wheel like a rag.

Every two inches alongside the road we see decorated, white wooden crosses, memorializing people who have died on this stretch. Highway 2 is a statement of lost lives—a fucking cemetery. Chet and Suzanne stop at a pullout. The space is tight, not quite big enough for three vehicles. Our bumpers touch. The vehicles edge over the lip of the road. We unload our travel-cramped bodies out of the rigs.

Chet, Jack and I look over the side of the cliff. The three of us have hunched postures and drooping heads. We see a heap of auto carcasses deep in the canyon. I imagine people inside a car going over the deadly cliff, screaming in terror, propelled through space, not having enough time to say good-bye to the lives they are about to lose. They hit the bottom with the violent crash of twisting steel and flying parts—they're gone—silence. All the shit in my mind about abrupt death is a repetitive performance and I'd like the play to end.

Jack curls his lower lip. "Their poor families."

We three war veterans stand. Heads craned, looking in the canyon's deep crevasse. What do my buddies think? The same goddamn thing as me. People caught in a split second twist of fate leading to an unforeseen end.

Diane interrupts our transfixed daze. "Why'd we stop?"

Diane is a natural looking woman in a tight white T-shirt and blue chambray skirt and leather sandals. Smart and healthy, with brunette hair cut shoulder length. I remember Jack said Diane's a maternal type—likes to take care of people's complicated dilemmas and troubles. Her body is slender. Shapely breasts outlined by her jersey shirt. Diane's luminous blue eyes and perfect white teeth make her a picture of vivacity. Her high school students must love her. And then behind the radiance, I notice her eyes are bloodshot.

Suzanne had the idea to stop. "Isn't that amazing? Let's see how the Mexicans decorate the crosses." She tilts her head towards the roadside memorials.

The six of us stand in a semicircle in front of one cross.

Jack says, "Memo, you have encyclopedic Latin American know-how. I recognize the Virgin of Guadalupe painted on the glass cylinder, but what's the encased candle called?"

I get a kick out of my pal thinking I belong to some sliver of the Latino intelligentsia. "It's a *novena* candle." I tell Jack the candles are used for a mix of reasons. Here, to keep vigil over the spirit of someone who has died, to memorialize that person, to ward off evil, and to bring safety and peace to the dead person's soul. "The grieving person lights the novena candle to relieve their own suffering and help the dead person make a connection to God." I feel easygoing—despite the death subject—being unhooked from the squeezed conversation with Kate.

Suzanne has a slow smile that builds up. "Maybe we should light it."

I faintly shake my head. "It belongs to somebody else's soul." The words come off my tongue like they were from the sensitivity of a person inside of me I don't know very well. My second thought is she wants to light it to relieve Chet's pangs of tortured agony.

Suzanne looks at me with one eye.

I study her. My eyes narrow. "How 'bout I get one for you to light?"

Diane stands close to Jack, wraps her arm around his arm, and pulls him close. "Memo, what's the little metal charm? The ear?" She gazes at the symbol, her look becoming focused through her soporific reddened eyes.

Chet looks down the road and off into the distance. He stiffly stands, looking isolated within himself as if he's cut-off from the rest of us. Chet taps his foot and crosses his arms.

Melancholic curiosity knits the rest of us together, letting the ache settle in of the infinite string of roadside crosses. And grasping how the Mexicans mourn and ritualize and manage death.

My spine straightens up, looking Diane directly in the eye. "The ear? It's a *milagro*—'miracle' in English." I tell her a milagro is for the supplicant requesting divine intervention; it symbolizes a specific pathway to the supernatural. "The ear milagro could have been placed here by someone who wants the dead person to finally hear the voice of God. Or maybe a spouse who is hoping at long last to be heard when he or she joins the departed in Heaven. Or maybe for the dead person to hear the spouse here on earth…who knows?" I slump and start to feel tight, a tingling sensation radiates across my shoulders and down my arms.

Their heads nod, as if they're eavesdropping on a supernatural talisman.

My lips move without volition, and feel disconnected from the rest of me.

The questions continue to decode and fathom Mexican death rituals. Chet has dull eyes and blank features. Everyone else listens.

Suzanne crosses her arms and bends forward while observing the adorned white cross. "What is the little painting on the square piece of tin?"

Suzanne's and my eyes make a bridge. I regain connection with what I'm saying. I tell her it's an ex-voto, and sometimes things are so mystical in Mexico it's hard to follow the exact meaning in the mind of the person who painted it. "Strange and wonderful—all ex-voto art has a surreal quality and a feeling of suffering and a hope for wholeness with God, despite the ultimate outcome of healing or death."

Each of us ponders the iconic details of the makeshift altar and cross. I wonder what they're thinking.

Diane squints and considers my words. "Death and mysticism," she says like her consciousness is in some cosmic world. I study her bloodshot eyes. Diane is tripping on pot.

I shrug. "Mexico is a risky place—fewer chances for survival. So, down here, a cat has seven lives, not nine."

Jack twists his right hand around his left wrist. "I'm sick of risky places." He bites his lower lip and then says, "It's all too goddamn close."

There is a collective agitated hush. Everyone's eyes stick on Jack, except for Chet, who turns and looks over his left shoulder at the auto carcasses deep in the canyon. He pats his pocket like he's looking for something that's lost.

Suzanne lets go of a breath and breaks the silence. "So what do you think this ex-voto means, Memo?"

"What does it mean? This one has someone praying to an image of the Virgin of Guadalupe—probably praying for protection and a miracle." I rub my chin. "I'm not sure what an ex-voto is doing here. Ex-votos are used to wish a living person back to health or save someone from death. The ex-voto on a cross is for a person who is already dead." I shake my head. "I don't get it."

Kate jerks back, "Oh, my God!" She fights to catch her breath.

"Kate?" I pause. She' stunned. "What's wrong?"

"It's nothing. Absolutely nothing. Nothing." Color drains from her face.

Stupefied and stoned Diane examines Kate with her glazed over eyes.

Vertical creases form between Kate's eyes. Three sudden empty blinks are full of what she is not saying.

I'm left to guess what's wrong, but I don't have an answer.

Diane dazed, looks quizzically at us. She draws in a breath, opens her mouth, and starts to speak, but Chet takes the moment. "Come on, let's go." He has a sharp tongue. "It's okay if we go now." He raises his eyebrows. "Let's go."

I'm relieved Chet finally said something. I need to leave, too. Enough of the death quiz.

We plunge down the abrupt zigzag mountainside road, taking one curve after the other. Every few seconds blazing taillights flash red as we go into a tight curve.

Kate braces herself with her hands on the dashboard. "You're on top of Chet's bumper," she says intermixed with convulsive breaths. Kate jerks from side to side at each turn.

I ignore her, keep going. My eyes are glued to the road. I love the danger. The risk makes me relax from Kate bugging me. Scorching brakes smell singed. Transmissions whine. We muscle the steering wheels to push into and pull out of hairpin turns.

"After all those twisted wrecks and crosses we saw and—you're scaring me!" Kate is shrieking.

I look in the rearview mirror. Jack is a couple of curves back.

"Memo, slow down!" shouts Kate.

My maniacal feeling subsides. I slow down.

Chet slows down.

"I didn't realize—" My chest pounds. I loosen my grip on the steering wheel. I see Jack close in. Now he is three-car-lengths behind us. My pulse regains a regular beat.

Kate sits back in the seat. Her hands are on her thighs. She lets out a lung-full of air. "I want you to stop scaring me."

CHAPTER 2

HERE'S THE JUMP

I DIDN'T EXPECT THINGS TO BE SUCH A MESS. I had an innocent, yet unsuspecting plan: to pick-up where Kate and I left off before my exodus for war. I counted the days and hours and minutes. Marking time to return to the solace of our marriage. In my guileless mind I crossed out any possibility of change between Kate and me.

A few sex-starved women who worked for the U.S. government on joint military-civilian missions tried to tug me in. I was randy right down to my bone marrow, but the true blue me came through in spite of those frantic moments of start and stop wavering. Kate—the permanent fixture in my mind—kept my ballast even and me going. She's the one I love. Her striking image in my mind was always the last answer.

There are the other parts of my war homecoming. I have the ambition that has turned into a longing to resume my architectural internship with Frank Gehry. And I'll cash-in on the GI Bill to get my masters in architecture at my alma mater, the University of Southern California. Some people say USC stand for the *University of Spoiled Children*. But that isn't the category I fall into. As an undergraduate I could've eased off, but I worked hard and was serious and had reserve and embraced modesty.

Anticipations have changed. And there's a reason. The basis is what happened during my absence. Now I'm daunted by the possibility

I've pissed away my marriage. There's an undying dark smear permeating the way I think and feel that forces the reckless ways I act.

Fleeing to remote Mexico is a way to be with my buddies who carry the same war in their minds. Taking our wives is a way to put them in the picture. The expedition down south is a stab at finding an unspecified thing to bring back a sensation of connection—from being disjointed to repositioning what's under the surface to find a sense of order. Though conceivably this solution is likely artless and unsophisticatedly green. But we'll take the plunge and give the jaunt a shot...the opportunity for an opening.

There are other reasons to break out. The escape to Mexico is to dodge the truth that I'm not getting any traction in my life back home. It's cheap, short-lived relief from the evil ricocheting from side-to-side in my mind. Part of my escapist plot is to find datura. It's a plant—a drug—that grows in Mexico. The shamans use it to treat demons and nightmares. It could be a panacea. Or it could be one more form of running away. Or a way to put back into place the splintered fragments of my soul.

OUR CARAVAN STRAIGHTENS OUT once we hit the pancake floor of the San Felipe Desert. After a couple of miles we see the K-28 highway marker that is our landmark. We turn south. Faint roads only slightly better than footpaths crisscross the desolate tract of the Laguna Salada desert. I point out what appears to be the best one to take. Maybe it's an incautious choice. The track could peter-out or go sideways. But shit, someone has to make a decision. Besides, if the pathway doesn't work we can realign our way to Cañón de la Virgen de Guadalupe.

The three-vehicle caravan continues for ten minutes. We stop at a cluster of acacia to double check our course. Smoke trees and creosote bushes give the desert setting an unexpected lush feeling.

Chet and I survey the mountain range to the west and south. He points out the location of Cañón Virgen de Guadalupe, more than 25 miles across the desert floor, at a southeastern leeward spot of the mountain range.

We stand separate from the group, next to the acacias. Chet's arm is parallel with the ground, his entire hand outstretched and palm down in the direction of the canyon. "Memo, let's draw an azimuthal equidistant projection for the shortest straight line to the canyon. We'll need to figure the variations in our navigation path to keep on point." He glances back at me and nods.

Chet speaks military navigation lingo in the tone of being out in the bush. The speak loops through us and makes a knot. We have strong eye contact. "Sure, Chet. I see the azimuth and image the navigational adjustments needed to arrive at the objective." There's a soothing familiar, brotherly comfortable feel to the talk. Somebody listening might think we sound technical or logical but not understand the unstated military bond. It's just buddy talk. It's a simple briefing to set up a path to reach the mark.

The two of us move further away from the others to get a better vantage point. I see a shiny black bird, with a long tail and a crest, and white on its wings. It flies into the acacia tree. The bird plucks berries from the parasitic mistletoe latched onto the acacia.

I squint. "Hey, Chet, look at the bird in the acacia tree. It's a silky flycatcher."

The bird drops to the ground and slurps liquid left by an unseasonable rainstorm a couple of days earlier. Juice fills the curvature of the fallen mistletoe leaves. The flycatcher looks ataxic— unable to control its muscle movements.

Chet wiggles his eyebrows. He nudges me. "Memo, it's staggering around. Those berries were fermented in the rainwater. The bird's loaded." Chet arches his back and laughs.

I let out a quick breath. "No shit!"

A cowboy shirt with rolled-up sleeves, a leather vest, and jeans cover Chet's lanky, muscular body. He wears beat-up brown cowboy boots. His long, blond streaked hair falls from underneath his well-used felt Stetson. Silver Navajo rings—one with turquoise inlay—are on each ring finger. He has an impeccably trimmed Vandyke covering his upper lip and chin.

Chet—who goes in and out of being in a distant place in his mind and emotionally remote—has unremitting and unbridled pieces crawling above and below his permeable skin's surface. I know Chet's fever. I feel it in him. And I feel it in myself. The regnant war trauma sickness says I drive you and I'm full of haunting surprises. Chet wastes himself with whatever anesthetic he can find to cool off his twitchy mind. But getting loaded is like melting ice's impermanence that gives the illusion of relief, and the fever can fire-up at any tick of a second to trigger a revival of his satanic demons. We were chums in high school, and I know who he was then and how he is now.

I know a lot of things about Chet. Things he's told me outright and by inference that happened before the war and after he came home. The war bit lets me know I am completely like him. And our pasts before the war say I'm entirely different. Or I ascribe something in myself to him. And there's the confusing and distorted ways we hide to make our war-caused fever go away.

Chet puts his service medals out of sight. He finds they've been rearranged. Suzanne found them. She says nothing. Chet conceals his Silver Star and Purple Hearts, pretending his memories will go away. But they don't go away. I don't think he's ever considered getting rid of his medals. He can't. The medals are attached to fragments of knowing whether they are hidden or not. They're permanently burned into his chest's flesh.

Chet came back from war before me. I wrote him a letter while I was still in that hellhole. He sat on it. Months, maybe. He buried it. And then he had a vicious argument with Suzanne. Chet said the next day he found my letter on his dresser. Suzanne placed it there. He finally sent me a response.

Chet had a lucky break when he arrived at his war post. His military occupational specialty—his MOS—was infantry, coded 11B—*eleven bravo* it's called. Stateside, he's a mason. Being a mason turned into a magic trick. He was assigned to the Army Corps of Engineers. But there was extra duty. Night patrol. Chet went out with three other GIs. He was the only one to come back. Chet screened out what happened to the other soldiers. That's the way it is with Chet. I don't know what happened. You just know something noxiously injurious happened because of his fever.

Suffering like pariahs takes our voices away. We clam up about being veterans when we got home, driven by the disenfranchising antiwar sentiment. The impact of war gives us a removed sensation and the antiwar people's lack of acceptance and insight about the personal ravaging touch the war had on us makes us trapped in a cage looking out. We feel more isolated and detached, like pariahs.

"So Chet." I lower my head and flicker my eyes. "Have you ever heard of *nepenthe*?"

He wags his head back and forth. "No fuckin' clue." Chet hums. "But you're asking about something that sounds like a drug, right?" His eyes widen.

I nod. "You're clued in after all." I tell Chet it's a drug mentioned in Homer's Odyssey. Nepenthe, which comes from Greek, literally means, *no grief, no sorrow.* The drug takes away anguish. Makes you forget the things you want to dis-remember.

Chet cocks his head and eyes me. "This is leading to something good, not just some dumb fuck mental exercise?" For this wink of an instant Chet has undiluted concentration.

"Let me finish the story." I tell Chet nepenthe was given to Helen by an Egyptian queen to rid Helen of grief and sorrow. Helen's intoxication allowed her to overlook the pain she wanted to cut out of her mind.

Chet puts his hands on his hips and laughs. "Yeah? You want us to drink fermented mistletoe berry juice so we can get loaded like the bird?"

I shrug and my lips draw out to a thin line. "No. Here's the jump." I tell him about the Piapia Amerindians who migrated back and forth over the Sierra Juarez. I sweep my finger from south to north, pointing out the mountain range to the west of us. "They used a hallucinogenic plant called *datura.*"

Chet makes a snorting sound. "Datura is like nepenthe?"

"Yeah, rid yourself of grief and sorrow—and maybe more than that." I tell Chet the Piapia shamans took the drug in the belief their hallucinatory experiences were the gods using them as conduits to communicate with the indigenous people.

"Sounds like it could be a kick-ass high." Chet's words are a stoner's muse. But his face is dead serious.

I lean forward. "You've seen the freaky looking petroglyph art up in one of the canyons near Guadalupe?"

"Sure." The pivot of his exaggerated nod rocks his shoulders back and forth.

I tell Chet the shamans made the petroglyphs by scratching through the natural mineral coating—desert varnish—on the boulders and canyon walls. The petroglyphic figures are symbolic communications from the gods pipelined through the shamans. "I'm going up in the canyon with the petroglyphs and try to find—"

"Chet! Memo!" screams Suzanne. "Come on, let's go."

We're back at the rigs in a minute.

"What took you guys so long?"

"Directions can be complicated," snorts Chet.

"Yeah, we were sorting out the complexities of finding our way." I maintain a staid expression.

Suzanne looks askance, knowing how to read when bad boys have an agenda. She crooks her head. Her concentrated eyes narrow.

We get back in the vehicles. The course is fixed for Cañón Virgen de Guadalupe.

The sandy path beneath the Land Cruiser makes the ride seem to oscillate between rough and floating. The landscape is filled with bursage shrub and tamarisk salt cedar trees. I look at Kate, seeing the landscape blur past her through the passenger window. I turn back to keep my eyes on the dry sagebrush dotted laguna in front of us. "Kate, see that optical illusion? The mountains in the distance appear to be moving away instead of getting closer."

"I make it out." She clears her throat. "Life is full of what you see and don't see."

I stutter. "You're speaking in code. What do you mean?"

Kate looks straight ahead. A rough stretch of terrain radiates tiny jerking motions through her body. "Were you guys talking about drugs?"

Her hunch is uncanny. I tell her about the flycatcher, nepenthe and my plan to find some datura.

"Figures. Predictable, really. Chet likes to do drugs. And he likes to talk about doing drugs, if he is not loaded on drugs." At first Kate's voice has a loathsome resonance. And then her speech spikes up two octaves. Stiletto peaks punctuate each word. "Memo, I don't care if you take a drug if it helps get you back. I want you back." She sounds cavernous and needy. "I don't want somebody else in your body instead of you. So do whatever you have to do." Kate stops dead. She looks at me, the road vibrates her body back and forth in the passenger seat. "Do you still love me?" She turns her eyes back to the direction of our path across the barren desert.

"I fell in love with you, Kate, and I have never fallen out of love with you."

"You love me...but can't show it." Kate's hands pull into white knuckled tight fists. She glances sideways. Her chin trembles.

Kate's acrimonious bitterness spills out, making her agitated. I say, "Look, if you're still thinking about what happened in France—well—I said I'm sorry. Give me a break. After all that wine I was totally trashed. Come on, anybody can do dumb shit things when you're plastered."

"It's not about punishing you. It's just—I can't get over it." Kate takes three heavy breaths. "Getting polluted isn't an alibi, so forget it." She looks at me. Her eyes are cold and hard. "There's nothing you can do or make up some bullshit thing to say to make-up for what happened. Your little romp."

I wince and push my hand into my breastbone. "Come on. It was a bad choice. I was skunk drunk."

"It was stupid."

"That's what I just said."

"Memo, goddamn it, don't be cute when I'm pissed off." Kate crosses her arms. Her lower lip curls in to a little girl pout.

I clear my throat. "Look, nothing happened." My head shakes. "And I'm sorry that I tried to pull you into it." I hesitate and then nod. "The reason I got so blotto was...because I wanted to get in trouble. Get some release because of all the bullshit I carry inside and it's tiring holding on by the slightest piece of unraveling twine."

"Let me be." She sniffs. "Talk about something else."

"Yeah. I guess. Okay." I mull over what happened in France for a couple of minutes. Then try to unhook myself from Kate's upset. Rattled, I lower my eyebrows and a distracted feeling seeps in—a curiosity—why was Kate taken aback by the ex-voto laden cross? "Kate, why did you flinch and gasp when we stood by the crosses, and I explained the rituals the Mexicans used to memorialize the people killed on the highway?"

She coughs. "What? You're trying to change the subject so I'm not so torn up right now about your frolicking in France?"

I blink and then look wide-eyed. "You're right. Distract you from being cross and huffy with me. But I also want to know what caused you to recoil the way you did."

"Oh. That?" Kate turns pale. She looks taxed. "You said the ex-voto was for a dead person. Your words triggered a memory of a dream I had a couple of days ago." Kate hangs on for ten seconds. "I wasn't going to tell you about the dream. Just wanted to forget it."

I grind my teeth. "I try to erase my dreams, too."

She doesn't seem to hear what I said. "Okay, I'll tell you." She spins through the dream like a movie reel. Kate says she goes to the closet at our beach house. She opens it. She sees me in the closet, dressed in my Army olive drab jungle fatigues, jungle boots, black captain's bars embroidered patch sewn on the right side of my collar, and infantry rifles on the left. I'm wearing a helmet. I'm a dead man wearing a helmet with captain's bars on its cloth cover. Leathery black skin is pulled tightly over a bony skull of a face. "It scares the shit out of me. Your eyes are glowing against your drawn face like two burning sapphires; you're both a live person and dead... Then 'already dead' pops out of your mouth up on the grade."

A trapped feeling abruptly scours me. The Spanish word *esposas*—it means both wives and handcuffs—detonates in my head. I'm thrown off balance, staggering to the edge of careening directionless. I can't escape.

For a fitting reason my mind shifts to a scrap of thought about the San Andreas Fault. The fault line can't be seen. It's just there. The fault disappears below the alluvium in the Salton Sea to the north and continues south. It subterraneously runs close and beneath us. In eons of geologic time the fault caused Baja and mainland Mexico to split. This land, once one, becomes two and fills in with water, creating the Gulf of California.

That's us. The distance is like a gulf and a vast sea separates Kate and me. The span between us is one chunk. Unraveling our split's agonizing wounds, we're like a fleshy ripped fabric filled-in with infection, pus and ooze.

Kate spews an exaggerated sigh. "Memo...Memo, aren't you going to say anything?"

"Look, I'm trying to recuperate from your goddamn hallucinatory nightmare. I'm losing ground trying to get myself reeled in, but constantly get dragged back to the past. But for chrissake, what can I say? Your bullshit wicked dream blows me away."

"Why? Because it's the straight scoop."

"Realism. That's it, realism. It's too fuckin' much."

"You're going to have to tell me what happened."

"You're not ready for it."

"Are you shitting me? You're the one who's not ready."

I feel the angst of my emotionally choked voice. "I'm such a fuckin' wreck; I'll never be ready to—"

Kate fans herself with an open hand. "Okay. Well, listen, then."

I feel overheated and grip the steering wheel, trying to pay attention.

The dust from Chet's rig gusts over us. Jack's van is hazy image through the clouds of dust in my rearview mirror.

Kate says, "When we got together in college the only thing in the world that mattered was us—not the draft, not the strain of you leaving, not military training, not your decision to go to Officers Candidate School—OCS—not fears about being deployed to Vietnam, and not me being a military wife stuck in the States, waiting for the doorbell to ring with a message that you were wounded or dead. I want our life back. I want you back."

I grimace. "I want our lives back too." My voice is uncertain. "A timetable doesn't exist."

Kate rubs her temples with her fingertips. "So you want me to be patient after I've been tolerant for the past three years? While you were in Vietnam all I did was plan for you to come home, work, come home paint, go back to work, come home and paint some more. Yeah, I was totally turned on to developing my art—kept me alive. But everything else was a vacuous abyss."

Kate looks out the passenger door window. She turns back to me, stretching out her spite. "I ran everything while you were gone. The house, all our business. Managing, saving the money you sent. Arranging our European trip." She hits her thigh with her fist. "Now I want you to help me and be a part of things. But you feel like a guest who has stayed too long—a permanent stranger. I keep running everything because the way you deal with stuff is so black and white and calculated like a military mission. Or else you're bullshitting—shooting the breeze—telling stories with your surfing buddies. I'm not sure if I even want you to help me anymore."

"You want me to help you. And you don't want me to help you." There's a fluttery sensation in my stomach. "Kate, you are confusing the hell out of me."

Kate's body posture collapses. "Well, how do you think it feels like for me?"

I shrug and purse my lips. My grip on feeling tied to Kate and everything else feels like it's slipping away. I scratch for one piece of empathic connection. "You must feel confused."

Kate's lower eyelids swell with tears. "Yeah. I wish you'd be with me the way you are with our black lab, Shadow Facts. Funny, isn't it? You connect with the pooch. You're at home with her. With me, you're present and absent at the same time, but with that animal you're the old Memo."

My voice feels unsteady. "Shadow Facts is easy. There are no conditions with her. The longer I'm away during the day, the happier she is to see me." I force a swallow. "The longer I stay away, the more upset you become."

"Yeah, I know, she wags her tail—not exactly what I do." Kate gazes straight ahead. Nothing falls across her face but a vacant stare.

There's no talking to Kate now. And I get she's scared. Kate's still the frightened kid whose daddy left her. Nobody is going to undo the divorce wedge set in her life when her parents called it quits and right now her old kid pain complicates the hell out of our crisis. Her mom was so wounded she slimly attended to Kate's damage. And if her mom had been one hundred percent, it wouldn't have been enough.

I was supposed to be safe. Secure. And now, I'm nothing more predictable than a shake of the hand and roll of the dice. I could be right or wrong. But I have a hunch she feels I've abandoned her—just like her dad—even though I'm right here sitting next to her. Maybe it would be easier if I was just gone, rather than being a shell-shocked phantom person who makes Kate's life a daunting mess.

She grasps the vehicle's armrest. "Memo, aren't we going faster?"

My mind filters back to being contrite and my heartfelt regret. Kate didn't care I was repentant. I pushed our taxed and antagonized marriage over the edge and into a deep chaotic chasm by the disastrous stunt in France. I'd like to find an excuse or justification or some way to defend myself for what happened. I can't.

My head jerks back. "Oh yeah. I didn't notice." I look in the rearview mirror. The outline of Jack and Diane's dust enveloped van can barely be seen.

Kate squints. "Look, Chet is speeding away from us."

I glance at the speedometer. "I'd better slow it down. Wow, look, he's really movin' out—our speed is slightly more than seventy. We'll let him go. Besides, we've got to stay connected with Jack to make sure he doesn't get lost."

Kate shakes her head. "Yeah, it's not safe. It's a good thing Jack is a doc in case Chet crashes. Poor Suzanne."

My eyes widen. "It's always good to have Jack along." Then I catch the reference. "Poor Suzanne? Why—"

"Why what? I'm focused on the wrong person? Suzanne? You're right." Kate turns her head towards me. "Look. Everything's changed. I should be saying poor me?" She shakes her head. "Well, I'm not going to say poor me. Even with all the bullshit you've subjected me to and the fallout between us. I'm saying no to being pitiful."

Self-abasement sets in. I have to do something to turn around what's happening with Kate. "Tell you what. I'll call Frank Gehry when we get home. See if I can get my internship back. Check-out the USC graduate school." I take a quick deep breath. "Look, I'll get back on track."

"Oh yeah?" Kate sits stiffly. "So when are you going to call him, Memo? I'm turning darker shades of blue waiting for you." The blankness of Kate's face looks as if the glue between us doesn't make a seal.

A tightening in my chest makes an imploding collapsed sensation; like Kate stunned my heart and now it has gone into paralysis. What caused her to do it? Me.

CHAPTER 3

MEMO'S OPENING STROKES

TODAY IS THE BEGINNING of the tenth of January 1966, and the start of the end of hiding-out in a charmed life. Letting go of the way I was. Not a naïve life but a charmed one. A magic life, which has seemed almost ordinary to me because I'd never known anything else. Life will be unlike what went before. Something is going to make it come unhinged, which makes for an edgy and messy interior feeling.

There's something else. It's something I haven't been able to get by being athletic or hanging out with my good buddies or getting good grades or being the guy who stands up to everything. It's a blankness. An empty space that has a weighty feeling. Most other things in my life are light and easy. Or have richness and depth, but with a splinter of pointlessness.

She's somewhere out there.

THE CAMPUS IS SOAKED TODAY. I run over to a group of people standing around under umbrellas. It's my last semester in the architecture program at USC. It feels good to finish my degree—accomplishment mixed with a turbulent sense of dread. I'm supposed to be the confident guy. Nobody knows how scared I am. In a few months I'll head home to San Diego, maybe Mexico, to figure out the rest of my life. That is, if my luck continues.

The umbrella people are listening to a protester giving an anti-war speech on the steps of the student union. The speaker's long hair is drenched, sticking to his back. He's shouting with the force of conviction. The draft, he says, is a political intervention to take control away from the people and tramples our dignity. He says the war causes human wreckage that runs counter to true peace and security. Yeah, that sounds about right. My fear of the draft torments me. Maybe the war will get me. Maybe I won't have to think about my future. I'll just lose everything I have.

I glance up at the sculptural figures on the student union's façade. I concentrate. There are four figures I've seen thousands of times. This time, imagination spins them to life. They speak. Two sculptures are sages, one on each side of a window. One sage holds a crystal ball, the other reads a book. The two other figures are atop a pillar—a dog talking to a dragon. The cold and grey stone figures turn to warm pink flesh, black textured fur and green armored scales. High above the crowd, what do these figures say about this war? The crystal ball glows with insight into what is to come, and facts jump out of the sage's book. The dog wags the simple truth in the face of the fire-breathing dragon. They all poke each other. They jabber back and forth and dance around in circles. Each one is certain, which makes the other one wrong. Their frantic mess makes an opinionated smudge. The sky blurts out a black clap of thunder. The figures turn back to cold grey stone.

A few years ago, when I started at USC, there were no anti-war speakers. Now it's impossible to forget there's a war going on. And the war doesn't give a damn about anybody's college career, or any career. In fact, the draft will be glad to see my 2-S student deferment expire and vanish. Most likely, I'll be accepted into the graduate program in architecture. But it's doubtful whether that will extend my deferment and keep me out of the draft.

"Whoa!" My shoulder's getting really wet, and I turn to see the rain pouring off the edges of a big black umbrella.

"Oh!" The umbrella moves slightly to frame the face of a strikingly beautiful girl. She's looking right at me, smiling, and there's something beguiling about her eyes that makes me feel like falling in.

What color are they? Hazel? I can't figure it out even though I can't stop staring into them. There's a depth there, inside an angelic face framed by waves of honey brown hair. I think she is the person who should be in my life.

I want to reach out and touch her and think I feel the same vibe from her. But she drops her eyes, and then I drop mine. We turn back to the speaker, who's finishing up to scattered applause.

There's a racing pulsation in my chest from the mere presence of this girl. I look at my watch. I glance at the carvings again. Soothsayer, prophet with a book, and a creature that breathes fire. The dog's eyes shine with flickered layers of truthful purity—stay innocent, keep your dignity. Good luck.

Damn, I don't want to be late for this class; it took me too long to get in. It's the most popular class on campus, all about witchcraft, shamanistic practice, and hallucinogenic drugs. It's perfect for students just starting to explore their inner worlds and maybe finding some new dimension by smoking pot and experiencing hallucinogens. It's an upper-division anthropology class, not my major. I have familiarity with Latin American history and culture, so Professor Gould made an exception for me. I'd better not be late.

Now the girl is gone.

I TAKE A SEAT IN THE MIDDLE OF THE CLASSROOM and watch the other students filter in. Soon it's crowded. That's when the girl with the golden brown hair and mesmerizing eyes comes through the door, shaking the rain off her umbrella and taking one of the last empty seats, way up front.

The professor is already giving an orientation to the semester. I'm having trouble concentrating, but I pull myself back, figuring how I'm doubly lucky to be here. He's talking about *curanderos*, or Mexican folk healers—shamans—who believe hallucinogenic plants were put on the earth by the gods. These ecstatic plants create connection with the gods for us mortals, a channel for our healing.

"Mr. Muir."

I jerk to attention. Professor Gould is a large man with a booming bass voice that commands attention.

"I know you've had some personal exposure to healing practices in Mexico. Would you give the class an example of a malady a shaman might be able to cure?"

"Sure."

The girl turns to look at me, and it's like a shot to the heart. I have to force myself to look at the professor and get my brain in gear.

"Well, uh, there's *mal aire*—literally, it means 'bad air'—when the spirit of someone who has died a violent death enters into a person who witnessed the death. The result is *espanto, susto y tristeza*—shock, causing fright, sadness and grief. The person who's possessed by the spirit starts binging—drinking too much, eating too much, taking too many drugs. Acting crazy."

"I'll have to catch up with you on that one, Mr. Muir."

The professor is brilliant, articulate and charismatic. The students searching for meaning are drawn to the mystical way he transforms ambiguity into conviction. Everyone admires him, but I know there is a flaw. He is the sage reading the book, with the illusion of certainty. The world scholar knows all the literature that's worth everything, and nothing. His academic mind insulates him from the intimate rub with the world's shoulders. It doesn't matter. He has something for me.

I totally lose my concentration again thinking about the girl. I feel crazy. I think we'll always be a part of each other; maybe we'll always be alone. All she had to do was smile at me.

Professor Gould continues lecturing to the class. His moss-colored corduroy sport coat gives an angular look at the shoulders, worn unbuttoned and open in the front. "Many curanderos use *toloache*, a plant that contains a hallucinogen that causes the mind to bloom like a flower to release the negative spirits, thus healing the afflicted person. This practice accounted for countless applications. But it is a powerful drug that can cause numbing and paralysis, so don't get the wrong idea."

Toloache. I know he's talking about the datura plant. I've seen its flower many times in Mexico, where it grows wild.

"Now let's get back to Mr. Muir's example of mal aire."

I hold my breath, waiting to either be academically ground up in little pieces or acknowledged for giving an example I hadn't read about in a book.

"There are other non-drug methods shamans used to treat fright." Gould puts his hand in his pocket. His sport coat drapes over his forearm. "What the shamans in Mexico call mal aire, was called fright illness by the Yuki Indians of the Round Valley region of northern California. The Yuki healers—the shamans and sorcerers—used methods of song, dance and ceremony." The professor paces back and forth in front of the class. "The healers re-frightened the Amerindian by reenacting every detail of the traumatizing event while physically or metaphorically holding the person." He stops and faces the students. "In this way, they symbolically anchored the afflicted individual and spiritually reconnected traumatized human being to the earth. Healer helpers chanted, danced and made a mystical-spiritual container for curing and bringing the Amerindian to wholeness— possibly a new, richer wholeness than the person ever had before."

I try to listen as the professor continues discussing shamanistic healing practices, but what I'm really doing is staring at the back of the girl's head, willing her to turn around. But she's busy taking notes, and at the end of class she slips out the door. I don't know her. I've known her forever. I don't even know her name.

THAT EVENING, THE RAIN STOPS. I should get organized for the semester, but I'm too distracted to concentrate. I decide to drop in on my old surfing buddy, Too-Tan Bremmer— "Too-Tan" because he needs to be in the sun for only half a minute before he gets a tan. And he's in the sun pretty much all day when the skies are clear. Underneath the tanned skin is a passionate heart that fuels a creative and deliberate mind. He's another one with a charmed life. His father is a design engineer; his mother sings opera. Add up mom and dad and divide by two. That's Too-Tan. I introduced his folks to mine. They became fast friends.

Opening the door to the apartment, Too-Tan says, "Perfect timing! My new girlfriend's here with her roommate. Be a brother, would ya," his face beams excitement, "and entertain the roommate for me?"

Too-Tan's place is neat, Spartan—sofa, two chairs and a coffee table. The usual posters—Miles Davis, *Endless Summer*, and a couple of other surfing posters. The Frank Lloyd Wright, Frank Gehry and Le Corbusier posters give a wink at his college major. My buddy has taste, and there is an innate sense of composition in the way he thinks and designs. An LP with Dave Brubeck's "Take Five" spins on the turntable.

Too-Tan hugs his girlfriend and introduces me. "Memo, this is Mary Jane."

She's charming, with long blonde hair streaming down her back. I get the sense she is Phi Beta Kappa, knows how to write a thank you note, but isn't anybody's little girl. Perfect for Too-Tan; he met his match.

"Oh," he says as a girl walks in from the kitchen, "and this is her roommate. Kate, this is Memo."

It's the girl. A bolt of realization hits me. This is destiny.

"Maymo?" she's saying, rolling her eyes and laughing. "May-mo." She tries it in two distinct syllables. "I've never heard that name before. What is it?"

"It's Spanish. It's spelled M-E-M-O. It's a nickname for Guillermo—William in English."

"So your name is Guillermo?" She looks me over slowly, and I am suddenly very aware of my sun-streaked hair, my blue eyes, and my skin that is so fair that I obviously have zero Mexican Indian blood.

"No, it's just Memo. My mother liked the name. She's, uh, she's from Mexico," I add. My tongue is tripping on itself—too stupid. I can't stop staring at her. She's perfect.

"Well, nice to meet you, Memo." She shakes my hand, pretends to be serious. Her hand is so warm and soft. I don't want to let go. Ever.

Too-Tan and Mary Jane disappear into the bedroom. The honor society doesn't make Mary Jane forget she is a real woman. I'm dying to hear the thank you note she'll send to Too-Tan.

Without a word, still smiling, still holding hands, Kate and I sit down on the sofa. Her legs, long and shapely in faded cut-offs, are folded under her. I am speechless.

"This is weird," she says.

"Yeah." Weird is a good word for it. It's weird and wonderful. "You ran out of Dr. Gould's class before I could talk to you."

"Yeah, sorry. I don't know why I did that." She shrugs. "I was feeling, I don't know." She frowns, and then smiles, clearly just trying to get a conversation going. "So what did you think of that guy in front of the student union today?"

"Well, honestly, I didn't hear much of it. I was just trying to get out of the rain."

"You didn't do a very good job of it," she says and laughs again.

"Well, your umbrella didn't help much," I tease her. "What did you think? You were probably actually paying attention."

She shrugs. "Nothing new, but he had a good message. Vietnam is a complete mess. It's a war, but they don't even want to call it that. It makes me so mad! And my whole family is angry because I'm even questioning our country's right to be there." Her voice is rising, and her hazel eyes are suddenly filled, an almost amber-colored light. "My whole family is Navy. My grandfather was a rear admiral, my father's a captain—even my stepfather was a commander. All of them went to Annapolis. They were in the military when we were certain it stood for the right things, honorable things." She slowly shakes her head. "Now, I'm not so sure. There's not much of a connection between what the military authorities say and what the media say and what photo-journalism shows."

"Oh yeah—everything's messed-up—all the confusion. Nothing is going to be all right until this mess is over. Or will it be over? And the draft. Not knowing if I'm safe or on the edge of a disastrous precipice."

She goes quiet, far away, and then comes back. "How do you know so much about curanderos—anyway?" The inquisitiveness in her voice says she wants to know.

"From my mother, actually. She's from Mexico City, knows about practically everything—the Mexican arts, facts to intoxicate your mind, indigenous traditions. And my dad's a physician—not exactly a curandero—he's from San Diego. But we spend a lot of time in Mexico, and they're both the masters of curiosity, and so am I, so—"

"Did you ever take that, what did he call it—?"

"Toloache. No. I'm intrigued, but not quite crazy enough, yet."

"Glad to hear it!" She gets playful, pushes my shoulder with her free hand.

I know underneath her joking around is a person whose secrets I want to learn about. And there's something about being around her that makes me feel like I've arrived, like I'm where I have always supposed to be. I can almost taste the emotional connection Kate has to give me. "Well, I have my moments."

Kate smiles, running her fingers through her hair and studying my face. "You don't look like a Mexican."

"Yeah, I hear that a lot. My mother's family is originally from Spain, but they've lived in Mexico for generations." I think of my mother, tall and aristocratic, warm, the person everyone confides in, the trusted person you want to talk to, whether you're a pauper or a prince, the person people seek out. How can I even explain her to Kate? Maybe she'll find out on her own and love her. "She lives in our house in Mexico City for about three months out of the year. She's in the arts, so—"

"No kidding? I paint!" She points to her cut-offs, speckled with paint. Then, more seriously, she asks, "Are your parents divorced?"

I shake my head. "My parents have what you might call a mature understanding."

"Ah. Not Ward and June."

I laugh. "No, 'fraid not. I didn't grow up in a *Leave It to Beaver* household. My mother thought June was a closet alcoholic, Ward was a womanizer, and they covered it up by looking perfect all the time."

Kate smiles and nods. "I always knew June's pearls were too good to be true."

"Yeah. She also pointed out that these sweet, perfect people's last name was Cleaver." *Whop!* I slash an invisible cleaver through the air.

Kate startles and jerks back.

I say, "Look for the cracks in the façade, that's what she taught me. And she saw that show only once!"

"She sounds cool." Then Kate turns serious. "My mom's a little more, uh, problematic."

"What do you mean?"

"Well, my parents have been divorced for years, since I was seven. My mom's bitter."

"Yeah? Too bad."

Kate seems so delicate right now she brings to mind a flower that could be easily crushed.

We drop into a sudden silence.

"So," I say finally, "how about the most frequently asked college campus question?"

"I grew-up mostly in Carmel," Kate says immediately.

"No, not that one."

"Oh," she says and laughs. She laughs so easily. Maybe she can teach me that. "I'm a studio artist, but an art history major. Remember my shorts?" She points down. "Dada!"

"I was thinking Jackson Pollack."

She jokes, "Well, the art history major is to make my family think I've really learned something at college. And I'm twenty-two, graduating in June. Your turn."

"I'm finishing my degree in architecture this semester. Finally. "

"Finally?"

"Yeah, it took a little longer—five years. I'm twenty-three. Thought I'd have a career by now, or on to grad school."

"Oh, you're such an old man. What happened?"

"I had a track scholarship, but I got a bad hamstring injury after my sophomore year and had to drop track. I was pretty bummed, took the summer off and was thinking about dropping out, lived at home—"

"Which is where?"

"San Diego, where my dad grew-up. I surfed all day and hung out all night, then went down to Mexico City and had an internship in architecture. But I wised-up about losing my student deferment, and here I am."

"You lead a charmed life, don't you?"

I can't believe she used that expression. "For the most part, yeah, maybe I do." I don't tell her that I've always had a feeling that my luck in life would run out someday. I don't tell her that sometimes I feel I've taken a charmed life for granted.

Another awkward silence. We'll get over this, but maybe not today. I try again. "Where'd you get the interest in painting?"

"I've always drawn stuff. Carmel is something of an art colony. My best friend's artist parents kind of took me over when mom fell apart after the divorce and gave me what I needed to develop my art. And here I am."

"And I'm really glad you're here." We lean into each other at the same time for a gentle kiss. This is it, what I wanted. After a taste of her lips and a trace of her fresh, feminine fragrance, I'm melting into her when she pulls back.

"What? Did I do something?" I ask. She's still holding my hand, though. That's a good sign.

"I'm sorry," she says, blushing. "This is too fast for me. I need time."

"That's okay; don't worry about it. We have plenty of time. I'm not going anywhere."

CHAPTER 4

TAKING REDS TO SLEEP

THE RUGGED LAGUNA SALADA DESERT PLANTS give me the sense they don't put much credence in death. Instead, they adapt and survive. *Laguna Salada*—Spanish for salted lagoon—got its name from past storms, which pushed vast amounts of water from the Gulf of California into the desert basin. When the waters receded, they left a salted landscape on the sandy desert floor. Some vegetation pulled through and made it. The rest didn't weather the adjustment.

After almost twenty miles, we angle westward out of the salted lagoon and onto the last seven-mile stretch. It's the way to a different landscape—the eastern shoulder of the Sierra Juarez and the Cañón de Guadalupe. The hand-built, boulder-studded road eats vehicles not meant to be here.

We see Chet and Suzanne, who have stopped at the dirt road juncture. We pull up. I spot an old, broken, rusted-out driveshaft someone left at the side of the road. Chet's shirt is off—telltale scars on his shoulder and side—and he is leaning on the rear quarter panel of the rig. He drinks a beer and smokes a fat joint. Suzanne stays in the front seat. All we see is her long blonde hair; she faces forward listlessly frozen—more like a mannequin than having life circulating though her.

Kate and Diane decide to stretch their travel-weary legs with a walk. They invite Suzanne. She shakes her head to say no. Suzanne is stiff and vacuously sits in the rig. Kate slides her forearm between Diane's arm and torso. They pace arm-in-arm. Kate looks like she's shaking loose of the conversation with me and is relieved to get breathing space.

"You've got some muscles there, Chet," Jack says. "How much brick and stone do you lift in a day?"

"About a ton," says Chet with a stoner's chortle.

My eyebrows squish together. "You were flooring it across the laguna." Chet is nonstop full throttle, except at the time he's too loaded to move. With me the crazy rushes are only punctuation points and not fulltime. Chet is edgy all the time. With me it's a crap-shoot. It's hard to know what's safer. Chet's predictability or my capricious volatility.

"Yeah, just felt like it, man. You guys want a hit? Or a Heineken?"

"Not now. I haven't smoked any dope since Nam," says Jack.

"Dr. Jack, you got loaded in Nam?" Chet asks.

I look back and forth at Chet and Jack. I'll bet Chet thinks Jack is straight arrow because Jack has the uniform look of convention. But Jack can handle any upscale or trashy thing that comes down the pike. That's one reason why my guts keep telling me I can trust the guy.

Jack says, "No joke, GI. After we took care of the wounded in an onslaught, we'd smoke more dope than you could throw on a fire to stay warm." Jack stares at Chet. He peeks at me, and talks to Chet again. "All kinds of shit happened over there. So when we weren't all asses and elbows in the OR, no holds were barred. I made sure to have my shit together when I had to be on. A couple of docs got totally out of control, diverting morphine. The only thing I asked of those fuckers was to not be loaded or go through withdrawal when they were operating on kids whose lives depended on us."

Chet squints, pulls on the front of his hat brim and takes another drink of beer. He hands the joint to Jack.

"No thanks." Jack wiggles his head to and fro.

Like me, Jack tends to zoom in and out of here and now; only he tries to hold onto sanity as much as he can. Still, his gaze becomes hazy, faraway. I think Chet affects Jack that way.

"One addict doc wasn't loaded, but started to sweat like a pig and got gooseflesh from bad opiate withdrawal in the middle of an operation. He had such dreadful diarrhea he left mid-procedure. I had to

shoot him up with just enough morphine so he could keep it together."
Jack nods. His face looks stern, hard. "A severely injured soldier was
on the table. That doc needed to be front and center to save the GI's
life, not withdrawing from opiates like a fucking junkie with a scalpel
in his hand. I had no choice but to give that doc a fix—just enough so
he wouldn't be drug-sick."

At Jack's story, Chet has an involuntary agitated rush. He drops
the joint. It rolls over the toe of his cowboy boot. He picks it up and
takes another hit. He sucks in smoke making a noisy exaggerated
drag off the joint.

"Nobody else could take over for the doc, and I was up to my
elbows in blood myself. Later that day, when the onslaught of wounded
GIs was over, I kicked that son of a bitch's ass." Jack hits the palm of
his hand with his other fist. "And told him that was the last time that
was going to happen. I'd get him help or he'd get court-martialed and
go to Long Binh jail, maybe Leavenworth."

"What about the rest of the docs? And you? You said no holds
barred," I say, parenthetically.

"We knew how to party pretty goddamn hard, but that doc was
wrapped up in himself and way over the edge. The death or medical
screw-up of a wounded GI caused by my complicity with that guy's
addiction wasn't going to happen. Absolutely and for certain, I kept
an eye on the guy."

"You were up against a lot, Jack," I throw in. I feel stupid for what
just came out of my mouth. Of course he was up against a lot. Jack is
the real man. "I'm just the self-pitying asshole who didn't do shit to
help—"

"You want a hit, Memo?" Chet breaks in.

"No thanks. Maybe a rain check."

"You boys out in the bush had it tough," says Jack. His mouth is
downturned, and his jaw is tight. "But I'll tell you what. When we
were besieged in the OR it felt like unrelenting fire from a .60
caliber."

Kate and Diane come back into sight. We can't hear their indistinct chit chat about this and that.

Chet butts his joint and puts the roach in an empty aluminum
35-mm film canister. He takes a last swig of beer. Chet fiddles with

one of his silver rings and looks over his shoulder and up the dirt road. "Okay, let's take off, man."

Kate and Diane's cheeks have a pink tinge from the exertion in the fresh warm desert air. They return to the vehicles. Chet goes back to his Land Cruiser.

Jack and I walk back to our rigs. "Thanks, Jack."

"Thanks for what?"

"You don't know?"

"No, what?"

"What you did in Nam, for everything you did for every buddy we had over there, whether we knew them or not. You know, thanks."

Jack's eyes take on an empty stare. The muscles in his face look frozen stiff.

Again, I notice the broken driveshaft. It's not far from a boulder in the road that probably broke it—rusted out, since the driveshaft has been there for a while. Some guy driving the wrong piece of machinery for this unforgiving landscape. We all fire-up our vehicles' engines within four seconds of one another—the guttural sound of two Land Cruisers and the air-cooled whine of the VW van.

We make our way through the terrain on the eastern shoulder of the Sierra Juarez, which is strewn with alluvial debris and huge granite boulders. Chaparral, scrub brush, cacti and mesquite find earth to grow in amidst the rocky landscape. I spot caves on the mountainside. The canyons containing water west of Laguna Salada are El Tajo, El Cariso, La Mora, El Malomar, and after a few miles of rugged road we see our prized gem—Cañón de Guadalupe.

The canyon cradles the backdrop of palmas oasis—oasis palms— lush palo verde and hot springs. A fault brings up the nearly boiling water from almost eighteen thousand feet below the surface. By the time it hits the surface it has cooled to 50 degrees above air temperature.

We drive onto the site and see José Loya Murillo, the owner of the camp at Cañón de Guadalupe. Don José gives us the best campsite on the knoll at the northern corner, which has its private hot springs pool, mineral water gravity-fed from the mountainside.

"Jack, beautiful, huh?" We stand together and look up the canyon. The monumental rock spire juts above the mountainous ridge. An indistinct feeling comes and vanishes before I can distinguish what the feeling is.

Jack becomes suddenly still. "Yeah, I can see why the canyon is named after the Virgin of Guadalupe—the rock formation is quite a resemblance of the Virgin." The spire's silhouette dominates the canyon. The setting sun casts crepuscular red and purplish and mauve shades on the pillar rock.

The canyon temperature drops. We set up camp. Chet pulls out a bottle of Cuervo Gold.

"Who's up for a couple of shots?" Suzanne hesitates, but has one shot with him. He rolls another joint. Suzanne has one hit. Diane shares the rest of the joint with Chet.

Jack edges towards Chet. His eyebrows press together and release. "How you feeling, Chet?"

Jack is friendly towards Chet. And then the idea forms in my mind Jack is an all-purpose friendly guy. Right now Jack looks as if he gets a kick out of Chet being high. Maybe it's because nothing seems at stake, unlike the doc in the Nam OR.

Chet says, "Dr. Jack, if I felt any better, I'd hurt and you'd have to put me in traction."

Just then a wind picks up. The airstream blows east over the shoulder of the Sierra Juarez. Air pressure funneled through hourglass-shaped, tight spaces of the canyon creates a high wind–velocity, a venturi effect. The wind increases in strength, violently shaking the six-foot long desert palm leaves. The racket is deafening. The two Land Cruisers are solidly on the earth, but Jack and Diane's top heavy van starts to rock—looks like it's about to be blown off the knoll.

The wind's force grows. Thirty-mile-per-hour winds blow the palm leaves horizontal. The van sways back and forth, and it looks as though it's on the verge of tipping over. Chet straightens up for a minute. We join up to get some line and secure the VW van. The physical part is a two-man job, so Jack supervises. Chet fumbles because he is loaded, but manages to be on cue to help me get the job done. Jack helps us with the hard part, the brains, pointing out how and where to secure the lines to tether the van to the earth.

The howling wind's force becomes intolerable for the women, and they huddle in the vehicles. The airstream noise is so loud that Jack,

Chet and I have to scream at one another to be heard. When we're done fortifying the vehicle, Jack and Chet join the women.

The darkness makes the pupils of my eyes dilate. I imagine my pupils practically eclipse my irises. My night vision becomes acute. I walk the terrain of Cañón de Guadalupe, checking the perimeter in the violence of the night. In the blackness I make-out shapes of bats with nine-inch-bodies and three-foot wingspans as they swoop down, skimming the surface of the pool of water to get a drink.

A stabbing feeling infiltrates me. I see shadows of human figures holding something—silhouettes of AK-47 assault rifles—among the oasis palms and palo verde trees. And then I pull myself back from the illusion—replaced by a rapid succession of combat images that uncontrollably flash though my mind like full blast automatic weapons. My breathing is short abrupt pants. But I still don't feel like I can get a breath. Air is trapped in the upper part of my chest. There's a tingling sensation in my hands and numbness in my upper lip and chin. A crash comes from the thrashing trees behind me. I spin around. Nothing's there. A wind-muffled coyote howl sounds in the distance. Or is it close? A rabid canine or sign of a trickster animal? I link back to the actuality I'm in Mexico. And I finally can breathe deeply into my abdomen. Now there's a reprieve from my twitchiness.

At 0300 hours I head back to my rig and sit in the driver's seat, next to Kate. At 0430 hours I drop-off to sleep. I dream.

When I wake, the day's first sunlight creeps over Sierra Cucapá in the east and casts early morning shadows across the San Felipe Desert floor. I'm okay, I guess. The canyon air has turned completely still. Jack and I are the only ones awake, both of us sleep deprived.

Jack says he knows sleeplessness from all the hours of emergency medicine—stateside and in Nam.

I know sleep deprivation from OCS training, and from what seemed like endless hours being out in the bush.

On the camp stove I make good coffee so strong it rolls back our eyelids. Jack and I head up to the vantage point a hundred yards from our campsite to check out the spire that looks like it's in the form of the Virgin of Guadalupe.

WHERE THE PATH NARROWS, JACK WALKS AHEAD. A REVERIE OF OUR friendship's beginnings filters in. At first blush Jack was a friendly guy. And that's the way he turned out to be because that's the way he has always been.

Our first meeting was a simple start. Innocent. He's a surfer. So am I. He's a physician— gifted, mixed with strong touches of humility. I come from a medical family, which breeds a familiar feeling. Those first two comfortable cuts put us in sync.

Serendipity links us a second time—standing on a cliff overlooking waves so huge and treacherous and gnarly, you have to be crazy to consider going into the water, much less actually do it. We're equally on a trajectory to go into the Army—war biting at our heels. What's to lose? We look at the monster surf. And then at each other. We say screw it. The adventure is ours. At this moment I knew Jack was a buddy.

Jack wipes-out. He's in deep trouble—caught inside the impact zone's turbulent human devouring watery mess. Jack is on the doorstep of Davy Jones's locker. I save him. And I rescue him from something else—panic-driven paralysis. I push him hard to go back out and face the mammoth waves that annihilated him. Otherwise he'll freeze into an emotional paralytic disarray. It works. He rides one wave. Then another. His excitement dissolved into fear. And then he overcame it and reconstituted himself to feel excitement. This tells me Jack is a gutsy hunk of human protoplasm. From that juncture, our future is set for other big wave risks.

Rescuing Jack weaves us together and cinches the friendship deal. I've never had a blood brother. Now I feel I have one.

War veteran camaraderie brings more webs of brotherhood. War's conflicts assign us an exclusive way of knowing and a nod of reciprocated compassion.

Jack and I mutually have strong family ties. That trait presets our friendship's strength. But we're more impartial with one another than our folks are with us—one difference between family and friendship, where between us criticism evaporates.

Our connection makes for something. No bullshit. No disapproving fault-finding despite times of our individual stupidity—respect in the face of imperfection. And there's acceptance of flaws and blunders, minus the destructive forces of placing judgment. There's a secure feeling, being taken to task—held accountable—without feeling dumb or like a fool. This leads to trust. We're confidants.

The surf rescue isn't a debt. It made for a beginning that led to a force. I count on Jack to step-in when a cold ugly rain comes down hard and gives me a biting poignant soak to the bone.

When we're together our friendship is bigger than what we individually put into it. It's like an alloy of two synergistically mixed metals to make a more solid substance. I'm the guy who came from an advantaged life. I'm pure gold that's soft and Jack mixes in to make one tough piece of elegant metal.

There's a bit Jack does for me. Jack has a well-tuned way of bringing me to self-honesty. It has a big brother feel to it. Jack's perfect timing is an uncanny gift. I wish I could say I always listen straight away. Self-honesty permeates through on its own timing. In the end, I hear Jack.

When we're together there is always a touch of newness based on an accumulation of something old. Jack is my pal.

JACK AND I ARRIVE AT THE VANTAGE POINT. From the elevated point we look up the gorge over the tops of tall oasis palms and palo verde. We see the early sunlight fall on the rock formation at the end, framed by the hillsides of the canyon. The angle of the light composes a phantom silhouette of the Virgin.

Jack has an incredulous dazed look. "Holy smoke."

"Yeah, an impressive holy piece, Jack." A glimmer of a euphoric feeling comes—diffuse and good.

We stand in silence for ten minutes. The euphoria of the sight subsides, and we return to camp. The others emerge from the vehicles. Kate and Suzanne look beat.

There are lingering touches in Jack's voice. "How are you all doing?" Jack says to Kate, Suzanne and Diane.

The women are dressed in yesterday's clothes, except for Diane. She wears jeans, a tee shirt and a warm Pendleton shirt. Diane runs her fingers through her thick brunette hair and ties it back in a ponytail. She drinks strong coffee from a metal camp cup. "Not too worse for wear." Her dauntless and ready spirit has an attractive pull.

"Ugh," says Kate. Robbed of sleep, her good looks come through her tired face and swollen eyes.

The downturned corners Suzanne's mouth forms a slack and taciturn expression.

Chet winks. "I took a couple of reds. Slept all night."

"That's risky mixed with all the tequila, Chet," cautions Jack.

"Maybe for amateurs and lightweights," he returns with his now familiar stoner's chortle.

Diane refuels and pressurizes the camp stove. She whips together eggs, pancakes and luscious smelling camp bacon.

The smell of the meat cooking in the outdoors stimulates the animal olfactory recesses deep in my brain. This seems to be the nature of camping. Kate and Diane straighten up the encampment after breakfast.

Chet cracks open a Heineken and smokes a joint and sits in a camp chair to take in a cosmic desert view of his own private making.

Suzanne corrals Jack and me. We're alone with her. We look at Suzanne's translucent light blue eyes. And see that the lack of sleep turns the whites of her eyes to vein-swollen red. She has an earthy smell, the musky mossy scent of patchouli oil. Her fine, dense, waist length blonde hair accentuates the slenderness of her body. She wears tight jeans, a beaded black Indian tunic, and buckskin moccasins. Her long fingers and delicate hands are trembling.

"Memo. Jack. I'm scared."

Jack instantly clicks into what she means. "You have good reason to be scared. At some point a mixture of barbiturates and alcohol could be lethal."

"Yeah, or some lethal combination of something else." Ribbons of alarm pass through Suzanne's voice.

I tilt my body towards Suzanne. "So what's the deal with the reds?"

She breathes a couple of raspy breaths. "He takes them to sleep. A couple of times he wasn't able to get them, and he thrashed all around the bed. Screamed. Cried out, having terrible nightmares."

I don't take reds, but I dread darkness. It means nightmares. Like last night. Or it means waking up in the middle of the night and not being able to turn off my thoughts.

"He sleeps in a weird position, with his bent arm draped over his throat at the inner elbow." Suzanne's voice is sharp and pressured. "I kept asking him about it, and he finally told me he got in the habit of doing it in Vietnam in case someone wanted to cut his throat in the night. I've tried to talk with him more about it." Suzanne's face is uneasy. She winces. Her lips are drawn. "He tunes me out. Or gets angry. Or gets loaded. Or goes to some dark alone place in his mind. I don't bring it up anymore. Had to break off asking him." She stops dead. "You know." She pauses. "Because he scares me so much." Suzanne draws a breath. "But I'm still scared and stopping talking about it is a minor, minor fix that does nothing."

While I listen to her, I hear Huey helicopter blades whipping. A voice screeches in my head to stop the imagined Huey's vibratory whacking hum. Collect myself up.

Suzanne's brow is furrowed. She shrugs in exhaustion.

Jack has a focused look and examines Suzanne's hurt, agonized face. "There's more, isn't there?"

"Yeah." Suzanne gathers herself. "I was rooting around in his drawer trying to find his drug stash and I came across a bunch of Army medals—a Silver Star and two Purple Hearts. Chet has scars on his shoulder and on his side. I asked him how he got the wounds. He invented an excuse about a construction accident in Vietnam. Only partially believable. Doesn't ring true. I had to strain to accept it as true." She stops, takes a breath and looks Jack in the eye. "I can't get those medals and the scars off my mind."

My widening eyes feel like they're bulging. "That's something you can't get off your mind, Suzanne. The Silver Star is awarded only for major heroism during intense enemy combat. I'm tryin' to suppose what the fuck he did over there."

"Yeah, that's it. I don't know. What he'd do? I found out what's connected with being awarded the Silver Star. He won't talk about it. Or anything else. Just works, drinks and does drugs. And then more drinking and drugs."

Jack slowly shakes his head. "No clue?"

Suzanne raises her shoulders in a slight shrug and drops them. "Well, I know Chet drank down at the Long Bar. He ran into an old girlfriend. I guess he was pretty loaded. Chet told the lady about going out on patrol with three other guys." Suzanne looks down. "The

Vietcong killed his buddies, and Chet barely made it back to camp. The old girlfriend was pretty freaked-out, called Chet's mom. Told her about it. I heard about it through his mom." Suzanne's voice aches. "Chet keeps it way down deep. It's underground."

I say, "You don't get a Silver Star for that. Making it back and your buddies…well… wasn't enough to—"

Jack's face looks somber and caring and soft. "What are you going to do?"

My head tells me Chet must have taken out at least a platoon and saved his buddies, only to get ambushed on their way back, but I feel a choked spooky sensation. There are millions of scenarios at war, leaving us not to know what happened that shadowy night he was on patrol and had enemy contact with the Vietcong.

Her edgy facial muscles undulate beneath her lustrous skin. "I don't know. Damn, I don't know. I'm caught. He's too much to handle. I want to leave him, but I'd feel guilty. He abandoned me, but I can't abandon him now that he's so torn-up." Suzanne shakes her head and bites her lower lip. "Look, down here is not the time, but would you guys talk to him when we get home?"

"Aren't you worried," I look straight into Suzanne's eyes, "that he was confiding in an old girlfriend?"

Her brows pull in and she forces a swallow. "Yeah, but I—"

"But what?"

Suzanne's expression changes. Her eyes narrow. The corners of her mouth dip. Her words are clipped. "Promise me something."

Jack says, "Okay."

Jack and I look at each other. And then back at Suzanne.

"You won't tell him. There was a mistake. A fall from grace."

Jack and I nod.

"I wasn't perfect while Chet was gone."

"Oh," I say. I wonder the same about Kate.

"I was lonely." She shakes her head. Suzanne apologizes to us like we are the ones she's supposed to ask for a pardon. "I didn't know what I was doing, but—really—I blindly acted, but actually knew exactly what I was doing. I went to a party and Robert Chalmers— you know Robert?"

"Know Robert? You're kidding, right? Sure. His folks own a mortuary. He's in the business." I cock my head and look into canyon.

"He told me at times he'd do a bunch of coke before working on a body. And then went to the mortuary in the middle of the night to embalm someone. A trip. He'd be wired to the gills. Told me a cadaver's muscles contracted, letting out a lung full of air and making a moaning noise. Freaked-him-out."

Jack laughs. "Kind of amazing. A constriction in the chest cavity of a cadaver causes it to expel air and make a groaning sound."

Suzanne takes a breath and opens her mouth to speak. She stops. And she waits for a few seconds. "Well that was part of it. The coke part. But we didn't do any stiffs. I mean, deal with any dead people." She slows down for a second. "I left the party with him to do some coke. Jesus, I was the one doing the groaning." Suzanne feigns a smile, and then gets serious. "You know, I was a coke bitch. More like a vamp to get attention. But it didn't last long." She shrugs. "I feel just awful. I'd get lonely, call Robert to see if he wanted to do some coke. He had the stuff all the time. I wanted to be with someone. I wanted to be touched. I faked liking coke. Look, it was over long before Chet got home."

"Affairs aren't Diane's style, but she was smokin' pot every night while I was gone. She's dialed way back on it now."

Suddenly my posture stiffens. "I didn't realize Diane—"

Jack sounds like he's apologetic and reasoning things out. "Yeah, even the people who have everything going for them aren't flawless, are they?"

Suzanne squints and her lips draw thin. "So what about it? Will you guys talk with Chet?"

Jack says, "Mum's the word about the cocaine snorting mortician. It's hard to be perfect when times are tough. And sure, we'll talk to Chet."

I want to prop her up and be reassuring. "I want to help. There's a glue when you've been to Nam and—"

"Memo, did you get any medals?" Her voice has a shallow, high-pitched stroke.

Fuck, don't ask me that! "Look, I'm no war hero, just a guy who went to Vietnam and thanks to God I'm back in one piece. The worst wound I got over there was a bad cut from shaving. Maybe stubbed my toe once on the sidewalk in Saigon." And I know I'm fashioning the truth to be the way I want to remember what happened in country.

We hug her. She is a sponge for the love she is not getting.

Diane's eyes are wide when she sees us moving closer. Her head turns while she follows the three of us coming back into camp. She nods at Jack. To her, his thoughts are as obvious as if she were reading them off a page.

Kate wrings her hands as though she were washing them.

Chet holds a green Heineken bottle, sits restively, churning. He's covered by a thick brittle shell, which is made by layers of dope smoke, reds and ethanol.

Maybe I'll be able to sleep tonight.

CHAPTER 5

CHU-CHU-CHU-CHU-CHU

CHET IS BROKEN-UP INSIDE. But there's no dismissing the fact he's our buddy. He doesn't say boo—just shows himself by sucking up all the booze and dope and barbiturates and hiding-out, but a silver star is permanently fused in his core. Suzanne tells us about Chet and war and his trauma—so much so—I have disquieted and agonized spasm in my guts.

And what happened that night he was on patrol with his buddies is a mystery he's not going to talk about, at least not now. But there's the obvious, explained by being awarded the Silver Star. Gallantry in action against the Vietcong hostilities and he exposed himself to enemy fire. I want to know what happened, but I'm not asking any questions. If Chet tells me I'll have to open and bear what I'm not ready to face.

I check my hand. It's a clinched fist, fleshy white at the knuckles. My clue that I'd like to think Chet is the one who's is the whacked-out mess. He's the obvious one. It's haunting knowing I brought his same craziness back from war. I've gotta get away to the escape zone.

Kate, Jack, Suzanne and Diane sit in the camp drinking coffee. "I'm going to talk with Don José." I put my scabbard and Buck knife on my belt and head down the hillside.

"*Buenos días, Don José.*"

Don José, dark-skinned and burly, is in his sixties. His hands are strong. They have a weathered look. Don José wears a high-crowned, wide-brimmed straw hat with a tassel dangling off the brim's back. He's dressed in a cowboy shirt. It fits well, except it's tight at his stomach, stretching the shirt's cloth at the buttons. I homogenized his manner with the vaqueros and caballeros from the pueblos in rural Mexico that I came in contact with when I was a boy.

"*Hola, señor. Hizo ventoso anoche,*" he says.

We discuss how windy it was the night before. The familiarity of speaking with this kindly gentleman takes me back to my naïve and innocent upbringing, but I know I'm fooling myself because this brand of ingenuousness no longer exists. Rolling back to an earlier time is an illusion of safety that postpones what's inevitable.

Without volition, a picture of Chet abruptly pieces together in my mind. He slept all night, had a foggy barbiturate haze in the morning and most likely didn't have one dream from being snowed under with reds. He doesn't say zip about what's thrown around in his mind. And then my perimeter walk—dark, menacing and safe. My dream. Waking up to the weight of the night.

Don José catches my lapse. He says nothing, like a tolerant old sagacious man.

"*¿Los Piapias vivían en las cuevas, verdad?*" I ask.

Don José tells me the Indians lived in the caves during their migration across the mountains to the canyon.

I tell him I want to explore the caves.

He says shards of their clay pottery can still be found, some intact and exquisite. "*Cuídese, señor. Tenga sus pepitas bien abiertas.*"

I've never heard this saying before—doesn't sound like any Spanish I've heard. The idea is to take care of myself. Keep my eyes peeled. I already have my Buck knife. I head back to the camp. On the way I cut a six-foot, smooth bark, yellowish-green palo verde branch. The staff is forked at the end. I fashion the stave in case...

Back at the camp I tell Jack I'm heading up the hillside to check out the caves. I recount what Don José said. I ask Jack to come along.

Chet overhears me. He wants to team up with us. I hate myself for thinking that having Chet along will take an act of tolerance for me. And then the thought becomes a blur. Do I have to tolerate Chet, or myself to handle his inebriate stupefaction?

The three of us head up the rocky hillside, which is dotted with various sharp-thorny cacti.

Chet staggers and labors to make his way through the rugged terrain. He has a hangover and whatever he's been pumping into his system today pulls him down. Chet falters.

We arrive at a flat spot that leads to a steep, cliff-like embankment. We see a cave entrance. I creep closer and tilt my head to the side. "It looks tight."

Jack's gaze is focused. "Yeah, but let's check it out."

Chet is stoned. He's winded from trudging up the hillside. "I'll wait here and have a smoke."

"You still smoke Chesterfields?" I ask.

"Yeah." Chet pulls out a pack and taps out a cigarette, puts it in between his lips. The pack goes back in his left chest pocket. He lights it with an old, dented, brushed-chrome Zippo. The lighter's top is wobbly. The beat-up hinge is about to give out. "I like to have a good French Gauloises once in a while. They're hard to come by."

I tell Chet, "I bummed one off a French guy in the bar at the Hotel Continental on Dong Khoi Street in Saigon. Those dark Syrian and Turkish tobaccos made me so goddamn dizzy it about knocked me on my ass."

"Thought the Continental was off limits." Jack speaks from the top of his throat. My pal has a disappointed sound. "Memo, you smoked? The guy with the track scholarship at USC?"

"Yeah, it was a short-lived passing thing. Seemed to help at the time. No place to run in Saigon, only stints of humping it in the bush. Towards the end of my tour I figured I'd make it back alive and didn't want to kill myself from smoking and getting cancer so I quit before I came home." It relinquished its hold on me. I made the decision not to die in Nam and I sure wasn't going to die of lung disease or some other nasty blight.

Jack and I squeeze into the cave. I click on a flashlight. The illumination lights-up the cavern's hard pack dirt and stone walls, ceiling and floor. We bend at the waist to be able to stand in the eight-by-twelve-foot earthen room. There's a ghostly feel that the Piapia still have an invisible presence. Spooky shadowy figures dance outside the light's beam. I flash the light in their direction and their gone. Must only be my twitchy phantasmal invention. I drop my shoulders and exhale.

We see a small mound of dirt that doesn't conform to the rest of the cavern.

I carefully clear away the loose loam and clay with the blunt end of my staff and my hand. I find a six-by-five inch shard of irregularly shaped pottery. There appears to be the likeness of a butterfly or moth outlined on the shard.

Jack and I go to the daylight to have a better look.

The three of us huddle in front of the cave.

My mouth drops open and I jerk my head back, feeling giddy. "Holy shit. It's a monk moth painted on this damned pottery shard." Now I'm hollering.

"What's that mean?" asks Chet.

"The monk moth is an insect closely related to the butterfly that pollinates the datura plant."

Jack has a squint-eyed quizzical expression. "The what?"

"Datura." A second of lucidity seeps in. I've been holding back with Jack. Maybe he won't be sympathetic about taking the drug. "It's a hallucinogenic plant the Piapia shamans took. They used the drug to go into a state—enabled spiritual contact with the gods—bring the gods' message to mortals on earth."

Chet nods in a semi-knowing narcotized state.

Jack says, "The Indians made the connection between the monk moth and datura. This image says there must be some datura around here. That's what you're thinking?"

"That's what I'm thinking." I ask Jack, "You want to take some if I find it?"

"I'll think about it." Jack's voice has an equivocal flutter, ratting himself out that he too doesn't have any interest at all.

"I'm in." Chet is unhesitant.

I tell Jack and Chet, "The Piapia painted the monk moth on their pottery."

The two of them huddle around me acting like an audience.

"The monk moth symbol reveals they must have worshiped the mothy creature."

Chet says, "Yeah, if those Indians got loaded on datura, sure as shit they knew the fuckin' moth pollinated the plant. You gotta know how your assets work." He mechanically trails-off in his stoner's chortle.

Out of the corner of my eye I catch movement twenty feet away. My eyelids twitch. Then I see it. Suddenly my chest glows hot. Fingers are tingly. A snake slithers over a small granite boulder. Now it prowls its way onto the gravelly dirt.

Chet staggers backward. His movement conducts pulsation through the ground, enough to spike a threat reflex in the creature's sensitive, primitive nervous system.

The diamondback coils up in a semi-figure eight. The snake's tension is so tight its body vibrates. The rattler's senses amplify—it gets more of a read on us with the lightning in-and-out movement of its forked tongue.

Chu-chu-chu-chu-chu-chu-chu-chu-chu-chu-chu-chu-chu-chu-chu-chu. The diamondback's tail is straight up, shaking violently—signals a death threat. The snake is a big one—must have more than ten segmented tail beads.

My throbbing body drives a pulse into my neck so loud my ears turn into pulsating kettledrums. A mind-blurring screech says I have to terminate threat whether it's a deadly snake, or whatever enemy. My breath pumps faster, stomach muscles tighten; blood-engorged skin has a concentrated hot feel. "I'm going to kill that mother fucker."

"Let me have 'em," says Chet.

"Don't go near it, Chet. Dope's screwed-up your reaction time," says Jack.

"Back off, Chet, he's mine anyway," I say. I think this is my threat to bring to an end.

"Come on, Memo, just walk away. You don't have to do this. It's too dangerous," says Jack.

"Too dangerous? Bullshit, I'm doing it anyway. It's just a rattler. I'm gonna kill that mother fucker and we're gonna eat the son of a bitch."

Chu-chu-chu-chu-chu-chu-chu-chu-chu-chu-chu-chu-chu-chu-chu-chu.

"Memo, back off. This place is too far away from help, too remote to take a chance."

Movie frame images race across my mind—being stuck in the middle of nowhere and the only chance of survival is self-rescue or to neutralize the enemy. "Fuck, a lot of places are too remote to take a chance."

"Look, the rattler's venom is going to kill your ass. Really, let's split, just walk away."

"Watch, Dr. Jack."

Chu-chu-chu-chu-chu-chu-chu-chu-chu-chu-chu-chu-chu-chu-chu-chu.

I calculate the snake's strike gap relative to the span of the forked palo verde staff, plus the length of my arm. I creep toward the snake, fixing on its eyes and its threat-detecting tongue. I'm at the distance of no return.

"Memo, you can still back up and get out of here."

"I know, but I can't." A hushed shriek sounds in my head. "It's too late now."

Chu-chu-chu-chu-chu-chu-chu-chu-chu-chu-chu-chu-chu-chu-chu-chu.

I move three feet away from the reptile. It raises its head, the sign of an imminent hit. Jaw open, fangs exposed, it strikes. I see it in slow motion. The rattler springs through the air in a twisting gyration. I instinctively jump back two feet while the snake is airborne, staff poised. The snake lands six inches in front of my boot. With the forked staff, I pin the snake at the back of its scaled, triangular head before it can make its next move.

Behind me, Jack and Chet flank me on the left and right. "Yeah, yeah, ya got it!" shouts Chet.

The snake aggressively alternates between coiling and straightening, unable to free itself from the fork's grip. I reach down and grab the back of the diamondback's head. I drop the staff and bring the snake up within a foot of my face. I stare at its open mouth and fangs. There's a threat that could take me—yes, no, yes... I scream, "Fuck you, mother fucker!" The scream has a reverberating echo off the hillside.

Jack's head bobs back and forth as he tries to get a good vantage point, trying to keep in contact with what's going on. "Jesus, Memo, what are you doing?"

We watch the twisting snake defecate. I unsnap my sheath and take out the Buck knife. With one hand I grab the knife and push the handle against my thigh to lock the blade into position. I bend over, push the snake's head against the ground, and sever the head from its body. I grind the decapitated head into the earth with my boot heel. My scream echoes again: "You fucker!"

I wipe the blade clean on the thigh of my jeans, leaving a purpled-red smear. I depress the knife's tang, fold it and snap the knife back into its sheath. I coil up the snake like a rope. We head down the hillside, kicking though dirt and gravel and avoiding rocks and cacti. I imagine a soldier's blood on my fatigues—God, erase that picture from my mind.

Jack says, "Memo, killing the snake was…well, your rage shocked the hell out of me. I've never seen that in you before—came out of nowhere, and it came from somewhere."

"Yeah, no shit. I mean, Jesus, Memo," says Chet. For a slight instant he seems stone sober.

I'm a ragged variation, but as crazy as Chet. "We're all surprised." Warmth makes me moist all over. Tingling in my cheeks. My breath smoothes-out. "Flashes come from—"

"I didn't know," says Jack.

"Didn't know what, Jack?"

"You're a tough man, Memo. I think we're dreaming this will all go away."

I think Jack knows for sure. "No. The war shit isn't going away. Something like the rattler happens and it takes me back."

The mental picture of finding Walter and his severed member grabs my guts like an inescapable film clip embedded in my cerebral cortex. No, it's lodged deeper. The image lives in my survivor's reflexive reptilian brain. I see the enemy though the foliage. And now I feel the sensation of the M-16 trigger as I squeeze off the fatal round. Retribution is brought into being for Walter's death. And there's a twisted warlike veneration for the confusing maelstrom and snarled way his life ended. I'm a maniacal wacko the way I did the rattler simple kill, like being transported back to the bush for a few seconds. Jack touches my shoulder. I flinch, being brought back to the now by the reach of his hand on my scapula.

We're back at camp. We look like rumpled troops returning from the field. Kate, Diane, and Suzanne rush up to us and ask what happened.

Jack gives a tidied up edition, generously excluding what a nutcase I am.

The women crowd close to us and scrutinize the diamondback.

Kate is on my right, with her arm wrapped around my waist.

I hold the shard of Piapia pottery; explain the monk moth-datura connections.

They're wide-eyed and open-mouthed.

Diane says I should donate it to the Museum of Man in San Diego. She asks whether I'd break any Mexican laws governing antiquities if I took the piece out of the country.

Right now I don't care what rules I break or don't break. At times, victory is following your own rules and not sticking to external constraints levied by autocracies. And I legitimize in my mind taking the piece by knowing the conservation at the museum will be choice over letting the artifact stay buried in the nowhere land cave, conceivably to be found by someone else who doesn't know the meaning of the image on the pottery shard and making an oblivious decision how to safeguard and preserve the bit of Amerindian history…unappreciated and destroyed in someone else's hands.

I get firewood from Don José and return and make a fire to prepare the snake to eat. I cut off the segmented rattler tail, which turns out to have eleven beads. I shake it. It feels like a vague warning. I give it to Kate, along with the snake's skin. The fresh kill is on a grill, basted with a rich extra-virgin olive oil.

"Is it safe to eat, Jack?" asks Diane.

"Rattlers can carry parasites, but it should be okay with the cooking. Salmonella? Nope, too fresh," says Jack. He watches over the cooking.

"Eat it? That's gross." Kate grimaces.

"What's it taste like?" asks Suzanne.

My eyes fall in direct contact with Suzanne. "Something like rabbit, frog legs or tortoise. Actually, it tastes like rattlesnake."

Chet unscrews his aluminum film container. He takes out yesterday's roach, fires it up and starts on his second or maybe third or fourth Heineken of the morning. It's hard to keep track of how much Chet is boozing it. Part of the time he hides what he drinks and what we see is the result, a spaced-out mired mess. How much he uses is an object of obscurity.

I finish cooking the snake. Kate leans back, stroking her throat and mutters she'll pass on tasting it. The rest of us crowd around and strip the meat off the back of the snake like pulling string cheese off a round of mozzarella.

Susanne licks her lips. "Yeah, tastes like rattlesnake." She hardly blinks, looking at me.

"It's great." Diane shrugs, presses her lips together and makes a coquettish smile, cocks her head and her eyes are flirty. "If I ever get tired of teaching high school maybe I'll go into the gourmet rattle-snake business." She wiggles the middle of her body.

My voice goes flat, still gathering myself from a numb haze, feeling for splits seconds that I was back in Southeast Asia. "There are one or two more things involved than you might realize." This is confusing talk, the epiphenomenon of the inner workings of my war shock.

Diane eyes me. A quizzical look replaces her smile, tying to decode what I just said.

Kate pulls me to the side. She says, "Jack left out some pieces of the story, didn't he? He made up a sanitized version. You didn't just happen to see the rattler and decide to kill it for lunch. Come on. Fess-up."

I tell Kate about the rattler slithering across the gravely soil. Something sparked in me. Jack pleaded for me to stop. Dangerous, he said. We're in a remote place. He told me to walk away. What he said couldn't stop the chain reaction. Fuck logic. A full drive instinctive reflex took me over. Killing the threat—nothing, nothing could stop me once I was set in motion.

Kate looks at one of my blue eyes and then the other. "Where's the war aftermath going to end?"

My eyes flicker right and left. I turn. My view follows up the canyon to the Virgen de Guadalupe spire. I breathe heavily. Crazy thoughts rev-up, sparked by the Virgin-like rock formation. The Spanish conquest annihilated the Amerindian cultural ways and the brown-faced Virgen de Guadalupe apparition became a symbol that filled what was destroyed. And she became a symbol of death and life and protection and purity. Caught by distraction, I blankly blink once. I turn away from Kate. The Mexican belief sparks an anguished longing in me. To bring me back normalcy. To have my dignity restored. Maybe I'm just spinning and will never get traction. My gaze comes back to Kate.

She says, "Your face is dead-flat empty." Furrowed ridges form in Kate's brow. "You can't answer, can you?"

I crisply study the Virgen de Guadalupe spire once more. The want for normalcy has an elusive palpability that's beyond my touch. I can only say one thing now. "Not yet."

Kate's shoulders drop. She exhales a huge sigh. "I can't get off my mind what happened in France." Kate turns, and paces back and forth. She faces me again. Her speech is faster, weightier. "Something's really wrong. Yes, we had some really good times on the trip, but you were so distant. Okay, I have to tell you. I'm going to stop pretending." She stops. She's measured. "I had a dreadful time. It would have been better if we hadn't gone, because I hated faking a good time."

"I couldn't help it."

"Memo, I love you." The depth of Kate's inhalations and exhalations exaggerate her chest. "I don't know if I can stand what you are doing."

The site of the spire spins my mind to the different worlds Kate and I come from and my mom's Mexican heritage. But our early relationship had purity. Kate and I were singularly engulfed by our innocent love. How we felt about each other drove everything in us and seeped into every crevice of our uncontaminated lives.

We're physically together. That's it. I long for Kate—to feel connected—and to be how we were.

Lamentation fills me. I can't talk because if I talk about one thing, I'm afraid of a flood of everything. I feel like I'm on my hands and knees on a sheer hillside trying to scratch my way to the top. I keep sliding back with every move forward that I make.

CHAPTER 6

FAROLITO

"Kate, your stomach is growling."
Her expression and giggle segue into an adorable laugh.
"It's been awhile since—"

"If I needed an excuse to take you somewhere for the first time—
one has come up. Let's get a bite."

"Okay. I'm starved." Kate edges on being demure. Her striking
hazel eyes widen. "Your Latin American background is so...well,
intriguing. Being an American, and having your Mexican cultural
history. Architectural internship in Mexico City, family connections
in the arts...what's say we celebrate meeting each other by having
Mexican food." Kate draws in a breath. "Anyplace good near USC?"

"Anything excellent? Not really. Just border food—tacos, tamales,
beans and rice. No gourmet quality regional cuisine from the interior
or southern coastal areas." I look away. And squint. In two seconds
my gaze falls back on Kate. "I know what you might like. Let's go over
to the Brown Derby and get the original Cobb salad. Sometimes
movie stars hang-out there. Maybe we'll see one."

"Memo, take me to the most authentic Mexican place in L.A. What
is it?"

This girl is something else. I want to take her to a classy place,
but... "That would be *Farolito*, a hole in the wall. The Brown Derby

would be a safer bet. Farolito is the best authentic place north of the border, but it's in a very rough neighborhood."

"Farolito? What's the name mean?"

"They intended it to mean little lighthouse, but it really means paper lantern."

"Oh, come on. Let's go, Memo." She yanks me to my feet.

I'm melting. I feel like I'd do anything for this girl. First class Mexican food? Who cares? I just want to be with this woman.

We leave Too-Tan Bremmer's place and go out into the night for the first time. We drive to East L.A. I park a couple of doors down from Farolito. We get out of the rig. I double check to make sure the vehicle is locked.

Then we are in front of the restaurant, where a Latino in his early twenties confronts us. He wears a bright white t-shirt, sleeves rolled up to his shoulders. Chino pants and a wide belt with a big, square-frame brass belt buckle. Pointed shoes. A bandana around his thick, shiny black hair.

"*Oye, guapito, tu mujer es muy hermosa,*" he catches my attention by calling me little handsome one and tells me Kate is beautiful.

I knew bringing Kate here was a bad idea. Win or draw, I'm going to keep her safe. Losing is not an option.

"*Si, soy afortunado.*" My face is stern and rock hard as I nod, and tell him I'm fortunate.

The street and sidewalk are still wet from the rain and glisten green, red and white in the glow of street lights. The wet asphalt and concrete start to steam. My chest intensely pounds. My face turns to a heated blazing feel. My palms sweat; my mouth goes dry. I'm scared shitless. But I'd connect with full tilt street fighting to protect Kate.

"*Tu suerte va a combiar ahora mismo,*" he says with a street swaggered cockiness that my luck is going to change right now.

I glance at the side of his face, avoiding direct eye contact. His jaw is clenched so tightly that he looks like he is going to break his back molars. Chest puffed up against the tight drape of his white t-shirt.

"*Depende de tu percepción, 'mano,*" I say it depends on your perception.

"*¿Cómo me dices?*" He asked me what did I say.

There is no lying, manipulating or faking being a tougher guy than he is—just won't work. But the twist of me saying things depend on perception confuses him, shakes his street-guy concentration.

"*Nada va a cambiar, ahorita, y por favor no nos molestes. ¿Estas de acuerdo? Ahora la señorita y yo vamos al restaurant. Así que adios,*" I say nothing is going to change and don't bother us. Are we agreed? Now we're going in the restaurant and goodbye. I do this while my head is tilted back and I forge a booming laugh.

I take Kate by the arm and in less than two seconds I have pulled her into Farolito. I close the protective grillwork door behind us. The restaurant owner recognizes me. We sit down.

The restaurant is narrow and long. The bottom third of the slick shiny plaster walls is painted moss-green, and the upper part is lighter pastel green. Two clear naked light bulbs dangle from the ceiling— bright, but not bright enough to illuminate the dark corners of the room. One beam falls on a rectangular ceramic tile of the ubiquitous iconic symbol of the Virgen de Guadalupe. The piece fuses and is embedded flush in the wall.

Kate's face has a quizzical look. "What was with the guy outside?"

I reel myself into an easy going style. "He was posturing, trying to humiliate me by calling me little handsome one and challenging me by saying you're gorgeous." I begin waving my hand like a metronome, indicating what he said and what I said. "I told him I was lucky and he said my luck was about to change. I told him it depended on his perception, and this twisted up his concentration, wondering what the hell I was talking about. I said, don't bother us. I cut things off and scooted you into the restaurant before things could escalate."

Kate's cheeks glow and she has riveted eye contact. "You handled that well, sweetie."

Calling me sweetie? Jesus. "Handled it well? Thanks, but my heart was in my throat."

I ask her if she wants to order a couple of beers. She nods. My eyes flicker to catch the attention of the owner and signal with two fingers. He gets the idea.

I lean forward. "Thanks for your faith in me."

"I wasn't afraid." Kate's face looks innocent.

I don't think she knows how much danger we faced. "I'm glad. The guy's belt buckle was filed razor sharp for street fighting. He had a cylindrical bulge in his right pants pocket that was a switchblade, and his pointed shoes were designed for kicking. His accent told me he was born in Jalisco. He lives with his folks." Her wide, curious eyes light up, and I go on with my hunches. "I'll bet his mother runs the show, and she ironed the nice crease in his pants and bleaches his super white t-shirt. She's the real backbone of the family; without her, things would fall apart. His father is inadequate, and the only thing he can do is hit the mother once in awhile when he's drunk to show her he's the man he really isn't. The guy has a tattoo on the side of his neck, which says he's already been to jail, maybe prison. This guy is struggling to be a man in a culture where my guess is he doesn't have much of a chance. What are the options? Be a tough guy on the street. I could be right or wrong, but most likely that's what's going on with him."

Kate raises her eyebrows. "Wow, you feel a lot of compassion."

Across the room come layered smells of chipotle, other chiles, tomatillo, cilantro, cumin and pinto bean. Then the bittersweet chocolate smell of the molé comes at the same time Kate catches it. Her nostrils flare and her eyes slowly blink as the scent invades everything else.

The restaurant owner brings over a couple of open bottles of Bohemia beer and no glasses. In Spanish he says welcome back. He looks up and sees the young man peering in the restaurant window. The owner squints, and his face goes hard. With a sweep of his hand he dismisses the young man as if he were shooing away a fly. The tough guy turns, drops his head and walks off. "*A sus ordenes, señor.*" He goes back to the kitchen.

"What'd he say?"

"He said it was his duty to get rid of the guy. What you were saying about compassion?" I make a half shrug. "I wasn't compassionate, well, maybe partly. I was mainly scared. Trying to scope-out what I was up against."

"How do you know so much about that guy?" Kate slightly squints and she makes a little nod.

"Hints and intuition and suspicions. He's like everybody else, and he's like nobody else, and he doesn't blend in anywhere, except in the niche that will suffocate him. I grew up next to the Mexican border and knew some of these guys who tried to get used to being in the States. The guy's angry and feels like a cultural misfit? Oh, yeah."

"So, what happened out there?" Her cheeks scrunch up. "Why did things go the way they did between this guy and you?"

"Maybe speaking Spanish with an accent from Mexico City? That's what mostly got us out of it. Also, one of my high school track buddies, Gacelo, came from a Mexican-American barrio and taught me about street fighting. I had three options. One, make eye contact, but only make eye contact if you're going to engage. Or two, run like you are doing sub five-minute miles for 5,000 meters, which I couldn't do because you were with me. Or three, start talking and keep it brief. Number three was the only option."

"You made the right choice." Her body posture perks up. "I marvel at why you didn't go for option number one?" Kate tilts her head. "You're bigger, and, well, much broader in the shoulders."

"That goes back to, who's the adversary? Look, these guys win in less than twenty seconds. They're in the streets all day long, while we're sitting in class over at USC thinking about academic this and that. Even if I had gotten by the swinging belt and the razor buckle, the switchblade and the pointed shoes, this is his turf. His buddies would have been on me like stink on…well, you get the idea."

"Yeah, I've got it." There's that precious laugh again.

"So, do you still want the best authentic Mexican food north of the border?" I smile back. "It's not too late to go to the Brown Derby for the Cobb salad and maybe see some movie stars."

"Well, we're here. Maybe it wasn't a good idea to come, but I can't get away from the luscious smells. Besides, I feel safe with you."

I hold back what I'm thinking from Kate. If the chips are down on the street, I take care of business if there is no escape. I grew up an advantaged guy—not a tough guy—but I don't give a fuck what the risk is. I'm jumping in if there's trouble.

I straighten up. "Let's order."

KATE AND I SPEND EVERY DAY AND NIGHT TOGETHER. Things I love—studying, architecture, surfing and running—I love even more because of her. Time slows and stretches to accommodate us. She's always on my mind, making everything richer, making real more real. We have complementary minds that I have never experienced before in a woman. And likewise this translates to electrifying bodily sensations. We're always with each other. We can depend on each other. We're a team. We're lovers.

After a couple of months I want her to meet my family. The beginning is meeting my mother. We depart on the Aeronaves de México piston-powered DC-6 late afternoon flight between Tijuana and Mexico City.

Kate cranes her head to examine me as we near our destination. "What's that thing you're flipping back and forth between your fingers?"

"Look." I show Kate the medallion, one side white and one side black. On the white side is the iconic figure of *Nuestra Señora*, La Virgen de Guadalupe. On the dark side is an image of *La Malinche*. "It's complicated—the light-dark feminine icons of Mexican culture."

Kate raises her eyebrows. "La Malinche? What's that?"

I retell the story I've heard thousands of times in my past. "Nuestra Señora and La Malinche are like symbols for the good-bad mother." I rub my hand across my chest. "The Virgen de Guadalupe stands for purity, goodness and protection. She was an apparition, a miracle, a holy Catholic vision with the brown face of the indigenous people." I run my thumb across the dark side of the medallion. "La Malinche was the beautiful Indian translator for Cortéz. Ultimately, she had his child, a son, recognized as the first Mexican mestizo—a child with mixed Amerindian and Spanish blood. She is considered to have betrayed the indigenous people because she helped Cortéz against the Amerindian peoples, slept with him, but—"

Through the rotating drone of the propellers the overhead speaker comes on telling the passengers to buckle-up, we're about to land.

Evening falls by the time we take a cab to my family's home in *Pedregal*, the rocky place. It's located in lava fields of southern Mexico City. Kate looks out the cab window, stares at street lamp shadows of *los pobres*, the poor people. She smells trash's smoldering smoke mixed with humidity and other smells of floral and herbaceous freshness. A deep clamorous sound is a mingling of horns, people's chatter on the street, and the rattle of an old cab repaired with pliers and bailing wire. The scene turns into cool, clean, long, wide avenues and lush trees. The city street resonant sound of cars has a muted hum. A

Saint Christopher medal hanging from the cab's review mirror sways and jerks while we head down the boulevard.

The cabbie takes us on a scenic tour around the *glorieta*—the roundabout—surrounding the gold leaf statue, *El Ángel de la Independencia*. Kate's head is nearly in her lap as she tries to get the right angle out the window to view the night's glowing masterpiece.

I look at the luminous dial of my watch. Mom is waiting for us. The driver is extending the taxi ride for extra pesos. I'm edgy, but polite. "*Vamos a usar una ruta más directa, por favor, como ahora mismo.*" I tell Kate the cabbie is padding the tab with some extra kilometers, and I had asked him to take us directly to the house.

We come up to the quiet fresh Pedregal neighborhoods. Curiosity, imagination and fantasy make one wonder what people, gardens and beautiful homes are hidden behind tall broken glass-imbedded-topped lava rock walls and fortressed iron gates. The cab jangles over cobblestone roads and crawls over *los topes*, metal speed bump domes.

Kate's eyes wrinkle at the corners. "How does your father handle your mother being down here three months out of the year?"

I shrug and make a slight frown. "Handle? They adore each other. So, let's say that it's a marital bargain he's gotten accustomed to. His life is his medical practice. My mom is a swish city girl. She gets bored to tears in ho-hum San Diego. All together she's here three months out of the year and that does it for her. There's trust. He's down here part of the time. They make it work." The cab driver pulls in front of the gate of the Pedregal house.

We step inside the compound. Kate stops short, struck by something. She stares, studying the house with narrowed eyes. "Who designed the house, Memo?"

I lift up my shoulders to stretch my back. "Luis Barragán."

Kate turns her head toward me. "No kidding and that was my guess."

I shake my head. "Let's say mom has always been used to a certain type of life, so when Luis started developing house concepts in Pedregal, she…look, let's go inside."

Uniformed Pilar opens the door. "*Hola, Memo. Tomaré sus maletas.*" She asks if she can take our bags.

"*Pilar, la mujer es mi novia, Kate.*" I introduce Pilar to Kate.

Pilar slightly bows her head. "*Mucho gusto conocerla, señorita.*"

"What do I say?"

"She's glad to meet you. Just say, '*Igualmente.*' It means likewise."

"Igualmente."

Pilar takes our luggage. Kate and I enter the living room. We sink into the sofa, and then mother makes her entrance. We stand. Mom's always elegant, and understated, regardless of the informality of her long blonde hair that flows to her shoulders.

I give my mother a hug and kiss. She turns to Kate. Mom's blue-gray eyes are on her like Kate is an illumination. She closes them and gives Kate a welcoming embrace. Mom's acceptance makes my chest warm.

Kate pulls back after the hug, "Alita, thank you for having me."

Kate's happy, and nervous laughter kindles a rose-red blush in her cheeks.

"Kate, *mi casa es tu casa.*"

"'My house is your house,'" I translate for Kate.

"Let's have a drink. Kate, what would you like?" says Alita.

"A Coke would hit the spot."

"*Una cuba libre.* Add a little rum to that Coke, and we'll celebrate our meeting."

"Celebrate? Okay then, I'd like a glass of red wine," says Kate.

Pilar appears, used to the silent cue. "*Pilar, traiganos un vodka y agua quina, un vino tinto de Valdepeñas para la señorita y una cerveza,*" says mom who orders a beer for me.

"The red wine is from Valdepeñas," I say.

"What's Valdepeñas?" says Kate.

Mom has a rapturous feel. "It's one of the best red wine-growing regions in Spain. My family's from there."

Mom surreptitiously examines Kate's shoes. She inspects her hands and manicure. "What's the fragrance you're wearing, Blue Grass?"

Kate has a giddy pitch in her voice. "You have a good nose."

"I'll say she has a good nose." I laugh, knowing her perceptiveness and how she scopes people out. "Good nose, right mom?"

Mom and I laugh.

"Inside joke, huh?" says Kate.

"Pay attention and you'll become an insider," says mom.

We all laugh. It shakes-out a little of the tension from the three of us coming together for the first time.

"The inside joke is that mom always smells-out people; she's quite the interviewer. So Kate, are you ready to be interviewed? If you don't pay attention, you won't know it's happening." Letting Kate in on mom's ways is followed by a smirk.

"Oh, come on." Mom boisterously laughs, knowing I'm letting Kate in on how her curiosity about people is unbendable.

Pilar brings the drinks.

"*Salud*—cheers!" says mom.

We all raise our glasses.

"Hmm. The Valdepeñas is spectacular," says Kate.

"Opened it just for you. There's a whole bottle left."

"Alita, the room is so comfortable—the furniture, the lighting, and the design. Memo said the architecture was done by Luís Barragán."

Mom's face is adorned. "Did Memo tell you he broke away from surfing one summer and had an architectural drawing internship with Luís?"

Kate's eyes widen. "He mentioned an internship down here. He didn't say it was with Luis Barragán."

Kate catches my eye and laughs. "Barragán, huh?"

I'm almost embarrassed about how lucky I've been. And some modesty has stopped me from telling Kate about every good turn that has come from my parents' tutelage about how to move in the world.

Kate looks at a piece of hanging art. She moves to another, and then another. She stops at the fourth. I wonder how she's handling all this opulence.

Mom gives Kate a probing look. "Memo tells me you're completing your degree in art history and you're a studio artist."

"Yes." Kate has an enthused ring to her voice. "I love your pieces by Tamayo, Zúñiga and Siquieros."

They launch into an easy conversation about Jose Cuevas, Diego Rivera and Frieda Kahlo. I can tell mom's impressed. Kate takes a five second break and studies the Zúñiga painting. Mother's liquid blue eyes shine on me, and a secret approving nod meant just for me.

"Memo, go freshen up my drink. Kate, you look like you could stand a little more."

I leave the room. Thanks to my habit of listening intently to each part of a record—the vocal, the guitar, the drums, and maybe the harmonica or the piano or the sax—my hearing is acute. By happenstance or accident or some intention, I overhear the two chief women in my life talking about me.

"You've probably seen Memo's architectural drawings? And you've watched him surf and run," mom asks.

"The drawing and surfing, yes. Track was before we met. I've seen him run noncompetitively. His form is a nice fluid motion. Too bad about the injury nixed him from the track team."

"I'll let you in on something," mom says. "Having quit the track team at USC disturbed him deeply, but he absorbed it and doesn't bother people with how distressing it was for him. That's the kind of person he is."

"I've noticed that about him."

There's a pause and then mom says, "You have beautiful eyes. It's nice to see the two of you together. Memo's father—Dan—and I had a whirlwind courtship at Columbia University. I loved being in New York; I went to Columbia after graduating from the American School here in Mexico City."

I hear mom's chair squeak as I pour more dark-red wine into Kate's glass. I'm drawn in by the way they're connecting.

"When Dan and I got together," mom continues, "nothing else existed but the two of us. At the same time, life felt saturated with a kind of aliveness I had never experienced before. You know, Dan's a terrific physician. He's also a Renaissance man. He can discuss any subject; have any conversation with any person."

"I imagine Dan is very easy to be with—if he's anything like Memo. Memo told me a bit about why you divide your time between San Diego and Mexico City."

"He told you I'm a city girl, right? I love Dan, but San Diego is a little slow for me, despite all of our wonderful friends, really good people. What's happening in the arts and literature in Mexico City and New York is more my pace. I crave it. I have to have it. Dan's here a lot, so we're not apart that much."

"Sounds love-ly." The two of them laugh at Kate's comeback.

Mom takes a shift. "What do you think is important in a relationship?"

Silence peppers a few moments. Then Kate says, "What matters is what's important to the couple. If it doesn't matter to them, it's not important. If it's important to them, it matters."

"Memo wrote me that your parents are divorced. What mattered to them?"

"Not enough."

"You sound bitter."

"A kid who's gone through divorce is always bitter."

"Are you still that kid who's bitter?"

"Of course I am."

"You don't want to be bitter again, do you?"

"What are you saying?"

"You know what I'm saying."

"Yes, I'll love Memo forever. God, I love him, yeah."

"You're scared."

"Of course, I'm scared."

"You know he's never brought anybody here before."

I enter the room. My ears burn.

Mom takes her drink. She examines the clear vodka and tonic liquid. She doesn't taste it. "Memo, go put some more vodka in this." She hands it back to me. I leave. But I linger in the hallway, to eavesdrop a bit.

"Don't hurt yourself or Memo because you're scared."

"My mom was gloomy for a long time. But I think she managed to get her spirit back. She recently remarried."

"It's better to be happy than sad, but a little sadness gives yearnings to a woman's heart, as long as sorrow doesn't turn to bitterness when a dream is lost. Loving a woman who is only beautiful is empty because she doesn't have to think about the need to have hope. So what turns out to be true beauty? The surface? Or the heart driven by ache and desire?"

"You're not talking about my mother, are you?"

"Beautiful Kate, I'm talking about you. I'm talking about you being scared."

"I am scared. A kid never gets over divorce. What saved me were my best friend's parents who took me over. They gave me belief that marriage could work."

Kate must be looking at mom. "Aren't you scared?" Kate asks. "Your life is so perfect. Aren't you afraid it's going to be taken away from you?"

"There's no perfect life. So imperfection doesn't scare me. I'll tell you what does scare me. I love Memo more than anything. I'm afraid because Memo is an *estadounidense*—U.S. American—and the United States is sending its young to fight a war in Southeast Asia. That's what scares me."

"I didn't expect you to say that right now."

"I say it because it is constantly on my mind."

I can't stand to hear any more. I walk back into the room. "Here's your drink, mom." I put the bottle of wine on the table. "Did I give you two enough time?"

Kate puts her hand up by her shoulder. I take it. She looks at me, and I know she wants to be kissed. For three seconds nothing else exists.

"The interview isn't over," says Kate. "I don't think it's going to end."

She takes her glass of wine and leans back into the sofa. She takes a sip. She looks at the Zúñiga piece. She stands and walks to the work of art. Mom rises and moves to Kate. Kate turns to mom, and a velvety hushed look passes between them. Kate melts into mom's hug. Kate kisses her on the cheek.

"So I guess the two of you covered a lot of territory."

We leave mom and enter the bedroom. "Kate, she loves you."

"How could you say that? We just met."

"She loves you by extension. Something else happened, didn't it?"

"We just met, but I got that. I love your mom. Something else did happen."

I pull Kate close, perfect body contours. The rich, red wine taste comes across her lips.

Kate pulls her head back from our embrace. Her eyes are clear and sharp and wholly present. "I can't say I'll get over being scared." Kate's chin wrinkles.

"What can you say?"

"I want you." She nods. "All of you."

CHAPTER 7

MAMA-SAN, BABY-SAN NIGHTMARE

I DRAG MYSELF BACK TO THE RIG after continuously walking the perimeter for hours. It's 0300 hours. Nobody stirs in the dusky unlit early morning. The unremitting coyote howling, and deafening turbulent wind violently whips the palms trees from side to side.

I sit in our vehicle. Awake, riddled with agitation and exhaustion. My eyes have a sandy scratchy feel. My skin has an invisible thin layer on it, like a fine coating of microorganisms waiting to be scrubbed off. Random wind gusts shake the FJ-40. At 0430 hours my eyes close. I fade, having a floating feeling that slumps into a dream.

The dream's vision is hallucinatory and jumbled and blurry and clear.

Night time. I slip into a 1966 palmetto green GTO coupe parked in front of the Continental Hotel in Saigon. The car has been mine to use for my year-long tour in Vietnam. It never would start. I'm about to DEROS—date estimated return from overseas—a month to go in Nam—a charter jet waits two blocks away to take me home. A generous spirit of optimism pushes me to make another attempt to start the muscle car. I put the key in the ignition. The engine turns over with a ferocious rumble.

Now, enemy fire completely surrounds me. Must be only a few blocks away. The sky is lit with orange, casting a gray-orange, eerie, flashing glow on the sides of the city buildings. A volley of gunfire and mortar rounds thunders, echoes and reverberates through the city streets.

Then the images take me somewhere else; in a sea of demonstrators protesting the draft lottery at the USC campus. Classes are cancelled. The university is shut down. Each person in the teeming crowd in the quad is holding a candle and chanting, "fuck no, I won't go." The Tommy Trojan statue is wrapped-up in thick sheets of padded gray-black material for protection against vandalism. A man in the mob turns toward me. It's Too-Tan Bremmer. He looks like the terrified swirling figure in the Edvard Munch's painting *The Scream*.

Another place, another horrific buzz. Hippies put flowers in the rifle barrels of National Guard soldiers at Kent State. Weapons flash. A succession of cap-gun-like blasts attack the crowd. Protestors lie on the grass—dead.

Celluloid-like frames switch to form a different movie reel. I walk into the bar at the Continental. A Vietnamese woman who's a ringer for a hot Vietnamese secretary at my Saigon post, the USAID II Embassy Annex—Ha Ti Nu—sits down next to me. She wears a tight red silk sleeveless dress, high collar, dress hiked up her thighs and overstated spike heels. "You number one, GI. You buy me tea."

"I'll buy you tea, but I'm number ten," I say. "Maybe number ten-thousand."

The bartender brings her a shot glass with tea instead of booze. She drapes herself over me and rubs her body up and down my side. She's a turn-on tease. I leave like a page turning to a new story.

I walk down Dong Khoi Street in Saigon's District One on my way back to the bachelor officer quarters, the BOQ. I take a side street. The narrow lane feels safe. And then an ominous oppressed feeling permeates the thick air. The street closes in. The sky comes down on me as though it's a roof.

I step on a heap of feathers—nearly miss a severed rooster head— a fleshy, reddish, serrated-looking comb runs down the center of the chicken's head. Over a fire on the sidewalk a refugee from the war saddled countryside cooks the freshly slaughtered fowl.

There's a reek of old rotting fruit mixed with used motor oil dumped in the gutter. In the humid suffocating night, my moist fatigues cling to my body.

A Vietnamese man wearing civilian clothes makes eye contact with me. It's Charlie—it's an eye lock—the death look. He draws a pistol. The weapon has an exaggerated two-foot barrel. He aims it at me. I gasp, knowing I'm fucked and everything I've loved in my life is about to end...

Kate, my folks and my black lab, Shadow Facts, appear in front of me. And then in a flash they vanish.

I pull out my M1911A1 .45. Charlie is the first to pull the trigger. I feel the bullet whiz past my bicep and rip my fatigue shirt. He's a frenzied deranged sniper. His eyes disappear in the dark. I shoot him once on the right side of his chin. The impact spins his head to the left. I squeeze off a second shot. It hits the side of his cheek. Charlie's head twists off his neck and bounces on the sidewalk. The shots send the rest of him reeling two feet backward. His body collapses. The walkway is dimly lit. Charlie's head and body lie in a pool of oozing black-violet blood.

I turn around. Look behind me. I see Charlie's bullet has completely ripped through a Baby-San and also killed Mama-San, who was holding her infant in her arms. The mother had been leaning against a wall, and she has toppled over. They lie on their sides, lifeless, blood streaming on the damp rotten sidewalk. They're gone. Nothing left to do for them. There has to be more VC. I have to escape.

I run toward the bachelor officers' quarters. I run. I run and run. Where's the BOQ...where...where? A vain frustrated feel, like running in quicksand. Can't make it back to the BOQ.

My eyes twitch open. I catch a sudden half breath. My head jerks upright. Choke back a scream. I take several rapid breaths and look around and blink. Different dream—same dream—constant dream. Killing Charlie. Witnessing Mama-San's and Baby-San's deaths. Again and again. When will it stop?

The wind has died down to stillness. It's perfectly hushed outside the rig. The motionless palm trees are at rest.

I turn towards Kate.

Her eyes are open. They have red and puffy sleep-deprived look. "I've been watching you for some time. You cried out. It awakened me. And you thrashed around."

For a moment, I'm too dazed and disoriented to say anything. I choke on a shadowy object in my throat. And then it's like I am spitting out the images of when we met and being at Pedregal for the first time and her fear and Kate wanting everything that terrified her about making a commitment to me to be eclipsed by what I could give her.

I look forward and scan the rocky desert landscape. My eyes become uncontrolled and begin to horizontally twitch back and forth. First, the images of Mama-San and Baby-San flicker, and then being in the field with Dunner and Swiney and the black kid—permanently etched and temporarily covered over—involuntarily break-through. My body feels disconnected. My breath is shallow and rapid and my heart races.

I scan the landscape again. And close my eyes for a second. I feel my body's contact with the seat. My breath slows. Sweet Jesus, help me. I turn towards Kate.

Kate clutches herself. "Are you back with the living?"

I clear my throat. "I need to pull myself together." I take a breath and drop my shoulders.

"You okay, now?"

"Almost."

"Can we talk?"

"About what?"

"I've been awake thinking about France."

"Give me a few…I need to gather myself up a little more."

Kate's shoulders roll forward. Her head drops. She checks out for a minute. Kate raises her head. She stiffens her back and sits upright. "How about now." Kate regains her expression.

My stomach churns. I'm braced. "Okay, I suppose."

"Remember when we were staying in the little country cottage in France? In Provence? It must have been a few weeks after Nam—those two days where we spent hours drinking wine and having really rough sex. It was a full throttle turn on. We hadn't done that before. Maybe it was wrong, but at the time it was so unconditionally right. I was saying, yes, yes, yes and maybe it was too brutally animalistic for me."

After the Mama-San, Baby-San nightmare the switch to talking about France unnerves and rocks me. My mind swirls for two seconds. And then I take the chance that talking about France will be a distraction and an escape from the nightmare. I pull together a fragment of resilience and tell Kate our trip to France had a new and a familiar feel to it. New because we hadn't been there before. Familiar because of my exposure to the remnants in Southeast Asia left by the French occupation—Saigon's architecture and old big fendered black Citroën cars and rebuilt yellow and blue Renault taxis and French food and hearing two words of French coming off an Asian tongue.

Kate says, "I was intent, listening to the language being spoken when you took me to the Vietnamese restaurant in Paris."

"I watched your face."

"Yeah, following the rhythmic low octave to high octave to low octave Vietnamese language melody."

"And—God—it was a strange flip leaving the restaurant—with all the Vietnamese rattling away—and going to the opening of the film *Woodstock* with French subtitles."

"Makes it hard to put two and two together, doesn't it?" Kate lets out a short forceful lungful of air. She shakes her head from side to side. "One minute eating Vietnamese food and listening to the language, and the next minute taking in the movie's peace and love and drugs and being colored over by antiwar rage."

I glance at Kate, and then look forward. I feel cramped sitting in the FJ-40. "Spare me for a second." I step outside. I lean against the vehicle and take in the vista. The morning sun casts the beginnings of warmth across the desert floor. I think, making my chest compressed and tight. Chic Paris doesn't have the grimy overload of war refugees crowding Saigon's streets, swelling every quarter with human protoplasm and the displaced people from the war-torn countryside living in the jam-packed swarming city in makeshift tin-roofed shacks or millions of Honda 50s buzzing like devouring locusts or the heat or the humidity or the gunships fighting at night on the perimeter of the city.

The French countryside is serene. A nontoxic and unharmed and protected feel. I see the rolling vineyard hillsides and quaint villages and quiet corner cafés. I imagine Kate's touch. Her gorgeous eyes look for reconnection. I have no fear of sniper fire. No ready alert—except the reflexive startled jump at the sound of a backfire. No toting an M-16.

What I see in France is bizarre and illusionary. A kind of removed and detached feeling, like color and depth are there, but I can't see it—like I'm separated from the outside world. Then I wonder if I don't know if France is dreamlike because a few weeks earlier I was in the Vietnam hostilities. Or if I'm the one who's unreal and alienated which makes everything around me surreal.

I open the door and sit next to Kate. We look at each other.

"Memo?" Kate has a wary, watchful expression. "Something spinning in your mind?"

"Just thinking about France."

"The sex in Provence?"

"It was too soon for me to go to France after coming back from war."

"One part of it was good."

"I think of the full throttle sex, too." Zigzag thread, an oblique inkling, comes the sense that the carnal bestiality was bound to my shell shock like an engorged blister that needed to be popped.

"Well, maybe we could do it one more time. Or just being held by you would be good, too."

Tension waves through and penetrates my body. "One more time, Sweet Cakes? Yeah." I let go of a breath. "Hold you? Okay, like spoons in a drawer." My eyebrows push together. I stutter, my voice having an uncertain inflection.

I scan the expanse of the desert floor. And then think the Mama-San, Baby-San dream revives itself like a relentless and surreptitious organism that defies relinquishing its hold on me. And I dread falling asleep, scared knowing the haunting nightmare will bring horror's trepidation back again.

CHAPTER 8

HAS A LIFE OF ITS OWN

THE SIX OF US SLIP into the hot mineral bath's ordering sense of tranquility. Diane's alluring natural beauty has an eye-catching pull that presses on me. She's somebody I always feel comfortable with. I feel upheld and bolstered and fed by Diane, like being taken care of by just being around her. My buddy, Jack, has the ultra cool utopian mate. Easy enough for me to push away her slight kink. She puffed a lot of pot while Jack was gone? In my mind I give her a pass, knowing it's tough being starved for the one you love. Who takes care of Diane? Jack does. She was desperate enough to get habituated to blowing the green-bud and getting loaded when Jack wasn't around. The picture perfect person isn't perfect.

I lean back, up to my neck to soak in the temporarily sedative effects of the hot water, and close my eyes. My mind drifts to the freakish human figures and geometric petroglyphs etched into the prehistoric Piapias' canvas—the desert varnish covered granite.

My eyes blink open. I sit up and tell the group about the figures. Jack is quizzical, and he likes to interview me. Smart people are like that. I look at him and say desert varnish is a weathering feature caused by iron and manganese containing dust. The dust mixes with night dampness and settles on the granite's surface. During the day, the mixture bakes on the rock—for countless and countless years. The result is the blackish-reddish-brownish thin film into which

Amerindians scratched their surrealistic rock art. The punctuation point that ends the explanation is that datura must grow nearby. The quiz is over.

The hot mineral bath softens my top layer. Underneath, my edginess still scratches at me.

I sit up and turn towards Kate. "Do you want to head up to the petroglyph canyon and help me search for datura?"

Kate shakes her head. "Pass. I'm going to let the mineral water penetrate." She exhales a soothed breath. "You're on your own." Her eyelids drop.

Kate's hair is pinned-up; her skin has already turned pink from the hot water. Her eyes flicker open. She sits up and squints at me. "Do you want a mystical experience? Or do you just want to get loaded?"

I roll my shoulders up. "Don't know."

"Well, don't hurt yourself. I might take some, too, if it's a good trip."

"Anybody else?"

"I'll go," says Chet. He bends his right knee, tries to push himself up with his right foot flat on the floor of the bath. Chet's fumbling push-off is short of the mark. He slips. Splash. "Double thinking it, I'll just slip into a tad bit more bliss right here."

Jack says, "I'm still unplugging from work. I gotta a good book to get into."

"I'm sticking with Kate," says Diane. "Maybe bum some of Chet's dope off of him."

"No takers?"

I grab another look at the Virgen de Guadalupe spire before leaving for the nearby canyon where the Piapia rock art is to be found. Jump in the FJ 40. I reach the mouth of the steep-sided deep valley and trailhead leading up the boulder chasm to the petroglyphs. One hundred and fifty meters south of the canyon is a lone vehicle. The stately looking lavish campsite set-up appears out of place. Three large tents, a table and chairs—more fitting for an imperial sheik than a Mexican desert oasis. I make out three figures. Odd place to be camped.

The figures move about, but stop when they sense me, the interloper. They stare at me. Two of them run pell-mell in my direction. I don't see weapons. Maybe they have pistols. They're aggressively running and now halfway to me. The bristling hairs on the back of my neck reflexively stand up on end in an involuntary piloerection reaction to the threat. Jesus, first the rattler and now two guys. I feel my heart throb in my chest. My breath quickens, my skin flushes, and there is a gnawing in the pit in the stomach.

Time to calculate.

Time is narrowing; think fast.

Automatic thinking: The first strike, the heel of the hand to the nose to throw the head back and reveal the Adam's apple for the second punch. The nose breaks, and there's potential for shoving the nose cartilage into the brain. This is followed by hit two, jamming the throat cartilage, causing the windpipe to collapse. Shit, how do I do two guys at once? I'll figure it out when they get here. Just like the snake. Just like Nam—no time to think—react—the job will get done.

The maneuver is from Hand-to-Hand Combat 101. The fatal move takes less than four seconds. Any more than that, and I'm the victim. They're almost on top of me. They slow down, fighting to catch their breath.

Like their campsite, they're out of place. The men are light-skinned Mexicans, handsome; the age spread and similar looks say they're father and son. Their clothes and shoes are casual but look expensive. They have fine-looking haircuts, ultra-thick-looking hair slicked back with pomade.

The two men give no sign of physical threat. The hairs on the back of my neck calm down, and my skin cools, leaving sheen of sweat on my forehead. This isn't a combat zone. But I can't purge the war from my mind. Compared with most soldiers, I saw little combat in Nam. And preoccupation with what I saw can make me transitorily dismiss what happened to the other men at war. For me, I've had enough combat for a thousand lifetimes. There's no dispelling that some men endured and suffered enough battlefield experience for a million lifetimes.

I address the older man: "*Hola, Señor. Buenas tardes.*"

They're sweaty, with flushed cheeks, and—gasping for air—neither one smiles. They're still trying to breathe after running only one hundred and fifty meters. I extend myself again: "*Permitame presentarme. Me llamo Memo Muir.*" I introduce myself.

The older man catches his breath for a second. *"Efraín Castillo y mi hijo, Cristián."* He says his name and his son's name.

I conduct the two-minute interview. They are from La Paz, and Efraín owns a nitrate mine there. Mexican nepotism, the son is involved in the business. It's all family. Not too hard to figure out which of the two Mexican classes these people occupy—*la clase alta*—high class.

He explains his daughter is up in the canyon. The proud father says she has two degrees from Tulane in Latin American studies. The family came here so she could examine the petroglyphs. And get a glimpse of the Virgen de Guadalupe spire. This explains the oddity of these people, who look as though they should be on a plush vacation in Paris, but are instead camped in a desert wilderness.

I'm going up the canyon to check out the petroglyphs and find if datura is there. They're not stopping me, daughter or no daughter. I tell them I'm an architect, past Army captain and here with my wife and friends. I share my mother's Mexico City background with them. They get the picture of what fabric I'm made of. Five minutes with these men, and they feel like anchors, weighing me down and preventing me from doing what I came to do.

I make an empty offer for them to accompany me, but *"No, gracias."* The one hundred and fifty meter run was enough. Their unstated agenda is effortless to understand. They're protective of the female family member up in the canyon. I pass their inspection, which surprises me and doesn't surprise me. They have no idea who I am. A few words and touches smooth them over. I am free to head up the canyon, unencumbered.

Something about them annoys me, something distasteful. Can't bring myself to shake hands. I didn't want to feel their grip. For a split second I try to conjure up a visual image of the daughter and then give it up. I'm curious. Petroglyphs, datura, and a partially explained Latina are in the canyon.

The origin of the name Baja California buzzes in my mind—think about Jack, the man with the quizzes—calling me the walking encyclopedia of Latin America. *Baja* is "lower." *Cali*—for *caliente*—means "hot." And *fornia*, a version of *horno*, stands for "oven." Put it together. Baja California means the "lower hot oven." Or is it a boiling cauldron? Strange muses visit me when I'm alone and walking.

Massive boulders guard the entrance to the canyon. I navigate my way around them. The vegetation is the same found in Cañón de Guadalupe and thins out to nearly zero a couple hundred feet up the canyon.

I reach a level area deep into the rift and come across the refined looking Latina. Her blue-black hair pulled severely back from her face, not a strand out of place. Her fair skin has the tender texture of a pinkish-white flower petal. She stands, framed by a fan of igneous rock, her head tilted to the side and one hand at her chest. The image of Botticelli's Renaissance masterpiece *The Birth of Venus* is all I see. And then a jarring recognition—she has the same tilt of the head as La Virgen de Guadalupe. Is she the persona of Venus or the Virgen, both or neither?

"*Hola señorita, acabo de hablar con su padre y hermano. Me dijeron que está en el cañón para buscar a las petroglíficos. Tengo la misma idea.*" I just spoke your father and brother. They told me you were in the canyon looking at the petroglyphs.

She makes an approving nod. "Your Spanish is fluent." Her eyes glisten.

A modest shrug is fastened to saying, "I come by it honestly—family from *El Distrito Federal*—D.F." I swallow. "Your father told me you're from Baja and educated in the States."

"Yes." She's bubbly. "Listen, I've already seen the petroglyphs. They're not far. Would you like me to show them to you? I saw some *metates* in the boulders, which the Indians used for grinding the piñón nuts they brought here from higher elevations."

I intensely connect with her eyes. "Sure. I'd love it." There's a friendly feel, like I could go along with whatever she suggests. "I'm Memo."

"A Spanish name? Mine's Lupe."

Lupe extends her hand. I respond. The handshake for a woman is to take the front part of her hand. Her grasp is firm. It's unlike the soft handshake I have felt with a lot of Mexicans. She runs her thumb back and forth across the tops of my fingers one time. I feel her touch. And then dismiss it as if my hand is disconnected from my body.

"*¿Lupe, el apodo para Guadalupe?*"

"Yes. Everybody calls me by my nickname, Lupe. The name Guadalupe has never felt quite right for me."

"Do you ever go by *Lupita*?" Suddenly, I'm self-conscious I've over-stepped a boundary—*ita* added to the end of a name is an expression of endearment.

"Sometimes. You want to call me Lupita?" Her eyelids flicker. "Sure, be my guest." She has an understated, but coquettish smile.

Lupita looks certain of herself. She's polished. The way she carries herself says she has the right proportions in every department. Her Mexican woven white blouse falls perfectly on her body. Her form fitting jeans could still have a U.S. price tag on them.

Lupita and I walk up the canyon. Her back and forth sway at the hips takes me back to a fleeting allusion—the girl I met in the hotel bar in southern France. Drinking Bandol with her and getting smashed. There was Kate's reaction when I brought the French girl back to the hotel room. I know why the French girl is popping into my mind—like a hint dazzling in front of my nose. I imagine Kate being here now. She would burn skepticism into hot suspicion and be pissed off furious. And then considering the fallout from Kate goes to a numb place in my mind.

I hate myself for lighting up the thrill of a smitten sensation out-side my relationship with Kate. Trapped by Nam's anguished shock leaves me isolated, except for the familiar tie aligning me with Jack. Letting my dreaminess of being with Lupita seep in is like a reprieve from far off aloneness, and in the moment I have the feeling of turn-ing the separation from my existence into feeling connected.

We reach the petroglyphs. There are numerous abstract geomet-ric patterns and human stick figures scratched into the desert varnish. We see the metates where the Indians ground nuts and seeds.

Lupita and I sit down. We talk. At first it's an easy uncomplicated conversation about the metates and the Indians' show of tenacity by rubbing the smooth concave depressions into the granite boulders. The indentations must have grown larger over time by grinding the life-sustaining nuts and seeds into meal. One subject leads to another, and then another. And we enter what seems to be a container that redefines time. I've felt so blunt and distant and on the face of it, desensitized or overly sensitized since I returned from Nam. And in this instant I'm so alert, tingly, a kind of ardent and hungry feel. I look at my wristwatch. Three hours vanished in to the ether. Nobody else but Lupita exists. Talk. Indians, culture, education, family and talk that's nothing that turns into everything. There's an unforced, sort of snug feeling with Lupita.

Lupita delicately grins. "You're looking for anything else besides the petroglyphs, Memo?"

The first four words out of my mouth are halting. "Why do you ask?" How the hell did she come up with that? She's quick on the uptake.

"A hunch." Lupita turns her head forty-five degrees, showing her face's lovely profile.

A smooth rejoinder slips off my lips. "Nepenthe."

Lupita turns her head back towards me and her eyes widen. "You mean the nepenthe that's in *The Odyssey*?"

I own up with an amiable nod. "Yes, *ne*, meaning no and *penthe*, meaning grief or sadness. The Piapia used datura to inspire their rock art." I lift one shoulder and then drop it, releasing a breath like I'm confessing to Lupita. "I want to find datura. It's a form of nepenthe, really, because the Indians used datura to gain spiritual direction from the gods."

Lupita raises her cheeks. "Memo, you know the word *borracho*?" She has a questioning uptick in her voice.

"Of course." My voice has an open and shut timbre. "It means drunk."

"You know, the derivation is from *borrar*, to erase. Drugs aren't specific. They don't erase one thing—grief or sadness. They erase everything. *The Odyssey* is a myth. I mean, really a myth—don't you think?" Lupita's looks deep into my face. "You must know what I mean." She has a lenient smile.

I feel permission. The French girl gave me permission, too. At this crossroads there are no barriers or chains and nothing to confine me. There's the canyon and the Mexican wilderness and Lupita and me. I've pushed Kate out of the picture and into a distant place, like she's tucked away in a box somewhere out of my mind. I'm heated by being with Lupita and at the same time I'm pelted by self-loathing for annulling Kate from my consciousness.

She says, "Listen, you know I went to school in the States. I've been caught up in the political and cultural revolution. I'm not straight when it comes to drugs or anything else. Memo, get to the point. What's going on that you need to rid yourself of grief?"

I wonder why Kate never had the intuition and discernment to ask me this question. Right now, it seems so obvious. "Meeting you is a one-time thing, isn't it? I'm never going to see you again. It's like introducing yourself to someone on a bus. You tell them your life story, you get off the bus and the door closes."

"Yes, today is it. We have only today. I have my own grief. My roots are in Mexico. But the reason my father sent me to Bishops in La Jolla was because the educational opportunities in La Paz were limited. One thing led to another and then I did undergraduate and graduate work at Tulane."

Lupita looks down the canyon, up the trail to the west and then back at me. I guess she's checking to make sure nobody is coming—that we're alone.

"Initially my father tried to do the right thing by sending me away to school. But the end result is that I fly in the face of his traditions and values. Unwittingly, he created a monster. Me." Lupita bites her lower lip. She has a pensive expression. "I can't turn back. I'm caught. I have my grief. What's yours? Today is it."

I lean forward, examining Lupita. "I'll tell you what my grief is." I edge closer to Lupita. "Tell me more about you."

Her mouth is pursed, and then her face eases. "Memo, you've heard the song by It's a Beautiful Day called "White Bird"?

"Of course. Written by David LaFlamme and—"

Lupita's expression looks like she's craving an elusive undefined thing that she could touch, but she's not ready yet to feel. "Right. 'White bird, in a golden cage, on a winter's day, in the rain, white bird, in a golden cage, all alone. White bird must fly or she will die.' That's me. Is that you, too?"

We sit in a vegetation-carpeted area surrounded by rock and boulders, more like a room than the Mexican wilderness. I am caught up in something uncontrollable. There is a weighty feeling in my stomach. It moves up to my chest, like terror and tears and fear. Then it's a vulnerable feeling wedged at the top of my throat. In an instant, Lupita and I are holding each other. It's happening—just is—unreal but real.

She pushes me back to look in my eyes. "Talk to me. Don't erase everything. Erase only your grief. For right now—not tomorrow or the next day—I'll give you what you need."

We stop holding each other and our eyes fix. "Lupita, what do you need?"

"I need to escape."

"Are you anti-war?"

"I am completely anti-war. But I am not opposed to the people who went to Vietnam, came back and are messed-up. They're not monsters. The people who created the war are the monsters. And that is you, isn't it Memo—loaded with grief about the war and trapped because of the reception you've gotten since you returned?"

A cinch to reckon Lupita is a smart cookie who has otherworldly perceptiveness. "How did you know—?"

"You have grief and ask me if I am anti-war. You must have gone to Vietnam. Look, we have different stories."

"But they share pieces that knit together, don't they?"

"You saw death, didn't you? And you feel guilty because you made it home and others didn't. I have only my petty dramas about cultural conflicts and being controlled by the Latino old guard conservatism's iron fist of my family—the grief of my past and maybe more grief in my future. Tell me one thing that happened."

"I…"

Lupita takes my right hand with her left, and I am drawn into the deep liquid pools of her eyes. Her eyes dance back and forth, first looking at one of my eyes and then the other.

"Okay." I have to turn away from her penetrating intensity in order to concentrate. Then a stabbing madness of irrational regret and contrition punctures my mind. "I was on a mission to evaluate the operations of some U.S. personnel. We were between Saigon and the demilitarized zone, the DMZ." I censor out the Phoenix Program and it's excruciating to skip it—hold it inside, stirring in isolation— until the day the operation is declassified. "North Vietnamese soldiers must have received intelligence we were in the area. They attacked us—stunning blows. Escape and evasion just weren't possible. We called for backup. We were two hundred percent committed to lighting up the enemy." My voice is raspy. "I killed one NVA soldier. And then another. Maybe more—a blur that makes it sketchy to put a stamp on what happened because the fight came in relentless fast bursting waves. The conflict was a constant frenzy of enemy soldiers. You lose track of what's happening, like the combat hostilities become vague shadowy impressions, a smudge that's wiped across your consciousness." I cringe, covering my face with my hands, and then I drop them and my eyes reconnect with Lupita. "Our troops were about to be overrun. An assault helicopter company appears out of nowhere. Must have been nearby. God bless them. They found a perfect landing zone—LZ—for the assault helicopter troops to flank the enemy." I stop.

Close my eyes. A cluttered flood comes from every which way. Dark green valley clearing. Rugged surrounding mountains. Light jade-colored undergrowth, shaded leafy trees pushed against the mountains. Sound of powerful horizontal rotator blades. Then small vertical whirling aft rotator blades. Smell of jet fuel. The woody grassland smell of tall, razor-edged elephant grass. Humidity makes mossy rot out of the damp red soil.

Lupita puts her right hand on my left shoulder and holds my hand tighter, cementing an anchored feel. "Okay, keep going. I'm here."

"There are a lot of mortalities on the other side. The enemy retreats. In the bush I hear one of our GIs crying in agonizing pain. I run in. Our men are around him, uselessly trying field first aid to treat horrific abdominal wounds. Another soldier and I carry him on a makeshift stretcher to a Huey for a dust off—medevac him—to a field hospital."

"I can't imagine what it must have been like to carry him." She puts her arm around me.

The sound of my heartbeat throbs in my ears. "I feel the heat of his body when we put him on the stretcher. Some of his blood gets on me. I feel his moist hot blood soak through my fatigues. The iron smell of the blood. His guts have the stench of rotten chicken. There is the stink of his skin—reminds me of my playmate when I was ten, and we got all sweaty in the summer—little boy body odor. The young black GI couldn't have been twenty yet. He's one of several GIs who saved my life and the lives of the field advisers with me." I bypass telling Lupita about Swiney and his animalistic henchman troops. Too damn classified. I keep buttoned what can't be leaked. And I spare her the other mind-corrosive pieces—just too much right now for her to hear or for me to repeat.

My shoulders roll over and my spine arches forward. I cry. It turns into sobbing. And then I begin to convulse. My throat constricts, trailed by opening up to a cleared-out feel. My stomach muscles contract so tightly it's an agonizing hurt. My cheeks are swollen hot—steamy and totally tear-soaked.

Lupita's body posture shows the strength of conviction. She stridently pushes me to mop up the rest. "Don't stop. You're almost there, aren't you?" A nod tags her certainty.

I wipe my eyes on the back of my forearm and passably gather myself up to spill out the finish. "I put him in the chopper and get in. There's the smell of antiseptic used by the medic, set against olive drab canvas reeking because of rot and the stench caused by humid jungle's bacteria. Outside is the *thwack-thwack-thwack* sound of the rotator blades. Inside the chopper the turbine-shaft engine whines—the reverberating hissing hum dominates the helicopter cabin. The GI looks at me, terrified. 'Sir, I want to go home. I want to be with my family. I miss my family, sir.'" I swallow. My voice quiets. "I hate pretending, having to come up with something reassuring to tell him, 'I'm going to get you home, troop. I know they love you. They'll be waiting for you.' The kid barely kissed life. His eyes go blank." I shake my head back and forth. I didn't lie, but I didn't say he'd be dead when he arrived home to his grieving family."

Lupita's eyebrows bridge together. "What did you do?"

"The surface troops took care of him when we landed at a base camp—don't know what happened afterward. Except, I confirmed with his CO the black kid would get a Combat Infantry Badge. I promised that to him before he died."

I take a breath. Stare into Lupita's eyes. "One problem. You witness people being wounded or dying. You order a dust-off. The injured person is gone. There's no conclusion. The hurt solider evaporates. You're left guessing what happened. All that's left is an anonymous body bag returning to an anonymous family. You have an accumulation of grief for persons you would not otherwise know, if it were not for war. What I imagined was this soldier's poor parents when they heard the military representatives ringing their doorbell or got a telegram and plunged into the depths finding out their son was dead."

Lupita looks like she's struggling to say what'll take the edge off. "There's the shock and agony of what happened. You think you should have done more?"

I've carried the weighty burden since the day it happened. "Yeah, what we were doing was based on having pinpoint intelligence, and it was all wrong. That attack shouldn't have happened. I should have double-checked our information about VC and NVA in the area—made sure it was correct."

"I'm naïve about the military." Lupita moistens her lips. "But do you really think you could have been on top of one hundred percent of everything one hundred percent of the time?"

"I don't know." I look down for a second. "I just don't know. One hundred percent grasp? War is being broadsided by the unexpected. It happened all at once. The death of the young soldier…a snapshot of what happened thousands and thousands and thousands of times to our soldiers, all of whom had barely kissed life."

Lupita sighs. "You're stuck with the blessing and the curse of war survival."

The pain lets up, like the spasms of my anguish are impermanently erased. Lupita catches what I'm saying. It penetrates her and she has a sympathetic grasp. "Blessing and curse? That's right. Simple. Complex. I'm here. All those dead soldiers aren't here. And there's the wounded that lived and suffer the guilt of surviving when others didn't. I made it. I'm stuck, baring the remorse of being alive."

We hug—tightly and tenderly—and then we let go. I get up and sit down on a boulder, hold my forehead in my hands and breathe deeply. There are more tears. An emptying out sensation, like a top layer being washed away. Grinding and rolling stomach convulsions twist me up for two minutes, and the contractions subside, leaving my abdominal muscles still hurting. I get to my feet. The beautiful Latina stands in front of me.

I have a searching gaze into Lupita's eyes. "What's your grief? Today is it. I'll give you what you need, too."

"Thanks, but no, Memo." She shakes her head. "Compared with yours, my problems are featherweight and feel like they don't have any merit."

"They're not inconsequential to you. You said you're the white bird who must fly or you will die. Tell me."

I stand, facing Lupita. My tears dry. We're in an otherworldly shielded bubble, open, vulnerable and safe. But she looks down the canyon. She's silent. I put my index finger on her jaw facing away from me and guide her eyes back to mine. "It's okay. You want to let it go, too, don't you?"

Lupita stammers for a second. "I'm getting married in a couple of weeks to the son of my father's business partner." Lupita hesitates, looks up and frowns. She turns back towards me. "My marriage to Alejandro is arranged. He's nice, has a MBA from UNAM—you know UNAM?"

"*Universidad Nacional Autónoma de México.* My mother being from D.F., of course I know it."

"Let me key into what I want to tell you. He treats his adoring mother and sisters well. Alejandro is nice in almost every way." Lupita's face is taut. Her lips thin out. "And he will never stop biting his tongue, nor does he ever speak an original word. He's habitually circumscribed by someone else." She stops, taking in anguished laden breath. "He's also a pivotal person in the business." Her voice trails off. "The marriage would represent—"

"A significant business power base."

"Yes, exactly." Lupita's eyes well-up. Her throat tinges red.

"You're saying he's perfect in every sense, except you don't love him."

"I don't mean to be critical. But, yes, that's it." Lupita's eyes switch from stern to bitter. Her voice turns acrid. "He bores me. I'm the monster my father created. The little Latina who went to the States and without all the dominating forces back home managed to cultivate a mind of her own."

"Fiery words. Your father wanted you to be educated but not evolved. Is that it?"

Lupita takes air in through her nose that makes a hissing sound. She stands straight and lets the air billow out. "That's exactly it." She stiffens, and an unsmiling determined look fills her face, leading to being matter of fact. "In our culture, women are seen as capable of keeping others safe from harm. Because their submissive goodness acts like a charm warding off evil. It's a parochial vision, one that binds and limits not only women, but ultimately men as well."

"You make *mejicanas* sound like La Virgen de Guadalupe."

"Yeah, that's the ideal. But too much praying to La Virgen for protection makes people stuck—no self-reliance."

Lupita's face softens to a resolute clarity. "Memo, women who show strength of character, daring or power are dismissed or are scapegoats, all of which lead to not knowing who we are. And then not knowing who we are extends to all Mexican people."

"Ever read Octavio Paz? What you're saying stands in the same way that he writes."

She looks astonished. "Absolutely. His work was key in my research."

"Yeah. Your father wants you to dance for him on the head of a pin?"

"Of course, if he only knew how much space I had at Tulane."

"The Latina women in my family do a good job handling feminine power." I'm soothing-out from being fragmented by the battlefield account. "They grew up in Mexico and move in artistic and intellectual circles. You see yourself ending up like Alejandro's mother and sisters, don't you? Let me give it a shot. His mom is matronly. She and her daughters wear loads of 18-karat gold jewelry and light a lot of candles at church."

"Yeah, that's it. It'll be a straitjacket."

"You probably tried to talk with your father about how the match didn't work for you."

"I did." Lupita's cheeks rise-up. "It was a dreadful conversation. Afterward, I cried for hours. Became depressed. The trip here is his attempt to make up with me. He told me what the marriage meant to the business. He said we couldn't cancel the wedding because more than six hundred guests were coming from all over Mexico. He talked about humiliation and family honor." She squints. Lupita moves her head two inches forward and speaks one octave higher. "You get the idea?"

"I get the idea you feel trapped and want to escape."

"I'm so alone. You understand, don't you?" Lupita lets up for two seconds. "Yes, you do." The push in her voice sounds like air that radiated up from her solar plexus. "I need somebody to understand. I'm so isolated—feel so alienated. There's yesterday's grief in my soul today and in anticipation of losing myself in the future."

I scan Lupita's drawn face. "It doesn't take too much work to see your grief. You have your own mark of pain, like a private battlefield with its victories and losses."

Lupita's eyes become pools again. I fall into them, dropping into an intrepid vortex that takes away the void. She pulls into my eyes like she's cascading, too. I grasp the tops of her arms.

She puts her hands around my waist and pulls to hold me tightly. "Thank you, Memo. Talking to you takes me out of an empty, lonely place. Let's leave. Come on. Let me show you some other petroglyphs farther up the canyon."

The breath in my chest burns down to my waist. Maybe it's the vulnerability. Maybe it's being understood. Maybe it's the closeness. Maybe it's the…I do not know what, except I want Lupita. I feel totally reckless. Kate comes to my mind and I feel like a shitty person because I push her out again.

"Yes, we're so close, let's do it." I'm incredibly awake.

Lupita walks in front of me. Her body. Is it a surprise package from a mysterious benefactor—a package I've been dying to receive for a long time?

We arrive at the granite rocks further up the canyon with the geometric shapes and human figures scratched out in the desert varnish. "They're more spectacular than the others, aren't they?" She leans into me.

I glance to side at her. "Yes, striking. Lupita?"

She faces me. "Yes?"

"We're out here alone. You're emotionally vulnerable, open. Aren't you afraid of me?"

"No, I'm not afraid. I have a sixth sense about people and have a good read of you. But I was thinking the same thing about you. Aren't you afraid of me, Memo?"

"No."

"Amazing, isn't it? We're out here alone, and both of us are vulnerable—and we're not afraid."

I'm afraid of Lupita's sense of invitation. But more so, I'm afraid that I'm losing control. "I've changed my mind. I am afraid of you, Lupita."

She's close. Lupita's eyes pull me. A visceral feeling. Her breath quickens. Her cleavage deepens with the depth of her inhalations.

"Memo, I suspect you're good at overcoming fear."

Her skin is warm and moist, with a fragrance that's nearly animalistic. Then comes the fierce electricity sparks. An urgency bursts open. Oh, God, her lips feel and taste so delicious. I run my hands down her sides and pull her close.

She holds me tightly, passion unzipped all at once. Everything ripped off and a flurry of scorching kisses. She screams between full-blooded breaths and gasps. Lupita feels so luscious. So alluring, magnetic.

I feel the wetness in the small of her back. Go, go and go forever. Echoes carom off the granite walls. Nothing else matters. Lupita's chest turns rosy. Turns red. Turns red hot. A scream from her pelvis shoots up her torso bursts in her throat—her convulsions are deep— we explode.

Exhausted, we hold each other, and our eyes meet. We laugh in disbelief of the furry that just happened.

Lupita looks in the sky checking where the sun was and to where it is now and calculates time passage. "Oh my God, Memo, my family has to be wondering what happened to me."

Like Lupita, my mind flips. Kate must be at the camp looking at her watch wondering where I am. Maybe she's tapping her foot on the ground. A momentary pang of wrongdoing sets in, making a wedge that inflames larger. There's a piercing feel at my temples and a weak feeling at the hinge of my jaw. Then the feeling is briefly reversed and evaporated by the excitement of being with Lupita.

We hustle down the trail to the place where we met. The excitement that vaporized gathers up again and I feel heat swelling in my chest. I stop and take her hand. "I've never been with anybody like you before. I've never had an experience like this before."

Her eyes soften. Our breath quickens, tension builds and it happens all over again. This time the edges are taken off the sharp corners, and the passion is deeper-rooted and longer.

She has to go. Lupita rips herself away.

I scramble to reconcile myself to Lupita leaving. "Today is it. We have only today." I grasped onto her, and now I feel anguished that I might dissolve into a more cavernous void.

"Yeah, today is it." Lupita wraps her arms around my waist and pulls me tightly towards her. "Memo, do you remember any other part of the song?"

I ransack my mind, trailed by the words reflexively swelling in my throat. "You mean, 'the sunset comes, the sunset goes, the clouds roll by but the earth turns slow, and a young bird's eyes do always glow'?"

"Yeah, that's the part I was thinking of." She lets go of my hand. "Goodbye, Memo."

"I hope things turn-out well." This feels like a trite and awkward and dumb thing to say after what's happened between us, all set in vague anticipation of the aftermath. I reach into my pocket. I pull out the medallion, one side white and one side black. On the white side is the figure of La Virgen de Guadalupe. On the dark side is an image of La Malinche. I pull Lupita towards me by the wrist and put the medallion in her palm. I release her wrist.

She flips the medallion from side to side. "The iconic symbols of feminine lightness and darkness."

We look at each other with torn smiles. "I knew you'd recognize the symbols. Keep the medallion to hold onto what we had just for today."

Lupita turns away and then looks back. "Oh, Memo. Your wedding ring—I saw it." Lupita turns and makes her way down the trail.

The first moment you meet someone it's uncomplicated—or, at least, it seems that way. And then the experience fills you. It has parts to it, like a puzzle with confusing pieces, struggling to fit together. It has a life of its own. She vanishes. Whatever happens, my memories will accommodate to the wash of the elation and buoyancy I have at this moment and Lupita's radiance will never fade, to be subsumed by the unknown cost of the consequences I'll have to face.

I sit back down on a boulder, put my forehead in my hands, and breathe as I did before. This time I'm purged and intoxicated at the same time. And not even a luminary has the leverage to reason away the unreal seam that was tied with Lupita. Her raw fragrance permeates my nose's passageways that feels permanently imbedded in my olfactory nerves.

I have the scent of Lupita on me—the man married to Kate. How could I've cut myself off from all of my feelings towards Kate to the point there was no stopping with Lupita? Kate hears my desperation, which differs from Lupita who knows it. She feels it. The sex with her took me out of being numb. But sex with her was one more self-destructive loop in my life.

Rippling through my mind is Lupita. She's a fanciful creature, edging on being make-believe. And now the dreamlike experience is smoothed over by being smitten. For an instant Lupita gives me connection. It could turn on me. Turn to disconnection by an omission and secrecy with Kate. And then the isolation of Lupita residing in my soul and the alienation of not having her. Or I could face my misadventure by being truthful and coming to terms with Kate. And her reactions to my betrayal would need a magic trick to undo it. So here I am in a quandary while a contentious argument battles in my mind like a tennis ball being slammed back and forth across a net.

I wait for half an hour. And then head down the canyon to my rig. I see four figures milling about the campsite. There's a strain trying to make out Lupita. There's the longing to touch her again, and also the pull to leave.

I drive off. My windshield is a blur. Nothing but dust to be seen in my rearview mirror.

The afternoon sun makes its way west, on the way to disappear behind the mountains lining the western edge of Laguna Salada. I slam on my brakes. Dust moves from the back of the rig over the roof to envelop my vehicle. Then the dust disperses, and I look northeast over the desert floor. The landscape changes to muted colors. Maybe I can abandon my rig, make my way across the desert to the highway, and hitch a ride deep into Mexico, to be lost forever. The thought comes and goes like a wave breaking on a steep beach—quickly reaching up, slowing down, pausing and receding in a rush back to the ocean.

I dread seeing the others as I drive back into the camp. An otherworldly feel returns. I want to be alone. I have to face them.

"Jesus, Memo, where have you been?" Kate looks me over.

I mentally step back when she inspects me. I hide—feeling like a fake—an imposter in our marriage.

She squints. Looking me over turns into an inspection. "Something's weird about you. Did you take some datura?"

I want to absolve myself. Stop. She won't understand. What wife would? "No, I'm just…slightly off. Where's Jack?"

"What! Where's Jack?" Kate's face is nerve-racked. Her voice is overwrought. "You've been gone for hours. And the first thing you want is to talk to Jack?"

I'm thrown into a self-forged panic. She has to suspect what happened. The smell of Lupita must be on my breath—all over my body. The musk of sex seeps through my jeans. Lupita is coming out of my pores. Jesus, she knows what I can't separate from the fragrant hints. "Please Kate. Give me a little time."

Kate stands, hands on her hips. She looks cross. "You've got some explaining to do, buster."

"Okay." I feign lightening things up. "Okey-dokey." I'm a frenzied jumble. Tell her? Hide it? "I need to talk with Jack first."

I search for Jack and pass Chet's Land Cruiser. A pack of Chesterfields and his beat-up old Zippo are sitting on the left front fender. I uncharacteristically take a cigarette and light-up. The rickety old hinge works one more time. I hot-box it for thirty seconds. Then I field strip the cigarette. I knock off the head and rip the paper down the side. Tobacco sprinkles on the ground. I ball-up the paper and put it in my pocket. My hands and breath smell like crappy cigarette smoke.

I find Jack. He's sitting in a camp chair reading a book and drinking a Jarrito tamarind-flavored soda.

"Hey Jack, can I talk to you? Let's head up the canyon and see the view of the spire from the base before the sun goes completely down."

"Sure, hold on. I've got two pages to finish."

Jack seems to take two hours to read two goddamn pages. My voice is silent. The voice in my head screams, come on, Jack.

We head up the canyon to the base of the spire.

"What's up?"

I tell Jack everything that happened. I finesse the explicit details for Lupita's privacy.

"That really happened?"

"Yeah. It's unbelievable. It's unreal," I say. Lupita gave me what I needed. How can I possibly reconcile my relationship with Kate?

"You want to know what I think?" says Jack.

"Yeah, I absolutely want to know what you think."

"I think you are a total fuckin' train wreck. But I love you, man. It's tough gettin' back, isn't it?"

CHAPTER 9

BROTHER'S-IN-ARMS

Our first acquaintance is brief and uncomplicated. Jack is a surfer, and it's one sturdy piece between us that makes the deal. It's the purity and passion, and the stoke.

I slip into the water. Morning's dark changes to the yellow-purple spectrum-colored crepuscular day's genesis at Sunset Cliff's Osprey. This time of the morning is sacred, dead quiet, with just the sound of the surf breaking. The smell of the salt and the seaweed draped over the shoreline rocks dig into my senses. Now a violet-orange glow of the sky's first light brings the day to life. The dawn casts a glimmer on the sea that gives it a pulsation.

The swells are well-shaped and overhead high, clean, crisp and glassy. A slight offshore wind feathers a spray back at the crest of the breaking waves. I paddle out. There's another guy out there, but we stay clear of each other, and then I don't see him anymore. After an hour of surfing, I make my way back up the cliff.

Another surfer, maybe a few years older than me, stands near my rig, leaning on his board.

"Hi. You really had a pulse on those waves," he says.

"Thanks. You looked pretty good too."

"Thanks for saying that. But I've been surfing only for a couple of years. I came out here from Chicago. We don't surf on Lake Michigan."

The man's body-hugging wetsuit accentuates his V-shape. The handsome guy's thick hair is salty wet.

My voice peaks up an octave. "Only two years?" I nod. "Well then, you're a natural."

"You a pro?"

I laugh. "Hell, no." I shrug. "Just surf because I love it. I've been at it just about all my life." My eyes must be bright from the surf session, the glow extending to my smile. "The ocean is a love affair that can turn into a drug. It's just you and the wave, you know?" I get a little serious. "Your mind gets focused out there."

"Yeah." He has a self-possessed smile and chummy expression. "I know." Jack has a poised expression, and he knows from experience. And Jack knows because he's the kind of guy who listens when people speak. Gets what people say behind only the sound of words. He'd probably would know what a person meant if gibberish were spoken. When Jack says he knows, it means he's taken in more than what has been said which makes him a sophisticated and cleverly bright guy. We stand staring out to sea, both of us wishing we were still out there.

He turns to me. "What do you do when you're out of the water?"

"Finishing up my degree in architecture at USC. What about you?"

"I'm a physician."

"Oh yeah? What's your specialty?"

"I'm a surgeon, mostly trauma surgery at—"

"Look at that!" I point out to the ocean. The surgeon spins around. We see the silhouettes of dark shadowy creatures clearly outlined in the face of a large, translucent green wave marching towards shore.

"Good god. What are those—sharks?"

I laugh. It's one of the most beautiful sights I know. I guess being a Lake Michigan transplant he can't read the ocean quite yet. "No, it's a porpoise pod." The porpoises dive down and resurface—freedom in their element. "Some old Mexican fishermen say that porpoises will try to help you if you get in trouble out there. Pretty much the opposite of the killer instinct and threat a small percentage of some sharks have."

"Yeah. God, what a sight," says Jack, watching the sleek animals disappear under the surf.

A second wave of the set comes through, and we see the pod again, leaping in unison, sun glinting off the water that sprays from their backs.

"Jesus, that's beautiful," he looks a little giddy.

The porpoise pod moves across the coastline. Their dorsal fins break the surface, become submerged and then reappear again and again, until they're too far down the coast to spot. Their silhouettes framed by the translucent waves is a lasting sight. And their images, lit by the bright morning sun, are burned into my brain.

I edge on feeling pressured for time. "Gotta go," I say, lifting my board onto my rig. "My name's Memo, by the way. Memo Muir."

"Jack Davey."

"Maybe I'll see you here again the next time I'm down from USC." There's something solid about Jack. Not just being a doctor or a salt of the earth Midwesterner—can't put my finger on it yet—something like a trusted older brother. And a seasoned kind of guy.

Jack affably says, "That'd be a real pleasure, Memo." I'm thinking Jack is a convivial man and then he turns and heads for his car.

I open the door of my rig. I'm charmed in a lot of ways, such an inherent feeling, and I bet I'll run into Jack again. An approachable and amicable guy like Jack just doesn't slip away.

A hippy drives by in a car painted in psychedelic colors. A bumper sticker says, *Make Love, Not War.* A second sticker spells-out, *Drop Acid, Not Bombs.*

My ingenuous feeling turns to a shadowy ominous sensation. A photojournalistic image flashes in my mind. A death scene from near the Vietnam demilitarized zone. An unclear future for me looms out there. My stomach convulses, coupled with a gagging sensation at the back of my throat. And then the charmed feel slips away, like it's elusive.

THE RUNNING SUBTITLE FOR FINISHING up my architectural degree at USC is dread. The culmination of academic accomplishment is met by the menacing threat of conscription, the Selective Service System— the draft— set off by the war a sliver of people stand behind and most everybody else hates.

Colliding storms drive a churn-up, a foul force that closes-out waves in front of Kate's and my San Diego beach house. Gray-black mountainously high cumulonimbus clouds breed an ominous day. The sandy offshore sea bottom terrain can't support the massive north swell and waves topple over all at once. The unseen sun lights the horizon, splicing the gray-black sky to a thin layer of gray-black ginger orange along the western horizon. And now the day is over. What's left is the thunder of massive rogue waves that rattle the beach house windows during the night.

The morning's ocean brings new extreme forces. Most would call it a tempest. I call it a sanctuary. There's darkness and lightness to it. The force makes you dig down deep to probe what you avoid, find out what you don't know about yourself and confirm what you do know. It's a wide open space and a private place. You don't have to enter it. But if you do go in, you'll feel a concentrated connection with another world that only you define.

At dawn, I am at the juncture of the dead-end corners of Sunset Cliffs Boulevard and Ladera Street, the northwestern corner of the Cal Western University campus. I get out of the rig and stand on the cliff overlook. The beginning daylight exposes monster twenty-plus-foot waves. Thick kelp outside the break makes for the glassiest early morning conditions. Not a hint of being closed out, unlike the beach break in front of our house. I hit on the right surf site. The undersea rocky reef embraces the mammoth swell, rooted by the marine shelf's configuration resulting in perfectly shaped waves and flawless conditions. Hell yes, I say, spilling out throaty laughter and I feel the glint in my eye.

I've got my surfer's sanctuary back. Yesterday's gray-black ominous no-go feeling disappears. There's only the ocean's invitation, the glassy surface turning from dark sunrise purple to twenty-foot walls of azure blue water.

Today is for those who have lived with the sea's potential and know it. If you're a man, the ocean is a mysterious woman whose name you don't know, but whose power you feel. And today is only for those who know how to read her and gutsy enough to march into her liquid. To the outside observer, surfing in these conditions isn't rational. For the waterman brand of surfer, it makes real more than real.

Another man arrives in his VW van. He gets out.

I do a double take and yelp, "Jack, Jack Davy! What a stoke to see you again. It's been over a year. Seeing the dolphins when we met was like a high that took over our minds, wasn't it?" I start feeling a little hyper. "Today is different. Today, the ocean is one big, strong, well-shaped muscle."

Jack throws his arm out and gives me a firm handshake. "Memo, terrific to see you." The sound of a crashing rogue swell reverberates through the still morning air. His head jerks in its direction. "Good God, look at those fuckin' waves pumping out there."

I bump my upper arm into Jack's deltoid muscle. "Yeah. The biggest waves I've seen here—the best conditions—what a stoke."

Jack scratches the back of his neck. "You going out, Memo?"

My senses are heightened. "Absolutely. It's totally bitchin'." I'm driven. Maybe desperate. Today I need to turn my jitters about the draft into being in my element, push myself to the max. Kate would think I'm insane for taking such risks. I think I am reclaiming myself.

Jack stands at the lip of the towering cliff. His hands are in his pockets. His head turns from side to side, examining the shore break pounding the rocks. He studies the cliff. I imagine he is calculating what it would take to scale down the cliff's treacherous descent. He looks up—studies the break and the glassy twenty-foot waves peeling off. I know the look. The excitement. The passion. Imaging what could happen. Stroking for the take-off, catching hold of the wave's power, grabbing the board's rails and pushing yourself to your feet. You make the twenty-foot drop. Weight on your back foot, pivoting your body at the waist and turning your shoulders the direction you want to go. Dynamic. Luscious. Watery bliss. This is what Jack must be seeing—the huge, flawless waves on the perfect day.

"You look pretty serious, there, Jack."

"I am serious."

"Take a little bit in of what I have to say. You're a fantastic natural at surfing. And you've got a few years of experience by now. I know this is going to sound preachy. But look, the surf is cranking. It might look easy from here. Out there, the sea tells a different story. There's risk. Danger. Lose your board and chances are it will be trashed, smashed to shit against the rocks and—"

"It could be too much. Maybe not. I'm a little on the fence. But, yeah, I'd like to get out in that big surf."

I clamp onto Jack being iffy about handling these surf conditions. I'm not going to push him to go out. "You have to figure that out for yourself. Assess risk versus skill, plus a little faith mixed with grit. I'm going out. I'd like you to go with me. But you have to do what's right for you."

Jack's brows knit in and he looks down at his feet solidly situated on the dirt. His gaze pulls back to the huge perfect surf. "My dad used to tell my brothers and me, 'No whining, no complaining, no excuses and put your shoulder into everything you do.'"

I cock my head to the side. "That must have made you aggressive with your brothers."

Still peering at the surf, Jack nods. "Yeah, and we're still competitive. They've done well in business. I'm the oldest of four boys and the only doc." He turns to me, having an intent look. "Memo, I always do the right thing. I was the good kid. Good grades in school. Did everything I was supposed to do in college, medical school, internship and residency." Jack shrugs. "My wife is wonderful, and we're faithful because that's the way we are. I drink a little and smoked pot a few times." He shakes his head. "But now I'm drafted, man. So you know what, those waves are looking pretty good to me. Some risk? Okay, fuck it, let's do it."

My eyes widen. "No shit? I just got my notice from the draft to appear for a physical and I'm blown away. Those twenty-foot waves have come at the right time. I'm itchin' to get my sanity back."

"I've never been in surf this big. Time to extend my parameters." I get that Jack is a doc because he says "fuck it" and then comes back with using a word like "parameters."

I tell Jack we'll have to help each other maneuver the boards down the cliff, and it'll be tricky getting across the rocks. I point out a narrow channel between the surf breaks, where we can paddle out. "Jack, we'll need to buddy up in these conditions." I pause for a second to collect up my thoughts. "The draft breathing down our necks doesn't make us rash about getting our sanity back. So let's just slip into those immense and polished waves."

Jack squints and surveys the ocean. "I'm ready."

"Okay, it's time."

We don our wetsuits and wax-up the boards with paraffin. Now the cliff. We take turns scaling down the cliff's narrow notches. We pass the boards to each other like two men on a bucket brigade. We're at the bottom. I'm right behind Jack to keep an eye on him. He makes his way across the rocks, through the wicked shore break. We're at the slim channel—fiery cold white water on either side tells us it wants us. The white water rumbles towards shore while we paddle out and gives the illusion we are accelerating faster than we are. I knee paddle my ten foot Dewey Weber surfboard. It's not the sleek, long gun board they use in the Islands, but it will get the job done. We make it out to the surf zone.

A huge clean-up set marches towards us. We scratch into position. I spin around. The enormous wave dwarfs me. The waves seem a hundred times bigger than when I saw them from the cliff. I take off.

The drop down the face of the wave is critical. A sharp bottom turn shoots me up to the midsection of the wave. The violent white water thunders behind me while I make a series of turns and cutbacks across the twenty-five-foot face of the wave. The face gets too critical and starts to come over. I kick the board out over the top of the wave. Nine feet up in the air, it twirls like a top in the back spray of the wave.

I swim to my board. Paddle out to Jack. "Jesus, I am totally stoked! I've got enough adrenaline pumping to drive a fuckin' freight train."

"I don't know if I can take off." Jack's lower lip quakes. "These waves are too goddamn big."

"Bullshit. Look, this one has your name on it. Spin around and take off. You're in perfect position—GO—GO!"

Jack makes the wave. I see him paddling back out to me. "Man, I've got enough adrenaline squirting to drive two freight trains," he says.

Jack is beyond himself. Nothing else matters. Not the draft. Not the war. Not the anticipation of being the doctor who is going to save bloody battlefield GIs on the brink of death. Today is today. The surf is pumping. Tomorrow—God help us.

We're jacked-up. Our exhilaration and our hysterical laughter don't stop until the next set looms like a moving mountain range on the horizon. I take off on a giant wall of cobalt blue water. The ride is a mind blazing memory.

I paddle back to Jack. Another set comes. "I'm in the right spot for this one," says Jack.

"No, no! The face is too critical. You won't make it."

Maybe he doesn't hear. He turns. It is practically a no stroke take-off. He disappears.

Jack couldn't have survived the drop.

I see the boiling backside of the winter wave. The powerful north swell is flexing its muscles. Churning white water takes over the blue-gray glassy sea. The wave pushed him towards shore. I see Jack's head pop up. He struggles to keep above water. He is crushed again and again by the succession of waves in the set. The wave mass mixes volumes of air with the water, so he has no displacement to keep him afloat. Jack can't stay up.

I take off on the next wave to move closer to him. Kick out of the wave. I see Jack struggling. Look for his board. It's not in the rocks. We've got a reprieve. The surfboard floats into the channel. There's a chance. I battle to get Jack's board before the next barrage. I paddle in the prone position with my foot on his board, towing it to Jack.

He is struggling to stay up. I get it to him barely before the next set comes. We scratch like hell back to the safety of the channel. His eyes are popping out of their sockets.

Jack has an ashen, morose look. "Let's go in."

I stridently shake my head. "No way. The completely wrong thing to do right now. Wipeouts are inevitable. Let's get back out there. Let's feel the force and power of that freight train again."

Jack's chin pushes up, forcing a frown. "I'm too fucked-up, Memo."

And I know I have to lead Jack on this one. My voice booms. "Okay, but you're already committed to being out here. And we already know you can do it. Ride one more wave. Let me tell you why." Waves are crashing in background. Jack's eyes lock onto mine. "You're going to be more fucked-up if we go in and you let the wipeout fixate in your mind. If that happens, there's no return from it. Let fear be temporary. Let courage be permanent." I hit my thigh with my fist. "Ride one more wave to get over your fear of what just happened. Now, Jack, let's get the fuck back out there. Judge the wave. Let the wave tell you how to ride it."

We're positioned in the perfect spot. Jack says nothing. His shoulders are rolled forward. His head is hung down. "Jack, watch me. Look at this wave. It's big. It's powerful. It's to be ridden." I'm swept up by the wave's ferocity and let it rip. I return to Jack.

We wait. "Jack, here you go."

Jack's mouth slackens. "No, it's too big."

I blow out a long breath. "Listen. There're no limitations on this one because it's perfect. It's powerful. You're in exactly the right spot. It's yours. Take off."

The passion of the wave pulls him in. I can't see what happens. All I see is Jack make strong strokes paddling back out after the ride. His chest is full. His eyes are filled with the energy of a full throttle freight train.

I'm mollifying. "We can go back to shore now if you want."

A spirited sensation seems to soak into Jack's face. "No. I've recouped. Let's stay out longer."

We catch one prodigious wave after another until an onshore wind picks-up, ruffling the sea's surface. Not even the dense kelp can keep the sea chop down. The surf deteriorates into a mess. I give Jack the okay sign and point to shore.

I climb to a narrow ledge on the cliff. Jack hands me the nose of his surfboard. I grasp the board and pull it up, followed by him handing me mine. He climbs up. We repeat the teamwork until we are at the top of the 80-foot vertical cliff wall. We're like brothers-in-arms returning from the surf zone battlefield, trailed by the last piece of getting our boards and our bodies up the face of the cliff to solid footing. We stand side-by-side at the top of the edge, looking back at the devouring surf.

I ardently say, "Man, was that ever intense." Comprehending more of what happened oozes in. "Did we ever take a lot in and spit it back out." I give Jack a lighthearted shove. "A total stoke."

"Yeah," Jack says. "Thanks for saving my ass. Being caught under those waves was bloodcurdling. And, hey, thanks for making me stay in the water, and so I didn't give in to my trepidation."

"We knew you could do it once you were committed. And you have to do it. Face the aftermath, no matter what it is. Or else you'll become paralyzed." I take a step closer to Jack. "You're too good of a surfer to be plagued with doubt when you go into the water. You'll remember today partly because of the wipeout and how you got over it, but mostly because of how stoked you are, Jack."

"When a dog runs at you, whistle for him." Jack sounds devil-may-care.

I wink and give Jack an easy nod. "Thoreau, right?"

"Good catch. Yeah, Thoreau. I'm glad I faced what chewed my brain after the wipe-out. I'd like to hang out with you, but I have to rush." Jack looks at his wristwatch. He speaks faster. "Got to get to the hospital. I want to stay in contact with you about the draft and what happens with both of us. Here's my telephone number. My wife, Diane, will always know where I am."

"What will Diane do when you leave?"

"She's a teacher—"

"You met in college?"

"Yeah, I was in medical school at Temple University, and she was finishing-up her degree. Funny. A mutual friend—a nurse—invited us to a party. The match making was a total secret to each one of us. The friend knew we'd fall for each other. And we did. It was like a party with a hundred thousand people, but after we met we were the only ones there..."   Jack looks down the road. And then he turns back to me. "I have to go. About the Army. I'll do the duty and come back." Jack gets in his van. Turns on the ignition. The rear-engine VW fires up. He rolls down the window. "Hey, I absolutely want to stay in contact with you, okay?"

"Absolutely? Yes."

Jack drives away. I watch the vehicle's rectangular shaped back move out of sight. The street is deserted. The empty asphalt is a blank movie screen. Celluloid clicks through each frame of what happened today with Jack.

What it was like when I met Jack a year ago played itself out today. He's like an older brother I can trust. Jack has spirit and fortitude and backbone. This man was scared out of his mind and had enough conviction he pulled himself out of it. He'd be the guy I'd go to if I were in a twist. Intelligence plus grit equals one hell of a guy you can count on.

CHAPTER 10

SELF-DESTRUCTIVE LOOPS

The beach house, nine days after Cañón de Guadalupe, 0830 hours.

THE GLASSY SURF ROLLS IN AND OUT, like the cradle swing of a baby's lullaby. The sea reaches to the horizon, made painterly by light catching ripples of azure blue, gold and silver. My love of the morning sea's effects seizes me with a spellbinding absorption.

Good strong coffee warms the core after a surfing session started at 0628 hours—the morning's first twilight. Now Shadow Facts stays by my side. She sits next to me and looks up when I stand. She lies down at my feet when I sit. Her eyes are on me anytime I look in her direction. Shadow Facts has dog world telepathy, intuiting the presence of Lupita in my mind and the wedge it's making with Kate. The dog still loves me. The dog still loves Kate. A loyal pooch, despite me being a traitorous rat.

Shadow Facts wags her tail and looks longingly into my eyes, letting me bracket off the faithfulness clash that fires back and forth in my rifted brain. I let the rustic beach house safety feeling spread into my thoughts. The place is a sanctuary, akin to the refuge of the ocean.

Reed grass wallpaper textures the walls. Two massive windows let in western and southern exposures; a twenty-inch world globe on a three-foot pedestal stands where two windows converge, anchoring the sea's vista. Bamboo stick curtains take the edge off when the afternoon sun's penetrating sea glare is too much. The rooms' wooden floors have been refinished a million times—unending old richness takes back its age.

Trying to keep one piece of my mind's dissension locked up in a compartment doesn't last long. What felt safe—out of harm's way— now is jarred. Today the house's sanctuary feel is cracked. I compromised everything. Emotions overran me and discarded my judgment. Lupita. Now I pretend with Kate. I trust Jack. Shadow Facts lies on the beach house floor and looks at me. Our dog's gaze confirms my self-loathing. Or it could be I assign her what I feel and imagine she feels what I feel.

I stand in front of a framed bathymetric map on the wall, which shows the depth and contours of the seafloor terrain along the coast, from south of the Mexican border to the northern San Diego county line. The map is used to help gauge surf breaks at different locations. Calculations depend on variations of wave directions—winter north or summer south swell and surge size. I look at the map, at the sea's surface in front of the beach house and back at the map. I sit down and return to gazing at the sand, waves and sipping hot coffee. I pet Shadow Facts. Escaping the uncertainty that surrounds me and eludes me.

I think of calling Frank Gehry about restarting my architectural internship. It's time to start assembling myself after coming home from war. But I stop myself. A dark numb feeling immobilizes me from lifting a finger.

The beach view pulsates with the day's life cycle—movie frames of wind-defined changing sea conditions, weather, birds winging and children playing on the beach. Decomposing seaweed, gulls, seals and other sea creatures are constantly reabsorbed into the planet.

I decide to give away the three bottle-green Japanese hand blown glass fishing floats I found four years ago in front of the house. I don't know why. I just have to do it. It took them ten to fifteen years to traverse the current's arc from Japan to Alaska to land on our beach. They're beautiful. They have history. They have a curiosity about them. But now in my mind they make for clutter. There's too much attachment to things I don't need. It was exciting when I found the fishing floats. They had a value, an importance and a novelty. Giving them away is part of a secretive final farewell.

An antique print of the majestic American race ship the Henrietta Vesta Fleetwing that won the 1867 Atlantic Yacht Race hangs on one wall. Next to it is a colored chalk drawing by Francisco Zúñíga of a Mexican indigenous woman. She is a sensual nude in a crouched position, sitting on one folded leg tucked beneath her; the flat foot of the other leg balances her on the earth. She's a timeless figure of earthy feminine nourishment and fertility, a piece of flawless line movement and composition.

I can't get Lupita off my mind, wondering if she's a sign of rescue and hope, or an illusion. Write her a letter? Yes, no, yes. Put off the decision. I sit looking at the ocean. Shadow Facts stands and rests her head on my knee. I know Lupita's family name. Her father owns a nitrate mine in La Paz. Finding her address would be the easy part. No, forget it.

The phone rings. "Muir residence."

"Memo?"

"Yes, this is he."

"Hello, this is Dotty Powers."

Hearing Dotty's voice gives me a reconnected and refreshed singular feeling. I think she understands war. And I think she understands men are changed when we come back from war. "I haven't heard your voice in eons! How are you?"

"Very well. Welcome back! When did you return?"

"In June."

"And how is it going, Memo?"

"I'm adjusting."

"Of course." Her voice is empathic sounding—weathering war and what remains in its wake. "Admiral Powers went through adjustments when he came home...during the days when he saw action." Dotty suspends what she's saying for a second. "Memo, I saw your parents at a party. They said they'd be in Mexico City for Thanksgiving. Admiral Powers and I would like to invite Kate and you to our annual Thanksgiving party at the Santo Tomás oak grove. You've heard of it? A musical event? Lots of people from the Fine Arts Gallery and the Museum of Man will be there."

"I've heard of it. Sounds wonderful." Dotty's invitation gives me a welcome and homey sensation. There's the overbalancing impression she understands the tribulations of returning from war. "I'll double-check with Kate and confirm. What do you want us to bring?"

"Well, you speak Spanish. You can go out to the coast and negotiate with the fishermen for fresh fish and lobster."

"You bet. And I'm wondering something."

"Yes?"

"I'd like to bring another couple." A tie comes that I'll need Jack. "My friend Jack Davey and his wife, Diane. Jack is a surgeon who served in Vietnam. He arrived home a few months before me. Diane is a teacher. They're great people. May I invite them?"

"Of course, Memo. Ted and I would love to meet them."

"Okay, I'll give them a call and see if it works. Is the admiral still on the board of directors at the Museum of Man?

"He is."

"I'd like to discuss making a donation. It's an artifact."

"Really! What is it?"

"A large piece of Piapia Indian pottery with a monk moth painted on it. I found it in a cave in Mexico. Such a remarkable piece. It's quite rare." I tell Dotty about the monk moth-datura connection and how the Piapia shamans used the drug. "I checked the Mexican regulations, and taking the piece out of the country doesn't break any of the rules governing antiquities."

"Sounds like quite a curiosity, Memo. I'll let the admiral know. He'll be very interested."

"Actually, it was Jack's wife, Diane, who had the idea of donating it to the museum."

"I look forward to talking with her."

"I appreciate you thinking of us, Dotty."

"Memo, it's so good to have you home in one piece." Dotty has the sound of an experienced military wife who knows the course. "I hope Thanksgiving works out for you and your friends. The pleasure is ours."

After we hang up, I sit motionless, my feet flat on the floor and my hands on my thighs. I look at the surf. An uncontrollable force comes. Out of nowhere, my mind involuntarily pulls up thoughts about Walter. I see his violet-red blood oozing and spilling out onto the muddy earth. We shouldn't have listened to him. We shouldn't have allowed him to go into the bush. We should have made him take a piss near the Jeep.

My recurrent dream works a path into a daydream. May 1970. Only one month before returning home, I was in Saigon's District One at night—stop. Don't think about it now. As it is, the dreams are too much. A lot happened everywhere. And there were the ironies. That month I received a letter from Too-Tan Bremmer, the guy who first introduced me to Kate. He told me about the protests at USC because the bastards running the war discontinued the general draft and started the draft lottery.

I should have been back at USC last May, when the university president shut it down because the protests had gotten so extreme. I should have been with my old university buddies, saying the war is no fucking good. Instead, I was in Saigon with my M1911A1 pistol strapped on my side. The tortured pangs of agony for what I should have done and what I did set my mind to racing without a shadow of forgiveness.

Images of Lupita dash to the front of my thoughts. Something which had a life of its own came over me—started by the reptilian brain breaking through an indefinable pressing down on my mind. Or on my larger spirit. Maybe both. I had no thought about Kate. No thought about the consequences. No thought about everything we're supposed to stand for. Jack's right. I am a train wreck. And I was hopelessly trying to find my ballast through Lupita, but I hopelessly made myself more lost.

The memories of Lupita's understanding have purity to it, despite my culpability for the infidelity. And then my mind shifts to one more self-destructive loop—my knife-like degradation when Kate and I are in France.

Kate and I have a delicious time in a cottage located at a chateau set-up for guests in Provence, replete with vintage wine and deliriously but delicious rough sex. Kate both loves and is scared of the rough sex because it is newly forged territory and she doesn't know what it means.

I know what it means. It's my way of handling war stress and trauma. It puts me on edge and that's what I want because I want to feel something. And seeking something intense—anything, even if it is destructive.

We go to Nice for a stay at Hotel Negresco on Promenade de Anglais, overlooking the sapphire shimmering sea of la Barie des Anges.

I want a drink. Kate is tired. She pleads with me to stay with her. I'm agitated. Then there's anticipation of boredom with the idea of sticking around the hotel room and doing nothing. I walk out.

Kate is sensitive to how detached I've been on the trip, combined with the sexual tumbles from the days before. She feels ditched and deserted.

I go to the bar. The wine list is outstanding. I order a bottle of Bandol that is from the coastal Provence region near where we're staying.

I glance at the bar entrance. A luscious young woman slithers though the door. A real looker. Our eyes click, leading to an on the spot flirtation. She is petite. Her knit top is nicely filled out. The woman has a saucy short brunette haircut. She comes like being pulled by a seductive magnate and charmingly saddles up next to me. Her short skirt hikes up her thigh when she sits down. She speaks English. Her accent puts me on a teased edge. Our smiles say we're fascinated. The bartender automatically puts another wine glass in front of the woman.

"Memo."

"Cossette."

I love the way the name rolls off her tongue. We work our way through the bottle of Bandol that spirits a tantalizing conversation.

I'm feeling lit.

Her cheeks are pink and getting pinker.

I ask Cossette if she wants me to order another bottle. She does.

I tell her my wife is upstairs. "You'll love her. She has a wonderful body. And the most exquisite legs in the world." I lean towards Cossette and kiss her. I think she clearly has the idea a ménage à trios is in the forecast. I whisper in her ear, "You'll love it."

She curls her head while I'm whispering and kisses my neck.

Cossette and I take the remaining bottle of wine and head upstairs. We stop in the hallway. We kiss. Our bodies grind together. I run my hand down Cossette's thigh and around her backside to pull her close. We start towards the room again. And stop again. The breathing becomes heated, intense.

I open the door. Kate is reading in bed. The sheets are draped across her breasts.

"This is Cossette."

Cossette eyes Kate. And then she smiles.

Cossette and I are in a flurry. We start to undress each other. I have her knit off.

Naked and flush-faced Kate jumps out of bed. She screams. "What is this? Get out! Get out!" Kate pushes half dressed Cossette out of the room. She slams the door shut.

Kate turns back towards me. She moves two feet in front of me and gesticulates each word she says with a pointed finger. "That's it. We're having the all-time shitty vacation. You've been so checked-out—with the exception of the last two days when we had animalistic sex and all the slithering between the sheets."

Kate—uncharacteristically angry—is so fervent she spits as she yells at me. "And now you bring Mademoiselle Tits and Ass to the room so we can all do it with each other. Or were you just going to fuck her in front of me? I can't stand this shit. We're going home. And we're going home now."

"But—"

"But nothing. And you better keep your goddamn mouth shut right now. Pack-up your crap and let's go. Right now."

I stumble around, trying to focus. I'm a little loaded on French wine, but feeling the dark cloud of Kate's anger weighting down the room. My stuff is gathered up and thrown in the suitcase. We check-out of Hotel Negresco within five minutes.

We have a stone chilly silent all night drive to Paris. I try to break the silence. "Oh, come one Kate. It would have been fun."

"Put an end to it, Memo. You're already tethered to the doghouse—on the verge of deep six." Kate raises her voice. "Please, you're making it worse. And by the way, what do you think Alita and Dan would say if they knew what you tried to pull?"

I know that I made a blunder. It was far-reaching and dangerous. I messed up. Then I muster up the sway to reason away what Kate is saying. "Our sex life is private."

"It's not too private if you're dragging some killer red-hot French chick back to our room who looks like she is going to fuck everybody in sight."

"Pardon me for talking." I recognize in advance that my manipulative maneuver is dumber than what a one-celled organism could engineer. "How about a little resilience on your part? You know, some forgiveness."

Kate's nostrils flare. "It'd be better if you just didn't say anything." She holds her chin high, spitting out words like daggers. "You're not excused, cancelled out and in no way overlooked."

The rest of the ride to the Paris airport is thick with impenetrable glacial ice. In the morning we are on the first fight back to the States.

NOW MY MIND IS A RUNAWAY TRAIN. No engineer at the controls. No internal governor to regulate the top end speed. No brakes to slow it down. A voice shouts in my head: Why the fuck did you go into the Army in the first place? You were smart enough. You should have tried harder to have gotten out of going to war. You should have been able to it. But you didn't. You should have done something useful, like trying to stop the goddamn war. You know peace, love and tie-dye are what's right.

Jack's clear candor is tough. Train wreck. Tough is what I trust. But I wasn't tough enough to say no.

Shadow Facts licks my hand. She nudges her nose under my arm so I'll pet her. Her warm brown eyes meet my tormented wheels spinning in deep mud.

CHAPTER 11

EVIL EYE

The day before Thanksgiving, 1970

KATE AND I HEAD SOUTH. We roll through the short line of cars waiting to cross the border at Tijuana. The Mexican border guards have a pitifully dismal brand of authority. Their looks are pro forma bland as though they're begging you to come into the country to spend money, rather than protecting something sovereign. It's our turn. They make a two-second inspection for God knows what—nothing. They might as well not be there, but it wouldn't seem right.

There's a disaffected cut off feeling between Kate and me. I have a hunch Kate has a sixth sense about Lupita oozing from my pores. I have to say something to cut through the divestment and separate feeling. "Kate, do you want to take the old road or the new toll road to Ensenada?" My voice is threadbare and sounds dull, like a thin flimsy cover uselessly trying to seal the gap between us and extenuate my self-reproach.

Kate sits motionless in the passenger seat. "Let's go the new way," she says. Her voice is frosty while she looks straight ahead. I feel like an anonymous taxi driver. Kate must be conscious I'm amiss, swimming in my Lupita-laden guilt.

We travel west and parallel to the border towards the sea in a convoluted path through Tijuana. We hit the ocean and head south on the new highway. I think of Chet on his suicidal boozed up motorcycle ride down the new toll road. His destination was Hussong's

Cantina in Ensenada. He drank more and rode back to the States at kill yourself Russian roulette speed.

I look out towards the sea. "Kate, see the Coronado Islands? We used to go tuna fishing out there. And we would take cigarettes and candy to the Mexicans living on the islands and trade them for gunnysacks full of lobster." The tug-of-war in my mind has a rest for a second.

We pass through Rosarito Beach. I crane my head to see the Rosarito Beach Hotel on the right. "Over the entrance to the hotel's lobby it reads, '*Por estas puertas pasan las mujeres más bonitas del mundo.*'"

"'Through these doors pass the most beautiful women in the world.' Is that what it says?" Kate turns her head. Looks at me. A faint smile lights her face. "You think I'm one of those women, Memo?"

I laugh and glance in her direction. "Goes without saying. You always have been. Nothing will change that." A flicker of a temporary relief comes from me being out of check and breaching our relationship. But it's an elusive grasp of blamelessness, kidding with Kate—not feeling I have to pretend.

Farther down the road we pass Puerto Nuevo. I tell Kate about the first day the restaurant opened. Family and old friends were there; eating loads of lobster, having drinks—fun times. Easy times in Mexico.

"So what's with Memory Lane?" Kate's edginess thaws out a couple of degrees. "All of this wistful reminiscing? Memo, you've felt far away, more than ever since Guadalupe Canyon. Right now, I feel closer to you." Kate reaches out with her left hand and tenderly squeezes my thigh.

I made a mistake with Lupita. I made a lot of mistakes. The mistakes are all part of a stirred up agitation at my core that wasn't there before I went to war. Now I feel like I'm granted an impermanent stay of execution. "The familiarity is like home. Wistful reminiscing? Sure, I'm in deep need for nostalgia. I'll take it in."

A glint of sunlight catches Kate's eyes and they flicker from hazel to amber. For a split second I let all the bad ingredients and trappings hide in memory's cavernous recesses.

We pass La Misión. The spot marks the start of the cliff highway that towers above the ocean, bringing azure sea vistas stretching to the western horizon. No civilization will be seen for miles until we approach San Miguel, just north of Ensenada.

Rocks have fallen from the hillside on the east side of the trans-peninsular stretch of road. My imagination spins a visual clip of Chet riding north on the highway at night, loaded, hitting a rock and smashing into the hillside—motorcycle parts and body parts scattered all over the nocturnally desolate road. Blood smeared on the pavement—somehow he cheated the odds—luck's trick. And I wonder how much longer he is going to be able to bluff the probabilities.

Kate tilts her head towards me while keeping her eyes straight ahead. "Memo, I called Frank Gehry." The news spilling off her tongue jolts me.

Pithiness resurfaces in me. The thaw between us hits a roadblock. "It must have been a social call, wasn't it?"

She turns towards me. "He said you could come back to the architecture firm." Her voice has a pressing timber. "Frank told me you could complete your internship with him, and there would be a place for you afterward." She soothes out. "Frank understands. He's a veteran, too."

"Yeah, I know he's a veteran." I speak twice as fast. "So you've been working behind the scenes?"

Kate's voice raises an octave. "Your dad is concerned, too."

I squint. "Who else have you talked to?" I clutch the steering wheel so forcefully my hands ache.

"Don't you think—"

"Look, what do you think it's like coming back?" I'm in a flurry of words. My eyes have a pressure behind them. "Give me some time. This ordeal isn't like a day and night light switch you can turn off and on. Look, let's take it easy. Let's just chill in Mexico. Not have any worries for a few days, okay? How 'bout it, Kate?"

"Okay, okay." Kate faces forward, looking strained. "I mean, I'm not a light switch either, you know." She looks heated, intense, like she can't curb her impulses, driving her unpredictably headlong to a forbidden place. "Memo, there's something I have to—"

"What? What do you have to say?"

Kate pulls in a breath and exhales, sinking back into the passenger seat. "I'll find another time. Tomorrow…maybe…goddamn, I don't know when. Please, give me a little time, too. And ease up on me."

We're silent. But we're not silent, like two spheres spinning in their own stirred up orbits.

The feeling is too much to tolerate, stirring me to take a stab at weaving in a conciliatory distraction to disarm where we're heading. "Kate, let's stop at Hussong's Cantina. You know, that's where the margarita was first concocted. Let's treat you to one." My voice settles.

"The margarita originated at Hussong's? Are you sure?"

I want to get my wisp of a reprieve back. Reconnecting with Kate is the only way to pull it off, even if it's no more than a fragile and tentative grasp. I'll bargain for what I can get, even if it's a shaky hold on her. Maybe a little storytelling will entice her, reel her back in. Hopefully she doesn't think I'm bullshitting her, like my lies of omission about Lupita.

"Sure, I'm sure. The drink is from the early forties. The bartender, Don Carlos Orozco, dreamed it up." I tell her he created the drink at Hussong's for the daughter of the German ambassador to Mexico. Tequila and lime are central parts. They originally used Damiana. I tell Kate purists now use Cointreau, but others substitute some kind of triple sec, shaken with ice with salt on the glass rim. "Yep, two shots of tequila, a shot of Cointreau, half a shot of lime juice, shake the hell out of it with ice and you have a bitchin' margarita."

Kate tilts her head my way. She looks at me from the top left corners of her eyes. "Catchy story. Is it for real?"

"Guess so. Heard the legend thousands of times when I've been at Hussong's with my surfing buddies. You never know. A lot of bullshit gets cooked up at bars. Who cares? Good story. Great drink. Hussong's has always been a blast."

Kate and I shape a stopgap for the tautness betwixt us to mesh with the peaceful coastal highway. My little detour from the fractured feeling gives us a makeshift mend to our cracked shell that penetrates deep.

We arrive in Ensenada. The buzz in the streets is mind rattling. Kate and I land at the people-filled cantina on Avenida Ruiz. Music charges the place with a mariachi fusion of violins, trumpets, Spanish guitar, *vihuela*, *guitarron* and a *jarana jarocha*.

We squeeze into the last two places at the bar. It's the same old place, bottle-green beaded wainscoting on the walls, wood floors, sheet metal ceiling, funky Mexican art, black and white photographs of celebrity parties and the old fireplace, which probably has not been used since the turn of the century. Through the noise of all the people and loud music, I order a margarita made with Cointreau for Kate and a Carta Blanca beer for myself.

Kate doesn't realize the good-tasting drink is lethal since the smooth alcoholic mixture slips down the hatch so easily. She sways back and forth to the mariachi band trumpet and strings. I love seeing her have a good time. "Kate, you want another one?"

She sounds mildly smashed. "Sure." A faint slur comes off her tipsy tongue. "Positively."

I order her another margarita. Good to see her a little juiced, and off my back. "La margarita, señor," says the rushed, but grinning bartender. I slap the money on the bar. Kate drinks half of it. She's in the spirit of Hussong's—the loose contagious soul of the cantina. Maybe we'll dance on a tabletop. Maybe everything will be okay. Maybe we're back to normal. She's a little lit. She's feeling fine. I nudge anticipations out of my head.

Kate recognizes the Mexican folk song "La Bamba" from the rock n' roll version Ritchie Valens sang in the 50s. Slapping her thigh, she keeps the beat.

Kate's happy, a little greased with tequila. I feel as though we're on our first date.

A short dark-skinned Mexican woman materializes. She's in black, head to toe. She wears a floor-length dress. A rebozo covers her head. The woman's bottomless dense eyes fix on Kate. The woman's eyes deliver a wicked stare though the dense cloud of the background mariachi music, which now sounds screeching. She hands a calla lily to Kate and lays her hand on Kate's upper arm. Her head slowly glides up and down giving a shadowy harbinger's nod, spooky and menacing. Then the dark Mexican slips into the crowd, seemingly transposing into sheer gray-black vapor and vanishes.

The blood in Kate's face drains out, and now she looks blanched. She's motionless, petrified like chiseled cold marble. "Shit, Memo, she gave me the creeps." A tinge of color creeps back into Kate's face. She breathes in rapid short stiletto breaths.

I squint and shake my head. "Where the fuck did she come from? She gave you *el mal de ojo*."

Kate turns to me and angles her head downward. "The what?"

"The evil eye—usually a curse, but different because she touched you."

Kate raises her shoulders and narrows her eyes. "What does that mean?"

"The mal de ojo followed by a touch means she's saying you're jealous and desirous at the same time. The thing you want is the thing you're terrified will disappear." I hear my voice quake and falter. A sliver of recognition lets me know I'm talking about myself and my fear that Kate will vanish.

Kate pushes her margarita away. "Let's get out of here."

We leave the bar. The sounds of the cantina's swarm of partiers and music fade-out as we walk out Hussong's door, turn right and walk down the street. We get into the rig. We're heading south to Santo Tomás. The silence between us vibrates the cab of the rig.

We enter the valley, *El Valle de Santo Tomás*, a Mexican wine region. Frames of a movie click through my mind. A luscious-dark and colorful picture sequence of Lupita ruminates through my memory. Lupita liberated me and put me deeper in prison. I replay the cantina dark Indian woman scene. Kate sits next to me. She's a wooden post covered with a sheet of ice in the shape of a woman.

"What's on your mind?" Kate's words are sharp and tartly mixed with bitter.

My voice is scientific. "I'm considering the major fault zones that run though this valley. They're deep fractures in the subterranean rock formations. They cause unpredictable movements."

Out of the corner of my eye, I see Kate's eyebrows arch. "You're really thinking about that?"

There's nothing I could tell her that would pacify her. "Think about it. I've known about the fault system in the valley. Just look at the surface geological panorama and it's pretty clear, right?" I can't do anything but shut up. So that's what I'll do. Shut up.

Kate looks suspiciously at me. "Right, unpredictable movements." She looks over the hood of the rig.

We turn west off the highway onto the road, which eventually meets the ocean. The landscape is riparian woodland. A few klicks down the dusty rutted washboard road we see the encampment at *La Arboleda de los Robles*—oaks interspersed with willows and sycamores.

We roll in under the ancient oaks. Fifteen campsites colonize this rustic patch of Baja. For the moment this backwater piece of Mexico is turned into civilized elegance. People have moved in—tents, fire pits and camp chairs. Tables are covered with plates of gourmet hors d'oeuvres, pitchers for martinis, margaritas, wine and Mexican beer. Everybody is milling around, tasting and pouring drinks, getting ready for the show. I welcome the sight of so many people, since it means I don't have to be alone with Kate and maintain a crafty stratagem to keep the tensions cooled down between us.

There's a little stage made from raked hardened earth. In front of it is a semicircle of several dozen one-pound coffee cans. On one side of the cans, a few inches of the metal has been cut and rolled down. The cans are filled with sand, into which candles have been planted. The open sections of the cans face inward to illuminate the stage.

A who-has-what assortment of instruments are tuning-up to play Swan Lake—marimba, violin, recorder, guitar, oboe and flute. Add the Brazilian instruments. A two-bell *agogo, ganza* metal shaker, *cabasa* wooden and metal bead shaker and wooden whistle *apitos* might make the music sound more like a Brazilian Carnival than what's on the program.

Somehow a ballet with musical accompaniment in the Mexican outback is going to come together. Percussion is an Afro-Brazilian timbal, looks like an African *djembe*. A leather-topped gourd instrument—the *cuica*—is open at the bottom, with a friction stick anchored on the internal side of the leather, which vibrates when the stick is rubbed to make a squeaking sound.

Admiral Ted Powers and Dotty Powers' granddaughter wears a white tutu and white ballet slippers. She's on the earthen theater stage. The flickering candle illumination lights the dirt platform like a Broadway production.

We're late. Nobody else stopped at Hussong's. We see Jack and Diane's campsite. Kate and I are jumbled, but manage to set-up our gear and make camp. The party crowd lightens Kate's somber mood.

Jack, Diane, Kate and I grab stemmed glasses and fill them with martinis from the pitcher. All set to join everyone at the Santo Tomás production of Tchaikovsky's ballet—the instruments and the music unlikely bed partners—resourceful people make a marriage of instruments and the music fuses into something beautiful and not totally planned. The people playing the violin, recorder, oboe and flute anchor the music's backbone, and the Latin instruments add a dissonant background of musical cool. The thirteen-year-old dances.

The candles in the sand-filled cans glow brightly, casting a magical light on the sweet ballerina and shining a glow on the underside of the oak canopy. She's talented. A subject fit for Degas, she spins and dances in her tutu and ballet shoes on the Mexican dirt stage.

We drink—intoxicated by the slight, graceful ballerina's dancing and imagining her perfect future, her destiny. The stylish audience smiles, each person holding up a glass at chest level. The music reverberates under the oaks as though we were in a concert hall. The swirling girl's elegance and the lambent glimmer of the candles fill our eyes. Everyone is captivated, which brings enchanted laughter. For the moment everything can be forgotten.

The onboard remnants of Kate's margarita are made plush by the martini slipping down her throat. She gets another one. Laughing and rosy cheeked, she flirts with the handsome men. Kate wears a chic tight pink sweater and a short skirt. No problem catching responsiveness—some guide their eyes down her body to the most beautifully shaped legs on the planet; men can never pass-up her good looks.

Jack jerks his head up slightly. "What's with Kate?"

The corners of my mouth are downturned. "I think she knows."

Jack and I watch Kate joke and laugh with three handsome, virile-looking guys, who stand around her.

"She's read your mind?"

"Yeah, I think so. Intuition." I shrug and laugh half-heartedly, trying to dissolve the uneasiness. "Maybe Shadow Facts told her." The attempt to kid comes off flat.

The men are called away, and Diane approaches Kate. The women talk. We can't read their lips. Diane listens more than she talks. There's a lot of head nodding and Diane grasps the top of Kate's arms with her hands. Five minutes pass. We see them hug.

There's a clicking sound when Jack opens his mouth to speak. "I wonder what the fallout is going to be."

My shoulders roll over. I sink, an interior collapsing feeling. The festive evening continues. I pretend to have a good time. But I'm like a double exposure photograph—one image is overshadowed by a dark image lurking in the background.

Kate retires early to our tent. I hesitate for a long while, but eventually join her.

She wants me. And I let up on my chaotic unglued feeling. The secret campground intimacy is hushed. I bracket my head and let my body feel good. Then I realize Kate is in her own orbit— disengaged from me—like two people not joined, having disconnected and separate individual happenings. She must be inventing romance with one of those roguish handsome men, letting her coquettishness rollout into her private fantasy. Kate recasts my body into someone else. I close my eyes to her self-arranged allusion. And I answer her vantage point by cascading into being raunchy.

We steam in an uncontrollable wicked heat. I automatically react by being rougher. And this is what she wants. Rough sex one more time. Kate digs deep. And then she's extreme. While she plunges her nails into my skin, I have the sensation her imagination is driving her to some other place instead of existing with me. Kate bursts. Afterward, she doesn't want to be held. She drifts away—far away.

CHAPTER 12

WHO CAN SHE COUNT ON?

1000 hours, Winter, 1967

I ENTER OUR BEACH HOUSE. My movement comes to a static stand-still. A furtive eye flickers in the direction of the desk. It's here.

No. Not yet.

I steer clear. Move to the picture window. Stare at the pounding waves. Damp hair, surf trunks, and sweatshirt, all crusted by salt water and permeated with ocean smell. Anticipation builds. It has a disturbing edge. A sharp edge. The type of edge that can nick, cut and score you. The sense of balance the sea just gave me spends itself and slips away, replaced by a sudden jittery warning making a throb that burns hot in my chest.

Out to sea a winter storm chases, pushing a bigger and bigger north swell towards shore. Waves saturated by blue-green and frothy white turn into the dimmest tint of pewter. Waves thunder.

I'm sucked back to the desk. Pick up the envelope. Return to the window and look out across the sea's jumbled surface. Shadow Facts sits at my feet. She's like a vibrating tuning fork, sensing my wretched helpless effusion. She's studied, taut and keen. My chest is tight. My cheeks reddened. I can't breathe past the middle of my chest and pant trying to get air.

I slip the letter opener under the fold of the flap. The dog's big brown eyes fix on me. In my ears the rip of the envelope paper hisses at a decibel louder than the rumble of the sea. The dog sits like a smooth statue. I take the letter out of the envelope. And then the dog curls her neck, and her fur turns from smooth to a texture saying, please touch me. I bend down and preen the coat on her back and Shadow Facts licks my hand when I take it away.

Kate enters from the bedroom. A soft, chemise-like white shift is draped over her. "I saw it."

One line stands out among the rest. *Order to Report for Armed Forces Examination.*

Pushing against the base of her left little finger, Kate puts pressure on her gold band with the tip of her thumb and twirls it counterclockwise around her ring finger.

I drop the letter.

The dog's head droops, and she watches the letter's feathery float down to the old wood-plank floor.

Kate comes next to me, bends down and picks up the letter.

Shadow Facts now licks Kate's cheek.

A sorrowful ache embodies me. The feeling mutates to throbbing pain. The hurt isolates in my stomach.

Kate stands, puts her arm on my shoulder and holds the letter with her free hand. While she reads, I look at the pounding waves, which take on a new monster shape and change to storm surf.

Kate's eyes well up. "I'm sorry, Memo. I know it's my fault. But I couldn't help it."

"You couldn't help it?" My steel eyes go buttery—kind of a puffy feel around them. "Your body must be upside down. We're both upside down. Our blood is lost in some nowhere place we can't touch or get back."

Tears roll down Kate's cheeks.

"Kate, losing the baby leaves a psychic stain. Things happen—no crystal-clear reason. It wasn't about you or me or how you took care of yourself. No defect of will or character or body."

"I know, I grasp it. But I don't know."

"It didn't take too much before you got pregnant, almost like I barely touched you. It was how it's supposed to feel, so right."

A few weeks after she was pregnant, I had been visualizing the two of us holding the baby. I replay and replay the night she miscarried. How I held Kate while she bled, cramped, and agonized in pain. Dad came in the middle of the night. All he could do was to give Kate

Demerol for the pain. And then it happened. Dad helped us with the first critical stage of letting go. It wasn't pretty for any of us. There's the upheaval Kate's body has gone through. I touch her now. We make love — nothing materializes. It's not time yet. It's not our time for a baby.

"Let's keep trying," says Kate.

"It's not about trying. Your body has its reasons. It's your body's timetable. I love you, and I want our kids." With the draft looming, I wanted to have them sooner. I hoped that I could get a 3-A family deferment after the student 2-S ran out. A family is first in our minds. Scooting out of the draft is another welcomed and secondary consequence.

"Your career is going to fall apart."

"The architectural internship with Frank Gehry took form from ingenuity and a stroke of luck. A lot's at stake. My career? No. You and I are at stake. No matter what, the most important thing is how we are with each other."

Her elegant face has a pure tempered look. But there is a brush of a telltale squint. "Well, at least we've got Shadow Facts. She's family. I'm so thankful your parents gave us the old beach house. Our island of security."

The dog licks the salt off my thigh. Shadow Facts rubs the side of her face on my hand. I bend down to pet her. "Yeah, I know, Shadow Facts. For you, we're mom and dad."

The boiling gray surf reaches higher for the sky and collapses in a turgid mush. We step back. The stirred up ocean's strength rattles the glass window, which separates us from the water's torment.

Kate hugs me. "I'm scared. I want to have our baby now so you don't have to go." Her voice is choked. "I don't want you ripped away from me."

"I know guys who've gotten drafted."

I tell Kate about the convoluted twists I've heard people go through when they receive the draft notice. The reactions. Trying to strike some bargain with the draft board or trying to find some bargain within themselves. Stories, a lot of stories with a lot of similarities. Stories twist and twist. They think it's going to end. It doesn't end. Time begs for more time, but in the end it turns out to be a short story.

First, it's as though it wasn't supposed to happen. They rage. They ramble. They conjure up arguments like a sophomoric second-year law student. Then the considerations come. Be a conscientious objector. Escape to Canada. Be a protester and burn the draft card. Go to jail for draft evasion, do the time there. Or just become a translucent ghost and disappear.

And then comes a frozen, anguished feeling. Fear generated by blood-red-oozing from a dark violet sanguinary imagination. No more stupid thoughts—just scared. It's not okay to be scared, because it's against some obtuse male code to admit you're scared. But fear overrides pretense.

Then there is a splinter of hope—a doc at the induction center will have compassion and say, *you're not our type. You're 4-F because once you took twelve hundred mics of acid.* They think, *I'll get compassion because I'm me.* But you're faceless, like the million guys the doc saw before you. The doc doesn't see the secret you, to be rescued because you're special. There's just the chunk of human protoplasm in front of the doc's fatigued eyes. The doc's compassion wore out a long time ago from all the guys who came before you and were herded down the Army induction center cattle chute to the precipice and free-fall into war.

The first steps are bad. So is the next step, self-recrimination for being drafted. Why'd it happen? Why'd I let it happen, not having stood up to the government in some unknown way that would have saved me?

There are the guys who take their bodies into the Army with a certain kind of numbness from the shoulders up, not knowing who's right or who's wrong or what to do. Everyone has a trapped feeling.

And then there's having choices inside of having no choices. Being caught in a steel trap and figuring you're not going to gnaw off your own leg to escape. Find ways to make bad work so it's not so bad. That's what I've heard about.

"What are you going to do?" Kate's eyes narrow. She frowns.

"Don't know. Except I know not to get into the same trip as everyone else. Except I know I'm angry and don't want to do something silly. Except I know I'm not leaving you tomorrow. Why do I feel like I'm leaving in two seconds? Or maybe I've already left. Let's see, there are two months between the physical and the induction."

"Call Dan. There must be something he can do."

Lydia answers the phone: "Muir Clinic."

"Lydia, this is Memo. Put my father on the phone." Too self-absorbed for politeness. "Please." My knees could tremble. They don't. "I need to speak to him. Please. Thank you, Lydia."

"He's with a patient." There's a supple, concerned melody to Lydia's voice.

"I'll wait," I say.

A weighted pressure builds, a tingly, scorching dread sensation.

"Dad. Finally. The draft notice came to appear for a physical."

"When?" Dad is matter of fact.

"Two weeks."

"What do you want me to do?" He sounds clinical.

"I don't know yet. Kate and I are terrified, anticipating God knows what. Can you help me?"

"I've been thinking of some medical reason to get you out of the draft. Your constitution makes it pretty goddamn tough."

"Whatever you can do, dad." My desperation transparently comes though.

"Okay. Let's slow it down." He has a soothing effect. "Give me a day to reason things out. Memo?"

"Yes." The one word response is pointed.

"I'm with you. The Vietnam War has changed the way many people and I feel about war—or, at least, this war." Dad has distain in his voice. "When I served in World War II, a soldier was a hero." I nod; knowing dad's distance from war turns it into a resonance of honor. "If a GI in uniform stood by the road and hitchhiked, the first car to come by would screech to a halt to give him a ride, even take him home for dinner. Now, people practically spit on soldiers wearing uniforms." He's voice is flavored by disgust. "I know you're up against a lot of agitation anticipating what's next. So I'll try like hell to get you out of the draft. If I can't, no matter what, your mother and I will always stand by you."

"I know, dad." My voice squeezes tight anticipating the future and attaching fear to it. "Right now, all I think about is being separated from Kate. She's not over the miscarriage. And there's the trepidation and suspicion and mistrust whether we'll have children or be left childless. Having to quit my internship. Getting my guts splattered all over the place by an AK-47, or being exposed to Agent Orange, or having my leg blown off by a booby trap. Or see it happen to the guy next to me. Dad, I'm too goddamn amped right now, too stupid, too jammed to make any sense."

"Sure you are. How else should you be? There's expecting to be shocked, and then there's being shocked. Not a theory, no more pretending it isn't going to happen, because now it's here. So slow it down right now. Give me time to think. We'll talk tomorrow morning. Okay?"

"Okay." Good to have dad to prop me up when I'm shaky and scared. His substance moves me across a transitory bridge. My charmed life just changed—turned from powder blue to thunder black.

THE BEACH HOUSE IS SITUATED ON A LAND SPIT on the southernmost piece of California coast. The Tijuana River is to the south, separating California from Mexico. The Tijuana Slough is to the east of the shoreline. The Pacific is to the west. Kate and I hold each other. The gray waves become swollen and turn to black like an ominous curtain across an endless stage. We give in to a dark sinking mood.

The formation of the ocean's sandy bottom in front of the beach house can't support the power and size of the storm-driven swell. Waves crash down all at once. It's what surfers call "closed out." Water builds to overwhelm the shoreline. The water looks the way it might in the opening scene of a tragedy—the stage curtain is blown open, revealing a crushing, churning sea of white-water soup. Just an hour ago, I was riding handsome blue-green waves. Their form changed. Now, they're devouring.

Kate and I step out onto the beach's dreary winter day with Shadow Facts. The unsettled air is saturated with smells of salty ocean spray. Uneasiness bleeds though my mind. The taste on my tongue changes from sweet, to bitter, to salt, and I gaze at Kate and the sweetness recovers its familiarity.

We aren't the only ones on the beach. Red-beaked white and gray California gulls squawk and dance around on their greenish legs. The sea birds seek the protection the beach offers from the storm, which is building in the northwest. But refuge is not enough for the gulls.

There's plenty of seashore sustenance, but they bicker over food. One gull already has a scrap. But he pushes the gull next to him out of the way to get that gull's scrap of food. We can't figure it out. Another gull swoops down, does his dance, and knocks a gull to the side to get that bird's food. They don't need to fight, but they do. There's plenty of space. They don't need to grab each other's territory, but they do.

Shadow Facts runs through the flock. They scatter. She finds a seal carcass. The lab rolls madly on her back in the decomposing fleshy tissue. She pants and smiles.

Kate smells the dog. "Ugh! Oh, my God, that's putrid and sickening. Why on earth?"

"Instinct. She's rubbing herself in the carcass to disguise herself so she can either hunt or protect herself from being hunted. Reflexive survival. Underneath it all, she's wild, in her element. Instincts woven into her—can't be undone."

Kate walks ahead of me, her arms folded across her chest against the chill. With a stick, I pull up the nose of the seal. The skin separates from the skeleton to expose millions of squirming maggots, breaking down the seal's flesh, doing their bit in nature's lifecycle.

Kate returns to my side.

I can't shield her from the sight.

She grimaces and turns away.

I'm fascinated by nature's universal truth and its order. What dies transforms into another living form.

We continue to walk south. Maybe I should swim across the Tijuana River and never come back.

The bottoms of our bare feet on the wet winter sand make us cold up to the knees. I stop. Face Kate. I feel tender, and I let it mix with the strain of her knitted brow. We hold each other. We have warmth at the fronts of our bodies. Our backsides freeze. Shadow Facts races around us in circles.

A sliver of panic rips though me. On top of the fear of Nam, I have to wonder if lovely Kate will stick around for the long haul. We have something special, sure, but I'm a realist, too.

We see the day pass into darkness. Any chance of a beautiful winter sunset begins to disappear, obscured by the gray-black cloudy sky. In the last three seconds of the day, an orange speck of sun ignites a thin filament across the horizon. And the sun is gone.

THE TELEPHONE RINGS. I PICK-UP THE RECEIVER. "HELLO." I LISTEN. Then nod. The feel of pallidness falls over my face. There's not much to say. "Thanks for trying."

Kate says, "Dan's attempt to pull some strings to get you out of the military didn't work?"

I'm stunned. Silent.

"Memo?"

"No, nothing worked."

Kate slumps into a chair. "Please turn off the light. I need...please give me a couple of minutes to collect myself up."

I step outside. The moon's glimmer wedges its way through a narrow break in the overcast cloudy sky. Huge colliding surf thunders in the unremitting darkness, illuminated by one band of light. I'm edgy, it feels like bubbling sensation in my arteries. I imagine the lightless room. She listlessly sits. I can't wait, which pushed me to return. Kate languidly occupies a chair. "Kate?'

"I'm not ready."

"But hang-on a second. There're a couple of things I want to say." I turn on one lamp.

Kate has a stained and reflective look on her face. "My grandfather and father were in the Navy when it was respectable. I'll wait for you. But I'll only wait for you. Not because you'll be connected to a cause I don't believe in." And then Kate trails off, sounding like she is conducting business, rather than talking to her husband. She perks up. "Tell me something new. I want us to feel in tune." Kate hesitates for a second.

"Yes. No bullshit. What's really circulating in your mind?"

"I took a chance on you. And, yes, in some ways the chance paid off. I thought I could count on you. But it was only a tease. It's not your fault."

"Not my fault?"

"It's history's fault. Like a rerun of a crappy movie. My father didn't just leave my mother. He divorced me, too. And she didn't mean to, but she ditched me to work at night." Kate looks in her lap. And then she turns her head up to square her eyes on me. "Look, men have always been very sketchy for me—never did I paint by the numbers and fill in spaces with nice beautiful colors to create a masterpiece. No. Just a sketchy story." She moistens her lips. "My friend's family rescued me when I was a kid. Her father was so nice to me it gave me a splinter of faith about men." Kate is open and exposed and vulnerable. Her face grows soft, while at the same time Kate's face looks like her spirit hurts.

"But the risk you took with me paid off."

"Does it look like it's paying off? Don't kid me. You're going to disappear." Kate's voice hardens. "I'll have to count on myself. Not you. Not anybody else. And there's nobody to rescue me like when I was a kid."

"My folks will help you when I'm gone."

"Your mom is in Mexico City all the time. Your dad's practice is beyond hectic. Sure, when they're around they'll help me. They're wonderful. And it's not enough. It's not like having you here. They have their own lives. Here I am again. I thought I was secure, but I'm screwed." Kate bits her lower lip. Her chin begins to shake. "I'll have to rely on myself, and…" Her lips draw thin. "I don't know what I'll do. I'm desperate." She looks away.

"Well, don't do anything desperate."

CHAPTER 13

ROTOR BLADES

BEFORE DAYBREAK AT ARBOLEDA DE LOS ROBLES I gather enough kindling to make the wet firewood blaze. Thick smoke wafts up. It struggles to escape through the dense foliated canopy, which is illuminated by the campfire. Phantom-like shadows dance in the glow above me. The oak wood fire smell fills the air. Water boils to make dark-brew, strong man's coffee. I put out two stainless steel camp cups.

Jack is still in the tent with Diane.

Come on. Finally.

The lush coffee aroma draws Jack from the tent. He looks as if his nerve endings are already excited in anticipation of tasting the brew.

Kate's fantasy sex last night has me disjointed today. Now there's seeing Jack. His substance eases me.

Our eyes talk. Lips don't move.

He downs half a cup.

"I'll make a second cup to drink on the way."

"Yeah, do that. Please. Killer coffee, Memo."

With the surfboards strapped to the roof racks of my rig, I turn on the ignition. We slink away from the sleeping campground, heading west to La Bocana. Dotty Powers's fish and lobster order is on the list.

"Lupita tuned my tension spring so fuckin' tight, I had to pull the trigger."

"You'd like to think it was about sex."

"Jack, hand me the pack of Camels in the glove box."

Jack has a disappointed look. "What's the deal with the smoking?"

"You know I smoked for a few months in Nam—gave it up before I came home. Made a decision I wasn't going to die over there, so I wasn't going to kill myself with cigarettes."

"Okay."

"But I had a lapse at Cañón de Guadalupe. Hey Jack, don't give me shit about it. I'll get back on the track team soon."

"You want to talk about Lupita?"

"I'll get to her. Hand me *los fósforos*."

"The what?"

"The matchbox."

The box cover has a picture of four playing cards—clubs, spades, diamonds and hearts. I slide out the matchbox tray, take out a wax-covered matchstick and scratch it against the striking surface. Mexican matches are the greatest. I take a deep drag off the Camel.

Jack turns to me. "Last night was quite a scene with Kate." He's concerned and questioning.

"Yeah. Sometimes when I wake up at night, I see her pacing the floor, muttering."

"What does she say?" Jack looks back to the headlight lit road in front of us.

"'I want you back.' Even though I'm physically there, my brain is somewhere else, in a minefield." What I think is her accusations are true. "My dreams wake me up at night. She stirs. Kate has a slippery grasp on me which turns out to be nothing but empty space filled with torment."

"Diane and I were rocking in the same boat. It's been a lot of work getting back. Things stand in the way." Jack draws in a breath. "We haven't gone into any detail, but she told me she imagined what it was like for me in Nam. She said it more than once. It's like she doesn't know, but she knows. Diane is the mistress of imagination and inference. And she's getting better. Her pot smoking has trailed-off to zero in the past two months."

"I was worried about her getting loaded." I take a huge drag off the Camel. The end glows so brightly it illuminates the rig's cab.

"My mind is in an easier resting place since Diane stopped."

"Diane aims to understand. She's always trying to take care of everyone else. Motherly, you know. Like you said, things stand in the way of getting back. Like Walter. He's pressing on me. Sometimes it's relentless." The Land Cruiser shakes when it hits a bad stretch of washboard on the deserted road. The road's vibration makes my voice shudder. "Those few minutes I had with you on the phone in Nam after Walter's deathblow meant a lot. I could have been sunk deeper in the path of harm's way, but your words helped to steer me."

Jack looks taken by surprised. "You didn't say a damn thing about it when we met in Vung Tau."

"I was in a state of I don't know what to call it—dis-embodiment maybe—by the time we pulled off that boondoggle and surfed in Vung Tau. Man, it was just so good to see you and catch a few waves. I couldn't talk about Walter then. I still—"

"We're talking about it now." Jack sounds brotherly.

"Okay. See, Walter got a letter from his wife the day before he died, saying she was doing it with some other guy. But I put together that she had been hacking away at his balls for a very long time."

A western brush rabbit runs in the path of the FJ 40's headlights. I hit the brakes. The rabbit narrowly gets away. Our heads turn left, following it as it disappears into the undergrowth and early morning darkness. I step on the gas.

"Charlie cuts Walter's cock off. Swacker wants to leave it in the bush. Jungle animals would have eaten it. No way was that going to happen. I stuck the damn thing in his pocket as a gesture of respect, maybe a weird way of restoring dignity to a guy who had none to begin with."

The sun starts to come up, lighting the hillside ridges, leaving the valley still in shadows. Valley fog casts a cloak over the meadow next to the washboard road.

"Yeah, there was one post-op guy who had his leg blown off. Same Dear John story. Happened right before the wounding. There's a connection. Being less watchful and vigilant and saying screw caution. He begged me to give him enough drugs so he could kill himself. You think Walter—"

I feel pushed by a sense of wrong. "Jack, Walter's wife told Walter to go shit in his helmet and put it on."

"Walter set himself up to get killed?"

"I don't know. I just don't know." I look at the headlights' glow on the fog. "If I was secreted away in his thoughts, I'd have to say yes, odds are he set himself up." My breath hits a center spot in my abdomen. "General Steele ordered me to go up to I Corps because Sam, the other officer I worked with, wasn't around to direct me. I tried to beg-off, leaning on the fact I was new in country. So then he ordered Walter to go with me. Goddamn, Walter was a numb nuts—had no business being out in the field. He was definitely not too tightly wired."

"So it was Steele's fault?" Jack is skeptical.

"No. I should have told Steele to fuck off, I'd do it alone and, yeah, Walter was a suicidal maniac. Steele didn't put that one together. No shit, it was going to happen."

"What are you saying?"

"It's my fault that Walter died, Jack. It's my fucking fault!"

Jack is to the point. "You couldn't have predicted—"

"I should have known, goddamn it. Walter shouldn't have been out there."

"Bullshit, you're working off of hindsight."

"Okay. What the hell should I have done?"

"You should have done exactly what you did."

"I'm not buyin' it, Jack. I'm just not buyin' it."

I slam on the brakes, cross my arms, rest my forearms on the steering wheel. I bury my face with my forehead on my arms. The Land Cruiser is idling. A light offshore wind blows dust in front of the rig, and the headlights beam through the cloud. I convulse and cry.

"Goddamn it, I had been in country four fuckin' days when Walter got killed."

The Camel burns between my index and middle fingers. I flick it out the window into dewy green grass.

Jack puts his hand on my shoulder.

"Tell me, Jack. Go ahead, tell me."

I wipe the tears off my cheeks with the back of my hand and turn to Jack.

His eyes well-up. This rock of a guy has tears streaming down his cheeks. "It's war. You can't always see what's coming, so stop fuckin' torturing yourself."

Jack and I hardly spoke when I called him to talk about Walter. But the few incisive words he said dug me out of sinking into quicksand. Jack couldn't talk much since he must not have been too available because of his own crisis. "What happened in the OR the day I called you?"

"I can't remember—a day like all the rest."

"Bullshit. You make it sound as though all the procedures you did in the OR were routine. It was anything but some regular medical practice with regular hours."

"I don't know. I swear to God, it's all a blur right now."

"Think."

Jack wildly shakes his head back and forth. He looks confused and exasperated and his words are short. "I can't think. There were so many cases the quick paced action turns into a vague impression and this very second it's a smudge."

I put the FJ40 into gear and we move out. The tires spin. I'm clutching the steering wheel so tightly my hands seem to hold the sum total of my body's force, jacked up by adrenaline squirting all over the place.

I say, "At one point, I was out in the bush. We had been pinned down by beaucoup Charlie in a firefight and radioed for help. An assault helicopter company—AHC—came over the horizon. A couple of shadow C-119 gunships dropped in, blasting away, with Hueys in tow. Those fuckers swooped down like the cavalry and saved our asses. It was smokin' hot in the LZ. GIs hit the ground. Those boys were two thousand percent into search and destroy. The place was lit up on both sides. I rock n' rolled—my M-16 had a mind of its own. NVA neutralized."

"I can't hear this shit," Jack screams.

"Why not?" I shout back. And I realize we're pouring our hearts out. I trust Jack.

"I don't know if it gets to me too much or not enough. What I can tell you is I've heard the same goddamn story a thousand times before."

"That's the idea, Jack."

Jack's eyes have a bead on me. "What do you mean?"

"I heard some kid in the bush screaming. I ran over to him, and he looked as though he had multiple frag wounds—MFWs. His buddies were uselessly trying to do field first aid. We used a Syrette to shoot morphine though a hypodermic needle attached to a collapsible tube—just like toothpaste. I found a vein and shot-him-up intravenously—did no fuckin' good. So much pain. Maybe about ready to slip into shock. We cradled him in a poncho—his blood all over his buddies and me—and we took him for a dust-off. Medevac him. There was another chain of enemy fire. A round whizzed within a centimeter of my ear. There was a volley from our side. The enemy fire stopped. Charlie *di di mau'd*—he took off. And then they opened up on us during the lift-off. Now I always hear that pinging sound. Rounds hitting the belly of the chopper."

"Memo, you're torturing me." Jack's voice is piercing. "What's the fuckin' idea?"

"Everything was no good with that kid—couldn't do anything. The terrified black kid whose face turns ashen. He begs to be with this family. Then he goes blank."

"Stop it, Memo." His words are sharp.

"Yeah, stop it. That's the idea. You've heard the story a thousand times, but the same exact fuckin' story happened fifty thousand times. That's what I mean, Jack. We've heard the same story again and again. The war isn't stopping. People are still turning blank. What am I going to do? What can I do? Nowhere to go."

On our right, we see a shanty structure that's a makeshift store. Two Mexican women are outside. One builds a fire. The other plucks a chicken. We slow down so they don't get engulfed by our road dust.

"Memo, for us, the war is a flood blasting down a gorge; we're like microorganisms caught up in that flood. You and I are helpless to change anything except ourselves."

"That's exactly what fucks me up—caught in the torrent—can't tell the difference between the flood and what I can do. I'm underwater."

"Yeah, no shit."

"Lupita said she felt trapped—she said she's the 'white bird in a golden cage.' As in the song."

"Yeah?"

"I've been thinking about it. There's a line in 'White Bird:' 'The leaves blow across a long black road to its darkened sky in its rage, but the white bird just sits in her cage all alone.' Jack, the white bird is a dove—peace. The black road, darkened sky and rage are war. If peace is trapped, it will die—it'll never find a way to rise above the madness of war."

Jack and I arrive at the coast and park on the bluff overlooking the sea. I take my hurting hands off the steering wheel and turn off the ignition.

We're hoping for good surf. There's a perfect offshore wind, and conditions feel as though the surf should be bitchin'. But the beach break is terrible today, with middle sections closing out. Nothing on the coast looks worth surfing. We sit in the rig, looking down at the crappy surf. The coastline is the grayest of overcast. There are spots where sun is laboring to break through.

I say, "Screw it. Let's go over to the fishing village and pick-up Dotty's fuckin' fish and lobster."

We head over to the village. I see a couple of men near the boat launch.

"*Nos gustaría comprar pescado y langosta.*" I tell them we want to buy fish and lobster.

"*Tenemos langostas en las trampas, pero los pescadores regresarán en dos horas,*" says the older of the two.

"What's going on?"Asks Jack.

"They have lobsters, still submerged in lobster traps. They say the fishermen will be back in a couple of hours. But the fish aren't on a schedule. And the fishermen are on Mexican time."

"We should probably wait."

"Yeah. Dotty and the Admiral were charming enough to invite us, but maybe we should have stayed home."

"Yeah, we could have stayed home. Doesn't matter, though."

"Doesn't matter. So Jack, what do you think is the best way to clean a lobster?"

Jack smiles and winks at me. "Break off the antenna, slowly insert the pointed tip into the lobster's anus, turning it clockwise, and continue to turn it as you push it all the way up the intestinal tract. Keep turning the antenna clockwise and draw it out. Pull out the guts."

"Okay, sure, yeah, that's the way to do it." I laugh.

It's a little after 1100 hundred hours and we've waited four hours. I pay the fishermen twelve bucks for nine lobster and eight more for yellowtail and white sea bass. We head back on the coast road to the valley leading to La Arboleda de los Robles.

"Jack, let's stay down here longer. Diane and Kate can go back in your van. We'll head down to La Pastora, Scorpion Bay, Todos Santos or some other place. We'll find good waves somewhere."

"I have to head back early Sunday morning because I'll be on call that afternoon. And next week, I'm going to be slammed. What's with you? What's up with work?"

"I'm still on unemployment. An Army captain, Vietnam veteran back from war who is on unemployment. Has Kate been talking to you, too? That pisses me off."

Jack's face is stone serious. "Kate? No."

"Are you sure? She called Frank Gehry to get my internship back. I guess she worked the veteran angle and got sympathy. He's a vet. The next thing she'll do is engineering me going to Harvard through Frank. He did his postgrad there. Can you imagine me living in Cambridge?"

"I can't imagine you living in Nam."

Kate has been working behind the scenes—scared I'll never get traction—and I think she is manipulating. I have to get this off my chest. "Damn it. And then she called my dad to enlist his aid. Are you sure she didn't call you?"

I pull the Camels from above the sun visor and fire one up. Take a lung full of filterless tobacco smoke.

"Sorry I struck a nerve," says Jack.

We turn east onto the washboard road running next to the Rio Santo Tomás. We're on the way back to our camp at Arboleda de los Robles. The sun has burned off the overcast. I space out on Baja's bright blue sky, cool and fresh, the late morning sun flashing through the leaves and branches of the gnarly oaks and brilliant yellow-green willows and sycamores that line the road. . .

"Jesus, Memo, slow down! Are you trying to get us killed? After all we've been through?"

Jack's voice snaps me back. The reek of fish and saltwater coming from the backseat fills my lungs, where it stirs around like hot oil. I muscle the FJ40 Land Cruiser around a sharp curve just a centimeter clear of a pickup full of pigs and chickens. Glancing in the rearview mirror, I see nothing but dust.

Jack white-knuckles the door handle in case I change my mind and drive us into the next oncoming car. "What's going on, man? You haven't said a word since La Bocana."

I take a last pull on my Camel and flick it out the window, all the while keeping my eyes on the road. Fine, I'll talk. "I should love this place, right? I did love this place. No goddamn Hueys beating up the air, no stink of jet fuel, no thousand-percent humidity, no Charlie trying to murder me in my sleep. But you know what?"

Jack waits. He knows better than to interrupt me once I get started.

"It's like Nam is right here. I close my eyes and those Hueys are going thwack-thwack in my head. I jump every time a twig snaps. And there's not a damn thing I can do about it. Every day, all day. Even here, in the most beautiful place on the face of the earth, I smell bodies and blood. There's a dense humidity—makes me sweat so hard and I feel like I'm choking."

I light another Camel and suck it in as the tires grind gravel into the road.

Finally, Jack says something. "You're an asshole, you know that? You came back in one piece, man. You're alive." He is pissed at me now. "You survived, Memo. You didn't end up like one of those pathetic pieces of meat whose life I was supposed to save, scared shit-less, screaming at me to help him or kill him, guts pouring out of him, arms and legs ripped off. . . . You weren't the only one who was there! I was just down the road, man, operating on near dead GIs in the MASH tent ... but we both made it. We're here. Dig it. We're alive!" He spreads his arms, feeling the magnificent texture that is Baja.

Jack knows what to say to make me feel stupid. Maybe he thinks the M.D. after his name or the fact he had the rank of major gives him the right to kick my butt. Or maybe he just isn't as crazy as me. "Shit, man. I'm sorry...I'm still tiptoeing though a goddamn minefield in my head, but yeah, you're right. We're in Mexico, man."

Jack howls his coyote howl. "Me-hi-co! Me-hi-co! Me-hi-co! Let's get something to eat." Jack points up the road.

"RIGHT." I SLAM ON THE BRAKES AND JERK THE RIG TO A STOP IN front of the rustic bare-wood shack. A hand-lettered sign across the door says *Refrescos*, meaning soft drinks. Maybe they have some ice trucked in for cold beer.

I punch Jack in the shoulder and manage a rough smile. "Time for Carta Blanca!"

We jump out of the truck and wander over to an open fire, where two small brown leathery-skinned women are squatting, cooking tortillas on a flat iron plate. They glance up at us. Little smiles. The smell of hot cornmeal and burning oak fill the air. This really is heaven. What the hell is wrong with me?

Jack says, "I'll get a six-pack and see if they'll make us some chicken tacos." We head for the shack. Half a dozen chickens jump out of my way, squawking. I can hear the sadness and grief in a scratchy old recording of Lola Beltrán from inside the shack. She is singing *El Crucifijo de Piedra*—"The Crucifix of Stone." I still feel twitchy, but yeah, it's good to be here.

"*Al contemplar mi tristeza*—" To contemplate my sadness.

Then something flashes in front of my eyes—there and gone—and the music is washed out by the rush of blood from my head to my heart. My eyes are popping wide to take everything in, and I see a dark, scrawny guy stumbling quickly out of the shack, carrying a rusty old rifle. Is it the weapon I'd once seen carried by a Mexican soldier? The Heckler & Koch G3 seems to glow, growing larger as my chest pounds—shit, oh shit, oh shit—the muscles in my arms and legs vibrate like ten-thousand-watt electric tension coils as the dumb *pendejo* raises the rifle up to his shoulder. What the fuck is wrong with this guy, and click, CLICK . . .

I'm back in the jungle with the Hueys from hell tearing holes in my brain. I grab the barrel of the rifle, the cold steel burning my hand like napalm. I jerk it out of his hands, lift it upward, rotate the butt down and back, and smash it forward full force. I hear a loud crack as his ribs break.

That's right, mother fucker, I think, *but why don't you scream?*

"Inocencio!"

At the edge of my vision I see a terrified young woman running out of the shack, carrying an infant and followed by two screaming children.

She shrieks his name again, "Inocencio!"

The man moans, staggering toward her and gasping for breath. But I'm not done.

Still holding the rifle in my left hand, my free hand swings around to drive a hammer-fist strike to the left side of his neck. His sweat and blood mix with mine. Now the man is on the ground, where I want him, and his wife is running at me, pushing me—

"Memo! Shit! Get off him!"

I'm standing over the guy, poised to finish him off with a rifle butt to the skull. And I'm the one who's screaming now.

"You motherfuckin' gook!"

"*¡Párese, Señor, párese!*" More bodies are pouring out of the shack. The tortilla ladies are running around. The wife is shouting for me to stop. The children are wailing.

"Memo!" Jack's voice is cutting through the rotor blades. For a split second my sanity flashes in, and I know how bad off I am. How did a guy who had every advantage—a charmed life—get this way?

"Memo!" Jack's grabbing me by the arm, trying to pull me off balance, and pounding on my hand so I'll drop the rifle. But I can't let go.

"Memo, stop! Stop! We're not in Nam! We're in Mexico! Stop before you annihilate him!"

I'm ripped back from the guy. I stand up straight and I pant with three-second intervals between inhalations.

The horror of injuring poor Inocencio isn't over. I'm holding his bolt action Remington .22. Inocencio's rifle is rusty. Can it shoot? How can I reconcile the dissonance of my delusion, which made me imagine this low-caliber old rifle was an assault weapon? I can't.

Inocencio is on the on the ground. He moans and wrenches and groans.

Inocencio's wife is hysterical. Crying. She screams, "*¡Váyase! ¡Váyase! ¡Váyase!*"

Jack shouts, "What's she saying?"

"To get the hell out of here." I look at her. Then back at Jack. I put the .22 on the ground.

The wide-eyed Mexican peasant bystanders are frozen in muted shock. And the roadside shack's record player stylus scrapes the old piece of vinyl, scratching out another verse of Lola Beltrán singing, "*Al contemplar mi tristeza,*" to contemplate my sadness."

Jack says he can't leave until he examines Inocencio. He moves towards him.

Beaten Inocencio strains with his trauma and pulls-himself-up. He stands. He twitches seeing Jack move towards him. Inocencio staggers back half a step.

His wife puts her hand up for Jack to stop.

"Tell her I'm a doctor."

"*Señora, él es médico.*"

The wife drops her hand. Nods. She turns to me. Her eyes draw thin. The corners of her mouth are downturned.

I say, "*¡Lo siento…lo siento!*" I'm sorry. The words are barren. I take in her appalling loathing look. I'm clumsy and sick and dim. How can I tell these poor rural Mexicans what I did was an incontrollable reaction—nothing to do with Inocencio. I can't. I brought a meaning-less vicious war to their naïve peaceful lives.

Jack examines Inocencio.

Now I'm graceless, having to interpret for Jack and Inocencio.

The report. No lasting damage. Broken ribs. But no collapsed lung.

Jack is stern. "You're still on the battlefield. He isn't."

My stomach convulses. My mouth waters like I am about throw-up. But I don't. The sickness just stays churning in my gut.

The wife glares at me. "*¡Váyase, señor! ¡Por favor, váyase!*"

She tells me to go away. I slink away.

We get into the rig and leave.

The washboard road rattles the FJ40.

Jack wants to know if the police will be involved.

I'm jagged. I pull my head together enough to talk. The nearest police are in Ensenada. I tell Jack Inocencio's wife might be able to get a ride from an occasional passerby, down the long dirt road to the two-lane highway and use a telephone in Santo Tomás to call the police who are almost fifty kilometers away. If she managed to get word to the police, then what? They wouldn't come to investigate a peasant woman's complaint of her husband who's been in a fight. No. Her only defense was to scream at us to leave. The peasant man and his family have no justice. And I'm the self-despising monster.

WE PACK-UP THE CAMP TO LEAVE ARBOLEDA DE LOS ROBLES. EVERY nerve cell is my body is weighted, and vacillates between numb and uncovered tormented vulnerability. I'm riding a streak of bad luck. I put camp equipment in the rig. Nothing fits right. Take stuff out. Repack. Still not right.

Jack neatly puts the last of his gear into the VW campervan.

We catch each other's eyes.

I stand motionless.

Eyes maintain connection.

Jack walks over to me. He puts his right hand on my left shoulder. "Memo, the key to recovering from the damage of war is to not make new damage."

CHAPTER 14

COMING TO TERMS

KATE AND I RETURN TO THE BEACH HOUSE. I have a crumpled, torn sensation pulling me apart.

She's still tucked away in a deep sleep.

I'm poised at the picture window looking into the predawn darkness. There's a hushed soundlessness. A vacancy in me has no choice but to be filled with an indelible smear of Santo Tomás and beating blameless Inocencio. The thought of him reappears as an image in my mind. And bleeds into repetitious ruminations. I can't stop the thoughts. I used to be in control of everything, or thought I was. Now control is sketchy, or it has turned into an unforeseeable mess.

The sun peaks over the eastern horizon. It projects an orange-pink luminous brilliance on the layers of clouds in the distant western horizon. Above there is a thin gray stratum. The beginning day-glow sunrise is over. It's light. The outlying clouds lose their color. All that is left is grayish clouds, lined on the bottom tier with threadlike blackness. A storm forms at sea. A torrent makes a gesture of its arrival. But for the moment, the sea in front of me is made glassy smooth by windless conditions that will be changed by the ferocity of what's in wait at sea.

The gray-blue waves are well-formed. Their smooth surfaces reflect the light like mirrors. I feel immobile. And then a strong pull steers me. I grab my surfboard and slip in the water. Today surfing—

the thing I love to do—feels like I'm going through the motions. Not living it. Just doing it.

I come back to shore and enter the beach house.

Kate is awake. A diaphanous nightgown drapes her body. Kate looks good any time of day. She's on the telephone and turns to look at me. Kate hangs-up. "That was Alita. They just returned from Mexico City. She'd like to make-up for not being here for Thanksgiving—have us over for dinner."

I have such an unsettled and unsteady sense about me. This leads to instantaneously settling into the idea of being around the folks' sense of permanence. I anticipate relief from a daunting malicious feeling inside that could make me crumble if I have one more piece of bad luck or misadventure. "What'd you say?" I step next to Kate.

"I was certain you'd want to do it. We're on for tomorrow night. Okay?"

I let out a breath. The corners of my mouth are upturned. A glint of a pardon rinses over me. "Very okay."

Kate tells me she has to work late at the stock brokerage. We'll need to drive separately and meet at my parents' place.

I WALK IN THE BACK DOOR. THE EFFUSIVE SMELLS HIT me like a red carpet. There's a busy sound coming from the kitchen. "Hi," I yell-out.

Mom is leaning over checking a standing rib roast in the oven. Her bright white apron is tied in a perfect bow. She stands upright and turns towards me. I love her smile—it says you're home. We hug. Then I become aware our embrace is lasting twice as long as we ordinarily hug.

Mom pushes back. She looks in my eyes. "That was nice." She lays bare a loving maternal-like expression on her face.

Sureness and security soak in. "Nice? I needed a little extra."

Dad walks in the kitchen. "I heard you talking." He shakes my hand. Dad then pulls me nearer and gives me a hug. There's a safe and sheltered feel. He's altogether confident and assured and predictable.

Having rooted parents is a piece of good fortune. But their solidness is a mammoth contrast to how I feel. The disparity lets me know how shattered I am.

Dad says, "We're sorry to have missed you for Thanksgiving. How was your time with Dotty and Ted Powers at Santo Tomás?"

Suddenly the smell of oak burning and the Mexican women cooking chicken overwhelms my transiently sane mind. Picture frames of thrashing Inocencio involuntarily flash through my mind. I blink. I hear his wife scream at me. Jack is yelling at me as he pulls me off of the beaten Mexican. "Santo Tomás? It was fine." I'm cognizant that my voice sounds flat, with no inflection to show the time was any source of pleasure.

Mom and dad look at each other. Then they look back at me. They're quizzical. A look of disbelief crosses their faces.

Dad and I go to the pantry where the liquor is kept. He makes a vodka and tonic for mom. He pours a single malt scotch for himself. I have a beer. We deliver the drink to mom. Dad and I go to his study while mom finishes up and we wait for Kate. He shows me his fly-tying projects. Dad is as intent describing the fine distinctions of each fly he has tied. He makes fly-tying sound like a surgical procedure.

I have breaks in concentration while listening to him.

He doesn't notice.

I take a fleeting look at his fine .30-06 hunting rifle, and the twelve-gauge and twenty-gauge shotguns in the English antique mahogany and glass gun case. They are perfectly maintained—makes me think of cleaning our weapons at war, which have been dirtied by being out in the bush, and in the grime and humidity and reddish mud. I listen to another one of his fly tying details. My attention goes back to the gun case. I'm thinking about weapons and war.

"Memo, I'm rattling on and you haven't said anything." Dad turns his head. He looks me in the eye. "Usually, you're very interested in this type of thing."

"I was just paying attention."

"Were you?"

We hear voices coming from the kitchen.

I sidetrack him. "I think Kate is here now." I was supposed to feel good being here. Now I feel like running away.

Dad quickly studies me. "We'd better join the ladies."

There's a perceptible once-over silent examination of me. Does he know, somehow?

Dad and I turn to leave the study.

I glance over my shoulder at the antique gun case. Nice looking weapons I say to myself. Then the recognition comes that I call the firearms weapons. It sounds too military to call a hunting rifle and shotguns weapons. It's like I can't get the Army out of my system.

We're all convivial in the kitchen. The family works together to get the meal on the table. Dad pours a vintage Margaux. The clacking sound of the silverware hitting the plates and chitchat fill the room.

All the smiles help me fake it to hide the agitated stir inside me.

Mid-meal eating slows to a snail's pace.

Mom turns to me. "We're sorry to have missed you for Thanksgiving. How was your time with Dotty and Ted Powers at Santo Tomás?"

Dad just asked me that verbatim. I can't breathe past the upper part of my chest. "...believe I said it was fine when dad asked."

Mom looks perplexed and concerned. "Is something wrong?" she says with a tender lilt to her voice.

Dad looks. He waits for me to answer.

Kate stares. She's not breathing. Two blinks accentuate her long eyelashes.

Then comes a rote explanation of the musical event and the Powers' granddaughter dancing, and Jack and I going to the coast to pick-up fish and lobster for Dotty. And the story stops.

We all look down at our plates. The silverware-plate clacking sound starts again. It's the only sound in the room.

There's an eruption in my chest that pushes up to my throat. It gets caught. I want to tell my parents about my uncontrollable reaction and beating the defenseless Inocencio. I'm stopped from saying anything. Stopped by shame and disgrace and embarrassment and dishonor and indignity. I feel as if I've disgraced my parents' influence on me. They would be mortified to hear what I did. I think of Lupita and spiral deeper downward. The infidelity with her is a different and further degradation adding to my humiliation.

Dad probes me. "Memo, something sounds missing."

Mom joins in. "I was thinking the same thing."

Kate blinks again.

I feel myself buckle under the weight. "Well..." I draw in a breath. "We had a nice time. The Powers were gracious to invite us," slips out of my mouth. The cover-up is too palpable and evident. It's a Pollyanna whitewash while I fight three heads of a dragon. One is what I did to the Mexican. Another is being dishonest with Kate and my parents. The third is the impact felt by war itself.

Dad takes the lead. He shows patience. "We are here for you whenever you need us." He sniffs and swallows. "I'll be frank. You look shaken. Leveling with us when you are ready would be to your advantage."

Mom nods. The center of her eyebrows is turned upward.

I drive home.

Kate lingers for a few minutes.

I think Kate and my parents must be discussing me—too clear something isn't right. I relive every second of beating Inocencio and the wife's screeching yells and Jack saving me from myself. Waves of alarm run through my body. And then I experience again the dread of what I did. It's like a skip in a vinyl long playing record that plays over and over again. The same sound I've heard for the millionth time oozes over me, like a sticky substance I can't get rid of. I should have told my parents what happened. Shame is a powerful stopper.

Shadow Facts greets me at the door. I pet her. We soothe each other. I breathe. An ominous feel says the dog master's reprieve will be brief.

I long for my parents. I long for their stability and solidity. I long to be honest with them.

Kate seems to be taking hours to get home. It's been minutes.

She walks in. Puts down her things. "Memo?"

There's the feeling a ton of bricks is about to fall on me. "Yes."

I sit petting Shadow Facts. Her big brown eyes watch Kate.

Kate is standing and positions herself facing me. Her weight is on her left leg. Her right foot is in front of her. Hands are on her hips. Kate tilts her head to the right. "Your parents and I are concerned." She sounds uneasy. Alarmed. "I think it's time you fess-up."

My shame brings a frothy nauseous feeling to the back of my throat. I swallow.

Kate says, "Don't stonewall me."

"I'm thinking."

"Think out loud."

Aching merges my mind and my body, and begs to get my soul back. I could figure out another escape, but it would only be temporary. Now is the time to let it go. I begin with the conversation I had with Jack on the way back from the coast.

Kate stands up straight. Then she sits down.

She hears each facet of what happened at the shack. Nothing is held back. No blocking the accuracy. The spigot is on.

Kate looks more horrified with each detail. The color drains from her face. Kate's mouth is open. She takes short quick breaths.

I push ahead. The story is short lived, just the steely facts. And it's over, like the rush of a hurricane strength wind.

Kate stands. She walks to the picture window and looks at the non-existent view in the darkness. Kate turns back in my direction. "You keep terrifying the crap out of me. I'm sick of being scared. We all know the war is wrong. I didn't want you to go to OCS. And here we are. You persist in dragging back shit back from war that's like a dead jungle animal that's left in our living room to rot and contaminate the place. Like I said before, I know you can't help it. But we can't get rid of the stench."

CHAPTER 15

RECKLESS AND DESPERATE

K ATE'S FATHER WAS A CAPTAIN IN THE NAVY, and her grandfather was an admiral. Both went to the Naval Academy at Annapolis, nothing like being a low life in the Army that I am taking on and brushing off because I get the drill of what the sergeants and officers are trying to accomplish with the troops. She probably has a hint at what the Army training at Fort Ord is about since she grew up on the Monterey Peninsula, but I am feeling it and thinking it, since I'm going through it, setting aside the top layer of bullshit the trainers pull to whip us into shape. I'd better let her in on it so she can get a clue of how it works. The letter gives the basics. I put a stamp on the letter and drop it off at our company's mailroom.

July 1967, Fort Ord, California

Dear Kate,

Lao-Tse wrote, "The is, is the was of what shall be," which makes me have to believe right now my charmed life of the past is somehow going to push me into a charmed future.

No matter whether life is charmed or not, I can't stand being away from you. I miss you and please pet Shadow Facts for me.

I let you down by getting drafted. Coming from a broken home, you don't trust relationships. I thought we would be able to get past that with our love. Maybe not. You feared I would leave you, just like your father left you through divorce. Now I have left you. Will I come back or be lost at war? Is that the question you're asking yourself? I know you are under so much strain.

You're making do in a situation where you feel compromised. You can't count on me and you have to count on yourself. I have to say that I'm sorry for all of the confusion and anguish this sharp turn in our lives has caused you. In retrospect, we were living in a fog, hoping the inevitable wouldn't happen, but it did. So, here we are and I want to write about how shockingly different my life is now from what we had together.

Please let me give you an idea of what is happening here in Basic Combat Training (BCT). They break you down, attack your civilian ways and cut through your whining. They teach you to think the military way. They teach you to react like a killing machine, willing to do anything —anything—for your unit. Go after the enemy, search and destroy. They want you to feel you are indestructible and operate without fear, but there is always fear.

The unit is your new adopted family. Your buddies are your brothers. Your brothers will die, and you will try to not think about it.

The sergeant in charge of our platoon got back from Nam a few months ago. He is a tough bastard. Underneath, I can tell, he wants to do the right thing for us, even though he is messed up by combat in Nam. When one of the troops is acting undisciplined, he will say, "All right you mother fuckers. Look around you—look at your buddy. Some of you guys are not coming back from Nam. If you don't pay attention—if you don't do exactly as you're ordered and fuck up instead—your buddy next to you is going to be dead. And you're going to be dead. Get your head out of your ass, troop!" I know he is dead serious. I can tell the sergeant is worried the men are asleep on their feet. I'm worried he is right.

There is a guy in my platoon. I don't know his first name. His last name is Stanley. He is a very tall, skinny guy whose ears stick out like a taxicab driving down the street with its doors open. Stanley is a farm boy from Hicksville and is basically illiterate. I am helping him with reading and writing. He reminds me of Shadow Facts because he has the same temperament. But the problem is Stanley has no survival instincts like our black lab. He is the type of guy who does everything the sergeant tells him to do. You tell Stanley to guard a post, you come back eight hours later, and he will still be standing at attention. I know they are going to send this guy to Nam. He is going to do everything they tell him to do. I know he is not coming back alive. The military tells you to think the military way and to take orders. But you are going to die if you don't have a survival instinct—if you don't think and don't work the system. I look in Stanley's poor, innocent face. I know he is a dead man. He will say nothing to take care of himself, and he will die.

Kate, you know I am not soft, but I have to say I love that guy Stanley, the guy whose first name I do not know. I grieve for him before he has died.

The company commander, drill sergeants, and sergeants are shaping up this hodgepodge of people, teaching esprit de corps and physical discipline where there is none. We march and sing the company song: "Kill, kill, kill, rah, rah, lizard shit." We are getting the killing mindset. The tune is ours alone and binds the men together, along with a myriad of other forces that nobody talks about—countering fear with bravado, being tougher than tough, and getting shaped up to face an enemy we have never seen. I know underneath everybody is afraid.

I am getting in a different kind of physical shape than when I was running track at USC and spending countless hours surfing. There's all the marching. We run three miles in the morning, march around and do double time while carrying forty to fifty pounds of field gear. My arms and chest are staying strong from all the pushups we have to do—a penalty the drill instructors impose for fabricated misdeeds.

A guy named Burt Wootten has the bunk below me. Nice guy. He also comes from San Diego. He calls me Sunshine Man because I remain positive despite the dark cloud of being jerked away from home and you. The nickname has stuck with the troops, drill sergeants and CO. I'm Sunshine Man despite being locked away in boot camp and despite the constant ominous subterranean threat of being sent to Vietnam.

Burt tells me I should go to Officer Candidate School since BCT is effortless for me, both the physical part and learning everything they have to teach. Carrying a guy who weighs fifty pounds more than I do off the battlefield (back strap carry, but I call it the "dead man's carry"). Or taking an M-1 apart and putting it back together blindfolded. I'll probably be getting the expert marksmanship badge because I am an accurate shot. I can cite all the Army General Orders while the drill sergeant is barking at me with his nose two inches from mine, etc. Whatever they throw at me, I catch and throw it right back. But I am still Memo, the Sunshine Man version.

Some of the men feel as if they are treated like a piece of meat and that the CO and drill sergeants are sadists. I am unfazed when the drill sergeants yell in my face because I get what the deal is and don't take it personally. They are breaking us down and putting us back together again to fight that god-awful war.

But I know that no amount of training is going to prepare the men to deal with what they are going to see on the battlefield. That preparation will have to come from somewhere else. Should I become an officer, Burt says he would want to be under my command if he goes to Vietnam. He thinks I am tough as nails but would never lose my humanity. I hope he is right about not losing humanity.

Kate, I can't imagine going to Nam with just a couple of stripes on my arms and being ordered into situations where I know I'm going to be screwed. Burt has worked on me, and I am serious about OCS.

Please, Sweet Cakes, don't feel like I've driven a stake into the heart of our marriage because of being scooped up by the Army. You said it's not my fault for replaying your history. But I can't help but shoulder the responsibility of re-enacting the hurtful parts of your life. You can blame me. But please don't do anything reckless because of giving into despair. I know your history and I wasn't sensitive to it by being smarter and shrewder in my attempt to get out of the draft. I have to face those facts. Now, there's no pulling the rabbit out of the hat. I'll have to do the best I can.

I love you,

Memo

I DONATE BLOOD FOR THE TROOPS IN VIETNAM, the tradeoff for a weekend pass to see Kate. Some of the red and purple fluid circulating through my arteries and veins could save a faceless buddy in Nam. Kate picks me up at the front gate of Ft. Ord. The feeling after giving blood is like a horrible alcoholic hangover, but without the party. It doesn't matter. I feel like crap. It's okay. The anticipation of seeing her—maybe we'll have the same excitement as when we first touched. Now is only about being with Kate.

I know Kate doesn't want me to go to OCS. I'll go anyway. I am not going to be a grunt pawn on the battlefield. She'll find a way to understand. Maybe she'll overcome the salt in her wound of being a military kid who had to endure the consequences of divorce. How else will the war disrupt our relationship?

We stay in her girlfriend's charming cottage in Carmel. We make our way up the path, made of yellowish Carmel Valley stone. The walkway winds through the lush English garden leading to the front door. Over the threshold and alone with her again.

Our bodies fit so well together. Her skin is so velvety, her fresh rose-like smell—no smell of spit shined Shinola Army boots or aging olive-drab blankets—just the texture of her sweet skin. My body and top of my head are sheet white, which exaggerate my crimson-sun-burned face. I smell like cheap deodorant from the PX. No matter, there's a reprieve. We're in love.

My mind goes into a spin—our connection—Kate's artistic brilliance and her passion for the arts. But that doesn't matter as much as the fact that she just gets me. Right now every little thing about her falls together in a blur and becomes one thing. When we look at each other today, we simply understand each other.

We have a pardon from the past few months. Now, it's only her and me together. Leave Ft. Ord Friday night and return late Sunday afternoon, just in time for the evening version of shit on a shingle.

"I don't want you to do the extra year to go to OCS. But you're going to do it, anyway. Okay, I'll bend. I get it. It's not a career move. You didn't go to the Academy like my granddad and father—not doomed to be a lifer like them. I just hope this thing will come and go." Kate lets go of a breath. A nod says concession.

I am smart enough to keep my mouth shut. She needs to talk.

"But sometimes I can't sleep at night. I wake-up trembling. What's happening in the war is too scary." Kate looks down and to the right. Her gaze returns and her eyes lock on me. "You have to promise that you'll come back to me."

"Promise? Okay, I promise." I sound like I'm pretending.

"Promise me, Memo. For real."

"Yes, I promise!" My fear is seeing my buddies die or screwing-up to protect another soldier in combat. But at this moment with Kate my fear is I'll abandon her through my own death. I promise her again. A false assurance—she has to know I'm faking it.

Her eyebrows arch up. Her anguished eyes show her fear and sadness and resignation. Kate wants to believe me. We're complicit, both knowing my assurances are an invention to get us past the moment.

We know Carmel. It's where Kate lived as a kid.

"Let's get something to eat," she says. "How about we go to—"

"I know this is weird, but I'm craving Mexican border food. I promise I'll buy you a swish gourmet dinner at someplace like Le Coq d'Or, but later. Let's go over to that Mexican joint on Dolores."

We soak in a thick veneer of happiness. I get rid of every thought of tomorrow.

We watch Saturday's sunset sky at Point Lobos burn orange and red and then turn to darkness.

We wake Sunday morning. A dreadful disjointed feeling starts. We anticipate the day growing thinner and thinner and the two of us dividing like a part of us was severed. The rest of our time together slips faster and faster downhill. Goodbye builds to a crescendo.

She drops me off at Ft. Ord's front gate. "Memo, you promise?" She wants to believe my clear blue eyes.

"It's a promise," I say.

This promise is a lie we hope isn't a lie.

OCS GIVES NEW CONFIDENCE. But Army olive-drab and a gold second lieutenant's butter bar on my collar don't replace irreplaceable old self-beliefs. For some, the identity of officer is a magic trick, a way to hide a person's vacant spots, hurts, or past abuses. For others, it's about being a patriot or having false pride, maybe arrogance or a family military tradition. A number of graduates are overachievers; everything they do is in excess. A few just get off on blowing up shit.

For me, being an officer is simple. It's a way of not being something else—a grunt.

There's one more thing. Slivers of subterranean instincts erupt, pushing earth and rocks and new materials to the surface. Instincts like aggression towards the enemy. Instincts like fairness to my own kind, the kind wearing a U.S. uniform. Life and death instincts. I had never thought much about my own death, but now I dwell on it. Thoughts of my demise have been driven like a spike into my mind. What's the path to death going to be—a short or long path? There's always a path. The specter of death makes my connection to life much more intense—may desire to survive and for my buddies to survive. I feel more alive when I feel I might die.

I hear about war veterans who survive and feel guilty because they're alive and their buddies are dead. They might numb themselves because they're alive but feel dead and bring on a kind of death through drugs, alcohol, and destroyed relationships. Some kill themselves. Shit, naiveté was a lot less painful than this.

I THINK DEPLOYMENT TO VIETNAM—YES OR NO? I know it's a stretch to ask Kate to relocate from the San Diego beach house to be with me at Ft. Benning.

We speak on the telephone. "It's another one of those crapshoots, Kate. There's no way I can give you predictability or promise permanence. But will you move with me to Ft. Benning?"

"In the military you get used to temporary. How temporary will the move be? We don't know. But sure, I'll be there."

Rank has its privileges—RHP—and the government pays for her relocation to Georgia. And then there's the start of a relentless, ambiguous undercurrent of apprehension. We make do living in married officers' quarters. There is no rustic old beach house or Luis Barragán–designed house in Pedregal or comfortable warmth of a childhood home. There is just basic, get-the-job-done military housing. The walls of the house are permeated with a blur of anonymous histories of the myriad people who have lived here before us. They lurk at night. Their faces vaguely come out of the woodwork, like formless hallucinations that appear and fade into nothingness. I take hold of what is now and what is with me—Kate and Shadow Facts.

"It's like we're camping, isn't it?" The harmonic tone in my voice is an apology.

Kate reads me like a sheet of music. "Yeah. And it's a nice feeling, a slice of normalcy enters our lives. Forget the circumstances." We have a go at not worrying. But apprehension is there. It's erased since we're together. And then uneasiness resurfaces after lurking in the background.

"You know, again and again I melt when I see your sweet eyes laugh. I'm too lucky to have you in my life." I must have a starry look.

Kate brings me back. "Memo, this is a short-term deal. That's the military. Remember me? The military brat."

Shadow Facts rounds the edges of military life. The lab's eyes and her receptivity to petting remind me not to lose myself, not to turn into a robotic military man. The dog stands for turning wrong to right, dishonesty to truthfulness and loathing to tenderness. All I need to do is look at her eyes.

After a few months Kate befriends the young wives of officers. We're at home one evening. She says, "I'm careful not to get too close. I know how transient military relationships are. Don't want to connect with something I'm going to lose." Kate is grave and somber.

I take a step at understanding what this means for her. "I don't want you to repeat the military blueprint of change on top of change like when you were was a kid." I nod and wait to see if what I'm saying is a fit.

"One thing is different from when I was a kid. I can't help but take on the panic of the women whose husbands are in Vietnam. I spend time with them. And I'm going to keep a distance. And then there's only one or two of them I feel safe enough to have coffee with."

I say, "The waiting and hoping and guesswork has to be pushed out of your mind or you'll go nuts."

"I'm getting more on edge, knowing you're at the critical point where you may be able to be enough of a short-timer to avoid deployment to Vietnam." Lines in Kate's face say she's worried.

"My unit's first sergeant—1SG McIntyre—told me, 'Don't decorate your foxhole.'"

She waits. Her face looks dour. After a couple of minutes she says, "I catch military sayings. McIntyre meant don't move in. Don't get too comfortable. You're the next to go."

In the next few weeks Kate changes. She seldom laughs now. Can't sit still. Always up out of her chair, moving around. Kate talks about when we met. She plays the Dave Brubeck album we heard the first night we were together. She doesn't want to talk about her day or my day or today. She plays "Moon River" from the Henry Mancini album *Breakfast at Tiffany's* again and again and again. She talks about what life will be like when we're out of the military. The house is spotless when I get home, like she's been cleaning all day. The varnish on the furniture looks like it is wearing off from polishing on top of polishing. Her cooking is elaborate. She makes dishes requiring sauces made with stocks and stocks are made from scratch—culinary detail inside of detail. There are always freshly cut flowers, arranged perfectly and rearranged to be more perfect. She can't relax; she's like a flying creature, constantly buzzing around until she is exhausted.

Kate's voice starts to sound tired. Still a young-looking beautiful person, but her face looks a couple of years older and tight. Sometimes sex is wild and crazy. But most of the time in bed, she just wants to be held, and nothing else. And then she wants me to hold her more.

Shadow Facts wakes me in the middle of the night to take her out. Kate is awake. Kate's eyes are wide.

"What are you thinking, Sweet Cakes?"

"Nothing. Just thinking." Kate keeps her thoughts private. But her private thoughts are so private I know what she's thinking. I'm leaving her.

We're taken by surprise. We think it's good news. I receive a notification from the Department of the Army. I'm being considered for a special assignment. I'm interviewed by the Department's representatives. They want to know about my fluency in Spanish. There are top secret background security checks.

The representatives come to our military quarters. They talk to Kate. They want to know every fragment about her military family. They perk up when they hear her father and grandfather went to Annapolis—her father a naval captain and her grandfather an admiral. They photograph us separately and together. The phone rings. They listen to Kate's manners and etiquette when she answers the telephone. They observe how we carry ourselves—style and graces. We're two hundred percent.

They leave. We wait.

Kate changes. Her laughing eyes are back. She sits in her seat for longer than two minutes. She sleeps through the night. Her voice is melodic. The house returns to clean, not spotless. Dinners are casual.

I'm smoothed coming home to a relaxed Kate.

We have dinners off base at an old shack where an aged black man barbeques ribs and chicken. We dip into pots of beans. We eat fresh-picked okra from the clay crock neatly placed in the middle of the beat-up wooden table. We drink Miller High Life. We chitchat with the barbeque owner's plump wife about her pickling recipe. She says her okra brings her local fame. Her starched white apron illuminates her smile and her pride. Kate and I ease into happiness. We linger at the shack, talk and get lazy. Under the surface there's a jazzy excitement.

I anticipate possibilities. "Maybe I'll be on assignment with the attaché to Spain—better work on having a Castellan intonation and give my Mexican accent an overhaul." I give it a cocky spin.

Kate is brushed by the fantasy. "Wouldn't it be grand to live in Madrid? I'll go to the Prado and see El Greco and Goya. I could study the Spanish masters who influenced the start of the Impressionist movement. Oh, and take Spanish cooking classes." Kate puts on airs. "We'll be invited to embassy parties—black tie and military dress blues. I'll have to be outfitted for a formal gown. Yes, you have a charmed life, Memo."

We wait for six weeks after the Department of the Army interviews. Finally I receive the news at my unit that is accompanied with my orders. I get permission from the CO to leave early for the day.

I walk through the front door.

"You're home early." Kate eyes me.

I must have a serious look.

"The news came, didn't it? It's not a romantic post. It's not Spain. It doesn't include me."

"I have the orders." My head is downcast for a moment. I look up at Kate. "It's Vietnam. I am assigned to the Military Assistant Command—Vietnam to work in a joint military-civilian mission with the United States Agency for International Development— MACV and USAID."

"Your—and my—charmed lives have turned to shit, haven't they?"

"I was stupidly stirred up, imagining a romantic life in Spain." I let out a blast of air. "It was dimwitted of me to think we'd get out of the Vietnam War."

Kate sits. She bends over and puts her head in her lap. Kate cries. "Somehow, I misplaced reality." Her voice is muffled. She sits up. Her eyes are swollen. "Those assholes."

We learn the Department of the Army has the same standardized interview process, no matter where the soldier is sent.

The house becomes disorganized. No more fun dinners at the black man's shack. Kate alternates between being distant to being warm and loving. The Army gives me a month's leave. We pack up in an hour. The movers come. I work on getting Kate and Shadow Facts relocated to the beach house in San Diego.

The month's leave is contending with the adversary of time—time slipping away—like we're parked in a gray riptide and trying to turn every second into easy light. We forestall thinking about being deployed for a year and being separated. Or thinking about coming home in a body bag or dying in some yet unknown way.

What else do I do with a month leave before going to Vietnam? Live in some crazy, drunken way? Say goodbye to all my family and friends? Hear their fears, hatred of war and attempts to understand?

WE TAKE EL *FERROCARRIL* FROM MEXICALI TO MAZATLÁN. The rickety Mexican train was built in the States in the 1920s. First class is comfortable enough. The berths are clean. The interior smells like old, dry wood and leather. The contours of the railroad car roof remind me of a coffin lid. The railroad car is shaped like a casket, one with windows.

Somehow we get on the wrong train. It's the milk run, not the express. The train stops and starts and stops and starts again. Minutes last for hours. The ride takes days, weeks, months—a lifetime. Our precious time before going to Nam is slipping away like grains of sand rushing though the neck of an hourglass. The trip will last thirty-six hours. It would have taken twenty-four hours if we had driven all the way from San Diego.

We go to the club car. Once classy, now it's worn out. We drink cervezas—Tecate in red cans—and refrescos—Cokes and ginger ale. We eat the pork tacos al pastor in soft, fresh smelling corn tortillas sprinkled with crumbly cheese, *queso añejo*. We skip the tamales, which look heavy—full of lard—they'd drop like rocks in our stomachs—we won't have enough time to digest them before I leave.

Kate listlessly stares out the train window. The desert tan and purple and muted green thorny cactus landscape blurs by.

"You look out of it, Sweet Cakes. How about a shoulder massage?"

"That'd be good." Kate sighs tired resignation.

Kate's shoulders and back are rubbed and kneaded for forty-five minutes. "I'm trying to get the rough edges off. You've got a few knots that are hard to untie."

"The tension is loosening up. Hey Memo, it can't all be undone."

"Want to try to get some sleep?"

"Maybe it would be best." Kate is a silent lump under the blanket.

I don't know if she's sleeping or occupying space in a state of paralysis.

The long haul is dotted with lone Mexicans in the middle of the desert. Throughout the night and day, the train creaks to a stop and then slowly crawls up to speed again. The train picks up one Mexican, one at a time, again and again.

"Say Kate, all this snail-like, stop-start is happening over and over a million times."

"It's agonizing. Where did these lone people come from?"

"I think the train conductors have nothing to do but torment us by this entire stop and start bullshit."

There are no villages, no houses, and no lights, just the isolation of the vast, slowly moving, sandy desert terrain. Lightning strikes in the distant night sky, illuminating the desert and violet-mauve mountain backdrop.

Thirty-six hours elapse. Kate says, "These thirty-six hours are wasted." Her voice is dragged-out.

"This not the way I want to spend time with you before leaving for Vietnam." It takes a lot more for me to knuckle under, but I'll admit this is a crappy deal. "Talk about miserable."

Kate is spent.

I begin to feel a second wind when we arrive.

Kate and I get a lift to Hotel La Siesta, along Olas Altas Bay at Mazatlán. We enter the reception area. Blaring brass and vibrating string mariachi music from the radio echoes off the hard tiled floor.

The clerk leans his shoulder against the foyer wall. He puffs on an unfiltered, moldy-smelling cigarette. He chats in a rapid exchange with another man about something inconsequential.

We wait. We have a strained feeling.

Kate's face is a shade of pale tiredness. She shifts her weight from one foot to the other, and then she folds her arms.

My love of Mexican time evaporates into the ether. "*Hola, señor. Necesitamos una habitación, por favor—una que es muy tranquila. Como ahora mismo.*" My voice is direct and polite. He gets the picture—we want the room now, not at the end of the conversation, which would last under a different definition of time than now.

Our second story, oceanfront hotel room overlooks the Olas Altas. Through open French doors, we view the azure sky shining on the iridescent sapphire sea.

Kate says, "The accumulation of this and that and an unknown something else is bringing me down." This translates to a torrent of tears welling up in Kate's eyes. The corners of her lips are slightly downturned. Her chin trembles.

"Kate this is a beautiful Mexican day on a beautiful Mexican bay."

"I know. I'm just so scared about what is going to happen." Kate's big, beautiful hazel eyes drip saline, making her cheeks completely wet. Her sweet body goes limp.

"The beauty of the day isn't going to save us, is it?"

"Just hold me, Memo."

A few minutes pass. I say, "Let's go to the bar."

Kate and I drink fresh Pacifico from the local brewery and knock back a shot of Cuervo Gold with salt and lime. We go back to the room. We have sex like the best of friends and soul mates. Connected. Readying ourselves to part. I hold her, and she's vulnerable and close.

South of the border is the place I love. But today I see it through a dirty lens, its beauty obscured. Where's the soothing charm? Our experience is like gears mashing together, never meshing. The next morning, we go the airport, fly to Tijuana and return to the beach house. We spend every possible moment together, except when I'm in the water, putting in some miles running, or communicating with Shadow Facts in her canine language. I run without feeling pushed or competitive, just for the love of its temporary freedom.

Freedom is illusive and transitory and collapses into fear about Kate. I'm plagued thinking about whether she will become reckless because of her desperation about me being gone—helpless and feeling urgency that will put her in some unknown dangerous situation driven by her despair. I have now become the sketchy guy she can't count on. And she's vulnerable to being rescued by an indefinite nameless somebody. I have to stop torturing myself. Have trust where ambiguity casts its shadowy light. But will she wait?

CHAPTER 16

DON'T TORTURE YOURSELF

Friday, December 4, 1970

THE DAYS ARE SHORT. SUNSET WAS AT EIGHTEEN MINUTES TO FIVE. Civil twilight—as defined by the law—ended at nine minutes after five. A light rain begins. I didn't think it would rain so soon in the season. I turn on the beach spotlight. Through the darkness I watch the rain come down in its beam. The wind blows the rain at a ten-degree angle. Kate is not home. I turn-off the spotlight and sit in the dark. Shadow Facts is next to me, with her head on my knee.

An hour passes. The sound of the rain on the roof is constant and stronger now. Kate is not home. My chest is weighty. I turn on the beach spotlight to see the heavy rain. The wind picks-up and blows the drops at a thirty-degree angle. I sit in the dark room and watch the rain.

The fear I had before leaving for the war and while I was there is now looking me dead square in the eyes. I involuntarily dredge up the unshakable intense dread that Kate would not be able to wait for me to come back.

Seven o'clock. Kate is not home. The beat in my chest surges, like its rhythm is racing claps of thunder. The beach house is silent, except for the driving rain and the throbbing in my chest.

Kate's schedule doesn't add-up. She fritters away time with girl-friends who seem more like phantom people than anybody who is real. There're countless hours in her artist's studio that don't match what materializes on canvas.

Then I think about our letter writing when I was in Vietnam. Our letters and their frequency bothered me. This made for a powerless feel. And then came second-guessing myself and a back-and-forth mental volley.

Our communications were hard to make sense of. Military's Vietnam culture clashed with the safety and security back home and put us at different places in our minds and changed perceptions. Within days of my arrival devastation came with Walter's death. It rearranged my mind. I felt disengaged, which led to feeling like I was failing Kate in some vague way.

Then there were the unmistakable cues that even my combat-strained mind could comprehend. The ratio of our letters was one-to-one when I was first in county. Then came an abrupt change. Letters were two-to-one. I'd be disappointed at mail call, which led to anger, and ended in sadness. Then suspicion added to my sadness when Kate's letters began to have a formal quality. I thought there must be someone else.

In this evening's darkness and the droning rain I feel alone. Isolated. I need to be filled with trust instead of doubt. I turn on a light. The well-known telephone number is dialed. I turn the light off.

"Hi dad, do you have some time, right now?"

"We're going out in forty-five minutes. Do you need more time than that?"

"It's a start." The muscles going down my neck and across my shoulders are taut. "I'm scared about my marriage."

"War has a high cost, doesn't it? Tell me exactly what's bothering you, son."

"It's hard."

"Just start. We'll see what happens."

I tell dad about the communication changes Kate and I had while I was in Nam. And how my combat exposure twisted my belief in what I saw going on between us. I couldn't tell shit from Shinola. Then the clearly identifiable signals hit me in the face that not even my war trauma could fog over.

"Right now I am sitting home, not knowing where Kate is. Freaked." I close my eyes for an instant. I take a breath. "I'm helpless. Filled with panic."

"Kate always kept in contact with us. We had dinners. She got busy with her job at the stock brokerage. Kate seemed absorbed in her art. She trailed off with us. We assumed she was expanding her life while you were gone."

"I'm crazy—frantic." I want to hit something. "Not knowing makes me rash."

Dad says, "Uncertainty is more malicious than the most horrible reality."

Dad has a way of pulling me together. "What should I do?"

"The obvious. The two of you have to level with each other."

"I have to go. She's here!"

At seven-fourteen, Kate slams the car door behind her. She runs in the door and catches her breath. She turns on the light. Her hair is soaked.

Shadow Facts and I stand six feet in front of Kate.

Kate's back is four feet from the door.

"What are you doing in the dark?"

"Waiting for you."

Kate's voice is short and impatient and icy. "You're usually busy doing something."

"I'm not busy right now. Where were you?"

She sounds dismissive. "Running errands after work."

"Where were you?"

"I had things to do."

"Okay, Kate. Where the fuck were you?"

She puts up a standoffish angry front, like a barrier to protect herself. "What is this? An interrogation?"

"You're avoiding me." I take one step forward. "This has to be settled."

Shadow Facts is frozen.

"Okay, I had to take care of some business." This sounds like a brush-off.

My face flushes. The veins in my neck pulsate. "I can't take this. Where the fuck were you?" I take half a step forward. I scrutinize her eyes, waiting to hear what she is going to say next.

Kate is rigid as a board. "I had to say goodbye to somebody."

"Who?"

"Joe."

I'm scared shitless that my fear is coming true. "Joe? Who the hell is Joe?"

"A stockbroker at the office."

"Why did you have to say goodbye to him?"

"Just did."

I have a slippery and elusive grasp on what's happening right now. Keeping myself in check is sliding away. "Okay. That's it, goddamn it. Now, what the fuck where you doing? Who's Joe?" I'm spitting out the questions. "What is your relationship with him? And you'd better snap out of it right fucking now and tell me just exactly what the deal is, or I warn you—I'm going to lose control."

Shadow Facts is petrified. She looks at Kate.

Kate puts her arms straight out in front of her, palms flat towards me.

Something about the gesture pulls me back from an abyss. I don't move any closer.

"I saw him a few times while you were gone."

"And what about since I've been back?" The tension makes me instinctively draw my right hand into a fist.

Kate blinks once. Her lips move like they're not connected to her face. "Well, yeah, a couple of times since you've been back."

"Did you screw him?"

"No." Kate sounds flat. Unbelievable.

"Kate, did you screw him?!"

"No, no, I didn't!" Her face is rigid, a cross look.

"What did you do?" I need her to confess. All the doubt about what she did is making me nuts.

Kate frees a speck of restraint. "I was lonely while you were gone. He asked me out for a drink after work a few times."

"And after I got home?"

Kate takes a step towards me. Then she does an about face and walks away. Kate stops, taps her foot. She turns back and stands in front of me. "You've been distant, and preoccupied since you got home. Goddamn it, I love you, but I'm still lonesome."

"You saw him again?"

"Well, yes, a couple of times. And tonight, to say goodbye. But I swear to God, I didn't go to bed with him." Kate sounds truthful now. But she's removed.

"How close did you come?"

Her iciness returns full force. "Stop it, Memo. Nothing happened. Don't torture yourself!"

That was what my buddy said. "Jack told me: 'Stop fuckin' torturing yourself.'"

"Just what exactly does 'Don't torture yourself' mean?"

"I'm not telling you right now." Yeah, I'm too jacked-up right now to fill-in any war details, much less the torrid time with Lupita. My deltoid muscles feel like knots. "Okay, Kate. Tell me what did happen."

Kate stops cold. The she erupts, "I came close. I was on the verge of going to bed with him when I found out Joe was a womanizer. Before that, I felt as though I was special to him. But I found out he preys on military wives whose husbands are gone."

"Oh, so you would have slept with him if he wasn't a womanizer?"

Kate folds her arms. "I was so vulnerable." Now she unfolds her arms. "I feel like a total idiot, getting sucked into his trip. I don't know. I just needed to be with somebody. Felt so deserted."

"What's his last name?" I'm going to find that mother fucker and get retribution.

She reads me. "Why?"

"Kate, tell me. It will be easy for me to find out if you don't tell me—one call to the stockbrokerage."

"It's Scanlon." Kate looks like she startled herself by the unfettered admission. Fright comes over her face. "What are you going to do?"

"Nothing." There's a roasting feeling in my chest and throat. "You wait here for me. Don't move. We'll talk about us later. I'll be back."

Kate sits down. She puts her head in her hands.

There's a collapsed feeling between us. Maybe she'll leave me. I stop—second thoughts about going. Fuck it. I've got a job to do.

I jump into my rig and head over to my parents' house. A combat-ready sense washes over me. I drive exactly the speed limit. Make a full stop at all the stop signs. All traffic laws are obeyed. Stoplights reflect the wet pavement. Windshield wipers work overtime. I pay attention to everything around me. When I arrive, nobody's home.

I go into the house. Use the telephone book. Joseph Scanlon, Spindrift Drive, La Jolla. I go to my parents' bedroom and get my father's .38. It goes under the driver's seat of the FJ40.

MY MIND GOES INTO AN AUTOMATIC DRIFT. I dredge up when I accompanied General Steele to I Corps near the demilitarized zone to evaluate the Kit Carson Scouts. In the evening he invites me to his quarters. He dismisses his entourage. We talk. He gets smashed on cheap bourbon. In what resembles a self-absorbed drunken stage performance he reveals too much. I find out he's a puppet for his father. And now I see he's a political military puppet. A blaring light illuminates who the people are behind running this war. I invent an excuse to leave.

I walk to where I am billeted. I am about to enter my quarters, and I smell pot. I turn a corner. There's a captain smoking a joint. "Give me a hit of that fuckin' thing," I said. He handed me the joint. I pulled the smoke deep into my lungs. Getting loaded gives me the sensation of catching the tail of an elusive dragon I'm chasing—trying to be okay, but not being okay.

In the morning I walk out of the mess hall with Steele and his henchmen. A fat gray rat that—to my eyes—is the size of a cat bolts out of the mess hall and waddles along the side of the structure like a mechanical prop from a movie. Its ash colored tail is the length of its body. I take out my .45 and free the safety lock. The rat runs across a narrow gap between the mess hall and another structure. There's nothing and nobody down range. Maybe I feel a little trigger-happy. I take a bead just slightly above and in front his eye to calculate the deadly shot and follow the rat running from left to right across the red-dirt compound. An easy touch of pressure on the trigger discharges a round. The top of the rat's head blows off. The huge rodent flips, landing on its back. It slides to a halt, its feet extended skyward.

Steele's head juts forward. His jaw drops. His lips move and are speechless. Steele stands motionless on the compound's red earth. His throat pulsates. Words seem to be stuck in his throat. What is he thinking? Sometimes you never find out with these high up military guys.

What I think is some rats justify having their heads blown off.

I PUSH THE BRAKES AT A RED STOPLIGHT. It turns green. I arrive at the La Jolla address. I'm jacked-up, but take in details of Scanlon's place. It's an expensive-looking, ocean view house with a completely uninspired design. Money can't buy good taste. A new black Mercedes sedan is parked in the driveway. I ring the doorbell. *Ding…ding, ding, ding, ding…ding, ding.* The chime sounds as though it were made for a dollhouse.

He comes to the door. Joe's a 6'1", two hundred pound, white guy with an Afro hair cut who looks as though he does a lot of pushups. His red polyester paisley shirt makes me sick.

"Yes?"

"I'm Memo Muir."

"Who?"

"Memo Muir. You know, Kate's husband. Kate's the woman you tried to fuck."

He tries to close the door. I push it open, and it bangs against the doorstop. I step inside. The door almost comes off its hinges when I slam it behind me. Joe takes two steps backward.

"I'm calling the police."

"You won't have time to call the police, asshole."

"What are you gonna do?" Joe is wide-eyed, like a schoolboy.

"You're going to listen." I feel as if I'm talking a pimply soldier under my command.

Joe's voice sounds higher pitched. It makes me nauseous, just like his polyester shirt. "Hey, man, I'm sorry. Nothing happened."

"A lot happened, you womanizing mother fucker."

"I swear to God! Yeah, Kate was lonely, but we didn't do anything."

"You go after women whose husbands are away on military duty."

"I'm telling you, nothing happened with Kate."

I step closer and Joe backs up. The way he's standing, he won't be able to maintain balance if I push him. He's a dumb shit. I grab his left upper arm with my right hand and squeeze, like a pair of Vise Grip locking pliers.

I'm screaming now. "Listen, you mother fucker. You prey on military wives whose husbands are over in Nam getting their butts shot off." I poke him in the middle of his chest with the index finger of my left hand to punctuate every single word I say. My grip on his arm stops him from being pushed off balance. "You son of a bitch. Fucking their wives in your kitsch La Jolla house with a black Mercedes in the driveway while those poor guys are bleeding to death in the sweaty jungle."

Joe's mouth is open. His eyes are like saucers. "What are you gonna do?"

"You asked that once before. Now I'm going to tell you. I'm going to keep track of you. This is what I'm going to do if I find out you're going after another military wife. I'm going to come back here and cut-off your cock. I'm going to shove it down your throat so you'll suffocate before you bleed to death."

I release his arm. Five more pokes to the chest: "You-got-that-mother-fucker?"

Off balance, he falls back with each finger jab, and then barely catches himself.

I pull back my left arm to make a palm-heel strike to Joe's solar plexus and think about the follow-up blow. Stop. No, don't do it.

"Joe..."

"Yeah?"

"Remember, I'm going to check on you. You're pathetic, you tasteless mother fucker."

I turn and walk out, pulling the door shut with a slam. I use enough force to rattle the door—just short of unhinging it.

It's stopped raining. I drive back to my parents' house. They're home.

"Hi, dad. I came to return your .38."

"I didn't know you had it." Dad's worried eyes are taut. They reflect an apprehensive concern.

"Yeah, sorry I didn't ask first. I had some business to do. Needed back-up. But I didn't use it."

"I don't like the idea of you carrying a weapon around. What happened?" Dad studies me. "You leveled with Kate. She told you who she's been seeing and you confronted him?"

"That easy to make out? It turned out there was a guy—Scanlon—who schemed on her. He took advantage of her loneliness. Didn't take her to bed. It also turns out he's a predator. Goes after military wives whose husbands are in Nam. It makes me sick. I told him I'd come after him if his predatory bullshit didn't stop."

"Did he get the picture?" His face loosens.

"Absolutely."

"I see the marital predicament—crisis—you're in. I'm worried you might be too reactive." Dad pauses. "Look, let's keep tied into each other. You don't want to be getting yourself in more trouble."

"You want to know what Jack said? 'The key to recovering from the damage of war is to not make new damage.' What he said stuck. I could have annihilated Scanlon—the womanizer. I didn't. I want the turmoil to stop."

"You won't be needing to borrow the .38 again, will you?"

"No."

"Let's keep tabs on what's going on."

"Okay." I stop. "Are you going to tell mom?"

"Yes."

"Okay. And tell her I'll talk to her myself."

"You do that." Dad's voice has a fine texture. "I love you, son."

Dad and I hug.

My parents are extraordinary. The advantaged life. God, I shouldn't be so messed-up. My blood has been poisoned time after time. Where's the antivenin?

I leave.

KATE IS WAITING FOR ME. I DESCRIBE EVERY MINUTE DETAIL of the scene at Joe's house.

I say, "Did you call Scanlon to say I was coming?"

Her voice is unnatural, as though she holding back a secret. "No."

"Why?"

"Just didn't."

"I can't believe the way that guy looked."

Kate sounds dismissive again. "Memo, I said I was an idiot."

"I forgive you." A hopeless and frantic feeling chokes in my throat. "It doesn't matter."

I take a step closer to her and see two suitcases in the hallway.

"What's going on?"

Kate's face is flushed red. She pulls in a breath. "You going over to Joe's house was the last straw. I'm worn-out and sick and spent putting up with all of your craziness. It started with you doubling-up on the letters you sent me from Vietnam and then demanding I should send you as many. I knew you were hurting. But goddamn, I didn't have that much to say about plugging along in my life here. I mean, shit, Memo, how many times can I say I'm lonely and I miss you and that I'm supportive. And your letters had those goddamn suspicious innuendos.

"But—"

"But nothing. And you were checked-out in France, except for the sweet parts. And the animalistic sex." Kate looks away. Her eyes move back on me. "And the super-sexed French chick you dragged back to our hotel room. Now our sex is either rough or non-existent."

"There are some reasons for—"

"Hold on. I suspect... let me finish something else first." Kate turns and steps towards the picture window. She turns on the beach spotlight. She surveys the beach for five seconds. The light doesn't carry all the way to the ocean's edge. Kate turns back in my direction. "Killing the rattler was knee-jerk craziness." She breathes hard. "And the way you went off on that poor defenseless man at Santo Tomás... good thing you didn't deck Joe in the same way, but there's no excuse for you going after Joe."

My guts are twisting. I don't care. I want to get this over with. "Let's get everything out."

"You do? Okay. Let me tell you what I suspect. You have been so distant. Distracted. And then there was Guadalupe Canyon. You came back after hiking to look at the petroglyphs. Gone for God knows how long. I thought you were loaded on datura. You weren't loaded on datura. You're loaded on another woman."

"How'd you know?"

"You had another woman's smell on you. And it was a sexual smell." Kate closes her eyes. Then she opens them wide. "I dismissed it. Thought I was imagining it. But then sex was extreme—on or off. I'm not stupid. In your own way you confirmed it with distance and conspicuous dishonesty over and over again."

I pace back and forth like I'm caged.

I tell Kate about Lupita, accompanied by some discrete and diplomatic omissions. She doesn't need all the details. But I don't leave out that Lupita took in what I have difficulty talking about.

"Are you kidding me? I listened and listened. And I would have listened more, but you did all that tight-lipped routine."

"The circumstances were...I just didn't think you'd believe—"

"No, Memo, I do believe you. The guy with the charmed life, who goes up some remote canyon in Mexico, meets a Mexican princess and screws her brains out. Well, I'll tell you what, you've just charmed yourself out of a marriage. Your going after Joe is the last straw. Well, you just pushed me over a fucking cliff with this deal with the Mexican chick." Kate's voice turns toneless. "I've always worried that we would split. Now it's happening."

"It's over with Lupita. I'll never see her again. What about a big dose of forgiveness?"

"Maybe I would forgive a onetime sexual mess-up. But there's too much stacked-up and we've toppled over."

"Please, let's figure this out together."

"I'll tell you the main thing that has me completely unhinged. It's the tension of not knowing what you're going to do next. I'm kept nerve-wracked waiting for you to snap. I just can't handle it, Memo."

Desperation goes deep. "Do you still love me?"

"I don't know. I'm so on edge all the time, it clouds over everything else."

Kate looks at me and shakes her head. She picks up her bags and walks out the door.

"Don't go, please. Please, Kate!"

"Forget it. I'm plagued by my parent's divorce, and always feared our marriage would fall apart. Now, my worst fear about marrying you has come true. Hurt by my parent's divorce. Now, hurt by you. Goodbye."

"You can't have Shadow Facts."

"You can have her. You love the dog more than me anyway."

"Ouch. That hurt."

Kate closes the door behind her. Shadow Facts paws at the door. She futilely tries to jiggle the door to get to Kate.

I stand in front of the picture window to look at the deserted beach. The wind has died down. Complete stillness. The ocean must be at minus tide. I turn off the spotlight.

There is a deep fathomless black pit in my stomach. I don't feel like living anymore. I'm cold, but I can't bring myself to make a fire. Shadow Facts licks my hand and nudges it to be petted. I give her a treat. I crouch down to pet her with both hands. I sit and look out at the picture window's cavernous blank emptiness.

An hour passes. There is a pounding on the door. Shadow Facts goes berserk barking. Is that Kate? I hope to God she has decided to come back. Please let that be her.

I turn on the interior lights. I go to the door. There are two uniformed police officers. "Yes?"

"I'm Officer Bradley and this is Officer Spiker. Memo Muir?"

"Yes, officers. Come in. Would you like a seat? Something to drink?"

"No, thanks. Do you know why we're here?" says Bradley.

"This must be about the visit I paid to Joe Scanlon, correct?"

Spiker is a skinny cop with an ill-fitting dark blue uniform. His badge is crooked and the way it lays on his chest looks farcical. He's pasty looking, with a long thin neck and a protruding Adam's apple.

You can tell Bradley is the senior officer. He has a soft face for a police officer. Ten more pounds, and he'd look like a teddy bear.

"He's filed charges against you for assault. We came to investigate. Tell us what happened," says Bradley.

"Scanlon's a con artist. I was in Vietnam. My wife was lonely and vulnerable. Scanlon tried to seduce her while I was away, took advantage of her situation. He kept it up after I returned."

Bradley and Spiker and I are standing near the front door.

The tops of their police hats and shoulders are slightly wet. The outside must have turned to a drizzle.

Spiker frowns.

Bradley looks neutral. "Okay, then what?"

"Kate—my wife—found out Scanlon has a pattern of seducing military wives whose husbands are at war. He's a womanizer. My wife saw the situation for what it was and dropped him. She said goodbye to him tonight. Then she told me about him—the whole story. So I went over to see him. Had to get some things straight."

"Spiker and I didn't know each other at the time, but we were both MPs in Nam. Mr. Muir, doing what you're supposed to do in Nam could be breaking the law here. Are you still in the military?"

"Bradley and Spiker are good military names. Spiker, kind of like Spike. No, I left the military six months ago."

Bradley says, "Why did you go to Scanlon's place if he didn't have a relationship with your wife?"

"Well, he did have a relationship with her, but there was no sex—they say. She was my wife, and he was trying to screw her. This is one piece. The other is that he has screwed a lot of women whose husbands are at war."

Spiker looks around the simple, yet tastefully appointed house. "Were you an officer?"

"Yes, a captain."

"You're going down for this," says Spiker.

"Going down for what? Look this guy rolls around in the hay in his expensive La Jolla house with other guys' wives while the husbands are dying in that hot, sweaty armpit called Vietnam. That guy is shit."

Spiker paces back and forth. "You broke the law. Think breaking and entering. Think assault. You're probably one of those fucking officers who deserved to be fragged—obliterated by your own men."

"Fragged? All I did was talk to the guy, Spiker. Excuse me, Officer Spiker."

"You made bodily contact in a threatening manner. You think you can get away with shit here just because you were an officer in Nam? Think again."

"Look, I was an officer at MACV working with CORDS. I evaluated manpower needs and slotted people into positions. I was out in the bush twenty times, at least a few of which were disasters. You understand what I mean by 'disaster'?"

"Bradley, let's take this guy in."

"I want to hear what he has to say."

"Fragging? Yeah, I've heard of it. Yeah, there were some big ego cowboy officers who were out for glory and made bad decisions. Really bad decisions. Made the GIs under their command shit bullets. Caused a lot of casualties. But there were only a few of them."

Spiker looks at me with icy sternness. How the hell could Bradley stand being teamed up with this guy?

"Go ahead, sir," says Bradley.

"Being an officer is a life-size responsibility. Everybody's continued existence is in the balance. You take care of your men. Get the mission done. Out there, leadership, coming through for the men, and trust is everything, no matter what the outcome. What did you do, Spiker?"

"I'm asking the questions."

"He was attached to the 720th Military Police in Long Binh," says Bradley.

"You were tucked away, working in a stockade—Long Binh Jail—Camp LBJ," I say.

"Okay, let's chill-out." Bradley's forehead is moist. "Sir, I know things got stirred up with the fragging comment, but let's get back on track. So you say that Scanlon is a predator who screws military wives while their old man is in Nam?"

I take a breath. My shoulders drop. "That's right, Officer Bradley. It would have been a different scenario had she gone off with some random guy. But this guy had cunning. He went after her."

"Well, you didn't do much to Scanlon. Just scared him. So we're going to make this go away."

"We're going to do what?" says Spiker.

"Spiker, shut the fuck up."

Spiker's Adam's apple goes up and down. "You're going to make this go away? Are you kidding?"

Shadow Facts goes over to Spiker and rubs her head against his leg.

"What the hell is your dog doing?"

"She does that to hurting people to try to help."

"Spiker, go have a cigarette, now," says Bradley.

Spiker leaves. "Officer, Scanlon's shit has got to stop."

"Sir, the complaint he filed is going to be lost somewhere. No problem. I'm going up to his house tonight and have a chat with him. Reinforce your position, you might say."

"That means a lot to me, Officer."

"It means a lot to me, too. Thank you, Officer."

Bradley walks toward the door.

The first thought of being without Kate flashes in my mind. I work off of impulse. "Maybe we can have a beer sometime."

"A beer? I appreciate the thought, sir." He has a polite and inferred way of declining my invitation.

Bradley and I stand. I walk him to his vehicle.

Spiker is in the driver's seat.

Bradley puts his hand on the passenger's side door handle. He stops. Bradley turns to me. "This whole womanizing thing that happened with Scanlon—the same thing happened to me when I was in Nam. I came home to no wife. Now I don't have anybody." Bradley opens the door. He shakes my hand.

I think he wants to hug me, but doesn't.

Bradley says, "Goodnight, sir."

I watch them drive away. The cop car's taillights get smaller and smaller in the night and finally disappear. I stand statue-like in the dark dank empty street. There's an unmoored sensation.

I take hold of the handle of the beach house front door—strangely afraid to enter my own home—knowing nothing is there.

The police visit made a commotion. It also made for a flood of distraction. Now the diversion is over. I quickly plunge into reckoning what Kate's exit means. It hasn't sunken in. The beach house is now dim and cavernously vacant. A fear comes. Will I go completely crazy without her? I'm a disgusting case of a human being. I'm miserable and despondent and angry. Pitiful. Why not just end it? I'd show her. But she probably wouldn't care.

CHAPTER 17

IN COUNTRY

Agitated HOLLOWNESS MAKES SLEEP IMPOSSIBLE. The night bleeds into a bleak overcast winter dawn. My all night restlessness is well known to me, like being out in the bush in Nam. Sitting in the vacuous twilit bedroom with the lights off. It's unfilled. I'm there. It feels like nobody is there. And it feels like ten of me are there. I'm unable to hold back the incoming tide of memories.

Kate is out of the picture. And she is a lasting picture I can't get out of my mind. Now I'm alone. The remorseful contradiction in terms fills me; I need her so badly and I'm the self-destructive guy who pushed her away. Now I'm engulfed by the memories that put me in this place.

All the clashing struggles dawned with my opening moves into the Phoenix Program. It was a special assignment from the Department of the Army. I didn't realize what special assignment meant. It turned a nightmare into a worse nightmare. All the behind the scenes secret trickery of the military took me—the naïve guy from an advantaged life—and turned me into an ugly unpredictable person who is frightening.

I DISEMBARK THE NONSKED—nonscheduled commercial aircraft contracted by the government. The stewardess says she'll look forward to seeing me on the return flight. She says that to everyone, knowing she'll see the lucky ones who weren't taken down by the enemy or medically evaluated.

The tropical humidity makes my jungle fatigues cling to my back. Ton Son Nhut Air Base is my welcome to Vietnam—fixed-wing air-crafts, F series fighter jets, C-130s, and the sound of Huey choppers that still reverberate in my mind. The next morning a Vietnamese national picks me up at my BOQ in a small green bus. He drives me through teeming, chaotic Saigon traffic to USAID II, which is situated next to a Buddhist temple. The swollen streets burst with people popping out every which way. Maybe four million people live in Saigon, including two and a half million refugees, driven by the war from the countryside into the city. Little makeshift towns, constructed of scrap building materials and populated with refugees dot the cityscape.

We enter the USAID compound. Stand-up, pillar-like Marines guard the place. They direct me to Daniels's office. I pass by an office and make note of the sign over the top doorjamb—Air America. I head up the stairs to the second floor. I knock and enter Daniels's office. The barrel-chested colonel looks up and closes the folder he's reading. I snap a salute and Daniels gives an obligatory return. "Howdy, son, you must be Lieutenant Muir." He disappears with the document. I'm left hanging. He returns in two seconds without the folder.

The colonel bellows from his diaphragm, "Now, then, I've been waiting for you. My henchman."

Henchman? "Yes, sir."

Daniels's jungle fatigues are loosely pressed, not starched. There's the bird embroidered on his collar, showing he's a full colonel. His wavy black hair is on the longish side. He walks with a saunter. Is this folksy-sounding guy really an O-6 officer?

"Okay, son, I am going to spend today and tonight giving you an orientation. Your record indicates that you have only a top secret security clearance. That poses a small problem, but we are going to iron it out and quickly."

I say nothing and know I will hear nothing past top secret. Plus, I won't know anything unless I need to know something; the military need to know security rule is always in effect. He's working on getting me a security clearance higher than top secret? What clearance is it? The name of the clearance must be classified. I guess I'll find out the name of the clearance when I get it, not before. Shit, what am I getting into? I wonder if my mother's outrageous left-wing friends in Mexico City are going to cause me trouble when the government does a deeper background check.

Daniels spends the rest of the day discussing the administrative and field operations for the U.S. Civil Operations and Rural Development Support—CORDS—Pacification and Phoenix Programs. We are going to handle manpower management and run the operation with the USAID people, who claim they are helping the Vietnamese because their country is underdeveloped. The manpower management is going to match highly credentialed people with specific strategic missions.

This is a lot to take-in. I'm befuddled. But, how dumb do you have to be not to know what the biggest USAID mission in the world is doing? I can't believe barely a few weeks ago I was in Mexico, sitting across from lovely Kate. Or spending time with dad and mom, hearing their words of support and sensing their anxieties about me being here. Where is Shadow Facts when I need her?

"The other thing you need to understand, Muir, is that our—your—area of responsibility will be special manpower evaluation and operations in the field. We'll set things up here, and you're going to check things out to make sure everything is running the way General Steele and I want it. You're going to make sure things get done for me. Have you got that, son?"

"Yes, sir."

"We have already cut your blanket travel orders. You are authorized to be anywhere from the DMZ in I Corps down through IV Corps—so anyplace in country at any time."

Blanket travel orders. The term seems to bode malevolence. In the field—does that also mean in the bush? Shit! A second thing pops into my mind. I'm going to use those blanket orders to connect with Jack, maybe do some surfing in Vietnam. Goddamn, am I crazy? Our troops are dying brutal deaths in the field. And then I think about what I heard—there's good surf in Vung Tau—how do you put those two things together? Yeah, crazy.

"Yes, sir."

"It's been a long day, Lieutenant. Do like you scotch?"

"Affirmative. Single malt or blended, sir?"

"I can tell we're going to get along. The choices are limited on this side of the pond. You have your ration card already, don't you?"

"Affirmative, sir."

"Okay, hustle on over to the exchange, get a bottle and meet me at my quarters."

"Yes, sir."

I know Daniels wouldn't be fraternizing with a lowly junior grade officer unless it was business. I ask one of the Marine guards how to get to the exchange.

The taxi ride is wild. The cab is a yellow and blue Renault; here years and years before the French occupation fell apart. The thing must have been rebuilt twenty times—its deafening rear-mounted engine grinds in my ear. I remember somebody told me not to put my arm on the ledge of a rolled down window, in case some guy zips by on his Honda 50 and rips the watch off my wrist.

I see Vietnamese women with the blackest hair, long and silky, and beautiful skin, rich from the humidity. They're slender and slight, clothed in the ao dai – a snug tunic with a high collar and long sleeves and a waist-high slit on each side, worn over loose silk black or white long pants. Conical woven hats, non la, or umbrellas shade them from the sun. Some men walk in pairs and hold hands. Are they homosexual or what?

French architecture is everywhere. A man, who looks like a refugee from the countryside, squats flat-footed on the sidewalk and plucks a dead chicken. The dense humidity brews rotting garbage and fruit into a putrid smell. It bleeds together with engine fumes and heat pushing up from the city streets. The mechanical swirling ring, ding, ding, ding, ding sound waves of small motorcycles bounce off walls and buildings, and amplify the feeling of being downed in nonstop honking horns. Millions of little motorcycles are swarming, buzzing gnats; they aggressively compete for road space with taxis and old black Citroens with big fenders, massive grills and running boards—congestion on top of congestion. My eyes are two peeled, hardboiled eggs. I can't remember the last time I blinked.

The ride is like schooling with a thousand sardines inside a can. The taxi driver—more like Houdini than a driver—squeezes through the choked streets. Jesus, I don't know how it happened, but we're at the exchange. I pay the driver in piastres—maybe I paid too much— goddamn, never again. Taxi drivers are the same, whether it's Mexico City or Saigon—exploit you if they can.

In the exchange, the tender is Monopoly money—Military Payment Certificates—MPC. I can't find any single malt. Will the blended crap do?

THE FIRST COUPLE OF DAYS IN NAM make for the next big adjustment to the military. The first adjustment was two seconds after entering the Army—bringing the civilian mind into conformity with the military mind. How the military mind works is easy to understand, but hard to assimilate down to your bones. You fight adjustment to the military because you fight yourself. It's a natural reaction to fight yourself—an automatic, screeching resistance in your mind to the military way. Resistance takes the form of bickering personalities in your head, like a cast of characters who take over. The military mind pits itself against the civilian mind. The big man pulls up the little boy. The strong guy bosses around the pussy. Strength says you can do it and fights weakness and weakness says you can't do it. Your tough part pushes you and doesn't let up on wimpy you, who wants to rest. The new and redesigned virtues with which you are being indoctrinated try to drown out old, well-established morals. The guys who washed-out fought themselves.

Resistance is painful. It is also stupid. Listen, and then decide what to do. Retain yourself, don't resist and you can find a way to deal with the military system. Do the drill—even if it is pro forma—and suddenly you have more choices.

I'm the stand-up guy who makes it through with no problem. No outward resistances.

But I have deeper voices baked into my internal war. More locked away than making the new adjustments to military life. Nobody hears screams in my head but me. The voices twist. They come from insecurities, like thinking I'm not good enough. And then there is the fear that someone will discover I'm not good enough. Nobody knows about the chats I have with myself because my life seems so charmed and perfect. But there's an involuntary voice that bleeds into a lot of things, like talking me into believing I'm chicken shit and it's the same voice that doesn't talk me out of believing I'm chicken shit. The volume turns up and down. Who would know it? I never act or do anything that's chicken shit. What will happen when I am in combat? Will I be good enough in the untried situation? I don't know. Maybe I'm just an imposter.

I struggle with the arrogance, hostility and power through domination on the part of the officers and rank-and-file NCOs. It pisses me off. I chew on my anger and chew on it some more and swallow it and don't throw up or digest it. It makes me more relentless and keener, and it's the way I keep hold of myself in the swim of the military current. Fuck 'em, I can take a joke.

One guy who drove home the military mind was Sergeant Decker. Decker was a fit, six-foot blond man in his early thirties. Back a few months from Nam. He was methodically going through the lesson in the basic combat training manual. I don't remember the instruction. All I remember is the field we were on, the smell of freshly cut grass, the afternoon sea breeze, and being suddenly caught by an acidic agitation in my stomach and the sensation of a band around my chest, which cinched tighter and tighter, threatening to cut off my breath.

A few of the troops weren't paying attention, and a couple of guys were cutting up. Decker stopped the training cold. His face turned a combination of colors. His cheeks blazed red, and his jowls turned cold waxen white. Later, I knew what was going through his mind. Decker said to the platoon, "Okay, you numb nuts, break up into your four squads! Each squad stands in a circle!"

He came to our squad first. "Look around at your squad. Next, look at each man. No fucking up—be dead serious." He paused. He closed the training manual and threw it on the ground. He stood at parade rest, with his feet shoulder width apart, arms behind him, and shoulders perfectly horizontal with the ground. One thing about Decker—he was no bullshit.

Each of us looked at every man in the squad. "Okay, imagine half your squad is dead. Who's left?" He waited.

I didn't dislike anyone on my squad or want anybody dead. The choice was like choosing sides for some strange athletic team that had rifles, grenades and more ammo than you could shake a stick at. This was when my stomach twisted, and my chest closed tight. I was fearful—couldn't rally any courage—because I couldn't catch my breath.

This wasn't any standard Army-type training procedure I, or anybody else, had ever heard of. It was Decker's way.

Then it got worse. "Okay, now you picked your favorite buddies, right? Now, imagine they're dead and the other guys are alive."

Up until that point, Vietnam had been more of a concept than a real thing. It was a series of images made up of a place created in my mind, influenced by newsreels, photojournalism, Time and Newsweek, anti-war demonstrations, and talk, talk and more talk.

Decker changed all that. From that point onward, I had strong reactions to him. I always listened to what he said.

But that day I felt warm blood oozing down my chest, followed by an excruciating feeling of being flat on my back with my guts spilled out all over the ground. The guys I liked and joked with—the guys who were my new family—were gone. The soldiers who were left were good guys, but they weren't my guys. And then I imagine my own death. One of the dead guys is me.

COL Sam Daniels's bachelor officer quarters—BOQ—are in the Rex. A guy at my BOQ said it's Saigon's landmark hotel. My taxi driver rounds a corner, weaves in and out of traffic on Nguyen Hue Boulevard, and then deposits me at the Rex. I've brought the scotch. The armed guards stationed in chest-high round cement barriers on each side of the hotel doors don't pay much attention to me as I enter.

The foyer is filled with correspondents carrying notepads. I didn't expect this. Some wear fatigues. Others are dressed in outfits put together for the bush or tropical street clothes. Their eyes are filled with alarm. They jabber, shouting to be heard. They posture and try to root-out information from each other. Activity on top of activity. It's a dense buzz and a weighty feel. I hear American, English and Australian accents. Japanese, French and German languages filter through. So much is taking place that I can't make-out the other languages. I overhear a British guy ask what's taking so long.

The correspondent next to me—a fit-looking man in his late thirties who's wearing jungle fatigues—has an American accent. "What's going on?" I ask.

"We're waiting to enter the press briefing in the American Information Service conference room."

"American Information Service? It's at the Rex?"

"It's headquartered here at the Rex. Disseminates daily updates about the war to foreign correspondents. Yeah, call it the governmental version of the Vietnam War's Associated Press," he says.

"What happened?"

"The U.S. just suffered major losses. Well over 200 casualties countrywide. Could be almost three hundred. And who knows how many wounded." Heaviness presses down on the correspondent's staccato speech. "Estimates are that forty to eighty were killed in a skirmish at Dong Ap Bia. That's about a mile from the Laotian border. In a couple of minutes, we'll be briefed on what's happened. We'll get more precise casualty numbers."

He pauses. Maybe he thinks he's saying too much.

My wordless stare says I'm waiting to hear the rest.

His eyes open, as if to say what the hell. "At Dong Ap Bia there was a horrific episode of negligent discharge. Some of the U.S. troops were killed by other U.S. troops firing M-60s from choppers. You know the disgusting military euphemisms. When soldiers accidentally shoot at one of their own guys, it's called friendly fire. If that soldier dies, it's called negligent discharge."

"Yeah, military euphemisms."

"There's more. I hear the battle at Dong Ap Bia gained nothing; the United States was trying to take some hill that had no strategic consequence."

"A disaster."

"A major disaster."

"You write for—?"

"Life magazine."

"What will your story say?"

"We're working on a photojournalism piece about the massive surge in the number of GIs killed. We'll print pictures of soldiers who were killed. Should be in next week's issue."

The confusion in the room changes to a concentrated stir. The swarms of correspondents leave the foyer and head down a hallway like a vortex of killer bees returning to their hive for an audience with the queen bee. The Life correspondent mutters good-bye and rushes to catch up. I stand alone. The foyer goes silent.

I find out later a correspondent went to the battle at Hill 937. Other correspondents followed. Now infamous. Now named, Hamburger Hill. Our military men were massacred for nothing. This ill-famed military shit takes my indignation about war and turns it into rage. Even our military guys are pissed off about it. Protesters and rednecks back home are enraged. My military mind is already fucked-up. Now it's more fucked-up.

I run up four flights of stairs to Daniels's floor. Knock. He greets me. I hand him the bottle of blended scotch. "There's something big going on, Sir. I saw a mass of foreign correspondents in the foyer going into a press briefing about major losses out in the field."

"The American Information Service has a press conference here every day at 1700 hours. It's nicknamed The Five O'clock Follies." Daniels looks at his watch. "It's late. Really late. The guys at the information service must have taken their time weighing-in on what was going to be released to the press."

"Makes sense that things have to be weighed before stories are published, sir."

"Yes, always, political and security considerations. You understand that, don't you Muir?"

"Absolutely, sir."

We sit at a coffee table in his bachelor officer quarters. Daniels empties the last of his ten year-old Macallan scotch into a couple of water glasses. We're about to drink single malt scotch. At this instant, some GI is most likely being killed or wounded out in the bush. This war is loaded with juxtapositions and contradictions pushed into an immense crazy whole.

"The exchange doesn't carry Macallan, does it, sir?"

"No, it doesn't, Muir. Smoke?"

"No, thanks, sir. Don't smoke."

Daniels flicks open his brushed chrome Zippo lighter. Its gold Army insignia is a standout feature. He lights a Camel, clicks the lighter shut, and leans over to throw the lighter the final six inches to the tabletop. Daniels's feet are flat on the floor, his arms level with the armrests of the chair. He looks like a ruler sitting on a throne—holding court while drinking scotch and smoking a Camel.

Daniels's quarters are comfortable enough. Nicely furnished. Spartan, though. Books about Patton, military history and war tactics sit on the shelf.

He doesn't use the air-conditioning. A fan whips around on the high ceiling, moving the room's dense air. The cool cream-colored floor tiles take a stand against the Southeast Asian humidity.

I excuse myself to use the latrine. The floors and walls have the same tile as his suite. I look straight up and see a yellowish-white lizard. The mechanical-looking creature almost disappears against the light-colored ceiling. Just at that moment, the lizard falls to the floor, breaking off its tail. It scuttles away to find some unknown place of safety, moving pell-mell. I notice that each foot's motion makes an independent and disconnected pattern from the other three.

"A lizard just fell off the ceiling and broke off its tail."

"Happens all the time; tail grows back. Think about it. Get your tail shot off and have the balls made of brass so your butt grows back. Got it, Muir?"

What he's saying is a precursor of things to come. I have a hunch it's a message that'll drive everything I'll do. I nod. "Got it, sir."

"So Muir, your given name is Memo. Tell me about that."

I fill-in Daniels on the origins of my name.

"You went to USC?"

"That's right, sir. And what about you?"

Daniels takes a drag off his cigarette. "West Point and two war colleges." The colonel finishes his glass of Macallan. He opens the bottle of blended scotch. Pours a couple of shots worth for himself.

"Lieutenant, I'm doing a little…well…boondoggle tomorrow. I need you to take care of some business."

"A boondoggle. Yes, sir."

"I'm taking an Air America flight to Thailand to get a couple of Asian elephants."

"Sir?"

"Ceramic elephants, Muir."

"Yes, Sir, ceramic elephants."

"Yeah, beautiful things, a little taller than knee high. Look, we have a new young buck, Donaldson, coming in tomorrow. I need you to receive him. Take him with my driver to the Research and Analysis Directorate, RAD. It's located at the Military Assistance Command,

Vietnam—MACV—headquarters. Donaldson is a new Ph.D. The Army recruited him. He's a computer expert. He got a direct commission. First rung lieutenant's butter bar on his collar."

"RAD? Computer expert?"

Daniels drinks half his scotch. He glances at the bottle of blended scotch. "Okay Muir, let's continue your orientation. Yes, RAD is our research division working with CORDS and MACV. We're using computers to track the geographic indicators of pacification, based on constant commander and advisor intelligence inputs. We use weighted measures to make predictions—based on statistical probabilities—to calculate attitudes, aspirations and loyalties of Vietnamese peasants in hamlets."

I try not to look stupid, while in my mind I'm sifting through all the jargon to get to the gist of it. What I come up with is that they're using computers and analysis to try to figure out what makes the Vietnamese peasants tick. Daniels downs the rest of his drink and pours another glass. I'm still working on the ten-year-old single malt.

Daniels smirks. "They didn't cover this stuff in OCS, now did they, son?"

"Negative, sir. You have a little more sophisticated way of doing business. It's also a lot to take in."

"You got that right, son. Let me clarify a few things. Here's how it works." Daniels tells me there is an item analysis based on two factors: security and development. The calculations keep track of a large portion of twelve thousand hamlets south of the demilitarized zone—the DMZ. The computers call-up vast amounts of data and use predictions to determine where security forces need to reinforce various hamlets and where to focus more on development. The two key systems now are Hamlet Evaluation Survey—HES, and the Phoenix file. "You with me, Muir?"

"Yes, sir, solidly with you. I get it—affirmative." Daniels sounds like a military textbook. Maybe that's what you get when you've been to West Point and two war colleges. My hunch is Daniels taught at a war college.

Daniels lifts his glass and I lift mine. Clink.

"Okay, Muir, let me tell you about your duties. You know Vietnam is a guerrilla war. Our specific mission is using a military narrative based not entirely on military might or conventional war. It's based on counterinsurgency."

This is going to be a long night. Daniels is articulate. I have no doubt he was a professor at a war college. Even polluted with booze, Daniels still has the clarity of a war wizard speaking from the podium. He tells me we will be working with CORDS and USAID and have major involvement with the Phoenix program. I start to understand the tactics used against the Viet Cong and North Vietnamese Army, the NVA. The strategy with Phoenix is neutralization of the Viet Cong and NVA by inducing them to desert or by capturing them and taking them prisoner. There's another piece, a more clandestine piece, assassinating them. Daniels explains the eliminations are targeted killings.

"Assassinating them?" The words roll-out in a higher pitch. "Yes, I see, sir." Does the slight catch in my voice betray me?

"Son, I hope you're not having some moral or philosophical problem with this. We're killing the enemy, Charlie. It's not the same as killing innocent civilians. That would be murder. We are killing soldiers, the enemy. That's war, son."

"No problem, sir. More scotch will clear my throat." I take a gratuitous sip.

Daniels' voice booms. It's forceful. "The key to a guerrilla war and counterinsurgency is to control the local population, the ones who support the infrastructure of the VC and the NVA. The Vietnamese peasants are naïve about core politics." He leans back in his chair. Drops his shoulders and takes a drink. Daniels lightens his voice. He sounds like a professorial soldier. "What they care about is *xa hoi hoa*—their sacred connection to the earth and land. You have to understand their culture to make this thing work."

"I imagine their worldview must not extend beyond their hamlets and villages, sir."

"You're getting the hang of it, Muir. All that those peasants care about is where their next bowl of rice is coming from and baby-san." Daniels turns harsh, an angry kind of harsh. "The VC are terrorists, who scare the villagers to death; they induce deep, deep fear through killing, kidnapping and torture. Saying the VC are cruel bastards is an understatement. We have to stop all that. Charlie's other tactic is controlling villagers with their brand of bullshit taxation—goddamn highway robbery."

"I see, sir. It's coming together now. The military works on security—protects the villages—and the civilian side, such as USAID, works on helping the villagers and improving their standards of living to rally them to the side of the South. Charlie loses support and the means to get things done."

"You're absolutely getting it, Muir. Damn good for a cherry."

"Yes, I'm very new in country, Colonel Daniels. My military training was mostly leading men in the field with just a smattering of military theory here and there. Unrelated college degree in architecture. But I do know how to come up with a drawing—a good blueprint, sir."

"Well, let's set the stage for you, son. Our strategy is based on the military design and structure of the Brits' successful counterinsurgency against the Communists in Malaya, 1948 to 1960. We're using this strategy and you must know why by now—Vietnam is a different kind of battlefield. The French fucked up over here when they lost the support of the people on the hamlet level. Commies used that to manipulate the locals into anti-colonial reactions. Our strategy will strengthen South Vietnamese alliances with us. Consequently, we will prevail against the Communists in the North."

What's underneath the plan? I'll come across as cool. No more lilts. "And our leadership, sir?"

"Leadership?" Daniels bends forward in his chair. His voice is hushed, but powerful. "Is your timing an accident or are you're right on cue? Look, Ambassador Colby is the station chief, and he's running CORDS. The guy's beyond clever, says his mission is to 'win the hearts and minds of the Vietnamese people.' We've studied the strategy the British used, so—unlike the French—we're not going to botch Vietnam." Daniels pours another dram of scotch.

The ambassador is running CORDS, the civilian and rural development side? Sounds mysterious to me. I say, "He must be deep in the Phoenix Program."

"Okay, Muir. You can connect the dots. In our operation, that's a major asset." He squints. Becomes incisively direct. "But remember, connecting too many dots could be a major way to screw yourself."

I get he's talking about working the military system. "I understand navigating dangerous waters, sir."

"Okay, then. The Phoenix Program is funded by the CIA."

I glance beyond Daniels' shoulder and into the latrine. I see the tailless lizard jerking along the tiled floor. The tops of my cheeks feel hot and frozen in place. Heat radiates down the broad muscles in my back, which run down under my arms, wrapping around to my waist.

My voice is emotionless. "So they don't pipeline money just for the hell of it. How are the strings attached, and how does Colby drive this thing?"

"Good thing you have a security clearance, son."

"I get the battlefield is on the local level, minus the boundaries of conventional war. Unlike a football game, there's no scrimmage line."

"You guys from USC always thinking about football?" He laughs and then gets serious. "This deal is no military football game. We kick butt with more cunning than you can imagine or you'll ever know about. The security of secrecy is central to this mission. Don't forget it."

Goddamn, this deal is the dark side of a sinister war nobody knows about. Does the president know? How the hell did I get here? I'm fidgeting, rubbing my thumb against my index finger. Stop it.

"Yes, sir. How does the 'neutralization' of targeted VC and NVA work? We're not in a field unit. Who's doing the hands-on stuff?"

"Muir, the Army's role is not to defend, but to build-up the South Vietnamese military side." Daniels sounds like he is filling in some blanks, a little less impassioned, but still focused. "USAID is working their butts off to develop you name it—hospitals, agriculture, roads and bridges, water sanitation. Also, they're dealing with displaced refugees. Etcetera. Phoenix is recruiting Vietnamese and training them to capture or eliminate targeted VC and NVA. They also suck Charlie into deserting and then extract intelligence out of them."

"Extract intelligence from deserters? That's how other VC and NVA are targeted?"

"Yes, it's fundamental. But it's more specific than that. We develop 'black lists,' which identify three levels of VC and NVA. On the highest rung are the political and military decision makers and the senior military commanders. Next are the less significant commanding officers. On the bottom rung, we have the VC grunts or VC living among the villagers in the hamlets in the south."

I begin to get the full picture. The Phoenix program has no direct military forces and the program is the scheme of the CIA. Basically Phoenix finds Vietnamese who are willing to be spooks, undermine, and even capture or assassinate VC and NVA. The end game is to drive a wedge between the enemy's political and military sides and destroy the VC infrastructure. I say, "The South Vietnamese do the work, and the program trains and advises them?"

"You're getting the hang of it, Muir." Daniels looks to the left and right like he has to be cautious because somebody might be listening. "Sometimes we use some of our boys to…do the work."

Holy shit. This deal sounds as though I am going to know maybe three percent about what's really going on.

There are three sharp knocks at the door. Daniels cracks it open. I can't make out who's on the other side. Whoever it is, whispers. The voice is too muffled to hear. Daniels' words have a dampened sound, "When can I get a hold of him?"

There's a hushed response out in the hallway.

"Okay. We'll nail it down then." Daniels closes the door.

"Do you need to go, sir?"

"Not now. We're taking care of some loose ends from the Tet Offensive. Nothing you need to know about."

Let's reduce me knowing maybe two percent of what's really going on. "Tet—the New Years—was one hell of a surprise NVA strike on our troops in the south."

"Nothing's going to make that one right. The Tet Offensive skewered us. Heavy losses. But those bastards didn't neutralize our command centers or topple the government in the south, like they had planned." Daniels sits, looks distracted. And then he frowns. He takes a drink of scotch. "Okay. Back to what we were talking about, Muir."

"Yes, sir…so what kind of neutralization numbers has resulted with the Phoenix Program?"

"Last year was the first year of the Phoenix Program. Just from the program we got about 2,230 deserters. We call it *Chieu Hoi.* That's 'open arms' in Vietnamese. It's an amnesty program. We try to get them to join up with the South Vietnamese, get intelligence from them and so on." Daniels' distraction from the interruption seems to vanish. "We took 11,230 captives, some wounded. Over 2,250 VC and NVA were flat out killed." He's staid and then laughs. "How's your math, son? That's somewhere over total of about 15,700. Not too bad for the first year's work, would you say, Lieutenant?"

"Yes sir. Impressive. How does Ambassador Colby handle the appearance of the program?"

"Well, Colby calls it advice and assistance. But of course, it's a little more involved than that. American soldiers pull together intelligence, and they plan and execute operations."

"Sounds surgical, sir."

"The truth is, Muir, we're not on top of it all the time. Now, this is a plus, and it's also a minus. Those South Vietnamese operating under the Phoenix program are on their own turf—they know the language, the culture and the VC-NVA animal that's at war out there. The downside is that they might do some things out of self-interest, take advantage of the situation or carry out their own agendas. There isn't a lot of supervision. Out there, there's… Well, maybe there isn't any supervision."

Jesus, this whole thing sounds like it could spin out of control. "Nothing is textbook in war, is it?" I say. Daniels was sounding like a textbook. Not now.

"Especially not in this war, son. The Cong are sly, vicious bastards and don't go down without one hell of a brawl. They do the worst possible things you can imagine to chop-up people. If the South Vietnamese allied forces get their butts in a sling, sometimes we have to rescue them when things get a little too…complicated. It's tough to use strong-arm artillery and aerial support and to send in units on the QT. But when our Vietnamese boys get in trouble out there—shit—we manage to pull it off."

I look at the books on military tactics on the shelf and turn back to Daniels.

"Sir, my next question is—"

"Where do you come in?"

Air is trapped in my chest. My stomach is a burning coiled spring. How bad is the news going to be?

"Ambassador Colby is running the shootin' match. Steele works for Colby. I work for Steele. You work for me. Most of the time, you'll be at USAID II with me, analyzing manpower needs and slotting people for the military side of CORDS. And we'll be coordinating with the USAID segment. We'll meet the new men when they come in country and give them the poop on their assignments. That's the bean counter part."

I shift in my seat. Shit, what's the other part? I simultaneously rub both my hands toward my knees and back. Daniels probably had no problem being a professor at the war college. He talks tirelessly.

"The rest of the time, you'll be going out in the field to make sure we're getting the staffing right…and check on activities for me. We're not going to make decisions based only on what the RAD data and our guys in the field are telling us."

"Sir, you said I would be working at USAID II most of the time. Does that mean I'll be working in Saigon fifty-one percent of the time? Or ninety-nine percent?"

"It depends. But count on something more than fifty-one percent. You'll be working at USAID II Embassy Annex, so most nights you'll be in the BOQ officers' club, drinking. You're going to get invited to some of the USAID parties. Believe me, our American civilian counterparts know how to have a wild time."

"Excuse me, sir." I go to the latrine. There is another lizard, this time on the wall. The bottom half of its tail—separated by a node from the top half—is a slightly different color. It must have broken off and grown back. I study the way the lizard moves. It looks as though the reptile's brain moves the front legs. The back legs seem to move through a spinal reflex unconnected to the front legs. I return to Daniels.

The colonel stands up. "That's enough for one night, Muir. My driver will pick you up in the morning."

A sensation spills over me like a thick gooey toxic substance. The field assignments are going to be the blunt starting place of nightmares to come.

CHAPTER 18

TOUGH AND SHREWD

KATE HAS BEEN GONE FOR ONE DAY.
    Dad invites me for a father-son dinner at a place where a handshake smiles familiarity. There's a homey and community feel when I walk though the country club entrance and see dad's name on the list of people who have made a hole-in-one. Fitting he scored it on the day he turned fifty.

Dad occupies a table next to a view window, which overlooks the first fairway and the eighteenth green. His hands are clasped, and he looks distinguished and as polished as ever. Dad has the best posture I've ever seen. Or his posture is the only posture I notice. He stands.

He gives me what starts to be a familiar fatherly embrace. I feel a tension. I squint, trying to put together what's up. Then I put it out of my mind.

Minutes and hours and days of my military life and homecoming condense into seconds. Seeing him makes me sort out my mind—tell him what's critical and filter-out what doesn't matter. And what's essential now will have a different slant to the story tomorrow because of what we've talked about.

We sit down.

Dad invites me, "Let's have a scotch."

"Sure. Suited, right? Two guys with a Scottish name having a scotch."

Dad catches the waiter's eye, "Nacho, is there any of my Balvenie left under the bar?" Something else out of character happens. His voice has a clipped edge to it.

Nacho leaves to check.

I take a second to sift though the shock of Kate leaving. It presses on me and stirs-up my whole body. The torment of Kate's departure makes my appetite fade.

"Memo, there's something I need to take-up with you—"

Nacho interrupts when he returns with the bottle. He puts two crystal scotch glasses on the table. Nacho pours a dram in each glass. He leaves.

Dad and I clink glasses. We take a sip.

I smile.

Dad feigns a semi-grin. He gets serious. "Getting back to what I started to say—"

"About Kate?"

"Yes, about Kate. Your mother and I are…displeased. Maybe disappointed is a better word."

"I have a hunch what you're going to say. I have never wanted to disappoint mom and you. The split is an enormous disappointment to… Look, our marriage turned into something I didn't want it to be." I take a huge breath. "And couldn't help—"

Dad cuts me off. I need him now. But I feel it coming—a ration of shit is about to get dumped on me.

"Please let me complete this thought. How do you imagine we're supposed to feel?" Deep lines form in his forehead and around his eyes. "The truth is Alita and I are disheartened by Kate leaving."

I stiffen-up. "It takes two to tango." Suddenly, this feels like a stale and hackneyed and stupid thing to say given dad's seriousness—and my feeling ruined.

"But you're the lead dance partner, so hear me out." Dad pushes his scotch glass away. He takes a drink of water. "Kate worked her way into our hearts, which was a pretty easy task on her part because of who she is."

"Trite, but true, you loved her like a daughter." Everything coming out of my mouth sounds too stupid.

"We still do." Dad glances to the side, then back at me. "I imagine we always will."

I look away and down at the floor. I bring my head up to meet Dad's eyes. "Dad, I came tonight because I need...look, maybe I should go."

Dad's voice is resolute. "No. Stick around. We'll handle this. That's what you and I are about, son."

"I love you, dad. I missed you while I was gone—like I wished you were in the next room to talk to." Fuck, I'm about to cry. I jerk in quick short breaths and get teary.

Dad sees me getting choked-up. His taciturn way of beating-me-up takes an about face—turns to relief in his eyes. "You're home. You're safe. And thank God. But being back doesn't remove you from harm's way."

I moisten my lips. "Look, I'm destroyed about Kate leaving and it multiplies all the shit about coming back from war. No sleep last night. I brood over whether my sleep will ever be okay. Sure, I made it back from Nam. But—Jesus—the fallout, like Kate leaving."

"I love you, Memo. Your mom and I don't understand the whole story. But we have an idea."

"What I'm doing has to stop. I stew over whether it's going to stop. I want Kate to come back. She's not going to come back." Kate being history is complicated and knotty, and hard to let seep in.

"I'd like to believe your utter hopelessness leaves an opening for something different and good to happen."

"I know. But that's too optimistic for me to absorb right now." I look down at the while linen tablecloth and the elegant table setting. I bring my eyes back to dad. "Please let me off the hook about Kate."

"Let me make sure we have some understandings." Dad settles on taking a drink of scotch. "First of all, Alita and I love Kate. There has never been any doubt in our minds why you married her. Her leaving is obviously crushing you." Compassion lifts one layer of dark clouds hanging over me.

"Beyond crushed."

"There're some reasons for that." He props his forearms on the table and clasps his hands. "What caused her to leave is more disturbing. Larger. I don't know the specifics of what you were exposed to in that god-awful war, except by context and inference and by the fact I treated men in the Pacific Theater during World War II." Dad leans back in his chair. "I know what shellshock looks like and how it makes people go from being numb to being overcome by emotion and being reactive. And the shock brought home from war changes marriages and makes them vulnerable to destruction." He sighs. "Maybe I thought you'd be above destroying your marriage. I guess nobody is. Not even my son who is a cut above—"

"I know you're angry about Kate leaving. No, I'm not above screwing-up. Forget me being the advantaged kid with the charmed life. That's over. I'm fucked and you see it." A twist of one underlying truth comes out of my mouth since he doesn't know about Lupita. I'll tell him. I'll tell mom. Maybe not right now. But it'll come.

"Okay. So from my side, what do I think you need? Let's start with this. I'll help you bear and hold up to the load and the strain you're carrying. Whatever it takes—despite our disappointment about your marriage—however long it takes."

My eyes puff up. They moisten. "Throughout my life, what you have done—not so much what you have said—has been what's helped me. And right now—being with you—touches me to the bone. We have to get it out in the open."

"Good. That's the idea. A start."

"This is a lot to take in right now. It's awfully close." I take a sip of scotch. "I think I need to back off a little. I'd like to talk about our family. Talk about what I do have. Not about what I don't have— Kate—and the war memories I have that I don't want to have."

Dad makes a sympathetic nod. The timbre of his voice takes a shift. "You like talking about your grandparents."

"Okay."

Dad tells me about granddad—whose family emigrated from Scotland—being the only doc in the teens and early twenties between San Diego and the Mexican border and being the king of barter with his patients."

The story is familiar. And familiar is a good hit. Our fireside chats have always made me feel as if my soles are planted on the ground, and like the space around me makes sense and it's mine.

Dad says, "But now more than ever, I hope I've been able to pass something onto you—the cloth my mother was cut out of. Her family was so persecuted. She instilled a lot in me. A main force is education. Because no matter whatever you lose, education can't be taken away from you. And to maintain and nurture the talents you have, irrespective of the horrendous realities one has that are inescapable. And to turn suffering into something that has a grander substance. She was a rock, despite what the Nazis did to her family in Europe. It was horrific for her to be here and safe while—"

"You wanted to have dinner tonight to tell me this?"

"Yes. Certainly. And your mother and my feelings about Kate walking out. And to help you."

There's a glimmer of recoiling from taking the heat because Kate left. "Dad, there are two things I have gotten from you, though I never met grandmother. One is the meaning of having strength, which supplants suffering. The other is to always keep your dignity, no matter what type of adversity you face, including humiliating, sadistic death."

Dad wrinkles his brow. "Change is inevitable. Bending to change is the critical part, isn't it? Alita and I will try to adjust to Kate being gone." He clears his throat. "As far as your grandparents go, there're two things. Put this in your pocket and always keep with you. Scots are tough in times of hardship. Jews are shrewd by necessity. Got it?"

"I know it." There's trust in dad that can't be destroyed by the ragged feelings over Kate leaving. "Tough and shrewd." My attachment to the family value is there. But I lose it. And I get back. And I lose it again. Like it deteriorates amidst the confusion of intrusions I have little control over. I struggle to hang onto what my family represents. "And tough and shrewd doesn't mean getting divorced, does it?"

"Let's give our disappointment over your separation a break right now."

I think about my adolescence—the fights and arguments and debates with my dad, which helped me form what I value. Not easy. Painful most of the time. When I was a kid, I thought he was unfair, but he was something to fight against, so I could see things more clearly. Now I realize what he did helped shape me.

Dad nods. "I have a proposal—to help get you straight."

All of a sudden there's another pressure. I stiffen up. "Proposing something sounds like a demand."

"No demands. Help. That's it—help. You want to listen now? Or maybe later?"

I take a sip of scotch. I look out the window and barely see the eighteenth green dimly lit in the shadows. "Okay, but I'm too stunned from Kate leaving to—"

"Just hear-me-out. I won't be bulldozing you this time, like my antagonism about Kate leaving. I think it's time for you to get back in touch with Frank Gehry and get your career going again."

"Now's not the right time. I'm not ready."

"It will give you purpose. You have a void that makes it impossible to land since you returned from Nam. Of course you're not ready. But if you get in the saddle, you can start to approximate being ready. Gehry is a veteran and—"

"Did Kate talk with you about this? Did you talk with Gehry?"

"Kate and I did talk about it. Independent of one another we were thinking the same thing. So did Alita. And despite Kate leaving, in our minds she still has credibility. Did I call Gehry? No. There are limits. Getting in touch with him is up to you."

"Is this part of being tough and shrewd?"

"You need to be tough and shrewd to redeem yourself. And you can be more than you were before."

"I'll mull-it-over."

"Okay."

"Actually, I'll call him. Check-in."

"That's a start." Dad takes a swallow of the Balvenie. "Would you like me to call Dutch Higgs to put in a good word?"

"Dutch?" Dad's willingness to call his old family friend who has considerable influence gives me a stable feel. "I see where this is going. Sure— terrific."

"Tonight was men's night. Would you like to see your mom?"

"That'd be good about now."

"She wanted me to ask you to come over tomorrow."

"Can do."

I stand in their living room, looking at what's in the bookcase— medical books and the classics and politics and Latino culture. I hear mom and turn to see her. She makes a flowing entrance. "*Hola, Memito.* Let's have a drink first. Make me a vodka and tonic, dear. Do you want a *cerveza*?"

"Tonight, I'll bump-it-up to a vodka martini." I go to the pantry and make the drinks.

When I return, mom is sitting comfortably, staring at Mt. San Miguel in the distance. She's as beautiful as ever, wearing a loose, floor length, flowing red, green, and white silk dress. The swirling pattern of the dress matches her elegance. Mom has the fragrance of Joy—rose, tuberose, jasmine, and the musk smell of aldehyde. The tuberose takes me back to the enveloping scent of flower-filled vases at the Pedregal house.

Now is the time to get Lupita off my chest. I begin by telling mom about what happened with Scanlon.

She says my judgment stunk when I borrowed dad's .38 without asking.

That item took less than zero convincing for me to get the point.

"Dan told me you covered a lot of territory last night. He took you to task. I could beat you up again, but I won't. I just have to say—though—I am completely heartbroken our family is losing Kate." Mom takes a drink of vodka and tonic. "Now then, there are a few items I've been thinking about that make a certain context. Are you ready to hear them?"

"I was upset last night listening to dad. I'll try to handle the next installment."

"Okay then. You know I ran in particular political circles in D.F. which influenced how I color things." She nods. "You were sent to war to fight for political ideologies and—whether right or wrong—to demonstrate the sovereignty of the United States." Mom stands. She walks across the room. Then she turns to me. "The quick political piece is over. Dan told me about Scanlon. He's another type of enemy who is vector of disease that attracts the vulnerable, like Kate." Mom permanently maintains her ballast. "And he is a very personal enemy—no political ideology for you to defend—only your love. Only to protect what's precious, and what's treasured—Kate." She nods. "Your father and I are sad Kate left. And I know there are private parts we don't understand."

I tell Mom about Walter and what Bradley said and how Suzanne's loneliness drove her to stray.

Mom answers, "War makes our needs go crazy, whether we're the ones who stay home or who go to war." She sits down. "It's a question of how we manage our needs and hurts and vulnerabilities, isn't it?"

"I haven't done a very good job of it. Disappointing and failing you."

Mom's face is kind and snug and it has the power of taking a grown man back to the womb. "You haven't done a very good job of managing? Nobody does. There's no perfection. There's only being deep in the soup and working at finding a way to swim to the surface."

We discuss what happened the evening Kate left. Mom guesses right about Kate's jumpiness, caused by the unpredictability of what I'd do next. Mom sees how the tension between Kate and me became too much.

Now for the bloodletting. I tell Mom about Lupita—but minimize the details. I fail at lessening what happened. I say I met a woman near Cañón de Guadalupe and she provided me an afternoon of understanding. Kate knows and it adds to her list of distresses about me. When I say she provided me an afternoon of understanding, I realize my stab at minimizing the full story is a slip-up and it sounds stiff and lame.

Mom is the mistress of nuance. Our made-up family nickname for her in Spanish is *La Matrizera*—the reader of tones and traces and touches of people and what is said. She pins my bullshit with a look. Mom knows what happen with Lupita was a sexy liaison. She doesn't need a bunch of words to understand. Her nod and eyes and curl of the mouth say everything.

"Let's have another drink," I say.

"*Totalmente*." She says absolutely.

I'm back in two minutes with fresh drinks.

"Mom, I hope you don't blame me for pushing Kate away." I listen to my words. The stupid feel I had last night with dad comes back.

"Let's not think about blame. Blame is an inadequate solution to any situation, isn't it?" Alita takes a drink of her vodka and tonic. "Kate has always been scared, having come from a family of divorce— trepidation betrays her—always on the underside of her beautifully painted outer exterior. You were heaven sent—the possibility of lasting love and having a family. And the war damaged love's promise for both of you. And how you are now? You're playing with a new deck of cards—dominated by clubs, then spades, but you need hearts and diamonds." She looks at the drink in her hand and puts it down. "Now you have a changing set of circumstances. Blame is not part of it. Instead, we will have to live with the pain of losing Kate. The lasting thing you can count on from me? I love you."

My mouth waters at the joint where the jaw connects. I feel a twinge at the corner of my eye. My folks are tuned to saying what touches. "Coming back has been too crazy."

"Don't be fooled by what Dan said last night. World War II damaged us because of our separation and the impact his duty had on him. We painfully absorbed it. Your war tells an unbecoming story, unlike the righteousness we felt during our struggle." Alita scans the books on the self, like she's looking for the right thing to say. She looks back. "Memo, you are a very resilient person. You are intelligent and good-looking and young. I have a lot of trust in you, despite your situation. My experience with war is through your Father and now you. Dan saw combat in the Pacific by extension—being a physician on backlines and treating the shell shocked and wounded and nearly dead troops. I'm more experienced with one thing. It's on the frontlines. And that's being your mother."

"You're a touchstone. Gives me faith." I feel like someone else said that. It didn't feel like me. I stand. Go to where my mother is sitting and take her hand. I pull her to her feet. We embrace. And for a fleeting second, time has no beginning and no end. Time is only in the present.

I walk to window. I see the dark purple majestic Mt. San Miguel. Mom sits.

I pick-up the stemmed martini glass and have a drink. "I called Frank Gehry today."

"Good. How'd that go?"

"One thing led to another. No specifics. But I'm going up to L.A. to have lunch with him."

Mom and I spend the evening talking more about my separation from Kate. I tell her what Kate said before leaving. Mom's good at advice. She's even a better listener. And that's what she does. Listens.

Dad enters. They hold hands. It's good to feel their love for one another before I head off. They're disappointed about Kate leaving. I can't escape failing them. But I'm still their son. I've unhinged Kate from our lives. My parents can't be undone.

I leave.

My stomach feels as though it's caving in as I drive away. The thought of Chet bubbles up in my mind. I imagine him on patrol out in the bush. I've never known what he was really thinking. He doesn't have the backing of parents like mine. What's he thinking now?

CHAPTER 19

MOVE FAST TO OUTRUN YOURSELF

1630 hours. Sunday, December 6, 1970

THE SUN IS DIPPING in the wispy pink-colored western sky.
"Muir residence."

"Hi, Memo."

Jack's been occupied the entire weekend at the hospital. I've been waiting on edge for his call. "Hi, Jack. It's a relief to finally hear your voice." Tautness automatically loosens-up in my neck and shoulders, just hearing his voice.

"I was entirely engulfed at the hospital the past two days." Jack sounds worn-out. "I'm okay. Apologize it took this long to get back to you. I want to talk with you."

"You know about Kate?"

"I know. She's spoken with Diane. I hear bits and pieces. The big piece is Kate's call to Diane after leaving your place on Friday. How are you doing?"

"How I'm doing changes every two seconds." My voice has a cracking sound.

"How about this split second?"

I gather myself. "My parents are heartbroken and angry at me because Kate left. But they still stand by me despite being pissed-off. I am making plans. It helps. Makes me feel better right now."

"What kind of plans?"

"You remember I was accepted into the master's program at USC. Then Kate got pregnant, so I was derailed from starting the grad work."

"Sure."

"I'm engineering something. I called Frank Gehry. He's willing to pull some strings to get me into the architectural program. It'll take some doing. It's not as though they keep your application on file, just waiting for you to start anytime you feel like it."

"I'd say he's got a fair amount of influence." Jack laughs.

"I'll say. Plus, enrollments are down because of the lottery. No more 2-S draft deferment system. They want students. Vets have an advantage. Frank's a vet. That'll help. I spent time with my folks this weekend. They're going to make some phone calls. A family friend, Dutch Higgs, is on the U.C. Board of Regents. He has ties with USC. Dutch was a commander in the WWII Pacific Fleet and awarded the Bronze Star with Combat 'V.' Nice to have a guy like that ready to step in."

"A lot of people are on your side, Memo. And maybe you fucked-up, but you're a guy who lands on your feet."

"Well, I'm trying to land. The winter semester's the target. If not, I'm sure they'll let me take classes as an unclassified graduate student until the fall."

"You're the guy with the connections."

"In Spain they call it *el enchufe*, a plug. Having connections. I'd say I need a little juice right now." I look at the only blank wall in the house. "Jack, am I wearing you out?"

"No, just the opposite. I'll have my turn." Jack laughs with a wheezing sound through his nose. "Look, you're lucky to know people like Frank Gehry and Dutch Higgs. Your family. How many people have those advantages? Only a few." Jack clears his throat. "Maybe less than that."

"I'm lucky. But being advantaged has an oppressive side. Everyone expects everything is going to be easy for you. It's like you can't be fucked-up if you're an advantaged person. I'm sick of that. It's just not real."

"Like the perfection that's expected when you're a physician."

"Yeah. Probably like that."

"But still—"

"Look, everyone has connections of one type or another. And it's a matter of using them. Even if you have a crappy family. Even if you come from the most disadvantaged background. There's always help somewhere. Use what's available."

"That's awfully optimistic. Idealistic, maybe."

My voice changes timbre. "But people don't ask for help. Or are afraid to ask for it. Or are so messed-up they do the wrong thing."

"There's another slice to it."

"Yeah, admitting defeat. Having some humility. Like me, right now. I'm fucked-up from Nam. My decisions have been destructive. I know it. It's time to make things right. Right isn't perfect, but as right as right can be given what's happening."

"And then there are guys like Chet."

My tone gets gloomy. "Chet uses his connections, but they're the wrong ones. He's scary. You don't want to end-up like him. He's in a swirling downward sucking vortex."

"You're moving pretty fast. Trying to out-run what's happening?"

"I'm not going to bullshit you, Jack; it's been a rollercoaster ride this weekend. But trying to get something set-up is helping me. Kate's ditching me got my attention. I'm not going down now, not after everything that's happened. My father has encouraged me to move ahead despite Kate leaving. That's him—take steps to help yourself no matter what crisis you're in and without disowning the realities of what's taking place."

"So that's your dad? It's also the stuff good doctors are made of. You're going to do it with or without Kate, huh?"

"Yeah, without Kate if I have to."

"Keep paying attention."

There's a tingling sensation at the top of my cheeks. "I will. It's my fault she left." My voice gives out. I pause for two moments and get it back. "I squeezed her more and more until it was too much. OCS. The extra year. Away in Nam. I've had no traction since I got home. Being reactive." A rippling movement starts in my abdomen and hits my chest. "I think she knew what had happened the second after I was with Lupita. I fucked Kate over. I fucked myself over. No thinking. Done all on automatic pilot. So how I can I blame her? I'm a piece of shit, Jack."

"You think getting a master's degree is going to help?" Jack laughs like he's pointing out the obvious.

Jack has a way of steering me. "Screwing myself with Kate hit me. Shows where it hurts. A career will help me recover from losing Kate? No. But now I'll go forward."

"Get your self-respect back?"

"Yes. An attempt, anyway."

"I heard about the story with what's-his-name. You went to his house. It wasn't the same as with Inocencio, was it?"

"You heard? Okay. That guy's a womanizer. He preys on military wives whose husbands are away at war. Sorry piece of shit. But no, I didn't destroy him. I didn't destroy his house. But no shit, he definitely got the point. I told him I'd keep tabs on him to stop him from going after military wives. He's not going to forget."

"You've been thinking about what we talked about before I left La Arboleda de los Robles, haven't you? What's changed?"

"Do no more damage. Constantly. What's changed is I don't want to make people afraid of me. And screw myself in the process."

"Okay, good. My turn. Memo, will you do something for me?"

"Sure."

"Something's come up. My parents are having health problems. My sister can't handle them now, because of all her kids and her husband. I need to bring my parents to stay with us. If I left to bring them here right now, it would be too much strain on my medical partners for a lot of reasons. And Diane can't go until Christmas vacation."

I look out the window as I talk with Jack. The storm has passed. The sky and sea almost merge at the horizon. The muted line on the horizon is dark and ginger-gray-black. It's hard to see where one stops and the other begins.

"What do you need?"

"Will you go and close-up their house? My sister will help. Please bring them here."

Jack trusts me after all the shit I've done? He's either foolish to have confidence in me, or sees something I don't. "No question. I'd love to do that for you, Jack."

"That puts my mind at ease."

"But after everything—"

"Look, Memo, you're the guy I can count on, no matter what."

"Sure, I'll make it work."

"Yeah, that's what I mean. You'll make it work."

"When do you need me to go?"

"Day after tomorrow, okay?"

"Definitely. Can you hold on for a second? Shadow Facts is sitting here, wagging her tail. She wears a wristwatch. Knows the second it's dinner time."

"Sure."

Half-a-minute later. "Okay, back now. Can Shadow Facts stay at your place while I'm gone helping with your folks?"

"You trust me with your dog?"

"You trust me with your parents."

We say goodbye. It's dark outside. Harsh emptiness fills the room. The crashing surf is the single sound I hear.

I usually feel uplifted after I talk with Jack. This time is different. Maybe it was too much to cover. I feel the way I did when Kate left. It comes back again.

Jack said I'm a guy who lands on his feet.

Is that true?

Or just an act?

It's shadowy in the room.

A spontaneous feeling happens. I become overwhelmed. I blame Kate for her part in destroying our marriage—fucking around with Scanlon and turning me into a pitiful used condom thrown on the hot pavement to melt into ooze. Why couldn't she have more loyalty and perseverance and commitment to our marriage? Instead, she falls apart, just like her fucking mother. She comes from a family of divorce. She's going to do the same goddamn thing. Yeah, I blame her for fucking us over. It's not all on me, no matter what mom says about blame.

And then I step back from my twisted blaming mind. Turn my anger towards myself. I'm an evil piece of shit. I don't feel like living. Kill myself and be done with it.

But people are counting on me. They have expectations. Some things have to be done.

I don't feel like living. My body feels blank and absent.

I have to get Jack's parents. My good buddy is counting on me.

I'll paddle out to sea on my surfboard at night for miles and miles. Stop and push my surfboard away.

Frank, Dutch and my parents are working to help me get back into USC.

Let the sea take me.

Shadow Facts rubs her head on my hand. In her silent canine language she says, "No. Hold on a little longer."

CHAPTER 20

WHERE TO?

1100 hours. Memorial Day, 1971

IHEAR THE PHONE RING. I DROP WHAT I'M DOING and pick up the receiver. "Hello."

"Memo?" Suzanne's voice has a jittery terrified edginess.

"Hi Suzanne, what's up?"

"Jack and you have to come over right away. It's Chet."

I've been expecting a catastrophe. Now it's here. "You want to tell me anything now? Or should we just come over?"

"Chet got up before dawn, put on his jungle boots and pinned all of his medals on his pajama top. He started drinking bourbon and hasn't stopped. About an hour ago he got his .45. Took off his boots, threw them in the backyard and shot the holy hell out of them. Someone called the police. They cruised though the neighborhood and left."

"Didn't the police talk with him?"

"No. I should have gone out. Should have intercepted the cops and gotten some help. Now I'm calling you."

"So what's happened?"

"Memo, he's circling the drain. He's much worse than he was during the trip to Guadalupe Canyon. Like before, I don't know how much I can take. Went past my limit a long time ago. Really, I'm on my way out the door."

Suzanne has gone past her cutoff point, like Kate went over the edge with me. "Okay, I'll check with Jack and see if he's available and not glued to the hospital. I'll be there with or without Jack."

I ASK MYSELF WHY I FEEL RESPONSIBLE FOR CHET. It's easier to examine his problems and to avoid my own. But that's the kind of answer that floats on the surface. There are deeper reasons. We didn't serve in a combat unit together, though there's the communal secret code sewn in a fabric of our understanding—the scars of war make new scars back home. We know this fact.

Time and place doesn't erase being an Army buddy and I have a responsibility to watch his back. The shared experience makes me feel responsible for a buddy who is in trouble. And Chet is in trouble. And it's a different trouble than when we were high school chums. War is about responding to an immediate crisis. I'm used to responding. Chet is in an immediate crisis.

The trip to Cañón de Guadalupe is a punctuation point. Chet skated around the precipice of being a casualty. He wasn't over the brink yet.

Chet and I have linked-up after we returned from Mexico. We talked about what came before and after our trip to Mexico. He unveiled what happened in the days he arrived home from war. Numbing himself through whatever turn he decides to take. From there, his story says he keeps losing more and more, like his voice is becoming fainter and fainter as he travels an ill-fated distance.

Chet is discharged from the military without anything left in his reserves to reconnect with work. He feels too trashed. I nod when I hear this. Chet is telling my story, too. He shows-up at the unemployment office with an invisible and indelible Combat Infantry Badge— CIB—clipped to his civvies. He collects a few bucks for being an unemployed soldier, until he returns to his mason's job.

Chet still has places he fits in. He has more than one thing and less than a half dozen things in common with his party buddies. What he has in common is how to drink and use various drugs and talk shit. His party buddies support him to deteriorate even further.

Chet told me he hooked-up with an old main squeeze at the Long Bar in Tijuana. She's nicknamed *Queenie* for a good reason. She's the queen of drinking. And the queen of singing. After drinking twenty-one shots of tequila she sang opera to the accompaniment of a maria-chi band. Chet said she's a hoot. I know he means a hot hoot having sex with Queenie is slang for having sex and is one more attempt to cool his fever. Screwing her again made him feel so good, which ended-up making him feel worse. I know through my connection with Lupita and deceit-caused disconnection with Kate.

He has a lot of scary flare-ups. Chet told me what the fuck about getting loaded and riding his motorcycle. He had a few shots of tequila and a couple of beers at Hussong's Cantina in Ensenada. At night he rides back at eighty-five miles per hour on the Baja toll road—*carret-era cuota*—between San Miguel and La Misión. He nearly misses a cow on the dark and hellish road. When he tells the story, I imagine his bloody body smeared across the pavement and motorcycle parts scattered everywhere. Suzanne finds out about what he did. She gets ticked off and chews-him-out. The idea of pulling back the throttle on a 650cc Triumph on a sinister lonely treacherous road in Mexico is complicated for Suzanne to understand. But I understand dangerous desperate acts. That's why Chet told me the story.

Chet was clearly in an uncontrolled power dive when we went to Cañón de Guadalupe. At the time I was too lost in my own self-absorbed emotional agony to plainly see it. Now it's see-through. The infusion of pot and the tequila and the Heineken and the reds to sleep all said he was a disaster.

I GO TO JACK'S PLACE AND PICK HIM UP.

"Chet's situation sounds grim." I fill Jack in, report what Suzanne said.

"The dominoes are falling."

"Chet's going to be screwed if Suzanne leaves."

"Well, despite how he trashes himself, he's still a good looking guy. I don't know how he does it. Maybe by laying a ton of brick and stone a day. The only possibility is if he gets some other woman to take care of him, at least for awhile. And then she'll leave. Delay the inevitable." Jack shakes his head from side to side.

"If he lives that long." The sound of resignation in my voice turns into a frown.

"Memo, let's talk about you before we get over to Chet's place. How are you and Kate doing with the divorce?"

I think of how we have kept the practical side together. "It's been civilized. There wasn't much to split. For now, I'm letting her have the beach house. Works for me. I stay about three days a week up at USC." I realize my emotions are more turbulent than my factual account to Jack. "Her grandmother moved to the White Sands retirement community in La Jolla, and Kate is staying at her house. It's really a nice spot. She's set-up her art studio there. My guess is Kate will inherit the place. That's all I know, except I will move back into the beach house after she leaves."

"Okay." Jack clears his throat. "How are you actually doing, man?"

"Depends on the day. On average, I'm reduced to a state of ruin."

"Yeah, but it's good to see you in the salvage mode."

"Is Kate in contact with Diane?"

"All the time. They pal around."

"Is Kate seeing anyone?"

"Nobody. I see her at the house. She's keeping in shape. Looks great. Diane says Kate is working a lot in her studio, developing some exceptional paintings."

"I'm not surprised she's creating outstanding pieces. She's a real talent." I visualize her and fight feeling sad.

"Memo, I know a stunningly beautiful woman if you want a date. She's a post-operative recovery room nurse. When men come out of anesthesia and see her bending over them, they think they're in paradise."

Women fill my mind all the time. I look, but not set to touch. "I'm not ready for paradise yet. Maybe later."

"Right. Yeah, it was a stupid thought. You don't seem geared up for that yet. What was I thinking? Sorry."

We arrive at Chet and Suzanne's house. She comes to the door. We enter the living room. Chet's collection of antique fishing reels are displayed in an old-fashioned oak lawyer's bookcase with pull down, waterfall glass doors. The house is spotless, filled with his finely refinished American antique furniture. How could Chet be such a wreck and have such nice things, with the place so manicured? Suzanne must be racing around doing a lot of compensation. We walk though the kitchen. Less than half a fifth of Jack Daniels is sitting on the counter.

Chet is on a chaise lounge on the back porch, smoking a Chesterfield. A glass of bourbon, a pack of cigarettes and his beat-up Zippo lighter are on a table next to him. The lighter's hinge finally broke. He's wearing blue cotton pajamas with navy piping. The hole-filled jungle boots he's wearing are a mind-blowing contrast.

"How are you doing, Chet?" I ask.

Suzanne goes back into the house.

"If I felt any better, I'd hurt."

"Yeah, I've heard you say that before. So what's with the medals on your P.J.s? You're carrying a lot of weight on your chest."

The medals pinned to Chet's pajama top are in the right order. A Combat Infantry Badge on top. Below, there's a Silver Star, two Purple Hearts, an Army Commendation Medal, an Army Good Conduct Medal, a National Defense Service Medal, a Vietnam Service Medal and a Vietnam Campaign Medal.

"I'm celebrating Memorial Day, boys."

Chet takes a long drag and finishes his cigarette. Crushes it in an abalone shell. He gulps the bourbon.

"You look pretty loaded. You okay?" I say.

"Sure. You want a drink?"

"No thanks. Suzanne told us you got out your .45 this morning. Shot it in the backyard,"

"Yeah, remember, I'm celebrating Memorial Day."

I look at Jack.

Jack shakes his head. His eyes are a mix of sad and concern.

I think Chet is in danger—a big liability with devastating evil consequences. He's on a collision course that will draw the curtain across his stage.

I look back at Chet. "We're worried about you and Suzanne—"

"Memo, Jack, you know Suzanne is always overdramatizing every fuckin' thing. I can't move one goddamn inch without her trying to control me." Chet picks up his bourbon glass. He almost spills it. And then he manages to take a drink. "I try to get her off my back, and now she calls you guys. I'm sick of her bullshit. Give it a rest."

I look at the backyard. It's a simple clean landscape design, with a dense rich lawn and plants of three graduated sizes, the smallest in front. The guy is so messed up, and yet his house is so squared away.

"We're concerned about you, Chet," says Jack.

"I appreciate you guys coming over. And your concern. But look, I'm fine."

"Chet, let's get you into the V.A. Hospital," says Jack.

"No way. I said I'm fine. Besides, I hear they don't have a cocktail hour at the V.A."

"Come on, Chet. Just for a couple of days," I say.

"I said, I'm fine. I'm not budging."

"Okay, but let's do this just to be on the safe side. We'd like to take your weapon until things settle down a little," says Jack.

"Nobody's taking my weapon." A cross look sweeps across Chet's drunken face.

"I have to ask you something. Are you thinking of hurting yourself—having any suicidal thoughts?" asks Jack.

"Hey, are you Dr. Davey or my friend?"

"We're your friends. That's the only reason we're here," Jack says.

"I'm okay. You guys can give it a rest, too."

I think Chet isn't going to reason with us in his irrational state. "I think we should go."

"Okay. We're worried. You might need help," says Jack. "Chet, promise you'll call us. Call anytime. Day or night. Promise?"

"Yeah, I promise." Chet lights another cigarette and slurps bourbon. "Look, thanks for coming over. Memo, Jack, no matter what, you're good guys."

We walk inside the house. Suzanne is in the living room. She stands up.

"Is he still taking the barbiturates?" asks Jack.

"Yes. A couple of times, he ran out. He didn't sleep much. And when he did sleep, he thrashed around. Must have been the nightmares." She squints. The edges of her mouth are turned down. "Last month, he was out in the garage and I think he had a seizure, but he didn't get help."

"Where does he get the reds?" I ask.

"Off the street. Or in Tijuana pharmacies."

"The combination of barbiturates and alcohol scares me. I offered to help him get into the V.A.," says Jack.

"He's not going to do that, Jack." Suzanne folds her arms across her chest. "I have to tell you, I'm making plans to leave. I can't stand what's happening any longer. And I don't want to be here when he drinks himself to death."

Suzanne makes me think of Kate's exit. "It's going to be bad for you whether you're here or not."

"I know. I've thought of that, too. At this point, I've thought of almost every possible scenario." Every four seconds she looks back and forth between Jack and me. "You know, I used to be able to handle everything—make-up for Chet being out of control—but I'm at the end now."

"You sound bitter," I say.

"I am bitter."

Jack bows two inches and moves his head forward slightly. "Suzanne, do you feel safe?"

Her eyes open wide. "Yeah, I'm safe. He knows I'm not the enemy."

She uncrosses her arms. We each hug Suzanne and leave.

"It was a lot more fun hearing about the recovery room nurse. Chet's trip is not exactly paradise. Had no idea he would be that bad off."

I look at Jack. There are deep lines in his forehead. His face is drained. A colorless look. His jaw is jutted forward. His chest is sunken. Jack's breath has a hurting raspy sound. He looks as though he should be crying. But he isn't.

"I thought I would be leaving all this shit behind when I got home. Escaping it." Jack shakes his head. "I see it at work. And now with Chet."

"There's no escape. Remember what happened in Cañón de Guadalupe when I looked for an escape. Escapes are tricky. Dangerous, maybe. Want me to take you home?"

"No, not yet. Let's go over to Sunset Cliffs and look at the waves."

We drive to Osprey, the surf spot where Jack and I first met. We park. I turn off the engine. We say nothing. The emotions of two human beings occupy every small square quantum of space. Inside the cab of the Land Cruiser, the air is leaden and opaque.

My brain sparks. "Jack, did you notice there was something we didn't talk about with Chet?"

"No. What?"

"Something obvious."

"Can't think of anything."

"We didn't talk with Chet about him going out on patrol with three other guys and being the only one who came back. We didn't talk about his Silver Star. We didn't talk about his two Purple Hearts. We didn't talk about his Combat Infantry Badge."

I look in the rearview mirror. A Jaguar roadster drives by. It has a round metal and enamel British car club medallion attached to the front bumper. Why does the driver need the car? Because it's fun. It's cool. He has to have it. He would die some kind of death if he couldn't have it.

The Jag would be useless if you needed an olive drab armored M3 half-track.

I reel my mind in. "Jack, we just saw our drunken friend in pajamas and jungle boots, wearing his medals and chain-smoking. Our duty was to protect Chet from himself. But we didn't talk about what the fuck was really going on—why he was so beat to shit, eating reds and drinking Jack Daniels. We didn't make the connection between him being a suicidal maniac and being a fuckin' war wreck. We just talked around it. We weren't in the middle of understanding him— just looking at him being loaded and the dangerousness of him shooting his .45."

"Probably because he was too loaded."

"That's one reason." A vehement sensation runs across my cheeks. "The other reason is there's a lot of stuff we don't say about ourselves. So how could we face what's happening with him?"

Jack lifts his shoulders, closes his eyes and grimaces. Drops his shoulders and exhales.

"There's a saying in Spanish, *Estar en la boca del lobo*–'In the mouth of the wolf.' It means you don't have a chance. That's Chet. Doesn't have a chance because he won't let anybody else in. Brother Jack, you and I have a chance."

"You know, Memo, I don't purposely avoid talking about what happened in Nam."

"Yeah, a lot of stuff isn't done on purpose. It's automatic. I'm going to try to talk if I can. Maybe I can, maybe I can't. Don't know if I'm ready now or not."

The color returns to Jack's face. The lines are gone. I see breath return to his chest. He looks at me. His eyes are clear—receptive.

"May 1970—the month before I came back from Nam—was the Kent State massacre. The president of USC shut down the campus. All hell was breaking loose in the States. All hell was breaking loose in Saigon, too, but I didn't know it until after the fact. I was in it without knowing it."

I pause. Silent frames of what happened run through my mind for the hundred-thousandth time. I look out to the sea. I see a set of waves come in, one after another, breaking crisply. Like a child, I still like to think I have superhuman powers—the ability to make waves come or to stop them. But they just come. I can't stop them.

"War is an exclusive language. It's a curse. Everybody uses different vocabulary to construct their thoughts, but we speak the same tongue," I tell Jack.

"Today is May 31, 1971. Exactly one year ago was your last month in Nam. Memo, stop talking bullshit about languages, curses and tongues. If you want to talk about the war, don't numb-out. What happened? This is the first anniversary of what?"

"I was a real short timer. I had a drink at the Continental Hotel on Dong Khoi Street in Saigon's District One. I was heading back to the BOQ, using a side street.

"I thought it was safe.

"I thought wrong.

"That's where it happened.

"There was blood and feathers where a refugee had just slaughtered and plucked a chicken. He was cooking the chicken in hot oil over an open fire on the sidewalk. There was also the sickening reek of rotting fruit mixed with used motor oil dumped in the gutter. The humid suffocating night made the fatigues cling to my body.

"And then I made eye contact with a guy in civilian clothes. Instantly, I knew he was Charlie. His eyes were black and shiny and burned in the depths of their darkness. When his eyes met mine, he gave me a death glare."

I space-out, stare out the windshield.

"Don't stop. Tell me," says Jack.

"He drew a pistol. He aimed it at me. I said to myself, I'm fucked. This is it. I said goodbye to Kate. Goodbye to my folks. Goodbye to Shadow Facts. Goodbye to life."

I turn and look Jack in the eye.

"I pulled out my M1911A1 .45. His bullet missed me. I swear to God, I felt it travel past my bicep. I shot him once on the right side of his chin. The impact spun his head to the left. The second shot hit the side of his cheek. His head exploded like a watermelon—thought it was going to spin right off his fuckin' neck. He collapsed right on the spot where he had stood. The sidewalk was dimly lit. Charlie's blood was a purple and black lake, smooth and clean, on the dirty Saigon cement sidewalk."

"Jesus. Why didn't you tell me? You've been so fucked-up. I've read you. There's all the known stories and left out details like—"

"Well, the important detail comes next. Charlie's bullet missed me, but went through a Baby-San and then a Mama-San, who was holding him. Mama-San was squatting, flat-footed, behind me. Not doing anything. Just squatting. A mother holding her baby. Innocent. She was leaning against the wall of a building, the child in her lap—a scene I'd seen a thousand times. This time was different. Mama-San and Baby-San lying on their sides, lifeless, blood streaming out over the damp rotten sidewalk. They were gone. What was there to do for them? Nothing. Nothing at all. If there was one VC, there had to be others. I had to *di di mau*—leave. And I was right to get the fuck out of there. Jack, I found out the VC infiltrated Saigon that night. They killed four hundred people. Four hundred people in Saigon in one night. I didn't need to be there. I fucked-up. No enemy fire would have lit-up that scummy side street had I not been there. I killed a guy point-blank. The poor harmless mother and child. I was so helpless to do anything."

"I hate the term collateral damage—crappy vague expression to substitute for the callousness of war. But I'm going to use it. What the fuck do you expect from yourself? You were there. Charlie was there. Mama-San and Baby-San were there. Weapons drawn. Three people killed. Not you. Brother, there is nothing you could have done differently. The only thing different could have been—"

"No fuckin' war."

"Yeah. The randomness of war torments you, fucks with your mind. War's stray bullets fly. They kill mothers and children. That part has nothing to do with you. We're caught in the middle—hit by another kind of stray bullet."

"The stuff that happened in the field is a secret mess that has no outlet. And after the one night in Saigon, I've alternated between frozen and alive."

"Okay, Memo, all of them are gone now. You did the best you could in the horrific situation with Walter. And—the Mama-San and Baby-San—you absolutely did the right thing. You killed the VC. You got the fuck out of there before other Cong showed up while you were bending over to try to save the mother and her kid, who were already dead. Over there—well, I trust you did what was best no matter how fucked-up the situation was. Yeah, things have been messed-up since you got home. But I'll tell you, Memo, I see you putting things right. You're getting there. No matter what you can or can't talk about."

"Are you saying I'm going to get over it, Jack?"

"None of us are ever going to get over it. The way you'll be all right is to find a way to get used to it. Pretend to accept it until you can accept it. Do you know what I mean?"

"Yeah, I think so—maybe. But what about Chet? He's never going to get used to anything besides drinking himself to death."

"He's a war casualty. The collateral damage back on home turf. It's safe here, but he thinks he's not safe. The war chiseled debasement into his mind," says Jack.

I cry. My stomach convulses. Same shit's happening again. Can't help it. The frames of the dead kid and mother repeat, again and again and again. My mind—driven like a flash flood. Walter. The interrogation center in Phu Yen. Swiney. Dozer. The gaping slit in the Vietnamese girl's throat. The black kid. Five minutes pass. I lose touch with what's going on around me. My eyes swell. I look at Jack.

Jack's cheeks are wet.

"I've thought about what you said before you left Arboleda de los Robles," I say. "A key to recovering from the damage of war is to not make new damage. That's Chet, making new damage. New damage that doesn't end because the guy keeps fucking himself over."

Jack looks at me. His eyes blink. His breath is labored.

"I knew I wasn't doing well. I felt removed, dead inside. Going to Europe with Kate right after I got home was a real bust—had a bad time, tried to fake it. But the damage I did to Inocencio punched me in the face. It told me something was drastically wrong. Kate left me—more wrong."

"Look, you've been building a changed Memo since Kate left."

"But Jack, maybe a lot of the damage we do to ourselves when we get back from war is more subtle than attacking some innocent guy. Or going crazy with sex. Or having a wife leave you. Or, like Chet, taking reds and drinking yourself to death."

"This is going somewhere, isn't it?"

"Yeah, it's going somewhere. You're always right. You're the super-competent physician. You salvaged a lot people, while I helplessly watched them disappear. You're lucky to have Diane. Jack, without trying, you look good on the outside. Then there are those times we have together."

Jack shifts in his seat. He scans back and forth. His eyes look blank, as though he's not taking in anything he's looking at. Jack turns. He looks at the breaking surf and squints. Jack rests his hands on his thighs. And then he squeezes his thighs so tight his hands turn white.

"Jack, tell me what happened."

"I did."

"It's taken me a year to talk about the baby and mother getting killed by mistake when I was actually the target. And there's only one person I could tell—you. Maybe I was being pushed now because of the year mark, maybe because of Chet. Maybe nothing is pushing you. Maybe nothing ever will. Maybe you'll just erode if you don't talk about what happened in the OR"

"I already told you what happened."

"So why are you squeezing the crap out of the tops of your legs?"

"I didn't realize I was doing that."

I'm suddenly filled with a savage need to know how Jack can possibly cope with all his memories. "No kidding. You told me the guys you operated on were scared shitless. They screamed at you to either help them or kill them. Guts were pouring out of them. Limbs were ripped off. You were operating on nearly dead GIs, trying to save them. That's what I remember you saying."

"Isn't that enough?"

"No. Goddamn it, it's not enough. What does all that stuff that happened mean to you, Jack? I don't want to hear your story as though it were an article in some fucking medical journal."

"I'll tell you what it means. The goddamn injuries were so bad I started to feel as though I were only a witness. The patient and God were the ones really doing the work."

"Surgeons are supposed to be the ones in control, right?"

"Not this surgeon. Not anymore. Most of those soldiers were so young. I wanted to call their families and say, I did everything possible to save your kid. Goddamn it, Memo, I did do everything possible. And it was never enough—never enough. I thought the fucking chaos would never stop. The abdominal vascular injuries were so complex."

"What the fuck does 'complex' mean, Jack? Come on."

"I had to improvise without time or space to think. There was so much turmoil that sometimes I'd look at the scalpel and say to myself, 'Remember, sharp side down.'

"There was so much debridement. So many transfusions. They'd slip into shock or cardiopulmonary arrest—disappear. And with the guys who lived, there were always multiple injuries. I'd question myself. Had I missed something before a GI was evacuated from our OR? Did he lose a limb or die because I fucked-up?"

"Jack, there's a stench lodged in your brain, isn't there?"

"God-awful. It's stuck in the lining of my nose. Burned flesh, wounds, dirty feet, stale tobacco, and body fluids—urine and feces—from pissing and crapping all over the place from extreme sympathetic stress reactions. The smells were fermented by heat and mixed with humidity, antiseptics, disinfectants, alcohol, and Betadine. Weirdest thing was the sweat and the pus and the blood from my patients mixed with a good cigar or a joint after dealing with an onslaught."

"I don't know why I asked about the stench—came out of nowhere."

"Because you know about the stink caused by war. But the smells of blood and pus from the OR weren't the worst part for me. It was the constant sound of the anesthetic machine. And continually seeing a bucket with an amputated foot or a hand in it. Again, again, and again. Mother fucker!"

"I thanked you once for all that you did in Nam. Goddamn it, I'm thanking you again for all the guys you saved—all the help you gave everybody—you're a better doctor now because you worked in that hellhole OR. You have more perspective than the docs you work with. If any of my family were in the OR, I'd want you doing the cutting. Come on. Don't stop, Jack. A lot of those things in Nam were way beyond anything you could possibly control. That's what you told me."

Jack doubles over. Head in his hands, he wails. I see his stomach convulse the same way mine did. He lifts his head.

"Jack, there's a ton of snot streaming out of your nose."

I hand him a t-shirt from behind the seat. DEWEY WEBER SURFBOARDS is stenciled on it. He blows the crap out of his nose.

"You told Chet and me about the doc who was addicted to morphine. What other crazy shit happened?"

"What other crazy shit didn't happen. You know, the nurses and medics looked to me to help them deal with everything that was going on. Hell, I was too busy trying to stop some guy's bleeding or push his guts back inside, before I had to move onto the next slot. A couple of times I got so fucking pissed off I threw a scalpel across the OR."

I see Jack's mind racing. He's watching a two-year-old movie. And the spigot's on.

"We'd laugh at the most sickening stuff—the humor was completely outrageous. It was weird listening to acid rock, the Stones, or Mozart while up to my elbows in blood. Some people were smoking a lot of pot. Fuck, who wasn't? Yeah, there were people diverting drugs. And one nut case nurse was strutting around because she was fuckin' the priest—the chaplain. Hell, she was probably fuckin' everybody else, too."

"What's left?"

"A lot of stuff. I'll tell you what's left. A lot of sleepless nights and nightmares when I do sleep."

"You look spent, Jack."

"Spent and dehydrated from all the crying."

"You want to take off?"

"Sure. Where to?"

"Home."

I drop Jack off at his home. I feel a purged hollowness after vomiting toxic memories—and I'm scared by the tickle at the back of my mind knowing my memories will gain momentum and reappear.

A state of emptiness is magnified after being so close to Jack.

The surf in front of the beach house is choppy, blown-out by the afternoon wind. Emptiness changes to something else. Impressions of Chet grip and consume me. I can't distance myself. A sunken black-and-purplish red sadness swells with agitation's synergism—imagining the thrashing damaged creature, captive within the boundaries of Chet's mind. And the fragile scabs covering his immeasurable wounds are on the edge of deteriorating by the solvent effects of alcohol to expose an irreparable sanguine mess.

An eerie sensation falls just below my eyes, like shadowy smudges smeared on my cheeks. I go to the bathroom mirror. The reflected image is the same person in Kate's dream. Me, dressed in my olive drab jungle fatigues, captain's bars and infantry cross rifles embroidered on my collar. I'm a dead and alive man, wearing a captain's bars insignia-laden helmet. Leathery black skin is drawn tightly over my boney face. My sapphire eyes burn hot.

Like a robot on automatic pilot I go to the bedroom and pull out the dresser drawer. They're hidden. But they're there. I drag out my war medals and place them on the dresser top. I study them. And then I think about how all the nightmares began—with Walter—out in the jungle triple canopy. I can smell the fresh smells of the vegetation—and the rot.

CHAPTER 21

SLUSHY RED MUD

W E AVOID THE SUN'S PENETRATING HEAT by waiting under the overhang at the entrance to the USAID II compound's main entrance. Daniels's driver leaves to pull the car around. Walter Dunner looked skeletal, so bone-like as if parts of a whole man were missing. His uniform hangs on his loosely connected body. His eyes sink behind inflamed, puffy bags in a gray-skinned face.

Dunner must have the worst posture in the military. He looks like someone punched him in the chest, making his thorax concave. Dunner's looks are juxtaposed with nonstop smiling—a childlike smile—as if he is a limp noodle, wanting the approval that would supply him with his missing backbone. He's in his mid-forties and hasn't been promoted past captain. Maybe he got busted. Or he's so flaccid he gets passed over. Dunner is holding a cigarette with his wrist cocked outward. His other hand is on his hip. Dunner's military presence is dispirited and sadly nonexistent.

Walter's smile is gone, now. He lights a cigarette. Thick smoke drifts up and hits the eave and becomes trapped on the underside like a solid mass. He's hunched over, smokes and smokes and looks like he's in a caged morbid state as if he can't stop thinking about a black nightmare. The smoke can't escape or dissipate. It accumulates and grows heavier and murkier. It begins to be weighty, a cloud turning dark and thunder-like, capable of being a torrent ready to fall back down on him.

"Walter, I'm afraid that—"

"You don't have anything to worry about, Memo. You're not broken like me. I'm on the farther side of getting patched up."

The driver pulls the car up to the curb. He's immaculate, dressed in a blousy woven black shirt. His shiny black hair is rich with natural oil. The language we have in common is the name of our destination.

Walter opens the right rear door for me. "Walter," I remind him, "you're the ranking officer. You sit in the right rear seat." He gets in. I walk around the back of the car, open the left door and slide in.

I realize Walter can't discuss what men face when they're deployed to a war theater. In your mind it's the sound of a radio that's always on, broadcasting something only you can hear—doubts and fears and uncertainty and questions about trust. The volume blares or is muted. The sound ranges between static and clear. It could be a horrible grating noise or a symphonic masterpiece. The sound is the woman a man leaves behind. He prays all problems will vanish—only what's good will remain when he returns. She will be his salvation and safety. But there's the fear he will return to find a permanent stain. Or return to nobody and nothing at all.

Some men say, she shit in my helmet and I put it on. Or, I reached into a barrel of pussies and pulled out an asshole.

And then there are the men with good women who acknowledge—mostly to themselves but sometimes to their best buddies—trusting her and feeling her permanence is their shelter from the storm. I crave for the total confidence to believe in Kate. And then I can't control the doubts, wondering if she'll be able to wait for me.

We drive to the guarded gate. It's opened. We leave. What could be a ten-minute ride to Ton San Nhut is delayed by swarms of Honda 50 motorbikes and the need to thread our way through traffic.

"Walter, I'm sorry you got sucked into going up to Quang Tri. There's no reason I couldn't have gone on the mission by myself. I'm new, but I could get the job done—that's what I should have told General Steele."

Walter caves into the back seat. His shoulders are collapsed, and his elbow is on the door rest. His limp fist supports his chin. He goes mute. His head is turned forty-five degrees to the right. He's listless. A

directionless and empty stare doesn't seem to register the street commotion whizzing by.

I think Walter is never going to get his approval-seeking childlike smile back.

He breaks his silence. "Not a problem. It'll be over soon. Don't
worry about it."

I can't think of what to say. Then I hear my mother's voice in my
head: *¡Memito, di algo!—Do something!*

The words come from somewhere. Yes, my mother is the ventrilo-
quist, and I'm the dummy. "Walter, right now, you must feel as though
you're caught in a trap. You're here in Nam. Your wife's at home, doing
who knows what." No, mom is not speaking through me; to me those
words sounded stupid.

"That's right. We've been married for twenty years. I have no idea
what I'm going to do. Too mixed-up. Her sleeping around with the
other guy is too much to tackle. I just don't know because I can't get a
grip on anything."

The dummy speaks for himself. "I'm pissed off at a woman I don't
know. Aren't you?"

"I don't know who I'm pissed at. I don't know what I'm pissed at."
Walter's face turns from gray to dark.

"Some things are shocking—hard to comprehend at first." I catch
his eye for a second. "But Walter, there has to be an answer for you
somewhere." I'm scratching, but there's not enough friction to adhere
to something substantial.

"Yeah, maybe there is." Walter's flat timbre doesn't give reassur-
ances of something positive to put stock in.

We pull into the airbase. Within a couple of minutes, we board a
C-130 bound for Quang Tri Province. We're strapped into seats that
don't face forward but instead run parallel to the sides of the craft.
The reverberating bellow of the engines and whirling of the props are
so loud we have to shout to be heard. We end up not talking. It's a
relief not to have to talk, and the relief is mixed with a sore sensation.

It's painful to look at Walter, knowing he's twisting in the wind.
His gray-dark face and swollen eyes transform into a thick mask.

WE PASS OVER DENSELY VEGETATED AND sometimes mountainous landscapes. Bomb-pocked areas show evidence of U.S. B-52s. We land. We are transported to meet with the CO, Lieutenant Colonel Mitch Hupp.

LTC Hupp briefs us on the training of the Kit Carson Scouts by the Marines. The Scouts are of strategic importance because of their knowledge of the North and South Vietnamese behavior patterns, geography and language. Some of the Americans use translators or speak Vietnamese themselves. But Hupp says the Scouts understand the idiomatic expressions and the lore of the peasants in hamlets. The nuances are difficult to translate. The stateside Defense Language Institutes, DLIs, have a hard time teaching this. Lily white fluorescent-lit DLI classrooms can't teach what rolls off the Scouts' tongues and the underbelly ways of knowing and a sixth sense about the jungle. The Kit Carson Scouts are starting to sound like the magic bullet for the Phoenix Program. And there's the next chapter's installment.

We find out the NCOs working with the Scouts feel uncertain about the Scouts, don't trust them. In fact, they feel the Scouts have not truly given up their VC ties. Hupp couldn't cite any specifics, only the intuition and suspicion of his field staff.

Now Vietnam has certainty—in an uncertain kind of way. What you can be sure of is the presence of fuzzy ambiguities. You can be confident that you don't know who to trust and who not to trust. It's like walking though a minefield in the fog on a pitch-black night. Generals want sureness. Steele knows the vagaries of the Vietnam bush. That's why we're here. The Scouts have the potential for skewering the VC and NVA, but it's dicey using them. They might work for us or against us. Who the hell knows what they're really doing?

In the morning 1SG Swacker takes Walter and me in a Jeep toward the Scout's training camp. I sit in the back as we ride on a rutted dirt road, splashing through pond-sized potholes filled with water left by early morning hot rain. The land in Nam is made red by dirt rich in iron oxide. The steamy road goes through the tunnel-like jungle. We make our way across a river. The foliage is dense and green on top of denser and greener foliage, giving the canopy a layered look.

"First Sergeant, what is your DEROS?"

"Ninety-seven days, sir."

"Feel like a short-timer yet?"

"Yeah, plan on getting my fuckin' butt back across the pond, sir."

"Stop, First Sergeant, I have to take a piss," says Dunner.

"We're about half way there, sir. I recommend we not stop."

"Stop," Dunner repeats.

We stop. The vegetated area is green-packed understory and canopy. "I'll be right back."

"Where are you going, Walter?" My voice sounds like I'm beating him up not to go.

"I'm just going into the bush to piss."

"Just do it here, next to the Jeep."

"I can't pee near others—pee shy."

"Oh fuck, Walter."

Walter dismisses me. He steps out of the muddy-wheeled Jeep. He walks toward the green denseness. We keep the engine running.

"I'll be right back."

"No, Walter!"

He stops but doesn't turn around. "No? Why not?" His voice is flat. Walter turns and keeps moving.

"Something smells wrong. It's shit. Human shit! Could be Charlie. He could still be around."

"He's right, sir," says Swacker.

"I don't smell anything. It'll only take a second."

Dunner walks into the opaque, thick foliage. Swacker and I wait. We exchange looks of trepidation. Dunner is taking too long. Something is off.

I'm permeated by adrenaline-driven fear. My heart throbs in my throat. I'm scared shitless. I act.

He's out there. Go get him.

"This is taking too long, First Sergeant. I'm going to check-it-out."

I grab my M-16, release the safety and head into the bush after Walter. There's a triple canopy. I kick the ground vegetation, that slaps my shins. I push aside the dense undergrowth; sunlight barely filters through the upper layer. I walk through the enveloping vegetation for forty-five seconds. My heartbeat vibrates my whole torso. My legs are weak. I flex my leg muscles to know they are still there. I can't remember being this scared.

Holy Christ! Walter is lying face up on the ground, with his throat neatly slit. His still-beating heart continues to pump blood, which is spilling onto the earth. The red earth, mixed with blood, turns violet.

I jerk sideways and see his pants are unzipped and his severed penis is next to him on the ground. I narrowly miss stepping on the poor guy's cock by less than a fuckin' millimeter. My boot sinks in the slushy red-violet mud. Muck mixed with blood oozes over the top of my boot. The detached penis touches the side of my foot. Unlike what seems to be every other goddamn person in his life, I don't tread on Walter's member.

I look up, through a passageway in the vegetation. Fifty meters out I see a strip of black hair moving back and forth. He's running away from me. I'm afraid. There's a high-speed swirl around me. My eyes focus on the vanishing figure. Adrenaline shifts from fear to a strange purifying effect because nothing else exists. And then everything slows down. My legs change into steel coils. I stand at a forty-five degree angle from my target, with my feet shoulders' width apart. The butt of my weapon is snug against my shoulder, and my left elbow is straight down. Using an off-hand shooting position, I squint, aim, breathe into my abdomen, slowly exhale, and squeeze off one round. Two hours pass in a split second. The moving figure goes down.

Swacker hears the weapon fire. "SIR?"

"Mother fucker!" Everything around me speeds-up. Sensations of being contaminated and frantic run through me. "Come here, Swacker! Now!"

In a flash, Swacker is standing next to me. He carries both his and Dunner's weapons, so that the arms are not left unattended in the Jeep. He sees Walter's body. Walter's blood is still spilling out, mixing with the mud and with his severed penis.

"Good God, sir!" Swacker says. Then he vomits—projectile, frothy vomit gushing from the pit of his stomach.

"I made a direct hit on the guy who slit Dunner's throat," I let go of a breath. "Let's go check-it-out."

Swacker wipes his mouth against the back of his hand and straightens partway. "I don't know, sir." He gasps. "There are probably other VC out there, maybe a trip-wire, a booby-trapped grenade or artillery round, a bouncing Betty, or a punji pit. Or maybe they're sucking us into an *alpha bravo*, an ambush.

"Swacker, to me, this doesn't look like an area were troops would move though on foot. Does it look that way to you? Unlikely there would be booby traps. Ambush, maybe, if they're setting up for a convoy. For chrissake, I just got here. What do yeah think? Other VC, well—"

Swacker straightens up. His cheeks are flushed and his eyes are bright. "Shit, I don't know, sir. This goddamn place is anybody's guess. Fuck it, sir, let's have a look."

Swacker and I move forward. We find the dead VC, wearing jungle fatigues face down on the earth with a bullet hole dead center in the back of his head, like a bull's-eye. The next-larger circle is his head. And the largest circle is the blood surrounding his head.

"Adios mother fucker," says Swacker.

Any semblance of reasoning in my brain switches-off. A frenzy comes over me—snaps. I bring my M-16 diagonally across my body and up into the air. I bring it down and smash the butt of the weapon into the VC's spine.

"Sir, sir, he's already dead."

Swacker looks up from the VC's corpse. "Sir, check it out. There's one of the Scouts."

I look up. I exhale and take another breath. Ten meters out at two o'clock is a man wearing an Army of the Republic of Vietnam—ARVN—uniform. He's tied upright to a tree.

"They tortured him 'til he died, sir. That's the way those fuckers do it—tie 'em to a tree and put 'em though a slow, agonizing death."

Swacker takes out a knife. He bends over, grabs the top of the VC's ear and saws off the entire ear. He breaks a branch on the tree next to the VC, leaving a nub on the tree trunk. Swacker punctures a hole in the ear with his knife and displays the ear on the tree nub. "Let's get the fuck out of here, sir."

"I won't tell anybody you did that," I say.

"You must be a cherry, sir. I don't give a shit one way or the other who you tell, sir. Mother fuckers!" Swacker whacks off the VC's two middle fingers, turns him over, exposing a partially missing face and sticks the fingers in the VC's mouth, which is still intact. "As a matter of fact, you tell everybody what I did to this asshole."

"Shit, Swacker!"

"Fuck 'em, sir."

We run back to Dunner. "You have a poncho in the Jeep, don't you, First Sergeant?"

"I'll get it."

I wait next to Walter. I am shaking. Swacker is back in two seconds.

"I'm not picking up Dunner's cock, sir. Let's just leave it."

"I'm not leaving CPT Dunner's member on the ground for the animals to eat. All of him is going home with at least a little dignity. And I would never think of asking you to pick up his body part. It's my duty, First Sergeant."

I pick up Walter's jagged and bloody severed penis. I put it in Walter's front pocket and zip up his blood stained pants. Without thinking, I wipe my hand on my pants. I feel the blood soak though to my skin. We wrap him up in the poncho, carefully place him in the Jeep, and head back to the compound.

"I'm sorry for being such a pussy back there and throwing-up."

"First Sergeant, I'm about ready to throw-up any fuckin' second, but don't stop if I do. I was so fuckin' scared back there I almost pissed and shit in my pants."

Swacker hands me his canteen. "Here, sir, have a drink."

"I'm not thirsty."

"Oh, yes you are."

I uncap the canteen and take a big swallow. It's vodka.

"I don't know what happened back there. Smashing the butt of my weapon into the VC's back."

"Typical battlefield reaction, sir. A kind of panic. You've got so much fuckin' juice flowin' you can't help it. It just plain, flat out, fuckin' happens. Forget it, sir. Be glad you nailed that VC."

So it's normal to smash the butt of an M-16 into the back of a man I just killed. Maybe this is my new paradigm. Am I the same man Kate married, or the person my mom wants me to be? Was this the same barbaric shit my dad faced in WWII? I doubt it.

But I'm here now. Whatever it takes, I have to find a way to keep myself in one piece. It had better be possible. I'll bargain for mostly possible.

I look straight ahead at the road. I can smell Walter's blood. My knuckles grow fleshy-white, holding onto my weapon. I think about Walter lying on the damp ground, his blood draining from his body—staining the dirt. My body starts to feel numb. It's the vodka. Or maybe it's battlefield numb.

The return flight to Ton San Nhut is a deathly kind of vacuous loneliness. I reflect on Walter. His pain is gone. He doesn't have to worry anymore about his wife. He doesn't have to worry about anyone liking him. He doesn't have to feel the constant humiliation of people looking at his captain's bars, seeing his age, and wondering what's wrong with him.

I think about Kate and my folks and Shadow Facts. I'm so far away from them.

I have to call Jack.

I have to get a pistol.

I killed a man. Queasiness spreads out from the tops of my lungs to the back of my throat. No more military pretend training rehearsals. We are in country. We are here. And we are in the war theater.

CHAPTER 22

LOST

Saturday, June 26, 1971. The beach house.

DARK ROAST, JAMAICAN BLUE MOUNTAIN coffee aroma fills the house. A summer morning's thin layer of overcast sky waits to burn off. The start of the day is unusually warm for the sixth day of summer, which means today will be a scorcher. Precisely how the sunset will glow is unforeseen. I open the window to let in the sea air.

The telephone rings. Shadow Facts perks up. She turns her head in the direction of the sound.

"Hello, Muir residence."

"Hi, Memo."

"Hi, Suzanne. I heard about it."

There's a sharp edge in her voice. "Yeah, I left Chet."

"He told me."

She's black and white and frank. "Did Chet tell you another woman moved in right away?"

"He mentioned it, yes."

"No doubt she's turned on by Mr. Lovability—jazzed by his good looks and fine body." Suzanne sounds jaded. "Wait until she finds out he's like a child or a pet—has to be taken care of."

"Who knows? Maybe she needs to be needed by someone."

"That's the way it'll start. She'll love being needed until she gets burned."

I imagine a coarse look on Suzanne's face. "Your bitterness is coming through?"

Suzanne's voice is piercing and troubled. "Okay—yes—I admit it. Pissed. Worn-out. And disappointed after all I've invested." She changes to a tune of sympathy. "And it could get really bad for her. Chet's getting worse."

I wonder if Kate talks about me the same way. "Suzanne, tell me about you. What's up?"

"A few things are different. I got a fantastic cottage in Mission Hills. Spectacular views, English garden, really comfortable. Yeah different. In a tiny way." She laughs.

"Sounds as though your luck is changing."

"Well, maybe. We'll see. I hope it lasts." Suzanne sounds whispery. "Say, Memo, how'd you like to come over? See my new place?" She's sounds silky. Suzanne has a sexy lilt.

I bend at the waist. My head moves four inches forward in disbelief of how sexy Suzanne sounds. There's the mental picture of her clear blue eyes, luscious skin, and long hair—and how her beautiful ethnic clothes drape her body. I've always thought Suzanne was a turn-on. And I've always put a wall up because of my connection with Chet. Right now she's tantalizing me.

She says, "Keep me company. We'll have a couple of tequila shooters, smoke a joint—"

I pull back. Stand-up straight. There's an internal rebellion against my initial impulse to be pulled in by Suzanne's come-on. "Think it's a good idea?"

"Let's make it a good idea."

I don't think she gets I'll be the same disappointing guy just like Chet. And I don't want to mess-her-up like I messed-up Kate. "Haven't you figured out yet I'm a version of Chet?"

"You're not like Chet."

"You're right, I'm not like Chet. And I'm just like Chet."

"Oh, come on. Look, you lost Kate. I lost Chet. Just one-time—only once. Keep me company, Memo."

"You're never going to get Chet back, are you?"

"No. He'll never be back. He's a goner."

I want to go for what Suzanne is dangling in front of me, but it would be a betrayal of my buddy, Chet. It doesn't matter they aren't together—too messy. "You're a stunning woman. I'd love to keep you company for a night. Give you a good run. Could be torrid. Nobody else would know." I'll let Suzanne know how delicious she is. She has to be sensitive and insecure after the break-up. I can't hurt her—let her down softly. "You'd know. I'd know. Maybe you'd want me again. I'd want you again. Don't you think? It's not going to fit for us."

"Maybe too soon? How about a rain check?"

"A rain check?" I wonder if she didn't understand I was saying no. "Suzanne?"

"Yes?"

"Take care of yourself."

"Okay. I'm trying. It's a rain check, right?"

"Don't count on me. But you can count on you being beautiful, because you are beautiful."

"I love you, Memo."

"I love you, too. It's a tricky time, isn't it?"

Suzanne and I say goodbye.

I look at the blank wall. Think about the conversation. What stands out: Kate's gone. I close my eyes. And hear a line from a Gordon Lightfoot song about not being free, *As long as I'm a ghost that you can't see.* Kate's a permanent imprint—my mind forever changed by our chemistry.

Suzanne put the test to my vulnerable loneliness. Suzanne sensed it—easy because she clearly feels the same. My loneliness is the residue of my Kate-caused fear of being attached to someone else. I'm guarding myself from another loss by staying away from commitment. The binding cohesion of Teflon with some of the coeds at USC is about all I can handle.

I've been allured by a few brief encounters with women in the graduate program at USC. They were free of the inherent sticky entanglement of hooking-up with a buddy's ex. The intimacy was like putting the accelerator to the floor to burn out the carbon in the system. Nothing more. It was the same for the women. The sexual revolution's lack of prudish excess is well-timed. I'm still lonely.

I sit at the picture window. Look across a tranquil morning sea. Shadow Facts is at my feet. I drift into a daydream.

I'm unmoored which is a desolate feel. Lupita is an automatic thought. I think about finally writing to her.

I imagine her receiving the letter. She opens it with an exquisitely crafted silver letter opener. She is a vision. She stands at the French doors in her home in La Paz, overlooking the Sea of Cortez. Lupita reads the letter—lost in the thought of the moment and other moments.

Lupita is a recast of Vermeer's *Woman in Blue Reading a Letter*. She's pregnant. Her contemplation takes on a poignant inner tension, a fusion of eternalness and anticipation. Her head is slightly downcast, her lips faintly parted, and her breath quickened.

The vision, like the work painted more than three hundred years earlier: there is an empty chair next to her, waiting to be filled by her missing lover. A map on the wall allows her to imagine where he is. She wonders why she is not surprised to receive my letter. She asks herself why it has taken so long for me to write it.

Her mind is saturated with every pen stroke. She remembers every word verbatim. The letter animates rich colorful inner images. She looks out the two French doors, leading to the balcony, which overlooks a simmering, calm morning sea. One door is open.

Lupita looks at her reflection in the panes of the closed door. She studies her image. Her face is absent. An interior voice asks, what have you become? Who are you? Her eyes shift to the vista through the open door and the distant eastern horizon of the Sea of Cortez.

She strikes a match to the paper. The letter is another blaze in her consciousness, and a secret.

What a thunderstruck fantasy's vision fills my mind's eye.

My telephone rings. I jump. "Jesus!" The startling sound is a screeching siren that wrenches me out of my inventive daydream. Shadow Facts jerks her head up, peels her eyes and turns her head towards the telephone.

"Hello."

"Memo?"

"Hi Chet."

"My new girlfriend—Andrea—said she was going to call you. Suzanne gave her your number. I said fuck no. I'll call you myself."

I'm annoyed. Suzanne was so intent on putting the hot squeeze on me she spaced-out telling me about giving Andrea my telephone number. "Your girlfriend's name is Andrea? Okay. Why'd Suzanne give her my number?"

"Beats the shit out of me." The phone number exchange between the women is key, and Chet can't be that clueless.

I stand-up. Blink twice. The sun breaks through the overcast sky. I look out the window at the blinding late afternoon glare on the ocean. I squint from the brightness. I'm gripping the receiver—squeezing it. I feel its pressure against my ear. "What's happened?"

"My father called. He wants to hook up with me."

I hate Chet's father—Mr. Peller—despite hardly knowing him. Chet let me know bits and pieces when we were chums in high school. Enough is known. One thing is for sure. The man is an asshole. And he's an abuser. Peller physically and emotionally abused Chet and Chet's sister and Chet's sweet adorable mother. He terrorized the family in his drunken tirades, followed by abandoning them and leaving them in a penniless and emotionally weak position. "I hope you'll stay away from him. I could annihilate that worthless piece of shit for the way he abused and abandoned you and your family."

"Well, I can't stay away from him. I think he's changed. I may be nutso, but when he called I felt like a kid again. Maybe he can be my dad now." Chet's voice has a twisted whimpering sound. "I want to let him in."

I think Chet isn't shaping up the evidence about what he's getting into. "Oh-my-God, then what?"

"I hope for—"

It's confirmed he's checked-out in the judgment department. "No Chet." I see Chet disheveled and drunk and sprawled on his chase lounge with his medals pinned to his pajamas. "Letting him in right now—or ever—is too chancy."

"He's coming over tonight." Chet's voice has the suppressed sniveling sound of injured seven year-old.

"Cancel it." I'm emphatic.

"I can't." He stiffens-up. "Andrea will be here. It'll be okay." There's pleading in his voice.

I remember Chet telling me the horrid details of his father beating him in a drunken rage. "It won't be okay. It'll never be okay. He was physically cruel to you and then disposed of you." I pace back and forth as far as the telephone cord will reach. "I'll come over. When's he coming?"

"A couple of hours."

I'm on a mission to protect my buddy. I arrive at Chet's place. He has the expected telltale smell of bourbon on his breath.

Andrea is attractive. She looks like a brunette version of Suzanne. Clinging jeans on her well-formed figure makes it impossible for any man to escape a second look.

We wait.

Chet's father turns up an hour past due. Mr. Peller is in his late fifties—looks older. His family's original name was Pellegrini, but there was a surname modification at Ellis Island Immigration Station. His shirtsleeves are rolled up—the front unbuttoned which shows a heavy gold chain. There's liquor on his breath. I remember he changed jobs once a year after his used car lot business went bankrupt. Chet got his good looks, appeal, and being lovable from his mom.

Peller has a bimbo-looking bubble-haired blonde woman in tow who is in her late forties—ridiculously old to be wearing a micro-miniskirt and pink patent leather boots up to her knees. She delineates what it means to be cheap. I don't catch her name.

"Hey, Chet, what have you got to drink?" is the first thing Peller says when he enters the house.

"Bourbon and beer." Chet gets a glass. He pours a couple of shots, nervously spilling some of the bourbon on the counter. He lifts his knee and wipes off the bottom of the glass on his jeans and hands the glass to his father. Chet is visibly shaky. He's perceptibly scared shitless. His face is uptight and has an overwrought look. His little kid innocence was stolen years ago by the brutal thievery of his father. Chet is delusional if he thinks having a new relationship with his father is going to work. Cruel people are recalcitrant to change. It's patent Peller isn't an exception. It's an easy guess Chet feels abused again simply by Peller's presence. Chet winces and winces again, like a movie rerun in his mind that only he can see of his father's past abuse.

The best I can do is make sure Peller doesn't pull something.

Peller takes a swig. He looks at Andrea. "And what have we got here?"

"I'm Andrea."

"The Peller men know how to pick 'em." He grinds out a deep dumb sounding laugh. "So what you been up to Chet?" Peller says while he is still looking at Andrea.

The mini-skirted woman flits about the room.

"Not much." Chet's lips hardly move. His body is stiff.

Chet's father says nothing to me. He's worthless and disgusting mixed with haughty dismissive arrogance.

I initiate small talk. "It's been awhile." I try to be neutral. "I'm Chet's buddy, Memo Muir." I take a breath. "And how have you been, sir?"

Peller starts on an unintelligible discourse about a new business venture, too muddled and confusing to understand. He abruptly stops. Peller suddenly shoots his hand holding his glass towards Chet.

Chet flinches. He looks like a little boy who is about to beaten.

"Give me another drink." Peller snarls repugnantly.

Chet cowers. He's visibly shaken. And his hand wobbles when he pours one more drink for his ape shit excuse for a father.

Peller migrates in the direction of Andrea. He puts his arm on her shoulder, balancing himself on one foot, while making a figure four with his other leg. Peller is insensible to the strain he is putting on her shoulder—not being able to distinguish humanly unreceptive from leaning on a piece of furniture.

I notice Peller's sidekick girlfriend examining Chet's furnishings like she's an antique appraiser.

Andrea says, "You're hurting me."

Peller doesn't move. He grunts out a misguided laugh.

Chet's lips move. His vocal cords are frozen.

I wait for Chet to say something.

He's in a state of paralysis. And then he has a vaporous ghostly look. He's two superimposed images of a crumpled man and an abused boy.

I stridently object. "Andrea delicately mentioned you are hurting her. That's clearly a request for you to take your arm off her shoulder." I stand at attention. My eyes bear down on Peller. My body radiates heat to my fists.

Peller steps back from Andrea. He downs what's in his glass. "Chet, get me another drink," he huffs.

Chet shrinks. He handles the bottle of Jack Daniels—splashes some liquor in his father's glass.

Peller looks around the room. "Nice place, Chet. Real nice. Say, how ya fixed?"

Andrea reacts, "He's fixed well enough." She shields Chet from the question.

Peller can't piece together that Andrea finds him repulsive. "And what's that mean, you nice tall glass of cool water?" Peller wiggles his head. He's flirty. Not an appealing flirtation, but the coquetry of a baggy-eyed middle aged egotistical failure that has the charm of a stinging jellyfish.

Andrea winces. And then she heats-up, "That's all you need—"

Peller interrupts, "Where's the little boy's room?"

She points down the hallway.

He leaves.

Andrea goes to Chet. She cradles his chin in her cupped hand and looks into his disappearing eyes. She hugs him.

Peller comes back to the room. "Yep, job well done."

If I was prone to vomiting this would be the time I'd do it. Who gives a shit whether he does a good job at urinating and watching his bodily fluids swirl down the toilet bowl.

Andrea is still facing Chet with her back towards Peller. Peller comes near Andrea and slides his hand down her butt, starting from her waist to her thigh.

The mindless bubbled-hair girlfriend doesn't react.

"That's it! Leave. Get out." Andrea's face flashes crimson red. The veins in her neck are on the verge of exploding.

"You sure get stirred up easy." He shakes his head from side-to-side, slighting Andrea. "Besides, I've got some things to take up with Chet."

I backup Andrea, "She asked you to take off."

"Who the hell are you to tell me what to do?" Dagger looks.

"You abused Chet when he was a kid, then abandoned him and his mother. What is it—twenty years later you arrive on the scene? And show up with your pink clad blonde girlfriend. The first thing you can say is to ask for a drink. Next is scoping out Chet's wealth with the implication of extracting money from him for some new scheme of yours. This is crowned by leaning on Andrea like she is an inanimate object, followed by hitting on her." I take a couple of flared nostril breaths. "I am supporting Andrea's second request, which is for you to leave. Right now I am a pussycat. But please gather-up your slimy self, along with your short-skirted girlfriend and walk through the door." I clear my throat. "And Peller, don't call Chet and don't come back."

"Chet can speak for himself. Besides, this is his place."

"Peller, look at Chet. Right now he can't tell the difference between whether he is actually standing in this room, or if he is a kid who has just been beaten by his father."

Peller jacks his jaws. No words come out.

I glance at Chet. He's reverted to a defenseless four year-old.

I grimace and take a step toward Peller. Both my hands are clinched into fists.

The girlfriend's eyes open to perfectly round orbs.

Peller puts-up his hands, the palms toward me. "Okay, stop. I'm gone, like right now." His voice is shallow and speedy.

The two run out the door.

Andrea shuts it securely behind them.

We turn our eyes to Chet.

Chet tucks himself in the corner of the sofa. He pulls his knees into his chest. His chin and jaw tremble.

I know Chet has been on a swift downward drift. Now he's plummeted to the depths of incomprehensible deprivation of spirit and has no courage to rally back. He looks destroyed.

"Chet?" My voice is frantic.

He's mute.

"Chet, talk to me." I look to Andrea and say to her, "Help me here." I'm terrified Chet can't express his anger related to his father. Where will his anger go? He's going to absorb his anger—deepen how he hurts himself.

"Chet?" Andrea's voice is soft and loving. But a nervous fear comes through.

Chet's facial muscles ripple under the surface of his skin. He takes a bandana out of his pocket and twists it and twists it tighter. He's in an agitated snarl.

A powerless feeling overwhelms me—powerless to shelter Chet from his father's merciless attack. Peller is one more enemy. I have a flash of having an M-16 or a M1911A1 .45 and tracking down Peller and blowing him away.

Andrea says, "Chet—"

He stands up. Chet moves to the counter. Pours bourbon. All of his agitation turns invisible and dissipates into an eerie vapor.

Andrea and I look at each other. We have shocked and quizzical expressions. We look back at Chet.

Chet looks relaxed, as if he has made a secret decision that made all of his tension dissipate.

Andrea's emotions transmit a pained stare. "I'm on edge."

Chet turns to us. His voice is soft. "Memo, you've helped me enough. I don't need you to lend a hand any more. Thank you." Chet's eyes flicker to Andrea, then back to me. "Let's call it a night."

Somehow, I feel useless. A sensation of guilt penetrates me. I turn to Andrea.

Andrea has a shaky worried voice. "I've got your telephone number, Memo." Having my number pulls her up a tad to give her a sliver of security.

I leave.

It's a dark, quiet ride home. My thoughts are populated by Kate's absence. And Suzanne tantalizing me. And my transient brushes of skin-deep intimacy with the coeds at USC. And the scene's sickness at Chet's place. I feel an opening sensation in my chest—a longing for something pure. And I think of Lupita.

CHAPTER 23

ALL DAY LOVERS

T IME HAS WEIGHED A HEAVY LOAD thinking about Lupita. Now, it is time and I am no longer going to put off having further contact with her, since she glows like a fire in my mind.

July 3, 1971

Dear Lupita,

We have only today.

That's what we said when we met. It was a day that came and went. But it occupies an exquisitely passionate place in my memory. My memory of you—and that day—will last forever.

I write to check on two things. One is your marriage. Did it take place? Are you content? Are you happy?

The other is the lyrics, "And the young bird's eyes do always glow." Has our intense chemistry kept you aglow? Or were the moments we shared simply a transient stop while on a train ride to another destination?

Life changed after I met you. The feeling developed, and now it has a life of its own.

You saw my wedding ring. Five months after our encounter, I finally revealed to my wife what happened between us, which confirmed her suspicions.

She left. She's gone.

Our relationship wore thin because of my military experience and—more important—because once I returned home, I was still gone, emotionally absent. The damage to my relationship had been done before I met you. Our encounter was simply the last punctuation point.

The connection with you brought me back from complete numbness. I've started to feel alive again. In the canyon I was looking for nepenthe. Instead, I found my intoxication in you. I found a different way to begin to traverse the passage from grief and sadness to something better.

So your memory is now a permanent fixture in my mind, which I revisit daily. It's sweet. It's torture.

We have only today?

You might say the only thing we ever have is today.

Are you able to truly live life with unbridled passion, to have freedom and feel release? Or, Lupita, are you still caged and must fly?

Abrazos,

Memo

Signing off with hugs increases my feeling of a lasting touch.

ELEVEN DAYS PASS SINCE I WROTE LUPITA. I contemplate and deliberate and chew over and over whether she received my letter. And what was her reaction? Am I an enduring fantasy or an experience she has thrown away or someone she wants a life with or a muse for her to play with or did I entice her into danger once and now she has to hide or am I tormenting myself with my agony? Maybe I should make an act of contrition, rather than lusting and longing for Lupita. My run-away mind has no restraint, no way of keeping itself in check.

My unconstrained shapelessness is impermanent and braided together by the unifying effects of my beach house sanctuary. The touch of Shadow Facts' back is a concentrated textured feel. And I watch the ocean swells form into waves made thicker by the incoming tide.

I jump each time the telephone rings when I am in this state. "Hello. Muir residence."

"Hello, Memo. Are you glad to hear from me?"

Sweet mother of God. A sensation of euphoria surges to every part of my body. "Glad? Call it elation. It's wonderful to hear your voice."

"I only have a second. This is a very risky telephone call."

"Okay—"

"Can you meet me? It has to be far away."

"Yes. Anyplace. You name it."

"Paris?'

"Definitely."

We fire back and forth for twenty seconds making the arrange-ments.

"I'll see you then, Memo."

"It's hard to believe what just happened."

"I know. And believe it."

I sit in front of the window. The tide pushes in. Waves get thicker and thicker. I stretch myself out on the wooden plank floor. My eyes are wide. All I can do is stare at the ceiling. Shadow Facts licks my face.

I dream lightening will strike twice with Lupita. She has to be unhappy with Alejandro, otherwise why on earth would she meet with me? It's automatic to visualize her and to smell her skin and I can taste her. How will we take another step forward?

SATURDAY, JULY 17, 1971.

I rented a fourth floor apartment on rue des Petits-Champs in arrondissement une, the central district one in Paris. I think how the French divided Saigon into districts—like the arrondissement system in Paris—during their occupation of Vietnam. Private and quiet, the apartment couldn't be more perfect. The owners must be art collectors—nice original paintings, lithographs and antique furniture.

The trip to France and lack of sleep are exhausting. Doesn't matter. Anticipation gives me a sweet-edgy sensation.

Eight-thirty P.M. I arrive at Le Grand Vefour. I enter the restaurant. Her back is towards me. Strapless cocktail dress. She searches for me across the glowingly lit intimate setting. A man with two menus stands in front of her. I touch her shoulder. Her skin feels so sweet. She turns. Lupita is an illumination.

I slip my hand around her waist, delicately pull her towards me.

Our lips meet.

The time between when we met and now disappears.

The kiss is generous enough, and still fitting for where we are. Or maybe it could be more. This is Paris.

We're shown to our table. I see her bare shoulders and her sway as she walks in front of me. Seeing her body's curves and shape spark a dance between my neck and my knees. And Kate flickers in and out of my mind like one frame on an endless piece of celluloid. We're seated. Under the table she takes my hand.

There's a concentration between us. Who can read the menu?

We drink brut as an apéritif. The excitement between us is intimate. Somehow, we order.

"How did you get away?" I say.

"I said I needed to buy a couple of Hermes scarves. Memo, I brought my child and the...*niñera*. I forget. What's that in English?"

A distraction sparks. Her beautiful body defies the fact of giving birth to a child. I pull myself together. "'*Nanny*.' Will we be able to spend time together? Alone together?"

"I'm not expected back for two days. Officially, I'm visiting the cave paintings at Chauvet-Pont-d' Arc." Her smile is sensual power. "And unofficially, I'm with you."

Eating dinner is a waste of time. The first course is ravioles de fois gras with crème foisonnée truffée. My taste buds are somewhere else.

I tell Lupita about all the time I've been alone. She must be able to read the longing in my voice. And I realize my lack of commitment to women makes for aloneness. It's all driven by the memory-caused punishment I feel left over from Kate.

We are halfway through a bottle of 1947 Petrus Pomerol. We laugh. We look at each other seriously.

She squeezes my hand.

I move my hand across her thigh, feeling the consistency of the cocktail dress cloth covering her bare leg.

Her cheeks are flushed.

I nod.

She nods.

"Monsieur, s'il vours plait veuillez demander au maitre d' qu'il vienne a notre table," I ask the waiter.

"You speak French?" asks Lupita.

"Pretend French. It's make-believe. Hopefully it's good enough to get the job done. Put together with some words and grammar I remember from a French class when I was a kid. I really don't have the faintest idea what I'm doing. But it's fun for now, isn't it?"

Lupita laughs.

How can it be she's more beautiful than I remember?

The maître d' comes to our table.

"Veuillez apporter le reste de notre repas à mon appartement?" I ask.

The maître d' looks at me, and then at Lupita, and then back at me. He sees the heat is on.

I asked him to deliver the rest of what we ordered to the apartment. This isn't the type of request you make in Paris—elegant French food takeout.

The maître d' looks as though he feels our temperature rise—agrees to make the delivery. It's not too much of a push—Le Grand Vefour is in the same arrondissement as the apartment.

The cab ride is short. We kiss. Breathing rips the fronts of our bodies.

I start to unzip her dress. Stop. Wait. My hand is shaking with so much urgency I can hardly get the key in the apartment door lock—practically rip our clothes getting them off.

The canyon in Mexico is no match for Paris. She's the same woman, wilder here than in the wilderness. The next three hours are concentrated, extreme, and luscious. Her touch, breath and moist skin drive me to know what pulled me to be here with Lupita. There's the tension of a huge taut thick cable—stretching tighter and tighter and tighter. Neither one of us can hold on any longer. The force goes out of control—snap. We drop. Total exhaustion.

The morning sunlight filters through the high gauze covered windows. Her skin pressed to mine and the smell of her fragrant skin. I catch myself weighing Lupita against Kate. Lupita is exciting. She's here. And I have all my familiarity with Kate and history and inextinguishable caring.

Lupita moistens my ear with her tongue. She delicately blows into it. "Show me last night wasn't just a dream."

We laugh. It happens all over again.

I pour some of the Petrus Pomerol in the cleft between her neck and her shoulder blade.

She can't move.

I lick the vintage wine mixed with the taste of her skin—oh my God. It happens all over again—again.

We bathe. We have *petite déjeuner*—breakfast.

The rest of the day is passionate to tender to passionate. Last night's tension snap turns into today's suppleness. Now we're all day long lovers.

Five P.M. "I think it's time for some Paris sustenance. Do you want to go to the Ritz Bar? Have a drink and hors d'oeuvres?"

"That'd be lovely."

We take a taxi to rue Cambon. We enter the tasteful bar. We're seated. Order martinis.

"Memo, have you wondered about my son, Juan Diego?"

"Juan Diego? Yes. The Christian name of the Amerindian who had the vision of the Virgen de Guadalupe."

"I loved giving him that name." She has a faraway maternal look. "Don't you think it's a beautiful name?"

"Of course." So smitten, right now I'd agree to anything. And it's the truth. "I love the name—smooth and elegant. Timeless."

"Did you do the math?"

"You mean to calculate whether he might be our child?"

"Yes."

"Again and again for split seconds since you told me about him last night. And then I felt it was a possibility because of the force we had when we first met." I take a drink to wet my palate. "In June, before I knew you had a child, I had a daydream, a vision of you. It was Vermeer's *Woman in Blue Reading a Letter.*"

"*Ella está embarazada.*"

"Right. She's pregnant, reading a letter, and waiting for her lover to fill the empty chair. She wonders where he might be. There's a map on the wall. She tries to place him on the map." For an instant the anesthetic effects of love and passion evaporate. "He's not my child, is he?" I'm snapped back by a sliver of rationality that still exists.

"He could be," says Lupita.

"That's a wish. But he's not, is he? My intuition says—"

"You're right. And my intuition is more compelling."

"A mother's intuition about her child is always more compelling than anyone else, isn't it?"

"It is."

The next day Lupita leaves in the late morning. An hour later I meet her at Angélina on rue de Rivoli across from Tuileries Garden near the Musée du Louvre. She brings little Juan Diego.

Being with the child reminds me of Kate's miscarriage. And then I think how Kate wanted to wait until after I returned from war to get pregnant. She wanted the commotion to settle down. It never settled down. She left. We're childless.

Lupita's child is cute. His long black eyelashes almost touch is eyebrows. Juan Diego is wide eyed.

"*Hola chico. ¿Cómo estás?*" I say, knowing he can only register the music of my voice and not the words, saying hello to him and how is he doing.

We enter the restaurant. We're seated. We order Angélina's specialty, *chocolat Africain.*

I glance back and forth at Juan Diego sitting in his bolster chair and at Lupita. A pit in my stomach says I'm in the wrong place. I fight to fit in. I push my chair back from the table. My shoulders drop. I exhale when I think about sitting at the table with another man's son. There's a hollow sensation in my chest. I feel a wedge distance me from Lupita.

The hot chocolate is finished. We go across the street to Tuileries Garden and sit on a park bench.

I want to love Juan Diego. But I can't.

"Lupita, what did you do with my letter?"

"I took in every word, memorized the letter. Then burned it."

"Do you still feel you are in a cage?"

"The cage has doubled. My husband—Alejandro—has imprisoned me like my father."

"And Juan Diego?"

"My child ties me to so much responsibility. But it's strange—an irony—because he also brings me so much freedom—Juan Diego touches me like nothing else. I love him more than anything. He's Alejandro's and mine. But Memo, I feel as though Juan Diego is only mine."

We sit on the park bench. I look at Lupita. Soft skin. Touchable. Beautiful.

"Memo."

"Yes?"

"I have to go."

We stand.

"I want you again. I don't know when," says Lupita.

We glance at Juan Diego.

I touch Lupita's shoulder. I gaze down at her child. *"Hasta pronto, chico. Cuida a tu mama."* One more lingering look in Lupita's eyes. Goodbye.

I walk back to the apartment on rue des Petits-Champs. My hand doesn't shake this time when I put the key in the lock. I enter the room. The bareness of the richly-decorated apartment hits me. The bottle of the vintage 1947 Petrus Pomerol stands on the table like a soldier. Upright, but empty.

I sit in a wood-framed leather armchair facing the tall diaphanous gauze-covered windows. My arms are supported by the chair. My wrists are bent, with spread fingers pointing towards the wooden floor. She's gone. I'm like an old tomcat. The only thing I feel like doing in the most exciting city in the world is go to the Galerie Nationale du Jeu de Paume. It's Monday. It's closed.

The rest of the afternoon I watch the light change in the room. Sunlight to dusk to dark. At midnight I'm alone in bed. Sunlight returns, peeking through the gauzy curtained windows. I am the first one at the Galerie Nationale. I wait for it to open. Finally. I occupy the museum as though I were the only person there. The artistic vibrancy and color and genius of Monet, Manet, Degas, Renoir, Cézanne,

Seurat, Gauguin and Van Gogh saturate this empty soldier. The impressionists' works squeeze into some of the gaps left by Lupita.

Before long I sit in the serene garden refuge of Jardin du Luxembourg a couple of footsteps from the buzz of St-Germain-des-Prés. Scores of people stroll in front of my view. The only persons I'm able to see are couples pushing baby carriages. I slump thinking of my attempt—and misadventure—to steal married Lupita way from her little child. I'm overcome by a feeling of worthlessness and I feel sad, drained of energy and the pleasure I had with Lupita—now alone. The couples and their children pass back and forth.

A retrospection of Lupita forms. How does she match-up with Kate? It's defined by one thing. I still love Kate. And I think of the child Kate and I didn't have.

The dream of taking another step forward in the relationship with Lupita was an illusion that consumed itself by reality. Something else happened. It's what she gave me—a kind of salvaged sensation. I've been numb from war. Lupita helped me feel. But maybe I'm feeling too much.

Something splits open. I become conscious of a massive chasm opening-up. My remaining vexing war memories have a life that controls me because of my inability to avoid what's unavoidable. I'm only partially salvaged. A fear floods that going home will set-me-off to revert to my old primitive jaggedness and being overwhelmed again. That dread immediately triggers the memories—an overpowering driven force—of accumulated undaunted emotion. There's no waiting until I get home. I can't prolong the memories anymore. No more hiding beneath my loosely constructed patchwork shield. I have to relive what happened with Daniels and Gildner and Swiney. And right now.

CHAPTER 24

BLACK SHABU

DANIELS SITS AT HIS DESK.

I'm standing. "Sir, I think Ho Chi Minh wasn't just pushing his balls around in a wheelbarrow when he sounded off about having at least two VC in every hamlet in South Vietnam."

"Don't be afeared, son. We're driving our balls around in a half-track." Daniels's voice sounds like he's gargling gravel. "This brings me to something."

Where I anticipate he's about to take this conversation pushes a fluttering feeling in my chest. "Sir?"

"Lieutenant Colonel Nunnemaker had a little mishap up at the PIC—Provincial Interrogation Center—in Phu Yen Province." Daniels frowns. His whole torso expels a sigh. "We've known he's a lush. How bad though as been a nonstop question mark. But we suspected misinformation had come from his sector. And now the son-of-a-bitch gets drunk and flips his Jeep. Stupid shit. We're pulling him out of the field."

I sense bad news is going to drop on me. I'm going to get screwed. I pace back and forth. "Now what?"

"I have to figure-out where to park 'em. Nunnemaker is a highly decorated officer. But that boy has fallen apart around his drinkin'. I'm bringing him back here. Eye the situation for a couple of weeks. Figure-out a disposition. In the meantime—"

"Is that an order, sir?"

"I haven't said anything yet. Muir, you're turning into a goddamn mind reader." Daniels takes out a pack of cigarettes. Lights-up. "I have a new field grade officer coming in country next week to take command. I hope he doesn't get stalled. Until then, you go to Phu Yen and do intelligence collection. Talk to the acting CO, 1LT Gildner. There'll be a Special Forces unit moving through. Accompany them— check their effectiveness. And I want you to report back the status of the PIC. Right now, I feel like I don't know shit."

The VCI—Viet Cong Infrastructure—is the main problem. The VCI are the tentacles of North Vietnam's war effort. The VC are placed throughout the South and are the North's key weapon and backbone. Phoenix finds the VC bracketed with the North and neutralizes them by whatever means it takes. The methods are bad news. Really vicious bad news. Maybe fighting in a regular combat unit would have been easier. Less guess work. At least some of the time you know who is who if you're lucky enough to see the enemy is wearing field gear and toting weapons. Phoenix is spook-work and intelligence and deception and warlike draconian magic tricks. The folks back home think this whole war is being fought in standard military search and destroy combat units. All the secrecy and security keep the U.S. citizenry from knowing squat about the true deal that's coming down in Nam.

I look through the Plexiglas windows, past the barbed-wire topped wall to the sculptural orange and sanguine-red-colored blooming trees across the street. "Sir, there's a story—sticks in my mind—Steele told me. VC terrorists have their way of controlling hamlets. The terrorists went into a hamlet. There was a pregnant South Vietnamese woman and they dissected her. While she was still alive they pulled out her fetus. Showed it to her. Umbilical cord still attached. All the villagers were watching. And then the VC shot her point-blank in the face."

Daniels takes a drag off this cigarette. "How'd Steele know about that particular one?"

"Pissed off one of the villagers." I look at Daniels in the eye. "The identity of the VC terrorists was given-up to our district intelligence, who put the VC on the black list. And then they were incisively assassinated."

Daniels takes another drag. He blows out a cloud of blue-gray smoke. "That's the way it's supposed to work, son."

"You mean little Vietnamese women being disemboweled?" I have twinges of hating myself when I say something sarcastic. It goes against my style.

"Take a breath, Muir. This war makes you sick, it makes me sick. But we're getting a bead on those mother fucker VC whom are fighting the war underneath the one fought by the combat units out in the field. Our statistics about catching up to those VC bastards are looking good, son."

EARLY THE NEXT DAY I TAKE OFF from Ton Son Nhut Air Base in a fixed-wing, Twin Beach aircraft; a flight to go three hundred klicks—kilometers—northeast to Phu Yen. I look down. Pockets of land form an early morning moonscape where the first sunlight casts ghostlike shadows across the craters left from B-52s bombings. I remember the same landscape pockmarks from my flight with Walter.

A man from the Vietnamese National Police picks me up at the Phu Yen landing field. It's a silent three-kilometer ride to the interrogation center. The PIC is a sinister-looking place. For security the vegetation on all sides of the walled compound is denuded. It's a stark, wide, open space. We pass through the next level of security—towering olive-drab steel-plated gates. Four cinderblock-like buildings with corrugated metal roofs are configured around a courtyard. A tower is strategically placed in the interior of the PIC, giving guards a three-hundred-and-sixty degree observation and shooting range.

First Lieutenant Gildner receives me. He's tall, thin, wearing fatigues rumpled from the humidity. We go to an office at the interrogation center. Gildner is buried under a broad-brimmed boonie hat. The black-green walls give the dim room an awful tint of dread. He keeps his hat on.

"We lovingly call this room *Shades of Green*," says Gildner.

"Okay, I'll bite," I say.

"Yeah, because this place is a different kind of military operation. It's not military olive-drab. It's a different shade of green."

I hear shouting in Vietnamese. And then I hear a scream through the wall that grinds on my eardrums. "Jesus. What in the name of God—"

"You got the stomach for it?"

"I'm over throwing-up."

"Okay Captain, come on. I'll show you."

Gildner takes me to a cement-floored room where an interrogation is taking place. There is a blindfolded VC, strapped to a chair. An electrical cord is taped to his back. The interrogators light-up the gook's back each time he resists answering. He jerks and quivers when the interrogators hit the juice. I notice another separate electrical cord leading to the VC's genitals—must be the next measure. "Our guys got the idea from what the bastards are doing to our troops in the POW camps," says Gildner. "One bad turn deserves another. Mother fuckers."

Gildner's bitterness is palpable. And there is an ache covered over by a deadened feeling, covered over by something else I'm trying to put my finger on. Gildner's pupils are pinpoint to the degree that they almost look nonexistent.

We return to the office and sit at a rectangular wooden table with four chairs. I fumble, trying to pull myself together. "How—how long have you been here?"

"Too fuckin' long. That's how long. You have to find a way to carry on." Gildner's face looks labored. His skin has a mushy look, loosely stretched over sharp cheekbones. "Daniels wants you to go with the Special Forces guys? You're kidding, right? Not a good plan."

I knew I was screwed coming up here. Gildner just evaporated any doubt. "You make it sound like a stupid idea."

"Pardon my sarcasm. But yes, stupid begins to define it. Look, those guys only do the most dangerous and scariest shit in this fucking war. I don't know what those guys are made of, but I'll tell you what, back stateside they'd be a menace to society."

I try to shut it out of my mind. "Let's get back to the intelligence."

"Sure, but I'll fill you in on a few things first. Captain Swiney and his Special Forces guys are bringing in a couple of captives. They'll stick around for two shakes to clean their weapons and get supplies. And then they're taking off in the morning for a hamlet we have found to contain two VC who are masterminding some hideous strategic operations." Gildner nods. "You're going with them? Yeah, then you're going with them tomorrow. And you're going early because there's a lot territory to cover to get to the hamlet. So, you'll be front and center—take off with them for all of their heinous sports in the field."

"We're going to use a chopper?"

"Part of the way. Then you'll be humping the rest of the distance—about thirty klicks. Using choppers for the final assault is not their style. When they move in, they move in quietly. Choppers obviously make one hell of a racket."

"How extreme are they?"

"One a scale from one to ten—about twenty-five. Swiney and his men are fuckin' animals."

Another yelping cry comes from somewhere in the building. I sit-up straight. My back is rigid and cold.

"What's going on?" I say.

"You don't want to know."

"I do. That's affirmative. Show me."

Gildner takes me to another of the interrogation rooms. It's windowless. One glaring light bulb hangs from the ceiling. There are three, fiery–eyed, fiendish looking, South Vietnamese interrogators standing around a naked VC captive, body and legs tied-up, sitting in a chair. There's a dead VC propped-up against the wall in direct view and in front of the captive. A bloody hammer is on the floor. Two toes on each foot of the captive are smashed. One of the interrogators has a revolver pointed at the captive's genitals. They're screaming at him. He cries tears mixed with blood on his purplish-brown, distended face. The interrogator pulls back the hammer on the pistol—CLICK. The prisoner yelps.

"Seen enough, Captain?"

"Yeah. Enough."

We return back to the office, Shades of Green.

Waiting for us is the scariest man I have ever met. He stands.

"Captain Muir, this is Captain Swiney," says Gildner.

We sit at the long Shades of Green table.

I feel a peculiar and unexpected combination of stunned, sacred and morbid curiosity meeting this soldier. I'm dwarfed by physical power, despite the fact he is my height. He looks to weigh two-hundred-and-twenty pounds and has a size thirty waist. The sleeves are cut off his fatigue shirt, and an open front shows his thick tanned biceps and deltoids and immense pectoral muscles. His heavy brow rides over deeply recessed eyes. There is nothing about this guy that says Government Issue, except one thing. He's Special Forces.

"I understand we're under orders to have you accompany us, Captain Muir. This is—irregular. You see, the men and I have an understanding." Swiney's stare is enough to push me back—like I'm fused with the chair. "We operate as a highly cohesive unit. That level of organization is based on a discerning comprehension of our mission." He nods. Swiney's movement looks mechanical.

"Yes, cohesiveness to get the mission done. I see, Captain Swiney." I'm immediately self-conscious that my voice is two octaves higher than deep-voiced Swiney. I think his voice stings of an underlying predominant pattern of the darkest shades of sinister.

Swiney stands. "Enough for now. Be in the PIC compound area at 0600 hours tomorrow." He leaves. Swiney pulls the door closed behind him. The precision way he ominously snaps the door latch shut has a specter-like edge.

I look at Gildner. I get up. Go over to the window and look down at the dirt and vacant wall. Suddenly, there is a downpour that turns the red earth into soupy scarlet mud. The metal roof sounds like it is being pelted with rocks.

I turn. "I know what you mean about you have to find a way to carry on." Now it comes together. Gildner's ache and stinging pain are anesthetized by a wash of dope, the type that makes his pupils opiate-collapsed pinpoints. "You got some more of the shit you're taking?"

"Part of the report to Daniels?"

"No."

"Sure. It's primo. I'll turn you on to some."

"How do you fix it?"

"Pour a beer with a good head. Sprinkle a bunch on top. And then suck in the foam, and baby look-out."

"Don't you nod-out?"

"Not me. Gives me energy. But you'll probably nod-out. Usual reaction."

Opiates are Gildner's abortive stab at surviving the PIC messiness. "I'll pass. Not into nodding-out." I pause. "Are Swiney and his men into this stuff?"

"Not at all. But they do have some pharmacological enhancements to cue-them-up to give them a strategic edge. Maybe you'll find out about it."

"Fuck this. Let's have a few beers."

"You bet. Let's go to my private officer's club. You'll be relieved to know that the screaming can't be heard there."

Gildner is the acting CO who runs this operation—competent enough on the surface—in disarray underneath his overcooked exterior. I hope he cleans-up off drugs when he gets home.

I MEET SWINEY IN THE MORNING.

Swiney continues yesterday's conversation like there is a two-second break to take one breath. No hello. No good morning. There's only his exclusive language of his elite group. "There are certain elements which allow us to get the mission done. Those elements may be beyond causal observation and subject to misinterpretation to someone naïve as to how we conduct ourselves."

"I'm a quick study. I'll try not to fuck-things-up by tagging along." I smile graciously. I think I have backbone, but right now I feel like a timid skinny kid.

Swiney is lightly staffed. His troop is the size of a squad. Eleven men, plus Swiney, a radio operator and an interpreter. Three of his NCOs overhear our conversation.

Everyone under his command looks to have approximately the same body type. Different faces. Differently colored skin. Different ethnic origins. But all the same tough mother fuckers. And scary looking. They're all wearing self-styled uniforms like decorations, which have taken form from a countless amount of time surviving in the bush. And all modified Government Issue. Flak vests decked-out with grenades, incendiary devices, flares, ammo. A couple of men have M-60 machineguns.

Swiney introduces the men who are listening in on our exchange. "This is Eagle Shit, Fuckemup and Dozer."

From the looks of these men all those names had to be well-earned.

Eagle Shit gives me a fake smile.

Fuckemup has the longest arms I have ever seen. His knuckles practically touch his knees. He grunts.

Dozer has a funny way of making, "Howdy, sir," sound hostile. Dozer's lack of charm extends to his nose which is pushed in and nearly flat on his face, like a door had been slammed squarely on the front side of his head.

I imagine how Swiney and this trio would socialize at one of my mother's high society cocktail parties. Hello, I would like to introduce you to Eagle Shit, Fuckemup and Dozer. And to one of the dames, I say this is Captain Swiney. I can't tell you anything about him because it's clandestine and classified. But I can assure you it's stealthy and exquisitely nasty.

Swiney snaps me back. "Captain, we are going to move-out in five minutes. You do have your gear together, don't you?"

"Affirmative. I'm ready to move-out in half a second."

The Huey chopper takes us to a place between Qui Nhon and Nha Trang. We march ten klicks along rice paddies and enter the Tuy Hoa Valley. There's dense tropical forestation and rocky terrain creeping up the hillside. The tall trees produce a thick canopy that stops the sunlight from reaching the forest floor. There's a vulnerable feel. Apprehension shudders through my body. What would we do if there was an alpha bravo—an ambush—or if we came across a NVA regiment or—

"You're kinda quiet there, Muir," says Swiney.

"How do you survive if you come across Charlie out here? I mean, you basically just have a squad."

"That's the operative word."

"Swiney?"

"Survive, Muir, survive. I haven't lost one of my troops. That's an affirmative. You see these boys out here? They are highly trained. They don't think. They don't have to. They act. And they act so funkin' fast you don't see what happened. Those motherfunkin' gooks don't have a chance."

"They're the rebar of the Phoenix Program?"

"They are the rebar, the cement, the walls, the roof and the fuckin' doors that swing in and out and in any direction you want. Muir, if these guys didn't have a weapon, they'd have no problem killing the enemy with their index finger and thumb."

"I could kill the enemy with my index finger and thumb. Like sipping duck soup."

"No shit, Muir. And I took you for a pussy."

I snap back, "Swiney, I am a pussy. And please, Captain, never forget I am a total pussy. But, I can still kill the enemy with whatever means are needed at any given time. Daniels trusts me, and there is a reason he sent me out here. I know your distinguished track record. Your troops survive. Your troops are elite."

"I'm going to tell you, Muir. We're elite. And we have enhancements."

I think of Gildner putting the pharmacological bit in the picture. "Enhancements?"

"You want to talk some more?"

"I'm piqued."

"The higher-ups know our results. But they have no fucking idea what we use to get the job done. They want outcomes. They don't give a rat's ass about the means."

"No shit?"

"*Black Shabu.*"

We're walking two abreast on a narrow trail though the valley. The forest becomes more solidly vegetated and opaque; the mountains on both sides become abrupt. Who's out there? There's always tension. Walking the minefields in your head keeps you alert, if there is something there or not. Never relaxed, or you're stupid.

"What the fuck is Black Shabu?"

"Combat medicine. The Japs used it in WWII—Philopon—all the kamikaze pilots were pumped on it when they made their suicide attacks on our naval vessels. The German troops in Europe took the shit for endurance. Fuck, even Hitler's doc shot him up with Pervitin four or five times a day—took too much of the shit—made him a wired-up paranoid sex maniac, and it's all the same fucking thing. Just different names for the stuff. What's good for the goose is good for the gander. But we have tweaked it just right. Some of our flyboys use a touch of it on long distance recon runs."

"Yeah, and—"

"Hold up, there. Our shit is really exotic shit. Black Shabu is a fusion Philopon from Japan with kratom from Thailand. Got the right balance. You get a little narc-ed on the stuff, but mostly stimulated. Exceedingly stimulated. My guys are so enthusiastic, no shit they get the job done."

"All right. Roger that. Enhancements."

"You want to take some before we hit the village?"

"You're taking some?"

"How silky is mama-san's skin?"

"Silky, like milky smooth."

"Okay, then, you're on?"

"I'm on. I'll try some of your exotic shit."

"Sir!" whispers Eagle Shit. Our forward observer is Fuckemup. "Fuckemup is signaling us. There's a NVA company movin' south."

"Easy evasive maneuver," says Swiney.

He moves our unit into the bush. We disappear and watch the NVA company move through. My heart throbs in my ear like a throbbing kettledrum. They're gone. My breath is slower and deeper. "Jesus."

"Except for the VC we captured and took to the interrogation center, we haven't seen any enemy troops in a week. Maybe two." Swiney blurts-out. "Shit, it's been getting a little boring."

"I was afraid they could hear my heartbeat." I know that's a bogus remark and I smirk, I look at Swiney. "What about you?"

"Blood pressure's too fuckin' low. Need a jumpstart now and then." He surveys the troops. Signals them to move out.

Five klicks from the hamlet we move into a covered area and assemble. Swiney takes a metal shaving mirror out of his pack. He sharpens his bayonet. He then removes a grenade from his vest, unscrews the top and taps out white power onto the metal mirror. Swiney uses his razor-sharp bayonet to chop-out thirteen fat lines of Black Shabu. The radioman and interpreter are out of the count.

Swiney unscrews a ballpoint pen and hands the bottom portion to Eagle Shit. He uses it to snort the Black Shabu. His eyes immediately dilate to almost totally eclipse their green color. In a couple of minutes he starts acting twitchy, really twitchy and talking a lot. One by one, the other troops snort the white powder.

There're two lines left. Swiney hands me the tube.

Being twitchy and wired out here with Charlie is sounding like a bad idea. I decide to pass. "A strong cup of coffee, maybe two, is as stimulated as I want to get."

Swiney takes a line.

Dozer snorts my line, making it number two for him.

Swiney and Dozer become animated like Eagle Shit. Any fatigue from marching twenty-five klicks is replaced by energetic bliss. A few of the men disassemble and reassemble their field packs. Five GIs break-down their weapons and put them back together. The men get caught-up in every detail of their gear. Swiney has to herd the troops to get them to head out.

We approach the village. There's a Vietnamese farmer working a rice paddy on the outskirts of the hamlet. Eagle Shit and Fuckemup capture the man and bring him to a secure location where Swiney works with the interpreter to interrogate the farmer. The farmer takes short rapid breaths, and he's trembling uncontrollably. Swiney doesn't need much interrogation to determine this guy isn't a VC.

Swiney takes a set of black silk pajamas and a hood out of his pack. He makes the Vietnamese farmer strip and pull on pajamas and hood. The hood has cutouts for the man's eyes so he can see. One of the Special Forces GIs whispers to me the strategy is to disguise him so he's more willing to give-up the VC in the village.

There's a lot of information fired back and forth through the interpreter. The farmer says there're two VC hooches in the village.

Swiney tells him to nod when we pass the VC thatched huts. Swiney takes out his pistol, "You understand Papa-San?"

No interpreter needed. His hooded head jerks up and down.

We form a perimeter around the village. Half of us move across a levy and around a hedgerow into the hamlet. The rest of the troops stay in the bush, and then move in and regroup.

The villagers race through the dirt pathways. Crying mama-sans collect their dazed baby-sans. A flurry. Commotion everywhere. Piglets with corkscrew tails squeal.

Half the unit fans out. The rest of us march though the village. Swiney's powerful hand holds the framer's upper arm. We pass by several hooches. Finally, the farmer nods. We go by two more thatched huts. And then another nod. Swiney makes a hushed whistle, which vaguely sounds like some kind of nonexistent bird. His men catch the signal.

The unit reassembles into two groups. Swiney motions to the two VC hooches. Each group stands in front of a VC hooch for three seconds, and then two soldiers storm the thatched hut, followed by a flood of automatic weapon fire. The soldiers come back into view. Grenades are thrown into the hooches.

I think, sweet Jesus, mother of mercy.

They torch the huts.

I think it's the end. There's more.

Out of the corner of my eye I catch Dozer going into a hooch. I say to some nameless GI next to me, "What the fuck is he doing?"

"Just let him be, sir."

A second later I hear a woman screaming. I move towards the hooch. The GI grabs my arm, "Like I said, just let him be, sir."

I look back at him. I give him a death look. "Get your fuckin' hand off me." I shake him loose.

I enter the hooch. There's a girl—looks to be thirteen-years-old—whose been done, throat slit. All I see is Dozer's pants down and naked butt. He's on top of a mama-san. "Get the fuck off her, Dozer."

"Fuck you, sir."

All I can see are his butt muscles contract and release. I grab him by the top of his flak vest. I pull him off.

He struggles. Stands-up. "I'll kill you, you asshole."

"You've got who's going to kill who all wrong."

I punch Dozer in the solar plexus. All the air is expelled from his lungs makes a gasping sound. He doubles over. He's standing, and his head is on his knees. I hear the zinging sound tearing through the hooch. I holler, "What the hell is going on?"

At first I think it's the nameless GI firing on us. And then I hear Swiney barking orders. We're under enemy fire.

He's battlefield precise. Swiney yells our coordinates into the radio.

I come out of the hooch. The NVA company must have gotten intelligence of our location and doubled back. I see a couple of NVA soldiers in the rice paddy and don't understand why they've exposed themselves. I'm not too combat experienced. One thing I know. If something doesn't seem right, you're screwed. They must be some kind of sacrificial lambs. More are coming across the levy and behind the hedgerow.

The two Special Forces men with the M-60s start ripping. Hundreds of casings fly. They concentrate on the artery of our vulnerability—the levy. The barrels of their weapons start to glow from the heat of the relentless fire. They take out a complete squad. The ones in the rice paddy drop.

My heart is hammering, adrenal glands spurting all over the place. I have to concentrate. In single-shot mode I bring down two NVA soldiers.

We hold them off for twenty minutes, and Swiney orders the unit to retreat.

Dozer flashes in my mind while we move out of the village—his bare-ass-white butt.

The Special Forces troops begin to take cover in the bush at the same moment the enemy flank us. "How the fuck did they get positioned so fast? Damn it," shouts Swiney. What didn't seem right, now makes sense—an attempt to suck us in, with the strategy to surround us. Escape and evasion isn't possible. But our troops are two-hundred percent committed to lighting up the enemy. The Special Forces troops unremittingly expel countless rounds onto the enemy's holding zone.

I kill one more NVA soldier. And then another. The action is blurry fast. I can't tell. Maybe I took another down. I lose track of what is happening. Everything becomes a shadowy smeared impression, like a smudge across my consciousness. Troops on the left and right are either blasting in auto, or firing in single shot on clear-cut targets.

Our troops are about to be overrun. A sudden muscular burst of choppers from an AHC—assault helicopter company—swarms over the horizon's translucent cerulean blue sky. Must have been next door. Or maybe Swiney had them on tap. He's squawking over the radio to the AHC commander.

I thank somebody, and I don't know who. God, maybe.

The choppers are blasting the NVA who have flanked us. There's a perfect LZ for the Hueys to put down. Troops pour out. Heavy action and enemy moralities. The NVA retreat.

I hear one of the GIs from the AHC. Crying in agonizing pain. I go in his direction—into the bush. His buddies are uselessly trying to help him. A black kid with his front side blown open. I know he's gone. "Where's the medic?"

"He's on the other side, sir," one of the GI's buddies snaps back.

I think dead man's carry. No, all the organs in his cavity will spill-out—fall all over. I take my poncho out of my pack. "Let's get him to the chopper. We'll use the poncho as a stretcher."

His terrified buddies look up at me. One says, "Sir?" They look at each other and back down at their buddy, the black kid. "Thank you sir." Their hands are bloody.

One buddy and I pull the kid up onto the makeshift poncho stretcher and we head towards the nearest Huey and dump him inside. He's not dead yet. There's terror in his eyes. And then there's a brighter look.

I say, "Are you in pain, soldier?"

"Not now, sir. Will I get a CIB?"

"I'll see that you get a Combat Infantry Badge, soldier."

He tells me he wants to go home and see his family. "I'm going to get you home, troop." He fades. I look at him with remorse, but it's what I expected and then he jerks a couple of times before the end.

Through the sound of the whirl of Huey chopper blades I hear Swiney's voice. I can't make out what he's saying.

Dozer and he and a couple other men from the unit jump in the Huey, along with numerous rescue troops. The crew chief yells for us to take off. We lift up while the Huey's door gunner blasts at the NVA on the ground. There's a pinging sound as enemy rounds hit the armored underbelly of the chopper.

Dozer looks straight ahead.

"Dozer, you're a sick fuckin' asshole," I say.

I report to Swiney, "Dozer did a teenage Vietnamese girl and raped a mama-san."

"Well this whole mess was a bum fuck operation—a piece a toilet paper that disintegrated because someone pissed on it. Not the way the Phoenix Program is supposed to work. Dozer? Yeah, that was bad shit. But Muir, bad shit happens all the time, so get past it. Dozer knows how to do his job."

I feel like pushing Dozer and Swiney out of the chopper. "And the men just wasted the VC without trying to take them captive, get intelligence off them."

"The boys got a little too excited today. That Black Shabu was particularly good shit." Swiney straightens-up and inflates his chest. "And they blew away their families, too. Besides, those VC won't be around to hatch anymore of that evil shit. Fuck 'em. Grow-up, Muir."

"Lose any of your troops?"

"Still batting a thousand."

I LEAVE JARDIN DU LUXEMBOURG and make my way to the fourth floor Paris apartment on rue des Petits-Champs in arrondissement une. The room has a vacuous emptiness, filled with the smell of Lupita. I return to the wood-framed leather armchair facing the tall diaphanous gauze-covered windows. All I see are Swiney's eyes which are so dilated and recessed into his skull they look like two black bottomless holes. And I hear the specter-like precision click of the door closing behind him.

CHAPTER 25

THE LAST SUMMONS

1600 hours, Thursday, July 29, 1971

THE MEMORIES OF WALTER AND DANIELS and Gildner and Swiney and the black kid and Baby-San and Mama-San are an everlasting force. I'm a damaged guy piecing myself together—and what's the glue? No more hiding-out to avoid emotions that will overpower me in the end. But the truth is I don't face every detail of war and its minutiae because it would be too staggering and would inundate me. I settle for the big stuff. Items and their fine elements will surface sometime, and who knows when, like a surprise.

AT A PHONE BOOTH HEADING SOUTH on the coast highway. "Hello, Chet."

"Hi, Memo."

"I've been up at the university, on my way home. Listen, I'm in the neighborhood. May I drop by?"

"Yeah, I just got home."

I arrive at Chet's house. He looks as though he's just stepped out of a post-work, get-the-grim-off shower.

"Good to see you, Chet."

"How was the drive down from USC? You want a drink?"

"The drive? Okay. A drink? I'd like some iced tea."

The day is hot and dry. We go into the kitchen. "Sure you want iced tea? How about a beer?"

"Yeah, but let's hold off. There are a couple of things I'd like to chat about. Drinking won't mix."

"How long?"

"Few minutes."

Chet pours us both iced tea. We go out on his back porch. We sit on comfortably cushioned, old wicker chairs. His backyard is beautifully kept. The garden is lush. Beads of sweat trickle down the sides of the iced tea glasses.

"I like Andrea. She must be a good soul." I take a drink of the cool iced tea. "Tell me, how's it going with Suzanne?"

"It's tough with Suzanne. We've started the divorce." Chet has a dour look. "She's really putting a tight squeeze on me. And she's the one from the family with money."

"In different ways, we fucked over the women of our past." A nod and frown concedes to our mutual destructiveness.

"It wasn't deliberate." Chet's voice has a halting quality. "Suzanne was into the fun party times when we got together. Then she changed the rules."

Rules change by circumstances changing. "Yeah."

"So, why'd you come by?"

"To help. But all of a sudden I feel like shit."

"I know the feeling."

"The women we loved blew out of our lives."

Chet takes a long drink of iced tea. He blankly stares straight ahead at the middle of the lawn. In a way, Chet's good looks work against him. People see only his handsomeness, and don't take seriously how messed-up he is—except for the women he's connected to, who are stunned to discover his underneath layers. And then there's Jack and me who know the scoop.

"Do you miss Kate?"

I flash back to sitting on the park bench in Jardin de Luxembourg and sizing-up Lupita with Kate—then realizing the strand of love's permanence with Kate. "She ripped the heart out of my goddamn chest. Sometimes I think losing her was a piece of a larger loss that's going to take me a long, long time to comprehend. Sometimes, I think I get it. Sometimes, I don't get it at all—just too stupid."

"Coming back from Nam…Suzanne leaving fucks with my mind. Good to have my party buddies."

I appreciate my connection with Chet isn't in the party buddy set. "Yeah, you have a lot of party buddies to keep you company. Partying can give you some extra layers of skin—I guess—until the party runs out."

"The party crowd is wilting a little. But the hard core guys are stickin' around."

"How's your sweet lovely mom? She has to be one of the nicest ladies on the face of the earth. Always so concerned about everybody."

"Same-o, same-o."

"And your sister? She still into Jesus instead of junk?"

"It hasn't exactly been a straight and narrow path. But right now, she's doing the church trip."

Chet finishes his iced tea. He tilts the empty glass back and looks in the bottom. Rattles the ice.

"Memo, you ready for a beer, yet?"

"In a minute. There's something I'm curious about."

"Yeah?"

"What'd you think about that trip that went down with your father?"

His eyes bead. Chet's mouth is downturned. "It's the same old story. He's still a fuckin' asshole. I wish he hadn't started calling me. It was out of the blue. Andrea and you helped me see what he was after. That whole scene just totally fucked-me-up. He fooled me. I went for it." Chet shakes his head. His eyes look dark and swollen. "I mean, I denied it to myself, but I thought it would be different. I really thought he had a true interest in making good on what he did to me. God, I need that." Chet is yelling now. "He's an unchanged piece of shit. And you know it. You were there." He shuts down his anger. Chet drops his head and rolls his shoulders forward like he has swallowed indigestible rage.

"Andrea and I could see how you were totally blown away."

"He was his slick motherfucking self over the phone. I was really hoping for something else, but it was the identical old fuckin' thing— just twenty years later. He sucked me in, and then pulled the rug out from underneath me. I feel like I'm repeating myself."

"It's what you need to say. But, no shit. That's what happened. Repeating yourself? Tells me you can't it off your mind."

"Yeah. It took me back to when that fucker used to beat me and beat my mom. Then he disappeared. What he did to mom was shitty."

"She's so sweet, it's hard to imagine."

"Yeah, maybe that's it. He abuses sweet people, the fuckin' jerk."

"Maybe sweet people are more in danger of being abused."

"You have something there. Sweet people don't have a chance." Chet looks down at the floor. He goes limp. I think he's going to drop his glass. He raises his head back up. I see the muscles in his arm and jaw tighten.

"Goddamn him. He fucked-me-up the first time. He fucked-me-up even worse when he came back into my life. And now the son-of-a-bitch is gone again. I couldn't move. Andrea really took care of things when she finally got pissed off and threw him out. Thanks for the back-up." Chet glances sideways. And then back at me. "The weirdest thing was I was stuck to him, as though some sort of bonding agent glued us together. It was shitty, really shitty. I don't know what was wrong with me, but I didn't want Andrea to throw him out." Excruciatingly, Chet vacillates back and forth, impossibly trying to mend the cracks in his mind. "That fuckin' asshole. I wish he would have just stayed the fuck away—never come back into my life."

"It was disgusting the way your father hit on Andrea."

"Yeah. And that airhead bimbo with him who was waving her pussy around. When he started to go for Andrea, it pushed me out. I couldn't move. I couldn't do shit."

"You disappeared. And got plastered."

"Hammered? Yeah. Aside from that, it was like my head was disconnected from my body."

"What do you feel now?"

"Not a fuckin' thing."

"You must feel—"

"I don't. I really don't feel a fuckin' thing. Let's have that beer now."

"Okay, but…" I recognize Chet's open-and-shut blankness. "Yeah, okay, do you have a Heineken?"

"Does water come out of the tap?"

LATER THAT NIGHT I CALL JACK. I LET HIM IN ON THE CONVERSATION with Chet.

"Well, it's more of the same, but worse." An afflicted anguish comes through what Jack says. "At least he didn't drink for a little while. At least he opened up some with you. Sounds grave."

"I couldn't do anything for him." My eyes open wide, and then seal a second. "I'm afraid what's going on inside that guy is reaching a boiling point."

"You did something for him. Call it the human connection. But it's still dismal. I don't think we can count on anything working. And Memo, please I'm not being morose. I'm aiming at the visible effects of what's happening with Chet."

The room is dark. I look out the beach house window. When a red tide covers the sea, the algae bloom appears rust-red. But at night it has bioluminescence, turning the waves' white water into a blue-green glow against the pitch-black night.

I shake my head. "What should we do?"

"I don't know what to do. Wait and see, I guess. Chet's not at the point where there's justification to involuntarily hospitalize him."

"I'm itchy."

"Yeah, it's unnerving, all right. We're just going to have to be comfortable with uncomfortable, don't you think?"

I pull in tepid air and exhale a breath heated by worry. And then look over the ocean. After the waves break, the red tide glow leaves a fractured luminescent line across the wave's white water.

"HELLO, MEMO." THE FOUR SYLLABLES SOUND LIKE SHARP SPIKES.

I take a couple of seconds to recognize her voice. "Andrea?" Then a familiar threat about Chet sets-in.

"Yeah. I'm scared."

I turn to look at the sea. The window frames darkness. "What's up?"

"I left Chet last night."

Shit! He's completely fucked now. I leash myself from spilling out all over the place. "What happened?"

"The party turned into a wild mess. Chet's a nightmare."

"Is he okay?"

"Don't know."

"Fill me in a little." I fight to tone down my voice's quavering sound. "Please."

"Well, he had been fighting with his boss for a couple of months. You know, coming home at night and telling me what an asshole the boss was."

Chet, Andrea tells me, comes home one night and heads straight for a drink. A beefy shot of Jack Daniels bourbon. Looks as though he doesn't even taste it. The whisky does nothing to smooth-out all his shakeup. But Chet looks at the glass as though it were an old friend. And then he gets his loaded trigger-locked .45 and sticks the muzzle in the hip pocket of his jeans.

Chet opens the bedroom door leading to the garden. He takes off his work boots, covered with mason's mud, and hurls them into the backyard. She says, "Shit, I don't know, Chet starts blasting away, maybe four or five rounds. Misses the work boots. Goddamn Vietnam vet trying to blow away his fuckin' work boots, and he can't do it."

Andrea says the next morning she tells him not to go to work. Chet paces back and forth in the bedroom. Walks to one side of the room, turns on a dime. Walks to the other side, turns on a dime. She says it's as though there is some sort of private dialogue going on in his mind. He's tense and angry. A caged lion. Chet goes outside into the yard, puts his boots on and goes to work.

"How much does his drinking have to do with this?"

"He doesn't look like he enjoys drinking anymore." Andrea's voice is weighty. "Doesn't like it...does it anyway. He's up at five in the morning. I stay in bed. I hear ice hitting the glass. Every night, he leaves just enough bourbon in the bottle to have a shot in the morning. Otherwise, Chet would get the shakes. I can hear him making a sandwich, and then he's out the door. I know he's down at the liquor store when it opens at six. He buys a bottle of bourbon. Then he's off to work."

Shadow Facts sits in front of me. Her big brown eyes fix on me. "Andrea, could you please hold on for half a minute?" I feed the pooch—back in thirty seconds. "Okay, I'm here again. So what happened with the boss?"

"About two weeks ago Chet came home and said, 'I told him to fuck-off.' Chet hasn't worked since."

I could see Andrea cued to leave from a mile away. "You plan on going back to him?"

"Not a chance"

I think about Kate's departure and how Suzanne felt. "You're bitter?"

"Yeah, some. Mostly, I feel powerless—unable to help."

"Andrea, I can't tell you how much I appreciate your calling."

"Okay. I love him. Strange to say, but he was the love of my life—I just couldn't stay."

"I know. Couldn't stick around. You must feel guilty. Love and guilt mixed together are like a virus you can't recover from."

"Yeah, that's what it feels like. Thanks, Memo."

"Take care, okay?"

"Yeah, I'm tryin'. Goodbye."

I get the mail. There is a box. I open it. Two antique fishing reels are inside. A Combat Infantry Badge. A Silver Star. And a note.

Memo,

I thought you might like to have a couple of my fishing reels. The Matecumbe bone fish reel with a bone handle was made in the late 1800s. I don't know the exact date. The Farlow and Co. brass reel with the ivory handle was made about 1890. I hope you like them.

Your buddy,

Chet

One second passes. I call Suzanne.

"Hi Suzanne. I haven't heard your voice lately. Do you know if everything is all right with Chet?"

"I don't know. I've been fighting with Chet about the division of property. He didn't want to give me anything. All of a sudden Chet gives me all of the antique furniture. You know how he's tied to all that antique stuff. Did all the research, collecting and refinishing. Now, it doesn't seem so important to him for some reason."

"Well I just got a box in the mail with two of his fishing reels and his CIB and Silver Star."

"Something is not right. Really not right." Suzanne is stern, but I an also hear the shakiness in her voice.

The phone rings and rings. Chet doesn't answer.

I telephone Jack. I tell him about the conversations with Andrea and Suzanne and about Chet giving away his stuff. I put the CIB and Silver Star in the picture.

"I got something in the mail today. Hold on," says Jack. He comes back to the phone in two minutes. "Yeah, it's from Chet. An antique salt water reel and a big game reel. Hold on a second. His two Purple Hearts are in the box."

"This is too fucking poetic. He gives the doc the two Purple Hearts. Let's get the hell over to Chet's place. I'll be over to get you in a flash."

We arrive at Chet's place and knock on the door. Nobody answers. The door is unlocked.

"Chet? Chet!" I yell.

Jack and I walk in. The house is dark. We see a light on the back porch. We walk through a near empty house to where he is. He doesn't get up.

"Yeah, what do you want?" says Chet.

"Chet, you all right?" says Jack.

"I'm fine. What are you guys doing here?"

"We came to see if you're okay," I say.

"Doing just fine."

Chet has a drink of bourbon. He doesn't offer us anything to drink.

"I heard you quit your job," I say.

"Yeah, it was a relief after a lot of fighting with that asshole boss of mine. Everything's okay now."

"Your father contact you again?"

"No." Chet's face is relaxed. He gives us a deadened half smile.

"Chet, how about you coming to stay at my place for a few days?" It's a stretch, but I have to do something to help him.

"No, I'm fine right here. This is where I need to be."

"Okay then, I'll stay here with you for awhile."

"I'm okay. You guys can go now."

"Not a good idea, Chet," says Jack.

"I love you guys, but you don't have to be your brother's keeper. Go on. Go now. You don't have to be your brother's keeper."

"Chet, are you going to hurt yourself?" Questions Jack.

"Interesting question. I've already been hurt. How could I be hurt any further? Go ahead now, leave."

"Where's your weapon?"

"Around here somewhere. I never gave up a weapon to Charlie. I'm not givin' up my weapon now."

"What do you think, Jack?" I'm restless and not quite sure about what to do.

"I've had enough, guys. You can go. It'll be all right. Come on, just go."

I feel like a big piece of waterlogged drift wood. We walk out the door to my Land Cruiser. "This is bad, really bad. Christ, we can't just leave like this." My stomach goes tight. The tops of my shoulders and chest go from numb to tingling to hot. We open the doors to the rig. "Let's go back and physically force Chet to come with us."

"That'd be a bad scene. Could be dangerous for everybody. But yeah, we have to something. And it has to be right now. And quickly. Right this fuckin' second. Look, let's call the police. They can see that he's put on an involuntary hold and psychiatrically hospitalized until he is safe." We open the doors to the rig.

"Okay. Right. There's a telephone booth around the corner." There is a feeling of urgency that radiates electricity up my back and in my jaw. "Come on, let's go."

We hear the blast of a .45 caliber pistol from the house.

I look at Jack. Our eyes lock.

CHAPTER 26

ASHES

Two weeks later, 0945 hours, Black's Beach, La Jolla

DIANE AND JACK AND I ARRIVE. I rake a round section of the beach, fifty-feet across. I take the rake back to the Land Cruiser. Return with my old ten-foot Dewey Weber surfboard. Jack brings the urn and places it on the sand next to the board.

Being stunned by Chet's self-inflicted death is unshakable. I started feeling an interior isolation in Vietnam. The non-welcoming reception when I came home on account of being a soldier of an unpopular war made my isolation swell even more. Now the isolation has gotten bigger and more concentrated since Chet killed himself, but oddly his death makes for more connection with trusted people like Jack and Diane.

Chet's self-destruction started when his father beat him and ran out on the family. It was evident. I suspected Chet translated the beatings into thinking he was a bad kid—took it to mean he was a bad kid who deserved to be beaten. He was so young he got mixed up and couldn't decode his father was the bad one and Chet was an okay kid. The impact went all the way down to Chet's bones. You mixed a guy like Chet with traumatizing combat and the exponential equation was an ugly mess. We never knew what the slice was that drove him to risk enough to be awarded the Silver Star. Perhaps he was simply a risk-taker who in the moment had nothing to lose. Add booze and drugs to Chet's proposition and the result was an uglier inescapable spiral downward.

But Chet managed to get a good soul from a sweet loving mother who cared. And she cared too much and it wasn't enough. Nothing could be enough after the damage his father caused. The guy we loved was a striking contradiction—damaged with a good soul.

Chet was a hurt person. The situation and I were filled with remorse. I regret I couldn't get through to him—and this merges with knowing nothing could get through to him. Except for one thing. More damage could get through. Chet had only a thin layer of protection. He was vulnerable. War trauma got through to everyone. But Chet was more of a target, a casualty before he went to war. I'm angry about the destructiveness of the war—and, as Jack said—the collateral damage done back home—like to Chet.

For reasons of self-preservation. Suzanne and Andrea had to abandon Chet.

I ought to have been more available to help Chet. Being caught-up in my own tortured preoccupations stopped me. One more regret. One more piece of shame.

I have rage towards Chet's father. The physical abuse setup a trajectory for what we are memorializing today. What's worse is Peller skewered Chet by coming back in his life and making the abuse—and all the other damage along the way—resurfaced all at once. Peller's appearance at Chet's place made for escalating and devastating destruction.

What will I do if Chet's father comes today? Kill him or hide behind Jack's protection, or…

The swirling combination of feelings are magnified by relief. The mess makes a riptide. Not wanting Chet to be dead. There's an unexpected relief, like an eerie sort of gladness it's over. His torture is done.

One question is could I have stood up to his alcoholism and his addiction to barbiturates. Likely I would have chased him down a swirling whirlpool and be swallowed up myself. In retrospect, it was the final piece that killed him. Chet occupied his intoxicated hide-out. It made his self-pity more pitiful. And it made the depth of his isolation more isolating. Chet's addictions trashed his judgment. So, in the end his choice was the only one he could see—like a pilot in a power dive trying to pull back on the stick and the gravitational pull is so strong there's nothing left but to crash.

What remains is all of the death I experienced in Nam. Needless death. And now there's one more needless death—Chet—the soldier who didn't fall on foreign soil. He fell right here among friendly and hostile forces. I have to accept my own helplessness, spinning in circles straining to make a difference that wasn't going to happen.

THE AIR IS PERFECTLY STILL. THE OCEAN IS A shimmering sheet of glass. Today's meteorological anomaly rewrites the rules. There isn't the beginning of the usual onshore sea breeze, caused by circular air flows and set off by temperature variations between the land and sea. The warmth of the day is a gift from nowhere and everywhere.

A fine layer of high clouds makes the sky and ocean the same blue-gray. A threadlike black line defines the horizon.

Chet's friends, family and others he affected start to arrive. The first arrivals are two men. One is tall, dark and slender. The other is broad in the chest, with shoulder length hair. I know them. The last time I saw them was at a party—a good time—everyone was riotous, getting loaded, and in the moment. A time that became worn thin by the checks and balances since prudent judgment had been thrown out the window.

Kate turns up alone. She wears a silky black dress and a wide-brimmed black hat. She is barefoot. I hesitate. My first reaction to seeing her is Chet's death is a sensitive grieving time and I couldn't handle her rejecting me. The second reaction is I love her and I'll take the risk. I go to her. We hug. Her hat is knocked off and ends up on the sand. We give each other a fleeting kiss on the lips—makes me feel as though we have known each other since before birth. I pick up her hat. She puts it on. We laugh about the hat.

Kate softly and elegantly gesticulates with one hand. She's succinct and cogent and to the point. "We've really been a mess, haven't we?"

I'm short and pithy, too, "There are no fools like experienced fools, right?"

"I'll say."

I turn and walk away to attend to others. A force radiates up and down my backside. I turn back towards Kate.

Kate's look is fixed on me.

I move my lips and make an inaudible whisper, "I still love you."

She nods.

I'm not sure if her nod means Kate still loves me or she doesn't love me. She's likely acknowledging me without an admission of her feelings toward me. And then what passes through my mind is she's loosely being neutral because of the tender sentiments circling Chet's memorial. I'm at a loss about whether I can still read her.

The size of the group swells. People talk in hushed tones. I hear subdued laughs.

Suzanne walks toward the group. The cluster quiets. She has the presence of twenty people. Suzanne wears the ao dai dress Chet brought her from Vietnam—black silk pants and the top is a form-fitting dress with slits up to the waist. Huge black-rimmed sunglasses mask her eyes.

"I'd give anything for my buddy to still be alive." I hug Suzanne. "His suffering is over," I whisper in her ear.

"I feel sickened. But strange how there's a feeling of relief. I never stopped loving him, Memo." I can't see the expression in her eyes behind her sunglasses.

"We all still love him. The relief—" The whisper drops-off. I kiss her on the cheek.

Chet's mother and sister come into view from across the sandy beach. Now they're at the group.

The sister's eyes don't make contact with anyone and she looks absent and distant. She says Jesus is going to look after Chet at his final destination. Her words echo like something read off a page, or memorized, or rehearsed over and over.

Chet got his looks from his mother. She's beautiful. But today she's ashen. I go to her. I embrace her.

We gaze at each other.

She struggles to say something. She murmurs and stops. She whispers, "Memo, after his father left I wasn't able to give Chet what he needed. I really tried, Memo. I—"

"You gave him what you had. And the thing you gave him was why we all loved him so much."

She tears up and then cries.

Being touched by Chet's mother is biting and sweet and sweeps through me. She struggled desperately, but nothing she could do would act to compensate for something: make up for Peller's irreparable ruin pressed into Chet's everlasting bedrock. I take a new white handkerchief from my pocket and offer it to her.

She takes it. She covers her index finger with the handkerchief and then wipes her eyes, just under her lower eyelid.

People gather. There're almost a hundred. I see a beautiful slender woman with long rich brunette hair. I go to her. It's Andrea.

She says, "This is my fault."

"It's nobody's fault. And it's everybody's fault. It's the fault of more things than we could possibly have control over."

"Memo, we weren't together that long, but Chet was the love of my life."

"I remember you said that before. Yeah, easy to see that. And easy to make sense of that."

She hugs me. I hold her.

Andrea walks to Suzanne. Andrea puts her hand on the side of her shoulder.

Suzanne steps forward and embraces Andrea.

Diane and I stand on either side of Jack. The sea is at our backs. The assemblage present to memorialize Chet collectively looks out to sea. Diane holds the urn.

The overcast sky, sandy beach, cliff behind our gathering and blue-gray sea give an outdoor enclosed feeling of containment. For this minuscule period of time everything in life is held in the space we take up.

Jack takes one step forward.

Everyone is silent. A seagull squawks. The sound of the breaking surf is in the background.

"Chet's choice to die makes many of us contact the despair that is revealed during dark times of isolation. This despondency—this sickness of the soul—can make us lose a sense of meaning in our lives."

I hear Chet's mother cry faintly.

Suzanne wipes the sides of her face below her eyes.

Kate spreads a tear across her cheek with the knuckle of her bent index finger.

"We all must feel different things about Chet. Some of you experience the passing of a good buddy, and the betrayal or sadness of having one fewer first-class guy to have fun with.

"No matter what you are feeling about Chet's death, I hope you can ultimately find the compassion that will lead you to forgiveness. Those of us who went to war share a kinship with Chet. He was not killed by enemies on the battlefield, but rather by enemies created by the experience of war itself, which attacks the human spirit."

The ten veterans in the assembled group stand at attention. They mysteriously stand out. It is as if beams of light were coming from the sky to illuminate them.

"For many of us, we are a collection of fragments, which we are desperately trying to put together to form some semblance of a new whole. Chet struggled with an essential missing piece. It was puzzling and baffling to take in his struggle. Instead, we chose or opted to see the lovable guy who was always everybody's friend."

The muscles in my abdomen pound like waves on the shore. I see Kate listening. Her presence gives me comfort. I wonder if I'm a comfort for her.

"At first, Chet's choice left me feeling shock, betrayal, anger and sadness. This was followed by grief, confusion, and helplessness. And guilt, because I was unable to grasp his hand and lead him out of his deep alienation, a feeling he masked by being a good-time guy. But now I realize there was a larger picture, made up of constituent parts that no one person could have fought to save Chet."

Jack's voice is soft, strong and heard by everyone. I know why I love Jack. Today Jack and Diane hold the splinter in our collective existence in their tender, capable hands.

Twenty people talk about Chet—their love for him and their disbelief that he is gone. A couple of people talk as if they will be having a couple of shots of tequila with him that afternoon at the Long Bar. Neither Chet's mother, nor Suzanne, nor Kate say anything, looking frozen in grief.

I walk to the back of the group and disrobe, leaving on only my surf trunks. I walk to Diane. I open the urn. Take out the waterproof pouch. I paddle out beyond the surf break. Sitting on the surfboard, I open the pouch and throw a handful of Chet's ashes in the still, warm air. They filter down to the calm surface of the water. The mourners now line the shore, three rows deep.

Halfway through, I stop. I see movement in the dark water below me. What is it? A lone porpoise breaks the surface. Porpoises never seem to be alone, always in pods. It moves its nose up and down. It says something. What is it saying? I hear diffuse sounds of disbelief from the mourners, who view the scene from the beach.

I think about Chet putting the .45 in his mouth and pulling the trigger. I imagine his mother's tormented state. The dereliction of his father, who has not showed up. Chet being the only one coming back from patrol. Suzanne's desperation. Andrea's appearance in his life. The medals pinned to Chet's pajama top.

I sprinkle the rest of the ashes across the tranquil water. The porpoise disappears. I stroke back to shore.

PEOPLE MILL AROUND. THEY TALK REMEMBRANCES. I overhear comments. People are touched by Jack's eulogy. The moments stretch and contract. A couple leaves. Another person departs. A few more disappear. The group slowly melts away.

I watch Kate.

She hangs back.

I talk with Diane and Jack.

And now Diane and Jack and Kate and I are the only ones left.

Kate and I are paying attention to each other, nearly at the exclusion of Diane and Jack.

Diane eyes us. She scoots Jack down the beach and towards their car.

I accept that we are alone together, burying blame and excuses for Kate or myself. "I'm sure and not sure what came over me."

"Chet's death is an emotional time. And it's a time of connection with people that cared him. Like you and me. You still love me? Well, I still love you. It's just we can't be married."

I yield to acceptance of a conclusion I don't want. "I guess that's the way it is."

"Memo, you feel softer to me. Like some of those jagged edges you had when you came back from war have smoothed out a bit. Right? Or is it because of today?"

I drink in her validation, like a warmth oozing over me. "It's both. I've adjusted a few things in myself. Did some mending. But I'll still never be the innocent person I was when we first met."

"Yeah, you can't undo experience." Lines form on Kate's forehead. She cocks her head slightly. "You've changed since we split, haven't you?"

I want Kate to come back. But I'll play it cool so she won't bristle and think I'm coming on to strong. "There's constant change. You mean for the better? I think so. Yes."

Kate looks out to sea. And then back at me. "I have to go now."

We walk her back to her car.

I open the door for her. Kate turns around.

I own up to Kate for our agony. "I'm sorry I scared you so much."

CHAPTER 27

TIGHT SPOTS

Ruminative contractions end up collapsing me, set off by being stunned and putting up barriers against accepting Chet's death. My resistance's struggle is short lived. And then a feeling of expansion unfastens the recollections of Chet's irrefutable fatal signposts leading to pulling the trigger. I slow my impulse to rush the realizations of what his death means. There's a reason to not force a premature closure. To calculate the depth of Chet's death is only going to be measurable through time.

I think for today.

Chet marched to a misguided final end.

And now there's the aftermath. And the let-down which makes for exhaustion that I didn't anticipate. But the consequences make sense. I was always on edge about Chet's tragic course and the tidal movements that swept close and that I provisionally pushed into abeyance, until the final moments when the gunshot cracked and I heard Jack's eulogy and I let in our collectively defined and unsaid felt grief.

Relief says Chet doesn't have to suffer any longer.

The people twisted into his life are uncoiled by the release that it's over.

Chet left a thorny legacy.

The final statement is the people who cared, have to grieve his death in discrete individual ways.

All human beings have something bad happen in childhood. Some bad and some not so bad. What matters is the hurt that bad things cause and how long it's felt and what brings the hurt back to being felt over again. Like Chet, whose old time hurts forecasted re-feeling his hurts by hurting himself.

I think of Chet's sorry family situation. Add war trauma and—if the final answer is suicide—it makes for hatred toward suicide's circumstances and anger toward the person driven to suicide's abortive finality to life. That's me. I'm antagonized by Chet's old history and his new war story and the results of his homecoming. And I have a personal and direct fury toward Chet. It's an illogical feeling. And that's the way it is.

I ask myself what my role was in his death. Why? Chet's death produces guilt. I couldn't help my buddy—a sense of defeat. It's an irrational feeling. And that's the way it is, too.

I am a survivor of war and Chet's suicide. War's death and suicide share one thing—traumatic loss. And they're both about wars fought and lost. Chet's death is a loss which brings-up my other losses at war, and losing Kate when I returned. I think of my own despair which led to flirtation with ending it all. Now his death makes the bullshit drop away. Now I can start to live my life again. If truth be told, I can start to live life for the first time.

My war traumas were patently less harsh or brutal or as frequent as Chet's ordeals. War trauma upset my ballast resulting in a tilting list that edged on sinking me. Despite that, I was able to fan a spark that pulled me upright, a heat seeded in by my upstanding parents.

I pretended to feel better by returning to the USC graduate school. And finishing the internship with Frank Gehry has been an uptick. At first, I felt like I was faking it. In the end, I felt better for a simple reason. To be better I had to do things to make me feel better.

And then work as an architect began. Work changed me from feeling like a pariah to grabbing hold of reconnection. The pretending stopped. The isolation stopped. I think of Chet. His childhood abuse and boozing and taking drugs greased his grasp so he couldn't get a grip.

There's one untold drive for succeeding. Maybe Kate would come back if I rise in my profession. I've felt stirred-up since seeing her at Chet's memorial. She said we were over, but I sensed a turn in her voice—a possible invitation. Maybe it was my finger of intuition touching a sweet spot. Or maybe it's me lying to myself one more self-destructive illusionary time. Kate's on my mind. So much so, it's like she has come back to live in our house. But she's not here.

DIANE AND JACK LIVE ON A SOUTHWEST SHOULDER of Mount Soledad in San Diego. Their house owns the view—one hundred and eighty degrees takes in the Pacific Ocean during the day and city lights at night. The place—purchased in a fair market and modest in comparison to the rest of the nearby homes—is a lesson in unpretentiousness. It's like them. Comfortable and real.

A brick path leads across a patch of thick broad-bladed green Bermuda grass and ends at the house. Sometimes I feel more at home at their house than my own. Their place is so full. Mine is so empty.

I knock on the door. Walk in and holler, "Diane. It's Memo." Shadow Facts has a favorite spot. She flops down.

Diane's in the kitchen. There are ten minutes before she leaves for work. I need to get to the airport.

"Jack's attached to Shadow Facts," she says between sips of aromatic coffee.

"He can have just about anything I have. So, can Jack have Shadow Facts? Not a chance, Sweetie." We laugh. I shrug. I can't help it—get a little serious. "Shadow Facts has always been—"

"We know." Diane pets the dog. "So, where are you off to?"

"La Paz for a couple of days. Thanks for taking care of Shadow Facts."

"Sure. Mexico's always has a pull, doesn't it? You've been pretty busy with work. Doing well in the money department."

"Yeah. You know, it's a month at the new job. They're working me to death with overtime. But I feel lucky—thankful, really. Getting hired out of graduate school. Unbelievable group of creative people. And the design projects are incredible. But a couple of breaks are coming up between assignments. That part's good, too."

"We think it's great how you're landing on your feet."

"At first, the fall was rough. But the landing is getting smoother."

"And it's good you and Jack are surfing."

"Yeah. Okay...Diane—"

"Okay, what? You want an update? You haven't asked for awhile."

"Been distracted, I guess."

"Her art is going very well. Acrylics are working for her. Zúñiga continues to be a huge influence on her work."

"When we met, Kate was on the verge of bringing her anthropology background into her art. Meeting Francisco Zúñiga through my mom pulled it together for her at just the right time."

Talking about the dimensions of Kate's art makes me think of the night view from Diane and Jack's house; you can see the city lights shine and flicker and the ocean is one big dark mysterious vastness.

An outsider might think Diane was bragging about her friend. But it's an objective report. "Timing is everything. She does almost zero to promote herself. Kate put some of her pieces in the rental section of the Fine Arts Gallery. Got some exposure. Her work took off." Diane nods. "She's got a following."

"That's almost exactly what my folks said." I feel a buzz hearing good things about Kate. "Diane—"

"Yes?" She gives me a generous smile. "So what you really want to hear about is—a couple of men have passed by here and there. She hasn't been serious about anyone, Memo. And no new guy is on the horizon."

My curiosity about Kate highlights what I'm not saying.

"What about you?" says Diane.

Suddenly my defenses fall apart. "I saw a couple of women in the graduate program." My voice is weak. I destroyed my relationship with Kate. Now I'm a catastrophe with other women. "I picked women who were about appreciating style and design, rather than laying a solid foundation with concrete and rebar. Nothing lasted too long." I have an exposed leaden feel. The architectural metaphor is bullshit. I can't help it. "It's just that I didn't feel any glue." I sugarcoat saying the passing relationships were mainly for sex. And I found out that's what the women had in mind, too—a mutual understood handshake in the rack—an arrangement.

"A well-done foundation, style, design and love are all important. Put together, they create something. A marriage, for example."

I get my voice back. "Sounds like Jack and you."

"I love you, Memo."

"I love you, too. And Jack.

"Hmm." I look at the kitchen clock and then at my wristwatch. They say the same thing. "Gotta rush; same for you, right? Say hi to Jack. Take good care of the pooch."

MY FANTASY AND DREAM ABOUT LUPITA crumbled in Paris. But she didn't abandon her interest in me. Kate is at a distance. Nothing is sure. Maybe the understanding Lupita had for me at Cañón de Guadalupe can be rekindled. Maybe seeing her is a mistake. I'll have to see her to find out.

I'm on a seesaw, wondering if I should follow-through with my plan to go to La Paz. Talking to Diane brings back each slow-motion movie frame of seeing Kate at Chet's memorial service. I can't get her off my mind now—like a frantic singular fixated passion that won't let go. Lupita is tied to her child. My relationship with her feels like thievery. Seeing another man's wife. Being in the presence of his child. I need a regular life—I'd be okay with that. Jesus, I'll cancel the trip. Lupita is a striking image in my mind. No, I'll go. I'd be sorry if I hadn't check-it-out. My mind ratchets back and forth. The final dip on my seesaw-thinking tells me seeing Lupita is circumventing my confirmed feelings.

I arrive in La Paz in the late afternoon. I check-in at Los Arcos on Paseo Alvaro Obregon at *el malecón*—the seaside boardwalk. The room overlooks the picturesque bay, which is dotted with fishing boats in various states of repair. My arrival is on time for the La Paz signature explosive fiery crimson sunset. The red-orange horizon fades to surprisingly unveil an uncommon and seldom to be seen two-second green flash at the moment the last sliver of the sun disappears.

A beer at the Los Arcos bar hits the spot. I cock my head and take in a 1950s picture on the wall of Clark Gable posed with a marlin. It makes me think of Lana Turner and him, a steamy duo in a 1940s movie about WWII—*Homecoming*. There isn't too much identification with the film, except leaving war and the fallout from coming back to the States.

I remember my dad's words. Military people got a hero's welcome when they came home from war in WWII days. You get a hero's welcome when you come back from Nam only if you're dead—an honor guard—volley of shots, drumming, and flag-draped coffin, fold the flag and give it to the next of kin. The soldiers serving on the honor guard have no idea who you were. It's just another duty. Hardly anybody grasps what it was like for the soldier who went to Nam. Hardly anybody says it's tough getting back—unless the person has been to Nam. I drink a second beer. I return to my empty hotel room.

The next morning I go onto el malecón. The sea is a sheet of blue glass. Ribbons of orange reflect the morning's firelight sunrise. *La Paz*—The Peace—must have had the same feel when Sebastian Vizciano named it in the late sixteenth century. I imagine the old days, when the Pericú Indians dived for pearls in the Bahia de La Paz oyster beds. European and American greed caused the oyster beds to be depleted to the vanishing point. Sad—losses caused by greed—greed leaves less than it gains—motivated by a desire for power and dominance and control. No oysters—no pearls—but the bay's tranquil exquisiteness finds a sense of permanence.

I pass time. At the southern end of town there is a statue of two doves facing in opposite directions. Two symbols of peace don't see eye-to-eye.

I pass more time. I talk to the last of the fishermen to leave for the early morning strike.

I pass yet more time waiting for the market to open. Strong coffee mixed with hot milk. Flour tortillas and huevos. It's time for the market to open.

I walk away from the bay towards the heart of town. I ask a slender dark man in sun-bleached cotton clothes for directions to *La Plaza del Mercado*.

"*Siga derecho dos cuadras y doble a la izquierda.*"

I follow the street for two blocks and turn left. The vendors are setting up for the day. A slow crescendo of voices animates the market.

I can't wait.

I have to wait.

Where is she?

She won't come.

Will she come?

A whirr fills the morning market place—the smell of fruit, sweet pastries, tortillas, tamales and woven reed baskets.

Maybe she doesn't come here.

Maybe she doesn't live in La Paz anymore.

Maybe she has vanished.

Two sinking hours pass. Another hour falls downward. Then I see her. At the top of the cement stairs. A shot of adrenaline wakes me up. She descends the five steps as though she were entering a ball—her long dark hair and milky skin. She holds her little boy, Juan Diego who's too heavy to carry, but too small to walk down the steps.

A dark-skinned woman accompanies Lupita. She's dressed in a white peasant blouse and long dark *falda* that flows from her waist to her ankles.

Our eyes fix.

I turn away. Move towards the vegetables and fruit. I squeeze the red-rich tomatoes.

The dark-skinned woman minds Juan Diego.

Lupita moves next to me. She puts sweet fruit in her basket. She picks up a lime. She runs her thumb across the fruit's deep green skin, releasing the pungent citrus oils. She puts the lime close to her nose. She smells the acidic fragrance.

"This is dangerous," she says in a hushed voice.

"Of course it is," I whisper back.

Lupita cocks her head. She turns in my direction. "We can't meet here."

"Where?"

"Somewhere away from La Paz." Lupita looks down at the fruits. "I'm too well-known here."

"How about Paris, again?"

"It will raise suspicion. I can use a secluded place on the East Cape between La Paz and Cabo San Lucas. It's just outside of Los Barriles." Lupita looks straight ahead. "I want to see you right away. I feel...an urgency."

"Let's go right this second."

"Too risky. And I have obligations."

"I'll go back to the States. You contact me. Is that what you want?"

"Yes. It will be soon. Very soon. I'll get word to you."

She holds *la canasta*—the basket—with her left hand. Her right hand touches her hip. She runs her hand down to her thigh. She steals a glance. One look fills in the time we've been apart. She walks away, upright and elegant.

Something hits after the encounter with Lupita. I'm not the twitchy vulnerable wreck when we first met. The saccharinity between us has changed its flavor. I want to see what we taste like now.

The day lengthens until I step on a plane to head home. I'll hold on and occupy the hiatus until the message comes from Lupita.

I PULL UP IN THE RIG TO LOOK IN ON JACK AND DIANE. Jack is in front of his house. I open the door of the rig. Shadow Facts jumps out. She runs to him, stands and wags her tail.

"Lupita? It's really happening, Memo?" Jack is uncharacteristically awkward. He tells me Kate's in the house.

"I'm twisted-up, Jack. Okay, I admit seeing Lupita is crappy judgment, but I want to check-it-out."

"Might be shaky for you. Remember—"

"Make no more damage." My eyes are downcast. I look up at Jack's eyes. I shrug. "I haven't done too well in that department—women—damage—and …The truth is I could do more damage. There's risk. But I'm living in a straightjacket. The risk may be worth—"

"It's okay, though unsure. Just be careful." Jack hesitates. "Want to check that someone who's inside the house with Diane?"

Jack, Shadow Facts and I walk into the house. Diane and Kate sit in the living room. Shadow Facts runs to Kate. The dog's whole body wriggles. Kate smiles. She strokes the head of Shadow Facts with both her hands.

Kate's face is soft. And exquisite. She's consistently beautiful, ignoring the years. I think of the first day I met her—standing under the umbrella.

Diane stands. She walks towards the kitchen. She turns back and says, "Jack, help me with something? In the kitchen?"

I know right now that seeing Lupita is too stupid. Seeing her in the market doesn't feel as fresh as unexpectedly running into Kate. "I hear your art is going very well, Kate." I come across as interested, but neutral.

Kate lights-up. Her eyes brighten to match the texture of her voice. "Yeah, I like the way my work is turning out. I've seen Alita and Dan at a few art openings. Talked to them a couple of times on the phone."

"I'm curious why you keep in contact."

"You know Dan is still like a father to me. I love your mom. Those things haven't changed, even though we're divorced."

I think of my parent's anger over our split. They tell me directly and by nuance and innuendo that they still love Kate. "Yeah, I do know—the divorce...They're so fond of you, despite—"

"Memo, I hope this doesn't sound silly, but thanks for never being late with your support payments to me."

"Sure. Never occurred to me to—"

Kate knows being responsible to her is a comment on my lasting love. "Just needed to say thanks."

We stand. I take half a step forward. Stop. "Diane, Jack, I have to go!" I yell.

"Goodbye, Memo." Kate's face looks tender, yielding.

I go to the kitchen. Diane and Jack look up at the same time. They smile an identical smile—like being twins of a long-term marriage. We say goodbye.

I step outside. I exhale. Seeing Kate washes through me. And being with her tugs, and it tugs hard. It's more rooted than only familiarity. Her pull draws me to want our chemistry to break the surface— to come to light—to be unburied and known again.

I want her. And it terrifies me. She still loves me. And thinks we can't be married. Does that mean we're history? Or is there an opening? Or does she only want cordiality because a lot of the pain has subsided? Seeing Kate makes me confused. She has to be confused, too. I can't read her. I can't read myself. So that means, I can't read us.

CHAPTER 28

TEAR STAINS

I CRACK OPEN THE FRONT DOOR. "Jack, Diane, is anybody home?" I'm here to drop off Shadow Facts. Her body and tail whip back and forth. "I love you, girl." I always talk to Shadow Facts in grown-up human language, not like a lot of people who talk to their dogs in baby talk. I pet her. Shadow Facts' big brown eyes check me. She pants. Her tongue hangs out. The smiling dog.

Jack appears. He's has a curious look. "Let me in on what's happening."

"Hi Jack."

Four seconds pass before I say more. "I'm heading back down to Mexico to meet-up with Lupita. There's a secluded place she can use on the Sea of Cortez at the East Cape near Los Barriles. When I found her at the marketplace in La Paz she felt an urgency to see me. But she felt too exposed to be seen with me in La Paz. I think it's going to be the same deliciousness and heat as in Paris."

Jack changes to a concerned look. "That's what you're after—heat?" His voice sounds flat, with a twinge of a brotherly timbre that says I'm in a misguided direction.

I squint. "That's kind of a thud. Are you disapproving?"

Jack lifts his shoulders. "Just puzzled." He lets his shoulders fall.

"Lupita has been a solution for me. Maybe a wrong answer caused by desperation." I look away for a second. "I have some grasp on what's happening. I'm not totally thick." I sigh. "My foolishness with

Lupita has been based on illusion. A fantasy. But the illusion helped me. She gave me something to hang onto because I was so messed-up and didn't know what direction to go in. I'm bordering on confusion. What Lupita means to me is still settling in."

"Those are a lot of words. I'm still not sure—"

I shrug. "Okay. I escaped based on a fantasy. Now I'm confused."

"That's better. Confused? Makes sense. She didn't quite hook you, did she?"

"Hook me? We'll see. There are a lot of things I can't explain."

"You mean there are a lot of things you need to figure out?" Jack has turned into my big brother. No bullshit.

"There was one thing I didn't need to figure out. After Lupita left me in Paris I saw the impressionist pieces at the Galerie Nationale du Jeu de Paume. I was empty and touchy after she left. Somehow, being with the masterpieces gave me a safe feeling. Like I was a receptacle waiting to be filled with something else." I relive the dreamy intoxication. "Exquisite art filled me with its color, dimension, genius and ecstasy."

"Extraordinary experience. But I'm not sure where that leaves you."

"I'm getting to that. Before long I was sitting in the Jardin du Luxembourg. It's a place that brings a feeling of equanimity. There were people passing back and forth, but the only ones I could take in were couples with children. I collapsed into a gray state of mind thinking I was duplicitous being with Lupita and causing a wedge in her family."

"I love you, man." Jack is sober. "There's been so much to face."

"I love you too, Jack." I glance down, then back at Jack. "What do you mean? So much to face? Do you still think I'm a train wreck?"

"We're all train wrecks. Chet. Me. You—trying to figure it out. At least you're looking at impressionist art in Paris."

"You're the solid one, Jack."

"There's Diane, there's the substance my folks gave me and there's what I get out of helping people. Call that solid. Call it what I have."

"Yeah, what you have is connection. A lot of people came back because of what you did to save them. I was helpless and saw a lot of people vanish."

"Yes, we had different circumstances. You hung-on. There's a big piece in you that won't change—the well-bred way about you."

I think adversity changes some things and not others. I went from brilliant sunlight into a dark, seemingly never-ending space, which made me strain to see. I could have crept into a hole and died. And now I'm walking out of a pitch-black passageway into bright daylight, starting to see again, but I have to squint to see because the brightness of the light can be too much.

"Back from Nam for awhile," says Jack. "And we're still gettin' back."

Sweet and bitter tastes are on my tongue. I can't help repeating the truthful accuracy of what rolls off Jack's tongue. "Still gettin' back...always be that way, though it will lessen over time."

Jack says, "There's something else, isn't there?"

"Good read." A sickening and empty dark feeling brings on a swelling at the back of my throat. A weakness at my knees. The blankness of waste—war's losses. The unpopular war's handwriting on the wall. And I'm still stuck with all the classified secrecy. "You know, the Phoenix Program is a malicious response to Nam's wickedness. The public—and most of the military—have no conception that Phoenix exists. It was never evaluated, just swept under the rug." A pause. Jack listens. "Now there's the troop withdrawal. And now everything is going to collapse." I glance down again. Look back up at Jack. Draw in a breath and let it go, "I guess the question and truism is: what was it all for?"

Jack raises his eyebrows and nods. "Good question." He looks out the picture window at the afternoon glare on the choppy Pacific. He looks back at me and shrugs. "The revolution in the States put the pedal to the metal, you know, started to blow out all the shitty carbon in the jets of this country's staid political authority. All the losses? Nothing's worth that."

"We owe an apology to ourselves for going in the first place."

"Get over that. We don't need a pardon for what happened."

"It's more clear-cut for you. All the good you did. I'm still on the fence."

I made a commitment to meet Lupita. The promise to her restricts me in some ways and not in others. A lack of refinement and indelicacy and insensitivity comes over me about one thought. I could simply go to Lupita's hideaway on the Sea of Cortez and provide stud service for the married woman who feels an urgency. And the crass thought is merely a cover-up for the positive and negative feelings—like love and hate—about meeting Lupita which exist at the same time. My uncertainty about choosing to go is cancelled out by the agreement I made to see her. I give-in to the obligation.

The flight arrives at San José del Cabo. I get a lift up north, outside of Los Barriles. The hideaway is on an enchanting patch of beach facing the dramatic Sea of Cortez. Nobody or anything are around, except silence and seclusion and a dazzling sea. It's too perfect. It has the emotional suck of a swirling vortex. I knock on the door.

Lupita comes to the door. She's barefoot. She wears a silky robe. Her long dark hair falls on her shoulders, down to her breast. "I've been so built-up. And now you're here." Lupita's eyes are magnetic.

In the flash of the moment I'm inescapably drawn into her. Warmth surges in my chest. Images of Cañón de Guadalupe and the swirling time at the Paris apartment spark a want and an eruption of heat. I take her hand. A feather like tug is all it takes.

We're in each other's arms. We kiss. The link between us is blood boiling.

The power of the moment erases every fragment of indecision and besotted hesitation about coming to be with Lupita. I thought it was over with Lupita. This instant tells me the thought was wide of the mark. "You've been constantly on my mind." I recognize this is an ambiguous statement, which leaves out all the divergent clashing quarrels in my mind about seeing her again. My inner dialogue is finally timed-out. In this split second I have a singular focus—Lupita.

We shut the door behind us. The ultra private setting's panorama overlooks the Sea of Cortez. The afternoon sun reflects a bluish-silver shimmer on the sea's rippled surface. The rugged terrain around the whitewashed casita is sand and rocky and filled with thorn-spiked cacti.

"Lupita, I could use a shower."

"Let's have a drink first."

We stand in the casita's view-filled kitchen.

Lupita pours Cointreau and tequila and fresh lime juice into a shaker. She adds ice and shakes-up the mixture.

I think about when I told Kate the Hussong's story of the margarita's origin. I force the thought out of my mind.

Lupita and I toast. We sip the margaritas.

She coyly tilts her head.

I put my hand around Lupita's waist and pull her close. Another succulent-filled kiss rushes our breathing. We make it for the bedroom. Lupita watches while I undress. I pull the sash from her gown. The robe falls to the floor. I soap her body in the shower. It's a silky smooth touch over her chest and thighs. Lupita angles her head back. She groans. The rest of the afternoon brings one crescendo after the other.

Lupita and I gather ourselves up and go the main section of the casita. She makes us a laudatory drink. We laugh a lovers' laugh. And then touch, and laugh again. Lupita and I watch the Sea of Cortez late day sunlight transitions turn from blue to orange to dark pink to navy blue, and then black.

I feel a post-sex enmeshed vulnerability. "I've been thinking about where we go to from here." One blink. Maybe I sound too serious.

"I'd love to see you more." Lupita has a lovely smile. "More frequently. Could be a regular thing."

"Regular?"

"Sure. I can work out random times to meet you which would steer clear of Alejandro's suspicion." Lupita rises from where we are sitting on the sofa and walks to the picture window. She gazes at the early evening's three-quarter moon casting a shaft of light across the opaque and inky dark sea.

I study the form of Lupita's backside. "I see." These are the only words I can squeeze out.

She turns her head and looks at me over her right shoulder. A perfunctory smile comes across Lupita's face. Her watch returns to the shadows and the moonlit sea.

I have a grating feeling. This is followed by the comprehension that for Lupita our romance has progressed to a relationship of convenience. There's no commitment, other than to fill the emptiness caused by her starved marriage to Alejandro and to thwart the dominating control her father attempts to exert over her. The final score is I feel strangely rebuffed.

Lupita returns to the sofa. She faces me and straddles my body.

I open her robe and bring her close.

The heat is turned on full blast. My body says yes. But in my psyche the tie with Lupita fades a notch. A waning mind, combined with a willing body. And I think my soul is defined by being locked up in a box, occupying some other scene.

In the morning and throughout the day each turn with Lupita leads me to feel less and less connection.

I hear the horn from my ride back to the airport. When I leave the doorway frames her silky robed body in the same way as when I arrived. We say goodbye. Her exquisite alluring smile lasts for a time without end. But the goodbye lies in wait for a lasting closure.

Lupita's parting words are she wants me again.

MY BEACH HOUSE IS IN THE MOST SOUTHWESTERN corner of California. Painterly days ignited by the sunrise are moved by seashore animation until darkness. The view brings in a shot to the south—Mexico. Mexico and the thoughts of Lupita have a weight that feels as if Earth is off its axis. I have to see her.

Driven by an uncontrollable press, I'll make my way back to La Paz to meet Lupita.

I go to Diane and Jack's house to drop-off Shadow Facts. I knock, enter and announce myself.

Kate is talking with Diane in the living room. Seeing these two women who have substance for me makes me settle into the decision about Lupita.

Kate gives Shadow Facts a good loving.

Diane says, "Hi Memo, let me take Shadow Facts into the backyard. I'll play with her." She doesn't look back.

"Kate, you just about live here."

"Yeah, it's good to spend time with Diane. You look good, Memo."

"You have a custom of always looking good, Kate."

Kate looks pleased, intertwined with a fragment of the old charm coming through my voice. "Memo, do you trust in the fate of serendipitous meetings."

"Like we've had recently?"

"Exactly. Seeing you has made me think about the unfilled parts with you and me. The pieces we haven't talked about that are still circling around waiting to land."

Kate moistens her lips with her tongue. "There's something you want to tell me?"

"Tell you about what?" There's something obvious. She's not the type to be cagy. I feel emotionally dense.

"You've been on my mind. Please."

I look in Kate's face. I turn around and take three steps away from her. Fear over repeating the mutual hurt in our relationship makes me want to run away. I tell myself to stop being such a chicken shit. I turn back and move two feet from her.

Our eyes link.

I take the risk. "Yes, okay." It may not be what she wants, but it's what I have to say. "I've thought about this for a long time. You might say I've been scared to tell you. When I was in Vietnam you were the only thing that kept me going. I always thought of you. I reread your letters again and again. I smelled them. Sometimes I put a couple of your letters in my pocket when I had to go in the field. I'd read them. It made you near."

Kate shows she's stirred by my confession. "I reread yours' too all the time. I remember seeing what I thought were tear stains on some of them."

Kate, noticing the tear stains, breathes validation into me. And now we're finally talking about it. "There were tear stains after Walter died, and after I carried the kid back to the chopper but he died on me. Maybe sometime I'll tell you about the others. I always had tears about missing you."

There's a whispery serious feel to Kate's voice. She squints and blinks. "What happened, Memo?"

"I came home. That's what happened. I was always afraid when I was out in the bush. But I couldn't be afraid. I had to take care of things, be the captain. I was the guy everybody could count on.

"I appreciate being alive. I just can't forgive myself for being alive because thousands and thousands of our troops died.

"And what I saw was horrific. But compared with what the guys in the combat units experienced every two seconds? It was nothing."

My stomach aches as though I just did a million sit-ups. If I were punched in the stomach right now, I'm not sure if the fist would bounce off or if I would crumble.

Kate says, "Our marriage revealed what you weren't saying. We fell apart because you fell apart." Her eyes are teary. "We know it's a gruesome war. I think this is what you're telling me; there're the things you saw, your perceptions, and then your reactions and emotions. So what has unfolded is more than what you saw." She clears her throat. "But everything was clogged-up and only visible just below the surface—numb and twitchy when you got home."

"Kate, when I came home my skin was rubber, two inches thick. Everything bounced off of it. Nothing could penetrate it. But really, I had no skin at all. My love for you made me able to live through Vietnam. I came home. Vietnam's residual made me die inside, but made me have a jacked up existence in misdirected ways. I'm sorry what that conflict did to our marriage."

"I had to leave you, Memo."

"I don't blame you. Without knowing it, I squeezed the life out of our relationship. Kate, the word sorry is too thin. There is nothing I can say to you to make things better after being so destructive."

"I didn't understand."

"Do you now?"

"I guess I still don't understand. But I'm not angry anymore."

"Still a lot of missing pieces." I leave an opening for Kate. I have the sense she carries a weight—something she needs to spill. And something we've neglected.

Kate is poised. "You know the one I want to talk about now, don't you?"

"Yes. We lost our baby."

"Alita and Dan and you gave me so much at the point when the miscarriage happened. You were all great. Then it flipped like a switch—completely crowded out by you. The draft. The military. The scariness about you being in Vietnam. The fallout of shellshock when you came home. Your grief. And my grief about losing the baby wasn't like a real grief. It was circumvented by that goddamn war."

I feel sick. My face must be ashen. Everything that's happened feels like upper layers. The loss of our baby drives a stake deeper than anything else. "There're no memories. No pictures of our child."

"Right, no memories of our hungry infant pulling at my breast. No milestones like sitting up or crawling or standing or taking the first step." Kate cringes.

"What Kate?"

"I'll always remember this. The night it happened. I went to the bathroom. There was a huge splatter of blood. I was so drugged-up on Demerol for pain. I unthinkingly flushed. And then I saw something fleshy and seahorse shaped swirl down in the bloody water. I tried to grab it—too late. It was gone."

"Jesus, why didn't you tell me?"

"I had so much guilt and shame. That's why. I second guessed myself, not knowing if what I saw in the clockwise churn of bloody water was real or a medication-provoked misperception. After we broke-up something hit me. Loads of feelings of failure. Partly because I didn't pullout the little piece of a person who was you and me out of the blood-spattered liquid. I went to my OB/GYN doctor. I let him know what happened. He told me a large percentage of miscarriages happen in this way. Suddenly I started to feel normal again." Pained ridges form across Kate's face. "It's tough telling you this."

I have a sick feeling. I didn't pay attention, being caught-up in my own crisis about war—didn't see how much I needed to be present for Kate. I was a ghost. "Good it's out in the open now. Any relief?"

"No. There's been so much confusion about it. I didn't know who I was. The themes of my peasant woman paintings were inspired by a loss of my identity as a woman. Through art I got myself back. And there's still the incompleteness."

"We said there wasn't a crystal clear reason why it happened. Nobody's fault."

"I know. And that's based on logic. Logic doesn't account for the most important things in life, does it?"

I nod.

A tear rolls down Kate's cheek. It falls on the front of her blouse. The saline liquid soaks in to the fabric.

"Do you want a tissue?"

"No. That's not what I want."

And in an intent look our whole connection is there without saying what would happen next or having a prediction about our future.

After the wounds and pain and sadness and grief and my wanting Kate, there's finally a glimmer she wants me back. But I'm left in the balance with the fear I may not be the thing she wants. Now I have to leave. There's one thing I have to finish. "Kate, I want to stay longer. I have to go. Need to catch a plane."

She looks taken aback. "Where are you going?"

"La Paz. I need to go to La Paz to…take care of some business. And then I'm going to Loreto for a couple of days—fish for yellowtail and dorado."

"Going to stay at the Hotel Oasis in Loreto?" Kate guesses since the place that's an old family haunt.

"Yeah, that's it. Goodbye, Kate."

I walk out the door. And then I stop. Turn around. Take a step back. I shake my head, and change direction again and head for the rig.

I feel ripped away from Kate—again.

CHAPTER 29

OASIS

I LAND IN LA PAZ. Rent a car. I drive south of La Paz and pass Pichilingue. I reach the cove, Playa Balandra. Another solitary car is parked. I walk to the sand and approach Sombrilla—the umbrella rock.

Lupita is stretched out on a large blanket. The sand is the color and texture of salt. The sandy bottom casts is the color of pale turquoise to the sea. The water and the sand frame her body—and all her beauty. I've loved her womanly sweetness and sway and elegance.

Lupita and I met on the bottom step of our respective emptiness. We filled in and expanded each other and now I know it was a transient connection to piece in what was missing.

And now I have to come to one piece of honesty. The more desperate I was, the more drawn to her I became. Her passion pumped light and color into a dark and opaque soul looking to be moored. It was a temporary frantic move. And she was a fantasy that gave me an illusion of being self-possessed when I was shattered.

"Lupita, I'm glad you got the message."

"The beach is deserted."

"Feel safe enough?"

"Yes."

"I had to see you in person." My voice has the purple-blue color of absence, like being her lover who is dissolving into ether and becoming nothing.

Lupita reacts. Her face changes from tentative desirousness to serious. "I know. What's going to happen isn't going to be a surprise. I have a love for you that isn't going away. Thank you for Paris."

"How do you know?"

"When we were in Los Barriles you were so present in bed. Sex isn't everything, Memo. I felt you slipping away. I denied it. And now—in hindsight—it's all so clear. Afterward, you needed to see me right away. Something has happened. I don't need to know what it is. I felt a goodbye approaching.

"There's more. My father and Alejandro and my family have ruled me. You gave me freedom. You let me know what is possible. Did I think you'd be an everlasting love of convenience? There was the hope, but I'm grown-up enough to realize what I faced with you."

"You're making this too easy for me."

"I don't think it's easy for either of us. Do you?"

"Not really."

"You want to have sex on the beach—one last time?"

"Let me kiss you goodbye."

"Oh Memo, kiss me."

We kiss the way we kissed in Paris.

I feel pulled every which way, and rupture inside.

I leave.

Back north to the airport. Arrangements are made to go farther north to Loreto.

I check into the Hotel Oasis.

I make a telephone call at the hotel.

"Hello, Dad."

"Memo, where are you? The connection. It's scratchy."

"I'm in Loreto. I took care of some business in La Paz—tell you about it later—here for a couple of days of fishing." I gather myself up. "Dad, I realize there were horrific mistakes when I came home. Not taking care of Kate. I did a dreadful job. There's so much remorse over how I messed up our marriage."

"Alita and I love Kate very much. Yes, you didn't take care of her. There's a lot of non-doable damage. And remember what I told you about what war does to marriages. You didn't get a free pass when you came back from Vietnam. No one does. We feel bad for what's happened between Kate and you. Now, there's another side. Today, I can tell you with absolute certainty that Alita and I have so much gratitude that you are our son. And, Memo, always remember this. You are really a good man. You have the substance to persevere, no matter what's happened and what mistakes you've made along the way. We can see the difference since you have gotten home."

"And the gratitude? It goes both ways. Thankful you're my folks."

THE NEXT MORNING I GO FISHING. The strikes are good. The colors of the dorado when it is still wet are a brilliant gold and blue and green. Take it out of the water—out of its element—and the fish's golden radiance and cool colors turn to a muted-gray nothingness.

I go back to the hotel. Cleaning-up feels good after a day on the Sea of Cortez. The sea is so familiar, it feels like home. It is home. There's a knock at the door. I wrap the white hotel towel around my waist and answer the door.

"*Señor, hay una mujer en la recepción que le gustaría verlo.*"

Who could it be? Lupita. The goodbye kiss on the beach wasn't enough. She said it wouldn't be easy for either of us. What else does she need to say?

I get dressed.

I go to the lobby.

It's not Lupita.

"Kate, what are you doing here?!"

"I forgot to ask you something yesterday."

Yesterday Kate said she wanted something. I avoided asking what. There was the hope she'd say she wanted me back—followed by the fear it wasn't what she wanted. "Okay. I'm ready to give you the answer." This feels so risky.

"Okay. You know what the question is?"

"I hope so. No matter what's happened, no matter what I've done, Kate, I've never stopped loving you. It was obscured. But loving you has always been there. I'm sorry. I should have taken better care of you. And this is a major regret. I'm sorry for everything I've allowed to get in the way of my love for you."

I reach out and grasp the tops of her arms.

"I saw only what was on the surface—didn't understand. What do you say, Memo?"

"Yes, but what do you say?" I'm edgy for the seconds before her reply, to make out if she also wants me back.

"Yes," Kate answered.

That's what I wanted to hear.

EPILOGUE

THE FJ40 IS READY TO DROP DEAD. I work on bringing it back to life—a rebuilt engine and new drive train. Fresh rubber connects it to the ground. The wiring for the electrical system needs work. It'll have to wait until I get back. The interior calls for a redo. And the cosmetics—a few dents and faded paint. I could buy a new one. I'll keep it. It's something I know. The FJ40 will make it.

I pack the rig with what I have collected. There's a McCulloch chainsaw, chainsaw oils, two Jeep five-gallon gas cans filled with fuel, fishing gear, a Remington over/under .22/.410 shotgun, Hoppe's No. 9 gun solvent, patches, cleaning rod, gun oil, boxes of .22 shells and .410 shotgun shells, and a tarp. Ponchos, jackets and blankets. Beans and rice. Everything one needs for living in an isolated place.

I go back into the beach house after filling the FJ40. "Kate?" Her back is to me. She watches children playing on the beach. The ocean is at low tide. Maybe a minus tide. The afternoon onshore wind unsettles the sea's surface, making foaming white crests. Between the whitecaps the sun glares silvery and golden against the blue water.

She turns around. Lines form in her forehead, and edges take shape at her eyes that look like crow's feet. Kate cocks her head to the right. "You think it's a good idea to go? The timing and all?"

"It's not a logical thing, filled with specific criteria."

"I have to believe it's the right thing." She's soft voiced.

"My senses say it's right. I could be right. I could be wrong. But I can't shake it loose. Something inside me always remembers what's unfinished, and now I have to finish this one—at least in some way." I move one foot in front of her. "But you understand, don't you? It presses on me and keeps me from being in one piece." We hug. And then I look in Kate's eyes. There's an irrepressible flash. "Now's the time."

Kate's silent—studies my face. She looks over her shoulder at the children playing on the beach. Her eyes fall back on me, and she squeezes my hands. Kate waits.

"It's time for the self-loathing to stop," I say.

"Should you go alone?"

"You mean take Jack, just in case I need him?"

"Yes."

"I have to do this one on my own. You're scared."

"Of course I'm scared."

"What about trust?"

"What about it?" Kate's face flattens. She's stone-like under her delicate surface. "Look, I'm not going to be okay until you're back and I know everything has turned out all right."

The next morning I get up before daybreak. Kate's sleeping, and I kiss her goodbye. She stirs.

I head south and cross the border. The clouds are orange and pink, and the sky is thin crystal blue. I begin to make the trans-peninsular drive. Pressure builds in my chest the further the march goes south.

I stop to check-out the surf at K-38. I have something to eat. The need for fuel for the ride.

Seventy miles south of the border the highway crests into a pass. The panoramic view of the valley is framed by the windshield. The basin, brightly sunlit, extends invitation. A black-shouldered kite swoops down and then hovers to hunt along the side of the road. I wonder if the falcon-shaped bird is a sign. I make the decent.

The heat of the day rises, moves toward its peak. I hit the valley floor, turn west off the highway onto the rough dirt road. No moisture to dampen the dust.

After several miles I pull in front of an isolated roadside structure. It's the only punctuation point that dots this remote place on the road. No one is around. It must be siesta time. I find a place to stand and wait in the shade so the sun doesn't cook me. I hardly remember being here before.

There is a lone man in the distance walking slowly toward me. He looks like a wavy mirage in the heat of the day. The distant figure becomes larger and larger and finally he's here. A weathered looking man, bow-legged and wearing dust-covered jeans. He shelters himself from the day's heat with a sweat-stained straw cowboy hat. I ask for directions.

He points up the road. *"Siga derecho."* He makes a snake-like movement with his hand to indicate the bends in the road. *"Pase por dos curvas."* And then he makes a gesture for me to turn left. *"Hay un caminito como una pista. Doble a la izquierda hacia el rio."* He points to the ground to indicate the place to stop. *"Va a descubrir la casita."* He could have just used gesticulation to give me the directions and not have said anything.

The friendly local stops and stands-up straight. He's serious now. There's a spark of recognition in his eyes, but I've never seen him before. Maybe word got out. *"No señor. ¡No vaya!"* He must know about me. He tells me not to go.

I tell him everything is okay. I turn toward my rig.

He keeps telling me not to go and escalates into a scream.

I stop and turn. I tell him not to worry; everything is fine.

I head the way he told me to go and see a faint passageway on the left that looks more like a path than a road. I turn and head toward the river. There's the little house—la casita. The wife comes out of the house. Her face falls when she sees me. She's terrified and tries to run away. I call out to her, *"Estoy aquí para reparar la situación. No estoy loco todavía. ¡Lo siento, Señora, lo siento!"* Tell her I'm here to make amends, I'm not crazy anymore. I'm sorry, incredibly sorry.

She disappears for what seems forever. I'm not going to leave without doing what I came to do. The sun is slowly crossing the bright expanse of sky, and I start to hear the birds in the river thicket, and the river flows with brown sediment.

I'm about to give up and leave, but then, slowly, Inocencio creeps out of *la casita*. Surrounded by his family, they keep their distance, skeptical and maybe even scared of me. But who could blame them?

I go to the rig and pull out the rice and beans. I give them to the wife. I give Inocencio the boxes of .22 and .410 shells. He jerks back when I pull out the new over/under. I hand it to him, and he looks at it. And then he admires his new possession. I unload the chainsaw and gas cans. I see all of their faces relax and even light-up by the time I'm done taking everything else out of the rig.

I go to Inocencio, *"Ojos que no ven, corazón que no siente."* I tell him I was unaware of what I was doing—the eyes that don't see. It cut-me-off from the feelings of the heart. And that's where my words come from—the heart. He hears my apologies. There's forgiveness in his eyes. I look at his wife, and the terror is gone. I look around at all of them, and they're no longer afraid of me.

War was horrific. I went out-of-control. But what I did to Inocencio was countless steps beyond shameful, and I can never make up for it completely. Maybe today I made up for it a little bit. Besides, there isn't anything else I can think of to do. It'll never be over, but it's time to go forward.

I get back into the rig. Head out. The oaks, sycamores and riparian landscape take on a deep saturation of color. The sky seems bigger and the land more open. Yeah, I remember this place now. It's the place I've always loved.

Acknowledgments

First off, much appreciation goes to Guy Biederman who helped with the initial developmental editing. The editorial work and support from Ann Creel and John Paine were tremendous and their assistance is gratefully acknowledged. Jeanmarie Morelli proofread the manuscript and made insightful comments.

Additionally, Robert O. Woodbury M.D. was a war trauma surgeon who provided input for the elements of the book that covered medical intervention and also how medical staff struggled with the stressors of impact of war.

Waights Taylor Jr. and McCaa Books need to be acknowledged for the publication of this novel. I also wish to acknowledge Maxine Hong Kingston for her encouragement for the publication of *In the Mouth of the Wolf.*

ABOUT THE AUTHOR

Bill McCausland is a Vietnam War veteran who had a special assignment from the Department of the Army to work in a joint military-civilian counterinsurgency program in Vietnam. He was assigned to the Military Assistance Command-Vietnam and worked with the civilians of the United States Agency for International Development. He worked with a colonel in a two-man office at a U.S. Embassy Annex to assist a general who was the special assistant to Ambassador Bill Colby who later became the head of the CIA.

McCausland went to graduate school when he returned from Vietnam and earned a doctorate in clinical psychology. He attended the training program of the Veterans Administration at the National Center for PTSD in Palo Alto.

He was also on the best practices committee for PTSD as part of the Kaiser Permanente Medical Group for northern California. McCausland also has a masters of fine arts in creative writing.

www.ingramcontent.com/pod-product-compliance
Lightning Source LLC
Chambersburg PA
CBHW070047030726
47506CB00002B/380